City of Lies

Center Point
Large Print

Also by Victoria Thompson and available from
Center Point Large Print:

Murder in the Bowery
Murder in Morningside Heights
Murder on Amsterdam Avenue
Murder on St. Nicholas Avenue

**This Large Print Book carries the
Seal of Approval of N.A.V.H.**

City of Lies

Victoria Thompson

CENTER POINT LARGE PRINT
THORNDIKE, MAINE

This Center Point Large Print edition
is published in the year 2018 by arrangement with
The Berkley Publishing Group.

The text of this Large Print edition is unabridged.
In other aspects, this book may vary
from the original edition.
Printed in the United States of America
on permanent paper.
Set in 16-point Times New Roman type.

ISBN: 978-1-68324-655-8

Library of Congress Cataloging-in-Publication Data

Names: Thompson, Victoria (Victoria E.), author.
Title: City of lies : a counterfeit lady novel / Victoria Thompson.
Description: Center Point large print edition. | Thorndike, Maine :
    Center Point Large Print, 2018.
Identifiers: LCCN 2017045326 | ISBN 9781683246558
    (hardcover : alk. paper)
Subjects: LCSH: Swindlers and swindling—Fiction.
Classification: LCC PS3570.H6442 C58 2018 | DDC 813/.54—dc23
LC record available at https://lccn.loc.gov/2017045326

With thanks to my friends at Seton Hill University who helped me get this one off the ground: John Dixon, Don Bentley, Dawn Gartlehner, Genevieve Iseult Eldredge and especially my old friend Leslie Davis Guccione, who is the best mentor anyone could have.

Chapter One

Jake looked much too smug.

Elizabeth's hand itched to smack the smirk off his face, but well-bred young ladies didn't go around smacking people in hotel dining rooms. Since she was pretending to be a well-bred young lady at the moment, she made herself smile pleasantly and threaded her way through the mostly empty tables to where he was sitting.

He jumped to his feet and pulled out her chair, because he was pretending to be a well-bred young man. "Good morning, dear sister. Did you sleep well?"

"Did you drop the leather?" she asked.

"Of course, and he just came into the dining room. Oh, wait. He stopped to talk to someone."

Elizabeth glanced over, turning her head only slightly so she wouldn't be caught watching their mark. Jake had done the same thing.

"It's a woman," Jake murmured.

"Shhh." She could see that. She needed to hear what they said. If he had a friend in the city, someone who might advise him . . .

"Hazel, how nice to see you," Thornton said, although a trace of strain in his voice indicated it wasn't really so nice to see her at all.

"Oscar," the woman said. Her back was to

7

them but her tone was unmistakable. Elizabeth almost shivered from the frost in it. She'd have to practice that tone. It might come in handy someday.

"What brings you to Washington City?" Thornton asked with obviously forced enthusiasm. He'd also felt the chill and was trying to pretend he hadn't.

The woman rose to her feet, and even though she was much shorter than Oscar Thornton, she seemed to tower over him. How did she do that? "I can't believe that is any of your concern." She laid her napkin down on the table and walked away, making Thornton look like a dog. How on earth did she do that? But Elizabeth couldn't worry about that now. She had to salvage Thornton's pride.

"Start talking," Elizabeth whispered.

"So I told him I wanted to order a dozen pair," Jake said a little louder than necessary so Thornton would know they'd been talking to each other and hadn't noticed that woman cutting him dead so beautifully. Never embarrass a mark. "And he looks down his nose at me, the way those clerks in those fancy stores do, and he says, 'Sir, you will never have use for a dozen pair.'"

"He didn't!" Elizabeth said, outraged on behalf of her brother in this imaginary conversation.

"He did. So I told him I'd take two dozen instead."

She laughed the little tinkling laugh she'd practiced so many times and said, "Father will be furious."

"Why do you think I did it?" Then he looked up in apparent surprise to see Thornton approaching their table. "Good morning, Thornton. Won't you join us?"

Elizabeth looked up, too, and gave him a delighted smile that told him how pleased she was to see him, because she was pleased, if not for the reason he thought. His face was still scarlet from the woman's snub, but she gave no indication she noticed. "Yes, do join us and save me from having to listen to any more of my brother's silly stories."

Jake pretended to be affronted, but they soon had Thornton seated and responding to Elizabeth's subtle flirting. He probably hadn't forgotten that woman, but he was thinking about Elizabeth now, which was all that mattered.

"Oh dear, are those women still marching at the White House?" she asked, seeing the headline in the newspaper Thornton had carried with him.

"Yes, even though they're getting arrested almost daily now," Thornton said. He'd cleared the last of the humiliation out of his voice, she noticed with relief.

"I don't know why women would want to vote anyway. Would you, Betty?" Jake asked, using the name they'd chosen for this job.

9

"I can't imagine why," Elizabeth said. "Politics is so boring." She didn't have to lie about her opinion of politics, at least.

"And not something a lady should concern herself with," Thornton said with a condescending smile that set her teeth on edge.

Thornton told them the details of the suffragettes' latest brush with the law while the waiter in his spotless white gloves served them eggs and potatoes and bacon and refilled their coffee cups. When they were nearly finished, Elizabeth said, "Oh, I'm sorry, Mr. Thornton."

"For what, my dear?" he asked. He thought he was charming, and she let him think so.

"I stepped on your foot."

"No, you didn't," he assured her.

Elizabeth frowned in confusion. "It must have been you then, Jake."

"No, it wasn't," he said.

"Well, I stepped on something," she said, pushing her chair back a bit and looking down at the floor. "What could it be?"

She couldn't see because of the tablecloth, so Thornton obligingly bent down to help look. Then he reached under the table and came up with a man's wallet.

"You've dropped your pocketbook, Perkins," he told Jake.

Jake patted his jacket. "No, I haven't. Mine's right here. It must be yours."

Thornton patted his own jacket and shook his head. "It's not mine, either."

"Someone's going to be very upset," Elizabeth said. "Look how much money is in it."

Thornton had opened the wallet and discovered a large amount of cash inside.

"How much is it, do you think?" Jake asked.

"Several hundred at least," Thornton said.

"We need to find the owner and return it," Jake said. "Is there anything in there with a name on it?"

Thornton started emptying the wallet, which was stuffed with not only money but other papers as well. He laid the items out on the table, and Elizabeth and Jake moved the dishes aside to make room.

Jake picked up the stack of money and counted it while Thornton laid out several telegrams, a paper with rows of letters and numbers written on it and a newspaper clipping.

"There's over six hundred dollars here," Jake said. Two years' salary for an average working man.

"What does the newspaper clipping say?" Elizabeth asked.

Thornton read it to himself. "It's about some fellow named Coleman making a killing in the stock market."

"These telegrams are to someone named Coleman, too," Jake noticed.

"Is that his photograph?" she asked, peering at the clipping in Thornton's fat fingers.

"For all the good it does." He turned it so she could see. The photograph was of a man holding his hat to cover his face.

"We don't need his photograph if we have his name," Jake pointed out. "He's probably staying at the hotel. Let's take it to him. I want to see his face when he gets it back."

Thornton glanced over at her. "How do you feel about going to a strange man's hotel room, Miss Perkins?"

She gave him a mischievous smile. "It's scandalous, I know, but I'll be thoroughly chaperoned."

"Indeed you will," Jake said with a grin.

While Jake stuffed everything back into the wallet, Thornton rose and pulled out her chair for her. She thanked him with a coy little smile that promised things she would never in this world deliver. Jake went on ahead to the front desk to see if Mr. Coleman was registered at the hotel. Which he was, of course, and he also happened to be in his suite at that very moment, the clerk reported after telephoning to find out.

Elizabeth should have been pleased. Everything was going perfectly. Jake was doing his part and she was doing hers. So why did she have that hollow feeling in her stomach every time she pictured how it would end?

The two men allowed her to go before them to

the elevator, and Elizabeth felt Thornton's gaze on her like a slimy hand. She and Jake were pretending to be members of an "old money" family, but she was sure Thornton knew they weren't. She'd gathered that his late wife had come from one of the old New York families, so he'd know the difference. That didn't matter, though. Actually, it was better if he thought they weren't rich. He only needed to believe she was interested in him, and a young woman of limited means would certainly be interested in a single man of apparently unlimited means, no matter if he wasn't particularly handsome or very young.

And Jake had determined that Thornton had the means while they chatted in the smoking car on the train down from New York. If he was green in other areas, Jake was a master at getting marks to talk.

The elevator operator deposited them on the top floor.

"The rooms up here are pretty nice," Jake remarked as they walked down the hall. "I wanted to get a suite, but Betty wouldn't hear of it."

"It's a waste of money," she said, reinforcing Thornton's suspicions that they weren't actually rich.

"This is it," Thornton said when he found the room.

"Betty, you stand out of sight," Jake said, "in case this fellow doesn't take the news in a friendly way or something."

Elizabeth gave him a surprised look, but Thornton said, "Stand behind me and slip away if things get ugly."

"All right," she said, stepping back to allow Thornton to protect her. He was probably hoping they would have to slip away. Left to his own devices, he most likely would have just pocketed Coleman's cash and left the wallet for the hotel staff to find, so they'd get blamed for stealing the money.

Jake knocked.

After a few moments, the door opened a little and a suspicious man peered out at them. "Yes?"

"Mr. Coleman?" Jake said.

"Who wants to know?"

"I'm Jake Perkins and this is Oscar Thornton. We—"

"Stop bothering me. I already told you, I'm not giving any more interviews."

He started to close the door but Jake threw up a hand to stop him. "We found your wallet downstairs in the dining room, and we're returning it."

The man frowned at the wallet Jake held up. "I haven't lost my wallet."

"Are you sure?"

He patted his jacket impatiently, just the way Thornton had downstairs, but he didn't find the telltale bulge he was expecting. He patted some more and felt around in all his pockets. "You're right, I do seem to have lost my wallet. I'm sorry to be so rude, but I thought you were newspaper reporters. They hound me all the time, which is one reason I came to Washington City. I thought I could get away from them here. Please, come in, gentlemen." He held the door open. "Oh, and young lady," he added when Thornton stepped aside to allow Elizabeth to precede him.

"My sister, Miss Perkins," Jake said.

"Pleased to meet you," Coleman said with a nod. "Come in, all of you."

The suite was even nicer than Elizabeth had expected, with a view of the White House grounds across the way.

"I guess you can identify this," Jake said, holding up the wallet again.

"Of course. Let's see, I had a few hundred dollars, five or six, I think. Some telegrams, and a list of ciphers. Oh, and a newspaper clipping. Is that close enough?"

"Yes, it is," Jake assured him. He handed over the wallet with a little flourish he probably thought was cute. Elizabeth managed not to roll her eyes.

She watched Thornton's surprise when Coleman didn't count the money to make sure it was all there the way Thornton probably would have. Instead, Coleman pulled out the piece of paper

15

with the rows of letters and numbers and tossed the wallet with its wad of cash carelessly onto the table. "I can't thank you enough for returning this. I wouldn't have missed the money at all, but without this paper, I'd be out of business."

"We were wondering what that was," Thornton said. "What did you call it? A cipher?"

"That's right. Say, can I offer you fellows a drink? And some sherry for you, miss? I know it's early, but I feel like celebrating. Please, sit down and join me."

Jake gave Thornton a questioning look, and Thornton shrugged. She was sure he never turned down a free drink.

Coleman poured a generous amount of whiskey into three glasses and a small amount of sherry into a stemmed glass for her and handed them around.

"You have good taste in whiskey, Coleman," Thornton said after a taste.

"What kind of business are you in that you need a cipher?" Jake asked. "I don't even know what that is."

"Oh, it's all very hush-hush, but I think you folks have proved you're trustworthy. I work for a combine of Wall Street brokers who are trying to break up the branch stock exchanges and the bucket shops. They control the rise and fall of large blocks of stock, and they send me around the country and tip me off when to buy and sell.

16

You probably saw those telegrams in my wallet. They're written in code, telling me what stocks to buy and sell. Without this cipher, I wouldn't know what they were saying, and I'd probably lose my job."

"And they pay you to do that?" Jake asked in amazement.

"No, they don't," Coleman said with a wink. "But they do let me keep the money I make when I sell the stocks. Say, I feel like I should give you some kind of reward for returning my wallet since you saved my bacon. I know you don't need the money, but how about if I give each of you fellows a hundred to cover your expenses while you're in town at least?"

"That's awfully sporting of you, Coleman—" Thornton started to say, probably thinking a hundred sounded good, but someone knocked on the door and called, "Telegram!"

"Excuse me," Coleman said and went to answer.

"Say, Thornton, did you ever hear of a scheme like this?" Jake whispered while Coleman was busy with the bellhop.

"Sure," Thornton said, although he was most certainly lying. "Those Wall Street types are always manipulating the market somehow." Which was probably true, at least.

Coleman tipped the bellhop and sent him on his way. Then he hurried over to the desk and consulted his cipher to translate the telegram he'd just received. When he'd finished, he said, "I've just gotten instructions to buy some stocks, so I'm going to have to go to the brokerage right away. Before I do, though, I want to give you fellows your reward."

"We couldn't take a reward," Jake said, completely ignoring the black look Thornton was giving him. "Anybody would've done the same thing."

Thornton wouldn't have, Elizabeth was certain, but Coleman said, "Don't be too sure of that, young fellow. I know you're both honorable men, but I still think I owe you something. Tell you what—why don't I take the two hundred I was going to give you and buy stock with it for each of you? This order I just got is going to pay off big, and I'm going to sell by the end of the day, so you can keep the original investment and whatever your share earns. It should at least double."

Even Thornton smiled at that prospect. "I think I could live with that, Coleman."

"I don't know much about stock, but it sounds good to me," Jake said. "If it's going to double, I have a notion to give you fifty of my own, too, if you wouldn't mind."

"Oh, Jake, do you really think you should?" Elizabeth said with a worried frown.

"You're right to be careful, Miss Perkins, but in this case, you can't go wrong," Coleman said.

"I can guarantee your brother will double his money."

Before Elizabeth could protest again, Jake pulled out his wallet and passed Coleman a fifty.

"How about it, Thornton?" Jake said. "Don't you want to get in on this deal?"

"Mr. Thornton is as careful as your sister," Coleman said with a smile when Thornton made no move for his own wallet. "I don't blame him for hesitating. But I think I'll have your confidence by the end of the day. Can I meet you gentlemen in the hotel bar at around six o'clock to give you your earnings?"

They agreed that would be satisfactory, and Coleman tucked the money into an envelope. Then he thanked them again and sent them on their way.

"I can't believe you gave him your own money," Elizabeth scolded her brother when they were in the elevator.

"Do you think I made a mistake?" Jake asked Thornton.

"I guess you'll find out," Thornton said, apparently gratified that Jake was finally asking his advice.

"And maybe you'll be sorry you didn't give him anything yourself," Jake said with a grin.

"Oh, Jake, how could you have been so foolish?" Elizabeth cried, blinking back tears. Two days

19

had passed since they'd found Mr. Coleman's wallet, and Coleman's stock deals had turned the original two hundred reward dollars and Jake's fifty into over a thousand. Thornton had even given Coleman some of his own money to invest the last time. This success had led Jake to sign a check for a hundred thousand dollars he didn't have in order to purchase stock that Mr. Coleman had recommended.

And now he was in trouble.

"It's not foolish, Betty," Jake said. They were sitting with Thornton in the empty hotel dining room in the middle of the afternoon, discussing the situation. "This Coleman knows what he's doing, and the stock he told us to buy with that check did exactly what he said it would. We made a fortune! Just think what the Old Man will say when he finds out," he added, his eyes literally sparkling with glee at the prospect. She only wished she thought the Old Man would really be pleased by any of this.

"Then why can't you just collect your money? Wouldn't that cover the check, too?" she asked.

"Miss Perkins," Thornton said gently, "it's really nothing to concern yourself about. The brokerage is just being careful, and we did give them a worthless check when we bought the stock."

"We just didn't realize they'd contact the bank and find out we didn't even have an account there," Jake said, as if this were some unimportant detail.

"I told you not to put your name on a check so large," Elizabeth said, sniffling again. "You heard me say it, Mr. Thornton, but you let him do it anyway."

"All we have to do is come up with the cash to cover the check, and we can collect our profits," Jake said. "Betty, we made over a hundred and fifty thousand dollars."

"But only if you have a hundred thousand in cash to cover the check. How on earth will you manage that?"

Jake nodded at Thornton. "Our friend here is going to help."

Elizabeth let him see her admiration. "Oh, Mr. Thornton, we hardly know you. We couldn't ask you to do that."

"Why not?" he asked. "Jake and I are partners."

"And Oscar and I are going to split the profits," Jake said.

"Oh," Elizabeth said. "I didn't realize."

"Which is why I'm putting up half of the money to cover the check," Thornton said.

"But where will the other half come from?" Elizabeth asked.

"I've got those bonds Grandmother gave me that I can sell for about thirty," Jake said.

"But what will Father say?"

Jake waved away her concerns. "He'll never

know, because I'll buy them back when I get my money. And I thought we could use your inheritance, too."

"You want me to help you?" she cried, suddenly furious. "But that's the money Aunt Mabel left me for my dowry."

"It's only for a few days," Jake said.

"And you'll get back more than double what you had," Thornton said. "The stock had a return of a hundred and fifty percent."

"But I only have about ten thousand," Elizabeth argued. "That still isn't enough to cover the check."

"Mr. Coleman offered to lend us the rest of it," Jake said. "He's a good fellow."

"He must be," Elizabeth said, still not quite convinced. "Oh, Mr. Thornton, I don't know what to think. Tell me what I should do."

Thornton smiled and patted her hand where it lay on the table. It took all her willpower not to jerk away. "Miss Perkins, you should lend your brother the money. In a day or two, you'll be a very wealthy woman, and I'll be an even wealthier man."

"Are you sure?" she asked.

"Of course I'm sure, and then we can celebrate by taking a ship down south to where it's warm. Didn't you say that's what you'd like to do if you could?"

Elizabeth blinked the tears from her eyes. "Oh

my, yes, that sounds wonderful." She turned to Jake. "All right, then, I'll help you. But, Jake, you must promise never to get into another fix like this again."

Jake gave her an unrepentant smile. "She says that every time, but this time you won't be sorry, my girl. Now, we'll need to go down to the bank and open an account. Mr. Coleman will help us. They know him down there."

"It'll be just a matter of days before we have our money transferred into the account," Thornton said. "Then we'll take it down to the brokerage and pick up our profits."

"Take it down to the brokerage? You mean you'll be carrying all that money around with you in cash?" Elizabeth asked, horrified anew. "Isn't that dangerous?"

"You worry too much, Miss Perkins," Thornton said. "I'll have my boys watching us."

A frisson of alarm shivered over her. "Your boys?"

"Yes," he said with that superior grin he always gave her when he was explaining something he thought she was too simple to understand. "I always travel with bodyguards. They've been bored these past few days, so they'll be glad to have something to do."

Elizabeth had her bag packed, and she'd been pacing her hotel room, looking out the window each time she reached it. Not that she expected to see anything. All she had was a view of the rear of the hotel, where the deliveries came in. They hadn't wasted money on a better room, since Thornton wasn't going to be coming to see her here, much as he might want to.

Finally, someone knocked on her door, but it couldn't be Jake. She'd given him a key. Her apprehension hardened into fear.

"Lizzie, it's me. Open up!"

She hurried over and opened the door to Coleman. "What's wrong? Where's Jake?" she asked as he closed the door behind him.

"You need to get out of here, Lizzie. It came hot and Thornton went wild when Jake told him it blew up."

"You were supposed to cool him off," she cried.

"I warned you—when you play it against the wall, there's no way to cool off the mark. You just get out the best way you can. Thornton slugged Jake, so he ran."

"You were supposed to hit Jake!"

"I told you, Thornton went wild. He sucker punched the boy before I could do a thing. And when Jake ran, Thornton sent his goons after him. He's probably going to come looking for you next, so you need to get out of town."

"But he let you go?"

"Of course. Jake might be a fool, but he knows how to do a switch. Thornton still believes I was conned, too." Switching a mark's allegiance from the roper to the inside man was crucial to a successful con, and Elizabeth had to admit that Jake was particularly good at it.

"What about Jake?" she asked, picking up her suitcase.

"Just leave that. I'll bring it to you in New York with your share of the score. What the . . . ?" he said, looking out the window. Elizabeth hurried over to see. They were on the second floor, so they had a clear view of Thornton's two bodyguards finally catching Jake near the loading dock of the hotel.

"They're going to kill him!" she cried as the two men began to beat him.

"I'll take care of it, Lizzie," Coleman said, his voice high with terror. "But I can't save you both. You need to get out of here and go straight to the station. Get yourself on the first train out. It doesn't matter where. You can get back to New York from any place. Do you need money?"

"No, I—" She cried out as one of the men landed a particularly vicious blow and Jake doubled over.

"Hurry," Coleman said, pushing her toward the door. "Thornton is probably already trying to get the desk clerk to tell him where your room is. He'll be here any second." He grabbed her shoulders and looked straight into her eyes. "You're a woman, and you know they won't be satisfied with just beating you. Now go."

He checked the hallway and then sent her out. She didn't wait for the elevator, instead racing down the stairwell, nearly tripping over her skirts in her frantic haste. She took a deep breath before pushing open the door and entering the busy lobby. She didn't want to call attention to herself, but she couldn't resist the urge to at least hurry. She was nearly running when she reached the front door. The doorman had already opened it for her when she heard Thornton call, "Betty!"

She didn't turn. She didn't slow. She ran for her life.

Chapter Two

They were coming. She could feel them. She didn't dare run on the street, but she quickened her pace as she moved down Pennsylvania Avenue. People didn't hurry here. Washington was a Southern town, not like New York or Chicago. But she needed to hurry. She needed to get away before they caught her.

Damn you, Jake. Damn you to hell.

Which was probably where he was now, unless God was much more forgiving than she had been led to believe.

She'd told him the whole thing was going to curdle, but would he listen? Oh no. What did she know? She was just a twist, and women didn't know anything about the con. At least Coleman had gotten away. She hoped, anyway. And maybe he could still save Jake.

Maybe.

"There!"

The shout from down the street hit her like a blow between her shoulder blades. They'd seen her. They were coming. As she rounded the corner, she strained to see up ahead. Only another block and she'd be there. She could already see the tall iron fence and the white mansion beyond it, and the women were still there, thank heaven, marching with their purple, white and gold banners. And the police.

She hated the coppers, every last stinking one of them, but she'd never been so happy to see anyone in her life. They were just standing around, though. They couldn't just stand around. She needed them to act.

The women stood in clusters, a good three dozen of them at least, clutching their gaily colored banners demanding the right to vote and looking nothing like the harridans the newspapers had described. Just a bunch of upstanding ladies in their fashionable coats and ridiculous hats and skirts so rebelliously short you could see the tops of their high-button shoes. The newspapers had described the suffragette riots and the wild women who had to be taken kicking and screaming to jail, but these women merely looked determined. And calm. Much too calm to get themselves arrested.

Elizabeth slowed her pace, acutely aware of the men on her trail, but she had to appear calm, too, so she'd fit in. She joined the closest group of women and tried not to sound breathless or desperate. "What's happening?"

They looked at her in surprise, three respectable women who saw what they thought was another respectable woman.

"They sent us home," one of them said.

"Home?"

"The judge told us to go home," another woman

said in disgust. Younger than the others, pale and blonde and not quite pretty, she had blue eyes that burned like the heart of a flame, making up in passion what she lacked in beauty. "But we didn't go home. We came right back here."

Elizabeth frowned in confusion. "You were already in court today?"

"Yes, just an hour ago," the blonde girl said. "They arrested us yesterday. All of us." She waved to include the rest of the women on the sidewalk in front of the White House. "Someone said this is the largest picket line of our campaign. But they didn't have room in the jail, so they told us to go home."

"Can you imagine?" the first woman asked. She was older, well into middle age, but the same passion burned in her eyes. She seemed familiar somehow, although Elizabeth knew she'd never seen her before. "Of course we came back. President Wilson must take notice."

Elizabeth saw them then, Thornton's two thugs. He hadn't come after her himself. He was too good for that. They'd just come around the corner, their black overcoats flapping because they hadn't taken the time to button them. But they'd stopped dead at the sight of so many women and the cops milling around the edges of their demonstration.

"Yes, President Wilson must take notice," Elizabeth said. "I don't have a banner."

The blonde girl smiled and offered hers. Elizabeth glanced at the words, something about President Wilson sending men to fight for freedom in Europe when American women still weren't free. She didn't care what it said. She turned her back on her pursuers, silently daring them to accost her now, with so many witnesses.

She held up the banner, struggling to keep the raw November wind from snatching it. "We demand to see President Wilson!"

She strode toward the nearest copper, defiant and angry because she was just a woman and didn't dare let those two men catch her because she could never defend herself against them.

The blonde girl followed her. "Yes, we demand to see President Wilson!"

Others took up the cry and moved to join her, their bodies a living barrier between her and the two men. They closed around her as one creature, united in purpose, many voices with a single message, crying for recognition.

For one horrible moment, Elizabeth was afraid the coppers would ignore them, but then a shrill whistle rent the air, cutting through the women's chants. They'd just been waiting for an excuse. The coppers moved as one, too, their shouts and their shoves breaking the women's momentum, forcing them back. Rude hands ripped the banner from Elizabeth's grasp and threw it to the ground. The blonde girl cried out as she stumbled, and

30

Elizabeth instinctively grabbed her arm, holding her upright as the cops herded them backward.

No, you idiots, not toward the two men! But when Elizabeth managed a glance in their direction, she couldn't see them anymore. The roar of engines drowned out the women's screams as the police vans pulled up. The cops yanked open the rear doors of the Black Marias and shoved, pushed and, when the women stumbled or faltered, literally threw them inside.

Elizabeth didn't resist, but a fat copper with onions on his breath still sent her sprawling onto the dark, filthy floor of the van. The stench of old urine and vomit and fear nearly choked her, but female hands lifted her onto one of the rough benches that ran along the sides.

"Are you hurt?" the blonde girl asked.

"No, no." Elizabeth managed a quick glance at the other women's faces before the doors slammed shut, plunging them into darkness. The tiny windows up near the roof in the front of the van allowed only a few rays of light to penetrate.

"Thank you for helping me back there," the girl said. "I might've been trampled if I fell."

"What happens now?"

"Haven't you been arrested before?"

"No, I'm new. I just arrived in the city yesterday." A lie, but then, she hardly ever told the truth about anything anymore. Would she even remember how?

31

"I didn't think I'd ever seen you before. My name is Anna Vanderslice. I'm very pleased to meet you."

"Elizabeth Miles." A half truth. "I'm pleased to meet you, too."

Other women murmured their names, but Elizabeth couldn't make out their faces in the gloom.

"You were quite brave, Miss Miles." This was the first woman who had spoken to her, the one she'd thought was familiar. For some reason, she seemed even more familiar in the dark.

"I only wish I could have been here weeks ago." Another lie. "I don't want to make a fool of myself, so could you tell me what to expect when we reach the jail?"

"I suppose we'll go before the judge again," Anna said.

"They'll probably lock us up this time," another woman said.

"I would consider it an honor to be jailed," a voice near the door said.

"Are you frightened?" Anna asked.

Terrified, in point of fact, but not of doing a bit of time. "I would also consider it an honor to be jailed." But mostly a relief.

"You really are brave, Miss Miles," Anna said. "I only hope I can follow Miss Paul's example."

"Miss Paul?"

"Alice Paul. She's on a hunger strike."

"At the district jail," another woman said. "She went on a hunger strike when they jailed her in London, too. She nearly died that time."

"Why did she go on a hunger strike?" Elizabeth asked. "She won't be of use to anyone if she's dead."

"That's just it," the older woman said. What was her name? Mrs. Bates. "The government can't let her die. They would be humiliated. A hunger strike is the perfect way for the powerless to force the powerful to capitulate."

Elizabeth sincerely doubted that, but she wasn't going to argue with this bunch.

"They force-feed her, of course," Anna said.

"How do they do that?"

"They put a tube down her throat and pour milk and raw eggs into her," Mrs. Bates said.

Elizabeth felt Anna's slender body shudder beside her.

"Miss Paul is a true heroine of the movement," someone else said, and other voices agreed.

The women continued to chat about what an honor it was to go to jail, their excitement almost palpable. They were fools, of course. Elizabeth usually spent a good portion of her energies staying out of jail. Why get yourself arrested over the right to vote? Men voted all the time, and she'd never noticed it making their lives any better.

"Will they really keep us in jail this time?" Anna asked.

God, I hope so, Elizabeth thought. She didn't know where she'd go if they didn't.

"You brought your toothbrush, didn't you?" Mrs. Bates asked.

"Yes, and a few other things, just in case."

"I'm sure the judge will be angry to see us again so soon," someone else said.

In Elizabeth's experience, judges were always angry about something or other, but would he really lock up so many ladies? She might have to cause a disturbance in court to ensure that she was safely locked away, at least.

At police headquarters, the cops booked them, and those who hadn't had their photos taken before were mugged, too. Elizabeth scowled for the camera, hoping for a bad likeness. Another trip in the filthy, stinking police vans took them to the courthouse. As predicted, the judge wasn't happy to see them. One woman got up and made a speech about their cause, but Elizabeth just kept watching the door. Lots of people came in wanting to see the show, and she wondered if Thornton's thugs had dared follow her here.

After a lot of arguing, which was mostly the women pointing out how unfairly they'd been treated, the judge finally banged down his gavel to shut them up. Elizabeth wasn't surprised: judges rarely paid any attention to fairness. He pronounced them guilty of obstructing traffic.

Obstructing traffic? Was that all he could come

up with? Nobody laughed, so apparently it was. Then he started pronouncing sentences. The red-haired woman who had given the speech got six months, and most of the rest of them got three months, except for one little old lady who looked to be about a hundred.

"Mrs. Nolan," the judge said in a voice he must have thought sounded kind, "I am only sentencing you to six days in deference to your advanced age, but you may avoid even that by paying your fine of twenty-five dollars. I urge you to do so, since a stay in jail might be too severe and bring on your death."

She looked like twenty-five dollars might not be too hard for her to scrape together, and Elizabeth would have advised her to take the deal, but the tiny old woman pulled herself up as tall as she could go. "Your honor, I have a nephew fighting for democracy in France. He is offering his life for his country. I should be ashamed if I did not join these brave women in their fight for democracy in America. I should be proud of the honor to die in prison for the liberty of American women."

Most of the women nodded their approval, although Elizabeth wondered how many of them would be willing to die for the old woman's liberty. Even the judge looked ashamed of himself, but he didn't back down. They never did.

He sent them off to the district jail to start their sentences.

Three months. The district jail was a roach-infested dump, but she'd be safe from Thornton there, and she'd have time to figure out what to do next. Maybe she'd be able to get a message to the Old Man. The guards started herding the women out and putting them back in the vans.

Anna slipped her arm through Elizabeth's. "I wish I were as brave as you."

Elizabeth looked at her in surprise. "I'm not brave."

"Oh, but you are. The way you took my banner and marched right toward the police. And now, you aren't a bit afraid to go to jail."

"Of course I am. The trick is not to let it show."

Now Anna was surprised. "How do you do that?"

One of the first lessons the Old Man had ever taught her. "Just smile." She forced her face to obey, and she felt her own fear slipping away.

"But how can you . . . ?"

"Just do it."

Tentatively, Anna stretched her mouth, but it didn't look anything like a smile.

"Pretend I'm a fellow you want to notice you."

Anna blinked uncertainly, and her gaze locked with Elizabeth's for a moment. Then she smiled. She really smiled.

Elizabeth smiled back.

"It works!" Anna said.

"Of course it does. Don't let them see how

you really feel inside. Don't give them the satisfaction."

They were among the last to be loaded into the waiting vans. The other trucks had already left. Elizabeth scanned the busybodies on the sidewalk who had gathered to watch the suffragettes getting their just punishment, but she didn't see any potential danger in the moments before they slammed the van doors shut. Three months from now, she'd walk out of the district jail and disappear. She'd never have to worry about Thornton again.

But when the van doors opened a short time later, they weren't at the jail. They were at Union Station. The guards dragged them out, prodding the laggards with billy clubs. Elizabeth knew better than to resist a cop with a club, and she moved along with the others toward a waiting train.

"Where are they taking us?" Anna asked.

"I don't know."

One of the other women said, "They're sending us to Virginia, to the Occoquan Workhouse."

Elizabeth shuddered and swallowed down hard against the bile in her throat. She knew all about the Occoquan Workhouse.

Oscar Thornton looked up from his newspaper when the boys finally came back to his hotel suite. "Well?"

They exchanged a glance that told Thornton all he needed to know.

Rage boiled up in him, but he knew better than to let his anger show unless he could use it to his own advantage. He'd lost control once today and look where that had gotten him. "You lost her."

"She went to the White House," Fletcher said.

Fletcher was the short, dumb one, a sniveling whiner, always making excuses. "Are you telling me she got a presidential pardon?"

"She might," Lester said. He was taller and not so dumb, at least. "She got herself arrested with the suffragettes."

"What?"

"She got there just as the cops were throwing them all in paddy wagons."

Fletcher nodded vigorously, as if his opinion mattered. "Jumped right in with 'em, like she belonged or something."

Thornton managed not to sigh. "Why didn't you follow her and pick her up when they let her go?" He held up the newspaper he'd been reading and stabbed at the headline: "Suffragettes Released."

Lester looked offended. "We did, but the judge didn't let them go this time. He sentenced them to three months."

"Three months? Are you sure?" Those damn women usually didn't get sentenced at all, and if they did, it was only for a few days.

"That's what the clerk told us. I had to slip him

a fin. They wouldn't let us in to see, but afterward they put the women back in the paddy wagons and took 'em off to the jail."

Thornton swore eloquently. "What about that bastard Jake? What'd you do with him?"

They exchanged another glance, and Thornton bit back another curse.

"Don't tell me he got away, too."

"He was done for, Mr. Thornton," Fletcher said. "We had to leave him when you told us to go after the girl, but there's no way he could've . . ." He looked to Lester for help.

"He wasn't in the alley when we went back for him, but he couldn't've walked away by himself. I'd swear to that."

"So you think some Good Samaritan took him to a hospital?"

"The morgue more likely," Lester said with more confidence than he had any right to feel. "You won't see him again."

"You're right I won't, because you're going to find him and make sure of it this time. And then you're going to find Mr. Coleman."

Fletcher winced and Lester started studying his shoes.

Thornton thought he might explode from fury. "Well?"

Lester didn't look up. "Coleman already checked out."

Of course he had. Thornton had frightened him

off when he got rough with that Jake character. The thought of never finding the man made him ill. Coleman was the only one who could help him get his money back. Next time he wouldn't be stupid enough to use a worthless check, and then there'd be no trouble collecting his profits. In one or two plays he'd make it all back and more, and he wouldn't have to worry about Jake and Betty Perkins ruining the deal.

Meanwhile, all he had left was revenge. "Go bail her out."

Lester blinked. "What?"

"They must've given her a fine. She can pay it or go to jail, so if it's paid, they'll let her go. Get her out of jail and bring her back here. That should be easy enough, even for you."

"Yes, sir."

They practically tripped over each other in their rush to escape. When the door slammed behind them, Thornton crushed the newspaper into a ball and threw it across the room. Not as satisfying as throwing it into the fire would have been, but the fireplace had been converted into a gas grate. He looked around the luxuriously furnished room for something to smash, and snatched an oriental vase off the mantel.

Testing its weight, he considered the satisfactory way it would shatter against the marble hearth, and then he thought of poor dead Marjorie and how horrified she would be at its destruction.

His wife had been gone for almost six months, but he could still savor the pleasure he'd taken in terrifying her when she was alive.

And now he was looking forward to seeing that same fear in the eyes of that little chippie Betty Perkins. This time he savored the rage boiling up inside him. No female was going to get the best of him, no matter how pretty she might be. Not Marjorie and all her stuck-up friends, and not Betty Perkins with her idiot brother. Once he got finished with her, she'd be thinking about him for the rest of her short, miserable life. In one fluid motion he lifted the vase over his head and smashed it against the hearth.

By the time the train reached Virginia, the women had lapsed into weary silence. Anna had actually fallen asleep leaning on Elizabeth's shoulder, and she woke with a start when the train rumbled to a stop. Elizabeth's stomach growled, making her think how unappealing hunger strikes were. She hadn't eaten since breakfast, and she didn't expect dinner at the Occoquan Workhouse would be very satisfying.

"Where are we?" Anna asked.

"End of the line," Elizabeth said. The women started gathering their things.

Someone said it was half past seven when they started herding the women off the train and into the winter darkness. A line of wagons waited to transport them to the workhouse, and Elizabeth obediently climbed aboard one of them like the rest of the women. Once away from the station, Elizabeth could see little except the bit of road ahead illuminated by the lanterns on the wagons.

Ordinarily, Elizabeth didn't like having somebody hanging on her, but tonight she tolerated Anna's clinging for the warmth of her body. Winter-stripped trees loomed over them in the empty country darkness, reminding her of how alone she was. After a while, she caught sight of an American flag, of all things, visible in the light coming from the workhouse windows. The massive structure took shape as they neared it, sprawling away in every direction, its massive wings disappearing into the night.

The wagons stopped, and Elizabeth climbed out with the rest of the women and allowed herself to be herded with them into a large room that looked like some kind of office. A couple of battered desks sat at one end, the only furniture. A hatchet-faced woman in a gray dress introduced herself as Mrs. Herndon, the matron. Elizabeth knew the type. She would enjoy making their lives miserable.

"Line up and give me your names."

"We demand to see Superintendent Whittaker," one of the women said.

"You can see him tomorrow. Now line up and—"

"We are political prisoners, and we demand to see Mr. Whittaker."

"You'll wait here all night, then," Mrs. Herndon said with a smirk and turned her back on them. About a half dozen bruisers in guard uniforms stood around the room, ready to do her bidding, but she just sat down behind one of the desks and proceeded to ignore them.

Nobody was going to give an inch, so Elizabeth staked out a spot near the wall and sat down.

"That floor is filthy," Anna said.

"The cells will be worse. Better get some rest while you can."

"She's right," Mrs. Bates said, taking a seat on the floor beside her. "Very practical. You're a sensible girl, Miss Miles."

Anna lowered herself carefully on Elizabeth's other side. "Why don't they lock us up?"

"Mrs. Lewis asked to see the warden," Mrs. Bates said. "I suppose we're waiting for him to arrive. Where are you from, Miss Miles?"

"South Dakota," Elizabeth said, choosing a location least likely to be familiar to anyone here.

"You've come a long way," Anna said. "Do your parents approve of your work for women's suffrage?"

"My parents are dead. I live with my aunt, but I'm afraid I lied to her about where I was going. She wouldn't have approved."

Mrs. Bates shook her head. "So many of the

older ladies just can't imagine a world different from the one in which they've always lived. They actually consider themselves fortunate not to have to think about politics and government."

Elizabeth would consider herself fortunate never to have to think about it. That was all Thornton talked about, politics and government contracts and how he was going to make a fortune selling rifles to the army. Near as she could figure, government was just the biggest of the big cons, with everybody trying to get the best of it for themselves and sting the other guys. Thornton seemed to think he was the smartest of the bunch, too. "I've noticed that most older people don't like things to change."

Mrs. Bates smiled, probably because she was pretty old herself. "Change is coming whether anyone likes it or not."

"Where are you from, Mrs. Bates?"

"New York City. I'm afraid I convinced Anna to join me on this trip. I'm sorry to have gotten her into this."

"Nonsense. I'm glad I came," Anna said, although she looked completely terrified.

"Do your parents approve of your work for the cause?" Elizabeth asked the girl.

"My father is dead, but my mother knew I was going to march with Mrs. Bates outside the White House. I think she was rather proud of me for that. It's my brother, David, who doesn't approve. He thinks he needs to protect me now that Father is gone. Do you have a brother, Miss Miles?"

"No." Was that a lie? She couldn't be sure, and she couldn't allow herself to think about it now.

"Then you have no idea how overbearing they can be. David would keep me in a glass case if he could."

"He only wants you to be safe," Mrs. Bates said. "He loves you very much."

"Being loved can be a form of bondage in itself, don't you think, Miss Miles?"

Elizabeth had no idea. "If it is, I'll bet it's more pleasant than this kind of bondage. Do you live with a disapproving relative, too, Mrs. Bates?" she asked to change the subject.

"No, just my son."

"What does your son think about you marching?"

"Gideon believes in our cause."

Which didn't exactly answer the question, but Elizabeth didn't really care. She was only making conversation to pass the time.

"Will they really keep us here for three months?" Anna asked.

"I don't think President Wilson has the stomach for that," Mrs. Bates said. "He'll probably pardon us after a day or two, as he's done before."

A day or two wouldn't help her at all. "Can you refuse a pardon?"

"Refuse?"

"Yes, refuse to be pardoned and stay in jail."

Mrs. Bates considered this. "I don't know. They always try to make us pay our fine so we don't have to go to jail at all, but we refuse because that would be an admission of guilt, and we haven't done anything illegal."

"You sound like you want to stay in jail, Miss Miles," Anna said.

"Only if it serves the cause," Elizabeth said, pleased that she'd come up with such a pious-sounding lie.

Anna's stomach growled, and she pressed a hand to it. "I wonder when they'll give us supper."

One glance at Mrs. Herndon's evil smirk made Elizabeth think they'd starve before she took pity on them.

Gradually, the other women followed Elizabeth's example and sat or lay down on the floor, some using their coats as makeshift bedding as the room warmed from the massing of over forty people. Quiet conversations died away as fatigue claimed them. Would the matron really keep them sitting here all night? And if she did, what did Elizabeth care? At least she was safe.

After what seemed hours, Elizabeth felt as much as heard the disturbance outside. Someone was coming.

"Get up. Put your coats on," she said to her companions.

Anna had been dozing again. "What?"

"Get up! Someone's coming."

Then the others heard it, too, and began to stir. Before they could shake off their lethargy, however, the door burst open and an ugly old man strode in like he was the king of England. From the looks of him, he ate little babies for breakfast, so a few dozen suffragettes were no more than a nuisance.

One cruel man was a bother, but behind him, she saw a crowd of men straining to get at them, and for the second time that day, Elizabeth knew real fear.

Mrs. Lewis stood up. "Mr. Whittaker, we demand to be treated as political prisoners."

"Shut up! I have men here to handle you. Seize her!"

Like somebody had pulled a cork from a bottle, the mob outside surged through the open door. They wore no uniforms and carried no weapons, but they didn't need any to overpower the weary women.

"They've taken Mrs. Lewis!" someone screamed.

A brute who looked like an ape grabbed Anna's arm. "Come with me, sweetheart. We'll have a good time." Anna screamed and struggled, but another man took her other arm and they lifted her off her feet and whisked her away.

"You damn suffrager!" a mug said, clapping a

beefy hand on Elizabeth's shoulder. "My mother ain't no suffrager!"

Elizabeth thought of a few choice things she could say about his mother, but she clamped her mouth shut and forced herself not to struggle. It didn't matter. He and his buddy still nearly tore her arms from their sockets as they pulled her outside and across the yard. Biting back her cry of pain, she concentrated on keeping her feet. No sense giving them an excuse to drag her. All around her, women screamed and struggled and men shouted obscenities, but she saw only shadows in the pitch-dark yard. She tried to run to keep up with her captors, but her skirts tangled and tripped her, and she stumbled at last, so they dragged her the rest of the way.

For a moment she feared they were being abducted, but then she realized they were only going to the building where she'd seen the lights illuminating the American flag.

The front door opened into a long corridor lined with stone cells. The goons were throwing the women into the cells, three and four at a time. A man in uniform kept poking women with a long stick as the men shoved the prisoners in.

Two men pushed Mrs. Bates into a cell so hard that she smacked against the rear wall and slumped down in a heap. Furious, Elizabeth wrenched one arm free and threw herself into the same cell before her captors could make another choice for her. Before she could see if Mrs. Bates was all right, someone outside her cell screamed in agony.

The plug-uglies had Anna's arms twisted above her head, and they slammed her slender body over the arm of an iron bench, then dropped her onto the cement floor, where she lay unmoving.

"Anna!" Mrs. Bates cried. "Help her!"

Elizabeth scrambled to her feet and scurried out into the melee, dodging the other women and their captors. Anna's eyes were wide with terror on her chalk white face, but she hadn't moved a muscle. Just as Elizabeth reached her, she suddenly drew a gasping breath, and Elizabeth realized with relief that she'd just had the wind knocked out of her.

Grabbing Anna's arm, she dragged her toward her cell. Mrs. Bates hurried to help, and they got her inside. Mrs. Bates cradled her gently. "Anna, are you hurt? What did they do to you?"

She gasped a few more times. "I couldn't breathe!"

"They knocked the wind out of her," Elizabeth said. "It scares you to death, but no harm done."

Outside, the screams had died down as the last of the women were run past and deposited into cells, but no sooner had they finished than the women began calling out the names of their friends, checking to make sure everyone was safe.

"Mrs. Lewis!"

"Mrs. Nolan!"

"I'm here!"

"Where's Mrs. Lewis?"

Across the way, two women were lifting a third onto the single cot. She appeared to be unconscious, and the other two were crying over her.

"She's here," one of them called, "but I think they've killed her."

"Quiet!" a man shouted. The ugly old man was back. What was his name? Whittaker. He looked like he might have apoplexy. "Be quiet, all of you!"

"Is Mrs. Lewis truly dead?" This from the red-haired woman who had spoken up for them at the courthouse.

"Shut up!" Whittaker screamed. "Guards, handcuff her!"

To Elizabeth's horror, two of the big apes slapped manacles on the woman's wrists and chained her to the bars with her arms over her head.

Undaunted, she cried, "Mrs. Lewis!"

"She's alive," someone called. "She was only stunned!"

"Quiet, all of you, or I'll put you in a straitjacket with a buckle gag!" Whittaker cried.

Elizabeth didn't know what a buckle gag was, but the threat of it frightened the women to silence.

"Let's put her on the bed," Mrs. Bates whispered, and Elizabeth helped her lift Anna onto the narrow iron cot, the only furniture in the cell except for a toilet.

Outside, Whittaker was giving orders, and in a few minutes, the guards came back and started throwing ratty mattress pads and filthy blankets into the cells. Theirs landed with a cloud of dust, and the guards slammed the iron barred door shut on them. All down the corridor, doors clanged with a sound like the end of hope.

Elizabeth went to the barred door and looked out. As the guards withdrew, having finished their task, other women also came to the bars. In the cell opposite, the old lady who had been so brave at the courthouse tended to Mrs. Lewis as she recovered from her brush with death. Down a ways, the red-haired woman still hung from the bars, her arms stretched agonizingly above her head and the handcuffs digging into her wrists. A buzz of whispered outrage rose like a cloud of flies at the sight of her, and over and over they said her name in awe: Lucy Burns.

Elizabeth wanted to despise her. What kind of fool would put herself in a position like that? But then she saw the woman's face. Surely, she was in agony, but her expression was triumphant as she met the eye of every woman straining for a glimpse of her. Her red hair glittered like a flame in the light from the corridor, and her eyes glowed with an inner fire.

51

In another cell, a woman reached up and grabbed a bar with both her hands and stood there, mirroring Lucy Burns's position. She stood there half the night, even after the others had bedded themselves down, until a guard finally came and released Miss Burns.

What on earth was wrong with these women?

Chapter Three

Sometimes Gideon was afraid he would die in his office. Could a person really die of boredom? If so, today was certainly the day.

Even his law clerk appeared to be in danger of nodding off, lulled by the sonorous drone of Mr. Ernest Pike's reedy voice. How long had they been listening to Pike's tedious account of his life, a life that had culminated in his phenomenal success in the production of packing crates?

An eternity, at least.

"So you can understand, Mr. Bates, how important it is to make sure my estate is safeguarded for my daughter, Eugenia," Pike said. "She is my only heir."

At last! The man had finally made his wishes known. Gideon straightened up in his chair and smiled across his desk at Mr. Ernest Pike. "We can certainly make sure of that, Mr. Pike. How old is your daughter, may I ask?"

His clerk perked up, too, finally sensing something he could make notes about.

"She'll be twenty-two next Tuesday. She's a lovely girl, and so accomplished. She plays the piano and sings. Everyone remarks on how musical she is."

"You must be very proud." Gideon understood

now. His yawn evaporated. Eugenia Pike was of marriageable age. Pike would want to protect her from fortune hunters and expected the law firm of Devoss and Van Aken to be the guiding force in protecting the family estate. Gideon was on board to make sure these estates lasted for generations. This wasn't a kindness. The law firm earned substantial fees for doing the work, so it was in their best interest to make the money last forever. "Your daughter must have many suitors."

Pike blinked in surprise and hesitated just a moment too long. "Yes, of course she does, but she's very particular, you see. That's why she hasn't married yet."

Gideon took a hard look at Ernest Pike. If Eugenia Pike resembled her father, she might not have any suitors at all. But Gideon could assist with that as well. A large dowry could increase a young woman's appeal exponentially. "You'll want to make sure she's comfortable when she does choose a husband, I assume."

"Oh yes, and I'm in a position to make sure she is."

"But you'll want to protect her from someone who might squander her dowry and make continued demands on your generosity," Gideon said.

Mr. Pike gave him a grateful smile. "Yes, exactly, Mr. Bates. You understand me completely."

"We can accomplish all that with a simple

trust." Gideon explained how it would work, but he had the distinct impression that Pike didn't really care, even though he was nodding enthusiastically. "We can draw up the paperwork for you to examine before you decide, but I think you and your daughter and her future husband will all be very satisfied."

"Thank you, Mr. Bates. I can see I was advised correctly by those who assured me you were the perfect attorney to consult."

Gideon knew he hadn't done anything particularly impressive, but he accepted the compliment graciously. "I'm happy to be of assistance."

"I'd like to express my appreciation in a more tangible way, if I may, Mr. Bates. Perhaps you could join me and my family for dinner some evening. Eugenia could perform. I know you'd enjoy it."

This time Gideon straightened cautiously. So that's why Pike had asked to see Gideon specifically. Pike had done his homework, ferreting him out as the scion of one of the oldest families in the city, one of the families whose fortunes had faded through the generations until this scion was forced to earn his own way. And to close the deal, Pike had made it clear exactly how comfortable he intended to make his only child and the lucky fellow who married her.

Gideon was not going to be that fellow, but he also wasn't going to lose a client. "I appreciate your kind invitation, but I try to make it a policy never to mix business with pleasure, Mr. Pike. Perhaps when we have concluded with our business, however . . ."

"Of course, of course," Mr. Pike agreed happily.

Maybe the fair Eugenia would meet another eligible, if needy, young man before then. If not, Gideon was more than happy to make her acquainted with several of his friends who were actively seeking a wealthy bride to settle their debts and provide a nice income for them for the rest of their lives.

All three of the men looked up in surprise when someone tapped on the office door and opened it without even waiting for permission. No one at Devoss and Van Aken ever interrupted a client meeting unless the building was on fire.

"Excuse me, Mr. Bates, but you are needed urgently," one of the other clerks said, obviously terrified. Maybe the building really was on fire.

Before Gideon could even think how to take his leave from Mr. Pike, David Vanderslice pushed past the clerk and practically exploded into the room. "Gideon, Anna has been arrested!"

Not a fire, but certainly cause for alarm, at least for David. Gideon rose with as much dignity as he could muster. "Would you excuse me for a moment, Mr. Pike? Smith here will take down some information that will help us draw up the paperwork." Gideon cast his clerk a pleading look, which he returned with an understanding nod. "David, let's step into the conference room."

He took David's arm in a death grip and steered him, unresisting, out of the office and down the hallway. He glanced up at his friend, furious at him for behaving so hysterically, but when he saw how distraught David was, he didn't have the heart to chasten him. Instead he pushed him toward the open doorway to the conference room and followed him inside.

When he'd closed the door behind them, David repeated his lament. "Anna's been arrested!"

"Of course she has. We knew that yesterday."

"No, you don't understand. She's been arrested *again,* and this time she's been sent to jail for *three months!*"

"Where did you hear this?"

"I got a telephone call this morning from someone at the Woman's Party headquarters in Washington. They said forty-one of the demonstrators had been arrested yesterday, and that the judge sentenced them to three months in the district jail."

This was a much longer sentence than the women had ever received before, but still not cause for alarm. "I assume my mother was among them."

"They haven't telephoned you?"

"No, but perhaps they tried to reach me at home. I don't understand. I thought the demonstrators had been released yesterday. That's what the news-papers said."

"They *were* released, but they went right back to the White House, and the police arrested them again. At least that's what they told me on the telephone." David was a tall man, but he suddenly seemed to shrink, as if all the air had gone out of him.

"Sit down and we'll sort this out."

"Poor Anna. The thought of her locked up in some awful jail . . ." He rubbed a hand over his face.

Gideon took David's arm and forced him toward the closest chair. "Sit."

He sank into it wearily. He looked like he'd been running his fingers through his fair hair. Or maybe he just hadn't combed it yet this morning. "I didn't want her to go. I knew something like this would happen."

"Of course something like this would happen," Gideon said. "The women get arrested regularly, and just as regularly, they get released."

"They didn't release that woman, what's her name? The one who's on the hunger strike."

"Miss Paul. But she's one of the leaders. They won't keep Anna."

"How do you know? They've never sentenced any of them to such a long term before." David looked up at him, despair clouding his pale blue eyes. He was a complete mess. He hadn't even

58

shaved yet. "We have to get her out, Gideon. If anything happens to her, it will kill Mother."

"Nothing is going to happen to her. My mother is with her, and she'll look after her. They'll probably be released today in any case. I'll telephone some attorneys I know down there and find out what's going on."

"Would you? I'd be very grateful."

They both started when someone knocked on the door. The clerk who had escorted David stuck his head in. "Mr. Bates, there is a telephone call for you from Washington City. They said it's very important."

"That's probably headquarters calling to tell you about the arrests," David said.

Gideon followed the clerk out to the front office, picked up the candlestick telephone from the desk and held the earpiece to his ear. "Hello? This is Gideon Bates."

The operator connected him to a member of the Woman's Party, who told him what he already knew.

"They were sentenced to three months in the district jail, but they aren't there," she concluded.

"Then they've already been released."

"No, they haven't been released. They've been taken somewhere else, but we don't know where yet."

"Someplace else? You mean they're still in custody?"

"As far as we know. We have our attorney working to locate them."

Dear Lord, this was ridiculous. Couldn't anyone down there do anything right? "You know that I'm an attorney."

"Yes, I do."

"Tell whoever is in charge now that I will be taking the first train to Washington. You may expect me at headquarters later today."

Gideon took a moment to get control of himself before he went back to David.

David jumped to his feet the instant Gideon stepped into the conference room.

"They told me the same thing they told you, that the women were sentenced to three months in jail. Did they tell you where they're being held?"

David frowned in confusion. "I told you, the district jail."

"Well, they aren't there, and the women at headquarters don't know where they are."

"What does that mean?"

"I have no idea, but it can't be good. I'm going straight to Washington to see if I can get this straightened out. I'll telephone you the moment I know anything."

"I'll go with you!"

"No, I think it's better if you stay here, at least for now. I'm not sure who will be the most help, and I might need you to see some people here in the city. While you're waiting to hear from me, try to find out where Mrs. Belmont is."

"That harpy! This is all her fault. If she hadn't given the Woman's Party all that money—"

"For God's sake, don't say that to her! She might not be married to a Vanderbilt anymore, but she still has plenty of influential friends, and you'll crawl to her on your hands and knees if you have to."

David pulled a face, but he nodded. "I'll do whatever I must to save Anna."

"Good. Now go home and try to keep your mother calm. You'll hear from me soon."

Gideon opened the door to the conference room to find his clerk, Smith, ready to knock. "Mr. Devoss would like to see you, sir," he reported with a great deal of apprehension.

"Does he know I have a client waiting?"

Smith nodded. "That's why he wants to see you."

Gideon drew a calming breath and marched down the hall to the large office where the senior partner held court. The clerk in Devoss's outer office nodded and indicated he should go right in.

Devoss sat behind his enormous desk looking like a thundercloud about to explode.

"You wanted to see me, sir?" Gideon said with as much confidence as he could muster.

"Givens tells me you left a client alone in your office to take care of some personal business."

"David Vanderslice came to inform me that his sister has been arrested with the suffragettes in Washington City." Devoss knew David well. All the old families knew each other well. Devoss was even some kind of cousin to the Vanderslices, Gideon recalled.

"David allowed his sister to demonstrate with those women?" Devoss asked, outraged. "What was he thinking?"

"I don't—"

"And what did he think was going to happen if she paraded herself in front of the White House with those unnatural females? He's lucky she was only arrested. At least she'll be safe in jail."

"That's the problem, sir. Even though the women were sentenced to three months in the district jail, they've been taken someplace else, and no one knows where they are."

"What do you mean, no one knows? Someone knows. This is the American justice system we're talking about. Prisoners don't just disappear."

"These prisoners apparently have, sir."

"That's preposterous, and if they have disappeared, it's their own fault. They have no business challenging the United States Government. Why would women want the vote anyway? Men have taken perfectly good care of them for centuries. They can't believe they could do a better job of it."

Gideon didn't really agree with Devoss, but

the man wasn't completely wrong, either. "I can't speak for the women, Mr. Devoss, but I do know someone needs to find them and get them released from jail. With your permission, I would like to take a few days to go to Washington City and do just that."

For a moment, Devoss simply gaped at him, and Gideon knew a moment of satisfaction at having struck his employer speechless. Only one small moment, though, before Devoss's expression turned thunderous again.

"Why do *you* need to go to Washington? Surely, they have attorneys there who can see to this matter."

"I know they do, sir, but"—he hated admitting this to Devoss, but he had no choice—"my mother is also among the missing prisoners."

"Your *mother?*" Devoss echoed. "Hazel is a suffragette? I can't believe it!"

Devoss and Gideon's parents had been friends their entire lives. Gideon had even suspected Devoss would have courted his mother after his father died if she'd given him any encouragement at all. Gideon waited for the ramifications of his revelation to sink in.

"And she's missing, you say?" Devoss said, his anger dissipating a bit.

"Yes, sir, and naturally, I feel I must go to her assistance."

But Devoss's anger had only dissipated a little.

"I can't stop you, Bates, but I also can't approve of this conduct. I'll expect you back in three days."

"Yes, sir."

"And if you're not back in three days, you may consider yourself dismissed from the firm."

Why was she sleeping in the outhouse? Elizabeth wondered in that last shadowy moment between sleep and wakefulness. Then she opened her eyes and the memories came rushing back. She was in the Occoquan Workhouse, which only smelled like an outhouse.

She pushed the filthy blanket away from her face and rose up on one elbow. The straw mattress crackled beneath her. It had provided little in the way of comfort except as a scant barrier against the chill of the stone floor. At some point during the night, she had finally fallen into an exhausted sleep, but it hadn't done her much good. All around her the rest of the women were also beginning to stir in their cages.

Anna awoke with a yelp of terror and sat bolt upright on her cot. Mrs. Bates, who had shared Elizabeth's mattress, automatically reached out a comforting hand even though she was only half-awake herself.

"Oh, oh, oh, I thought it was just a nightmare," Anna said, hugging herself and rocking back and forth.

"I'm afraid not," Mrs. Bates said. "And we must make the best of it. Think of the stories you'll tell your children one day, Anna. They will be amazed to learn how brave you were."

"I'm not brave at all!"

"Then pretend to be," Elizabeth said. "Don't let them see you're afraid, or it'll be that much worse for you."

Mrs. Bates stared at her in amazement, but Elizabeth just pushed herself to her feet and tried to shake the wrinkles out of her skirt. In the light of day, their prison looked even worse. The cells were black with years of dirt, and the guards had told them they were in the men's punishment cells.

Not exactly what Elizabeth had signed on for.

"Mrs. Nolan!" a guard called.

"I'm here!" The elderly woman who had told off the judge yesterday came to her cell door.

He unlocked it and pulled her out.

"Where are you taking me? Are we being released?"

The guard simply locked the door, grabbed her arm and started pulling her along with him.

"Where are you taking me?" she cried again, but the guard didn't even glance at her. All the other women had rushed to the bars of their cells, and they called out encouragement in the moments before she and the guard disappeared from sight.

"Where are they taking her?" Anna asked.

"They're probably going to let her go," Mrs. Bates said. "As a mercy, because of her age, I'm sure."

Mrs. Bates wasn't a good liar, but she was good enough to fool Anna. Or maybe Anna just wanted to believe her.

But Mrs. Nolan was only the first. One by one, each woman was summoned by a guard and escorted out. None of them came back.

About half a dozen had gone when Anna started crying. Elizabeth wanted to shake her.

Mrs. Bates sat down on the cot beside her. "Now, now, there's nothing to cry about."

"What's happening to them?"

"I don't know, dear."

"They're either releasing them or moving them to the women's section," Elizabeth said.

Anna looked up in surprise. "How do you know?"

Elizabeth wanted to say that even a worm like Whittaker wouldn't dare keep a bunch of respectable females locked up in the men's section with male guards to ogle them for more than one night, but she couldn't appear too knowledgeable about jailhouse life. "It only stands to reason. What else could they do, sell them into slavery?"

Mrs. Bates said, "Miss Miles is right, dear. It only stands to reason."

"Elizabeth Miles," the guard called.

Elizabeth sighed. "Here."

It was one of the brutish guards from last night. He grinned, showing blackened teeth, as he unlocked the door. Elizabeth gave him her best glare and shook off his hand when he would have grabbed her. Annoyed, he gave her a little shove with his stick, but she'd been expecting it and hardly even stumbled. Head high, she strode past the other cells and through the door into the yard.

"Ain't you gonna ask where we're going?" the ape taunted.

She shot him another glare, the one she'd practiced in the mirror until the Old Man said she had it right. "No."

He looked like he wanted to crack her over the head with his stick, but he apparently thought better of it. Beating a woman last night during the confusion might be excused, but doing so in the light of day with possible witnesses might not be so wise. For all he knew, she was the daughter of a millionaire. She could certainly glare like one, as she well knew.

She'd been walking toward the building where they'd waited last night. When she reached the door, she stopped expectantly, and the ape actually opened it for her. One small victory, she thought.

Several clerks sat at the two desks in the large room, and one of them asked her name and checked her off a list. The ape left with the name of the next woman, and the clerk took her to an office down the hall a ways. Warden Whittaker sat behind a big, bare desk looking like a toad wearing a cheap suit. He didn't get up.

The clerk pointed at the straight-backed chair sitting square in front of Whittaker's desk. Elizabeth sat, folding her hands primly in her lap, and waited. The clerk handed the warden a sheet of paper and left.

Whittaker studied the paper for a long moment, while Elizabeth studied him. A small man who wasn't aging well, he seemed shrunken inside his clothes. A big black birthmark covered his temple, like a spider that had settled there to read over his shoulder. She bit back a smile. He didn't look like a man who would take kindly to being laughed at.

"You're a long way from home, Miss Miles."

"Women come from all over the country to support the cause."

"Pretty girl like you, don't you have a husband to keep you at home?"

If she was going to be stuck here for three months, she shouldn't make an enemy of the warden on the first day, so she swallowed the reply she wanted to make: that she didn't need any worthless man to run her life. "No, I don't."

Whittaker sighed, obviously frustrated with the suffragettes. "Your fine is only twenty-five dollars. If you pay it, you can walk out of here right now and catch a train for"—he glanced down at the paper again—"South Dakota this afternoon."

"Paying the fine would be an admission of guilt, and I've done nothing wrong, Mr. Whittaker." Thank goodness she'd listened to Mrs. Bates. "Did the other women pay their fines?"

"Yes, every one of them," he snapped. "I'm sending a wagonload out to the train station this minute, and you can be on it."

Mr. Whittaker blinked a lot when he lied. Most people did.

"Thank you for the offer, but I think I'll stay."

"Rogers!" he called, slapping the paper down onto the desk.

The clerk stepped in.

"Take her away."

Elizabeth rose and followed the clerk. Only then did she realize her hands were shaking. But she didn't have anything to be afraid of now. She was going to stay in jail.

A long walk with a female guard brought Elizabeth to the dining hall. Any hope they might be feeding the prisoners here died a swift death. No food in sight, and the matron who had taken such delight in ignoring them last night was doing some kind of paperwork for each of them.

Elizabeth saw the women who had been called out of their cells ahead of her sitting at a table on the far side of the room. So much for Whittaker's claim they'd all been released.

69

After Matron Herndon had verified all of Elizabeth's information, the woman sent Elizabeth to join her "suff friends."

Elizabeth happily obeyed. The other women, all as miserable and weary as she, greeted her with weak smiles. "Where's the old lady?" she asked after glancing around the group and finding it one short. "Mrs. Nolan?"

"We don't know."

"No talking!" Mrs. Herndon shouted.

The next prisoner came in, and Mrs. Herndon started questioning her, so Elizabeth felt safe to whisper, "Maybe they let her go."

The other women nodded, wanting to believe but obviously as unconvinced as Elizabeth herself. One by one the other prisoners arrived. They came more quickly now. Whittaker was probably tired of lying to them and asking them to pay their fines. He wasn't even seeing some of them at all. Eventually, Mrs. Bates appeared. The older woman scanned the faces of the other prisoners until she found Elizabeth and flashed her a radiant smile.

Elizabeth had the oddest sensation in her chest as she felt herself smiling back. It almost felt like happiness, but why should she even care if Mrs. Bates was glad to see her? And why should she be *happy* about it?

The table where Elizabeth sat was full, so Mrs. Bates took a seat at another one. Elizabeth found herself looking up anxiously every time another prisoner came in, not even sure what she was worried about. Then she saw Anna, and she knew. Relief flooded her.

For her part, Anna was craning her neck to see the other prisoners, not even noticing where the guard was leading her. When she caught Elizabeth's eye, her whole face lit up, and she waved. The guard jerked her around and practically threw her toward the table where Mrs. Herndon sat, but even that didn't wipe the smile from her face. She was still smiling when Mrs. Herndon had finished with her.

Taking no notice of the fact that Elizabeth's table was full, Anna hurried over and inserted herself into the nonexistent space on the bench beside her. The other women made room for her.

"I knew it!" she cried, slipping her arm beneath Elizabeth's and snuggling against her.

The other women instantly hushed her, but she continued to gaze adoringly at Elizabeth.

"I knew you wouldn't leave," she said more softly. "He told me you did. He told me all of you did," she added, glancing around the table. "But I remembered what Elizabeth said, and I knew she wouldn't have. You gave me courage."

The other women stared at Elizabeth in a way no one ever had before, making her want to squirm. What were they thinking? What were they seeing? She had no idea, and the realization puzzled and terrified her at the same time. Why should she care what they thought?

"No talking!" Mrs. Herndon shouted again, silencing the soft buzz of whispers coming from every table. Apparently, she'd finished with all the prisoners, and now she came striding toward them. "No talking is allowed in the dining hall. You are here to be punished, and you must be conscious of your guilt at all times. After you've eaten, we'll take you to your ward."

At the word "eaten," Elizabeth heard her own sigh echoed by every other woman in the room. She hadn't swallowed a thing since breakfast yesterday, and her mouth watered at the thought.

The female guards got them on their feet and began herding them toward a long window at the end of the room where some Negro women waited. Anna still clung to Elizabeth's arm, and for some reason she didn't mind.

The women ahead of her moved surprisingly quickly. When she had her turn, she saw why. One of the servers, a girl who looked to be no more than sixteen, handed her a small glass of skim milk and a piece of dry, cold toast. Swallowing the toast and milk was the work of a moment, and then she moved on, following the line of women down a dismal corridor until they came to the women's ward.

Here they found a double row of cots in a large room, but when the first women in line tried to sit down on them, the guards ordered them on their feet.

"Why won't they let us rest?" Anna asked.

"This is a workhouse, that's why," Elizabeth replied, and tried not to think about what the Old Man would say if he could see her here. Then she remembered his stories about being in prison and how after a month, he'd figured out how to run a con even there. What was it? Oh, yes, he had them paying for all the incoming supplies twice so he had a nice score when he finally got out. She almost smiled.

"Take off your clothes," one of the guards said.

Elizabeth looked around. This was clearly the women's section of the workhouse, and all the guards here were female, but Elizabeth didn't want to undress in front of them or anyone else.

"Take off your clothes, all of them!" Mrs. Herndon shouted. "Take them off or we'll take them off for you!"

Slowly and with obvious reluctance, the other women began to fiddle with buttons.

"Do we have to?" Anna asked in alarm.

"We're all women," Mrs. Bates whispered. "And it's for the cause."

That's not what it was for, Elizabeth knew, but she removed her coat and unbuttoned her dress and slipped out of it. The unheated air raised gooseflesh, and she shivered. Others around her were removing petticoats and unrolling stockings.

Beside her, Anna trembled visibly, nearly falling when she snagged her foot in the waistband of her skirt. Like the others, Elizabeth paused when she was down to her chemise and drawers. Glancing around, she could feel the wave of reluctance they all felt at this final humiliation. Then Lucy Burns, the red-haired Amazon who had been manacled to her cell most of the night, raised her bruised hands and determinedly opened her chemise. As if that were a signal from which the others derived strength, everyone followed suit. Elizabeth peeled off her chemise and let her drawers fall.

She stood there, naked and vulnerable and hating them, hating all of them, hating Whittaker and Herndon and Thornton and Jake and the Old Man and everybody who had brought her to this place.

When everyone was naked, the guards made them stand there a long moment, just to make sure they all realized how humiliated they were. The guards—women who in the outside world would have said, "Yes, ma'am," to those who were now their prisoners—leered and gloated. Elizabeth wanted to scratch their eyes out, but she stood like the others and refused to quail or even lower her gaze.

After what seemed an eternity, Herndon said, "To the showers!"

The guards prodded the naked women into

motion, and Elizabeth followed, shivering and furious, for what seemed like a mile to the shower room. The concrete floor was icy beneath her feet, and the smell of mildew and damp nearly gagged her. When they arrived, she saw there was no privacy here, either. A row of showerheads along one wall were turned on, each producing an icy trickle.

"Soap in the bucket," one of the guards told them.

Elizabeth glanced in the bucket and saw one sliver of soap, blackened from use and probably shared by every inmate foolish enough to use it.

"Don't touch it," she warned Anna. "Some of the women here have diseases."

Anna's eyes widened with terror as she followed Elizabeth to the shower. The women ahead of them shrieked when the cold water hit them, so Elizabeth knew to do no more than get a bit damp, which was fortunate, because there were no towels.

At the end of this ordeal, some of the regular inmates were passing out prison clothing to the suffragettes, and the women ahead of her balked.

"We are political prisoners, and we demand the right to wear our own clothes!" Lucy Burns said.

"Wear these or go naked," Herndon told them. "You won't get your own clothes back until you're released."

"I demand to see the warden," Miss Burns said.

"You want to see him right now?" Herndon mocked her. "While you're naked?"

In the end, having no choice, the women accepted their prison clothes. At least, thought Elizabeth as she accepted the pile the girl handed her, she knew they'd be warm.

Back in the ward, Elizabeth dropped her pile of clothes on an empty bunk and began sorting through them. She pulled out the thick, unbleached muslin undergarments and began to pull them on, willing to overlook the scratchy texture and be grateful for a barrier against the cold. She knew what the Old Man would say: "You can get used to anything, Lizzie."

Anna scurried up to the cot beside hers and began to do the same. In her street clothes, the girl had looked thin, but naked she was a waif, all skin and bones with her white skin stretched tight. Why would a rich girl be so skinny? Elizabeth had seen beggars fatter than she.

Next came the bulky, Mother Hubbard wrapper made of blue gray ticking, and Elizabeth buttoned hers up to her throat, adding the "matching" apron. The heavy stockings wouldn't flatter anyone's ankles, but Elizabeth rolled them on gratefully over her frozen feet.

Mrs. Bates had settled at a cot across the aisle from them, and when she sat to put on her stockings, she said, "I happened to notice that the girl passing out the clothes was dressed in rags. I mean, as awful as the things they gave us are, at least they're in good condition. I asked her about it, and she said that a few days ago the guards made them turn in the clothes they'd been wearing and gave them those rags to wear, so these clothes could be washed for us."

"That's terribly unfair," Anna said.

Elizabeth wanted to point out that she probably wouldn't like wearing the rags herself, either, so she should be grateful. But these women didn't think the same way she did, so she kept her opinion to herself.

"Yes, it is unfair, but that's not the worst of it," Mrs. Bates said. "The fact that they were getting the clothes ready for us days ago means that they intended to send us here all along, even before we had our trial."

Now that was unfair. The authorities had decided how to punish these women before they'd even been arrested!

Before she could become properly outraged, however, one of the guards shouted something that made the hair on the back of her neck stand up.

"Betty Perkins! Betty Perkins! Which one of you is Betty Perkins?"

Betty Perkins had been her name for the past few weeks, but only Thornton knew her by it. That meant he knew where she was, and he was trying to get his hands on her.

Elizabeth erased all expression from her face as

the guard walked slowly down the center aisle, looking at each woman in turn.

"Speak up, Betty!" the guard called. "Somebody's paid your fine, and you're free to go."

Oscar Thornton thought James Wadsworth looked exactly the way a United States senator should look, handsome and dignified, although he was a bit young for such a big responsibility. "More coffee, Senator?"

"Yes, thank you."

Thornton reached across the breakfast table the hotel staff had set so elegantly to fill the fine china cup. "I'm glad you were free this morning."

"I was a little surprised to hear from you again so soon. When you canceled our original appointment, I thought you said you were going to be away for several weeks."

Thornton had thought so, too. He'd been planning a little trip with that scheming Betty Perkins. They were to have left on a cruise to the islands as soon as the deal with Coleman came through, or so she'd said. She would be traveling someplace much less pleasant now, as soon as his two bodyguards bailed her out of jail and brought her to him. Meanwhile, he'd decided to move forward with his original business in the city. "My plans changed unexpectedly. You haven't said what you think of my proposal."

Senator Wadsworth smiled uncertainly. "I

really don't know what to think of it, Mr. Thornton. Everything about the war is so new and . . . uncertain. I don't think anyone really knows anything yet."

"But surely you know who's making the decisions about what to buy for the army."

"Of course I do."

He was lying, but Thornton didn't mind. Wadsworth was a senator. He could find out easily enough, and they both knew it. "And I'm sure somebody on your staff can make the introductions for me."

"Actually, I may be of more help to you in New York than here."

"New York City?"

"Yes."

"I thought you were from someplace out in the country, Senator."

"Yes, Geneseo, but of course I represent the entire state. I have many friends in the city, people who helped me when I needed it. I was the first of the New York senators elected by the general population, you'll recall. It required a lot of organization."

"I always thought it was a mistake to let the people choose their senators directly."

Senator Wadsworth smiled the way rich people did when they thought they knew something you didn't. "Some people felt having the state legislature choose the senators was too elitist."

Thornton smiled back. "Maybe it was, but you didn't have to pay off nearly as many voters that way."

Wadsworth looked like he might choke. "I . . . I'm sure I don't know what you're talking about."

Thornton didn't understand why rich men had to pretend that politics wasn't all about money. The thought of money reminded him of Betty Perkins again. "Say, speaking of votes, what do you think about those suffragettes? Is your wife one of them?"

"Good heavens, no!" He looked as if Thornton had asked if she was a prostitute. "I'm proud to say she's an Anti."

"A what?"

"She's anti–women's suffrage. In fact, she's very active in the National Association Opposed to Woman Suffrage."

Which left very little chance she'd been arrested with Betty Perkins yesterday. "An excellent cause. Heaven help us if we have to start buying women's votes, too."

Wadsworth nearly spilled his coffee. "Mr. Thornton, really—"

"These friends of yours in New York, are they involved in procurement for the army?"

Wadsworth needed a moment to catch up to the change in topic. "They are dipping their toes in the water, so to speak, and since you would like to supply the army, you would have much to discuss."

"I want to do more than discuss, Senator."

"Of course you do."

"And I'm prepared to pay a finder's fee for your help, of course."

"Oh, that isn't necessary. I'm just anxious to help a constituent," Wadsworth said expansively, which meant the senator got his cut from his friends. "What exactly is it you want to sell to the army?"

"Guns. Rifles, to be specific."

Wadsworth blinked. "Well . . . that's certainly something the army can use."

"Yes, it is, and I can supply them very reasonably." Wadsworth didn't need to know where the rifles had come from or why Thornton had gotten them so cheaply.

"I'm sure many people would like to sell rifles to the army."

"That's true, Senator. The government has lots of money to spend on this war, and anytime the government has lots of money to spend, lots of people are going to want it. Somebody is going to get rich in the bargain, and I figure it might as well be me . . . and you."

"I see."

"I'm sure you do, Senator. All I need from you is a letter of introduction. I'll take care of the rest, and your friends will be very happy they met me."

Wadsworth didn't look too happy to have met him, but Thornton wasn't worried about that. "Of course. If you stop by my office tomorrow, the letter will be waiting for you. I'm always happy to serve a constituent."

"And just so I know, who is it you'll be introducing me to?"

"I . . . uh . . . Well, various people are . . . Things are so uncertain now, you see, and . . ."

Thornton leaned forward. "Who?"

"Uh, well, I believe I know just the gentleman who can see that you make the right contacts."

"His name, Senator?"

"David Vanderslice."

Chapter Four

Gideon Bates went right from the train station to the Woman's Party headquarters on Capitol Hill. The house Mrs. Belmont had bought for the party to use as their headquarters was humming with activity when he arrived, and for a moment, he stood unnoticed in the foyer.

Finally, a young woman in a wrinkled shirtwaist peered at him with some alarm through her spectacles. "Who are you?"

Gideon gave her what he hoped was a non-threatening smile. He certainly didn't want to alarm anyone. "I'm Gideon Bates. My mother was one of the ladies arrested yesterday. I'm also an attorney, so I've come down from New York to see if I can help."

The young woman blinked a few times. "Oh, yes, someone said you might be coming."

"And now I'm here." Gideon waited, somehow managing to hold his smile in place even when she made no move to announce him. He wouldn't inspire much confidence if he shouted at her. Or started turning over desks, which suddenly seemed like an excellent way to vent his growing frustration. Instead he said, "I'm very anxious to help. Do you suppose I could speak to someone?"

She was still blinking. "What? Oh. Oh, yes.

You'll want to see Mrs. Stevens, I suppose."

At last! "Is she the one in charge now?"

"Yes."

Gideon waited, trying not to think about doing violence to the furniture, and when she didn't move, he said, still smiling although his face now felt more than a bit stiff, "May I see her?"

"Oh my, of course. Just a . . . I'll be right back." She hurried off. Finally.

Gideon set down the carpetbag he'd hastily packed back in New York and rubbed the stiffness from his neck. He noticed he was attracting some suspicious glances from the women working in the front room, so he smiled at them, too. They didn't smile back. They had a right to be suspicious of strange men showing up on the doorstep, of course.

The young woman who had greeted him returned. "Mrs. Stevens would like to see you. Follow me, please."

He followed her to the back of the house, where a room that might have once been a butler's pantry had been fitted out into a private office of sorts with mismatched furniture, clearly cast-off odds and ends. A plump, middle-aged woman, looking as if she hadn't slept last night, came from behind the desk and offered her hand. She had a grip like a federal judge. "Thank you for coming, Mr. Bates, but I'm hoping we won't need your help."

"Does that mean they've been released?"

"Please, sit down." She removed a pile of papers from one of the rickety chairs and set it on the floor, then took her seat behind the desk again. "I'm afraid they haven't been released yet—at least not that we know of—but our attorney, Mr. O'Brien, has gone down to Virginia to meet with the authorities there and ascertain the conditions under which the women are being held."

"Virginia? I thought they were arrested here in the district."

"I guess you haven't heard the latest news."

"I haven't heard any news at all since the telephone call I received this morning. At that time, you didn't even know where the prisoners were being held."

"Yes, well, since then we've learned that the women who were arrested yesterday were taken by train to Virginia, where they are being held in the Occoquan Workhouse."

"A workhouse?" This was worse than he could have imagined.

"That's right, and others have been held there before. It's a horrible place, Mr. Bates, filthy and cold and the food is rancid and full of worms."

"Then we've got to get them out of there. You say you have an attorney already working to free them?"

"Yes. We do not believe the government is willing to free them just yet, however, which is why they were sent to Virginia. We suspect they want to make an example of them in hopes of discouraging others from joining the protests."

Gideon considered the wisdom of that strategy for a moment, and his opinion of President Wilson's leadership abilities sank even lower than it had been. "They don't know you and your ladies very well, do they, Mrs. Stevens?"

She smiled grimly. "No, they do not. They thought locking up Miss Alice Paul would dampen our spirits, but since news of her hunger strike at the district jail has gotten out, new members are arriving every day to join the pickets at the White House. We have not missed a single day since we started our protests last January."

Someone tapped on the door, and Gideon turned as a well-dressed man came in. He looked harried and very angry.

Mrs. Stevens jumped to her feet. "Mr. O'Brien, what is the news?"

"Nothing good, I'm afraid. The warden wouldn't see me, and they laughed when I asked to see the prisoners." He gave Gideon a questioning glance.

"Mr. O'Brien, may I present Gideon Bates," Mrs. Stevens said. "His mother is one of the prisoners. Like you, he's an attorney, and he has come down from New York to help."

"I don't know how you can help," O'Brien said.

"I have friends here."

"Unless your friends work at the White House, I doubt they can do us much good."

Gideon didn't like O'Brien's tone. He sounded defeated already. "You think it will take a presidential pardon, then?"

"That's one solution, but it's starting to look like we were right about President Wilson wanting to leave the women in jail for a while this time, since he's tried everything else to scare them away from his front door."

"I'm afraid I don't understand why they were taken to Virginia," Gideon said. "If they were arrested and charged in the district, shouldn't they be imprisoned there?"

O'Brien rubbed his chin. "That's very astute of you, Mr. Bates. It is, in fact, illegal to incarcerate someone in a different jurisdiction, but the district routinely sends prisoners to the workhouse in Virginia because they don't have room to accommodate them here."

"If they are being held illegally, we have grounds for getting them released, at least," Gideon said.

"Not if the president doesn't want them released, and it seems that he doesn't," O'Brien said. "They may be there for a time, I'm afraid."

Mrs. Stevens said, "Oh dear," with such feeling that both men turned to her in alarm. "There's something I haven't told you yet, Mr. O'Brien. We had a visitor earlier today, a young marine. He's stationed in Virginia, near the workhouse, you see. Last night the warden there asked for help handling some unruly prisoners, so the commanding officer sent over some of the marines. This young man was horrified to learn that the prisoners were all female."

Gideon frowned in confusion. "The marines were called in to handle the demonstrators?"

"Not only the marines. The warden had also recruited a band of ruffians from the nearby town and aroused them to a state of fury, so that when he told them to put the demonstrators in cells, they treated them very cruelly and even injured some."

"Injured? How badly?" Gideon demanded. If they'd harmed his mother or Anna . . .

"We have no way of knowing, except that this young man did describe one of the women in particular, who could only have been Miss Burns. They handcuffed her to the bars of her cell with her hands over her head and left her hanging there. Another woman was knocked unconscious, but that's all he could tell me for certain."

Gideon could hardly breathe for the rage boiling inside of him. How dare this warden treat respectable women in such a way? "This is outrageous! When the public hears—"

"The public won't hear a thing if we can't verify this by seeing the prisoners ourselves," Mrs. Stevens said.

O'Brien nodded. "I'll go back to Virginia tomorrow."

"What if they still won't let you in?" Gideon asked.

"Then I'll have to try a legal maneuver."

"Could you get a writ?"

"You mean a writ of habeas corpus?" Mrs. Stevens asked.

"Yes, that's about the only thing that would work," O'Brien said. "At least it would force the warden to produce the prisoners so we can judge their condition and determine the legalities of their imprisonment."

"You'll need to find a friendly judge," Gideon said.

Mrs. Stevens smiled. "I'm guessing any *Republican* judge would be glad to help if it will embarrass the president."

"I hope you're right, Mrs. Stevens," O'Brien said. "In any case, it is our best hope at the moment."

"If you're going back to Virginia, Mr. O'Brien, I know of two ladies who would like to go with you," Mrs. Stevens said. "Mrs. Young is concerned about her daughter, and Miss Morey wants to see her mother."

"Is that wise? I don't know what I'll be facing when I get down there."

"It's not a bad idea to take them along," Gideon said. "They might let the women in for a visit where they'd refuse you."

"He's right, they may," Mrs. Stevens said.

"But if I have to find a judge, I wouldn't feel

comfortable leaving them on their own down there," O'Brien said.

"I'd be happy to go along," Gideon said. "Then you wouldn't have to worry about leaving them alone."

"That's very generous of you, Mr. Bates," Mrs. Stevens said.

"Not at all. My own mother is in that place, and a young friend is with her."

O'Brien nodded. "It's settled, then. Tell the ladies to meet us at Union Station at eight tomorrow morning. And wish us luck."

Elizabeth rolled over, trying without success to find a comfortable spot on the narrow cot. Exhausted from her nearly sleepless night and then sitting at a sewing machine most of the day, she realized that even her bones ached. She thought she'd fall asleep immediately when the guard had finally turned out the lights in the ward. Unfortunately, her stomach kept reminding her of how little she'd eaten that day. She'd hardly been able to swallow any of the rancid, nearly raw pork and weevil-infested cornbread they'd served for supper, the only real meal of that long day. Even worse, she could still hear the guard calling out the name Betty Perkins, which meant Thornton knew exactly where she was and would be waiting for her whenever she was released. When she closed her eyes, she could still see Thornton's thugs beating Jake. Had Coleman gotten there in time to save him? And if he hadn't, how would she ever face the Old Man again? Of course, if Thornton got to her first, she wouldn't be facing anyone.

Her head pounding from hunger and terror and guilt, she punched the lumpy pillow and tried rolling over again. She'd just settled when she heard an odd, mewling sound coming from Anna's cot.

"Are you all right?" she whispered.

"I . . . I'm so afraid."

Elizabeth sighed. "No one's going to bother you tonight."

"How do you know?" Her voice broke on a sob.

"Stop crying! You don't want the guard to hear you." No telling what torments those harpies might dream up if they knew Anna was so frightened.

"I . . . I can't!"

"You have to!"

She sobbed again. "Can I . . . Can I come over there?"

Elizabeth swallowed a groan. At least she'd be warmer with Anna in the bed. "Yes, but be quiet! Don't draw the guard's attention."

A rustle of cloth, and then she was sliding beneath the blanket. After a few moments of wiggling and rearranging, they were spooned together with Anna's back tucked against her.

The girl's slender body shuddered with one last sob. "Thank you so much."

91

"Don't thank me. I just wanted to shut you up so I could go to sleep."

Anna giggled. "You're so funny."

Elizabeth rolled her eyes in the darkness. "I wish I could be like you."

"No, you don't. Go to sleep."

"I want to be strong. That's why I came to Washington with Mrs. Bates. She was the strongest woman I knew, until I met you. You're strong in a different way than Mrs. Bates, and I want to be like that."

Elizabeth didn't want to know what that meant. "What about your mother? Isn't she a suffragette, too?"

"It's 'suffragist.' "

"What?"

"The term 'suffragette' is demeaning. We call ourselves 'suffragists.' "

"Oh." Elizabeth hoped she hadn't revealed her ignorance. There was a lot she didn't know about this business. "So isn't your mother a suffragist?"

"Not really, not like Mrs. Bates. She'd never march or anything. Oh, she wants things to change, for my sake, she says. She wants me to have an easier time of it. The world is a dangerous place for women."

How well Elizabeth knew. "Do you think getting the right to vote will change that?"

"Men will have to take us seriously then, won't they? It's not just the vote, you know. Women hardly have any rights at all. Legally, I mean. When my father died, he left everything to my brother. If David decided to put my mother and me out on the street, he could do it. We don't own anything, not even the clothes on our backs. What would become of us then?"

"You'd get a job, I expect."

"Doing what?"

What indeed? Anna gave no evidence of being able to fend for herself. "If you ever learn to run that sewing machine, you could do that."

Anna's body shook with suppressed laughter. "I'm better at it than you!"

Elizabeth recalled her trials today with the mechanical beast. Most of the other women knew how to sew, but Elizabeth had never felt the need to learn. "That's nothing to brag about."

"Which just goes to prove how hard it would be to make my own living. Girls don't get paid as much as men, either, even for doing the same job. I could never earn enough to keep myself and Mother, too."

She was right, of course, and Elizabeth didn't want to work in a factory any more than Anna did. That's why she'd convinced the Old Man to teach her all he knew, so she'd never have to worry about it. "I guess getting the vote will change all that."

"Of course it will. I heard Mrs. Pankhurst speak, and she explained it."

Elizabeth didn't know who Mrs. Pankhurst was, but she figured any self-respecting suffragist would, so she didn't ask. "What did she say?"

"It's all about the laws. Politicians make the laws, and they have to please the people who vote for them, so they make laws to benefit the voters, who are all men. Women don't vote, so they don't have to pay attention to what we want. If we could vote, though, they'd have to pay attention, and they'd have to pass the laws we want."

Elizabeth thought the reasoning was a little naïve. This Mrs. Pankhurst obviously didn't understand that there was more to politics than pleasing voters. You could lie to voters, but you really had to come through for the rich people. Being a successful politician cost a lot of money, and rich people expected a good return on their investments. Still, getting the vote might give women an edge they didn't have now. At least it couldn't hurt. She'd have to revise her opinion of the suffragists. Maybe they weren't completely wasting their time.

"You need to get some sleep," Elizabeth said. "Tomorrow will be just as bad as today."

"Do you think so?"

She knew so, but she said, "No, probably not, because we won't have to see Whittaker before breakfast tomorrow."

Anna giggled again. "You're so funny."

"Go to sleep."

• • •

Gideon couldn't ever remember being so angry. Or so frustrated. He paced the small room again, glaring at the armed guard, who seemed more amused than annoyed by his behavior. Which was probably a good thing. He was armed after all.

"Please, Mr. Bates," Mrs. Young said. "You'll exhaust yourself."

She and Miss Morey were sitting at a table, the only real furniture in what had been the parlor of this house. They were, according to the guard, a mile or so from the workhouse, but they had been allowed no nearer. When they'd been denied entry, O'Brien had gone in search of a cooperative judge and a court order to allow him to see the prisoners. That had been hours ago.

"I'm sorry, Mrs. Young," Gideon said, remembering the manners his mother had drilled into him since birth. "I didn't mean to distress you."

"Nothing you do would distress me under the circumstances, Mr. Bates," she said with a sad smile. "It was so kind of you to come with us today to look after Miss Morey and me."

Gideon hadn't done it out of kindness, but he could at least do a little more to look after the ladies. "Aren't you going to offer the ladies something to eat?" Gideon asked their scruffy-looking keeper.

"If I had anything to offer them, I'd eat it myself," he said quite reasonably, which only

95

irritated Gideon more. "Why don't you folks let me take you back to the train station so you can go home? Mr. Whittaker ain't never going to let you in to see your people."

"He'll have to when Mr. O'Brien gets the court order," Miss Morey said. She had been remarkably calm throughout the ordeal, much to Gideon's relief. Both women, in fact, had taken their situation far better than he. The suffragists, he'd noticed, tended to be sensible women not given to emotional outbursts, no matter what the newspapers claimed.

"If we don't get in to see them today," Mrs. Young said, "I'll make sure Mr. Tumulty knows about it."

"Who's that?" Gideon asked.

"He's President Wilson's personal secretary and an old family friend. He's known my daughter, Tilly, since she was an infant. Surely, he'll be as upset as I when he hears how we've been treated and what's happened to Tilly and the other prisoners."

Gideon could hardly believe she'd allowed such a valuable contact to go unused. "Why didn't you go to him first?" Gideon asked.

Mrs. Young dropped her gaze, and Miss Morey frowned at her. "She did."

"He has no idea this is happening, I'm sure," Mrs. Young said a bit defensively.

Miss Morey did not acknowledge her remark.

She said to Gideon, "He told her all the reports about the poor conditions at the workhouse are exaggerated. He said the prisoners are very comfortable there, and she shouldn't worry about her daughter."

"Tilly wasn't dressed warmly enough," Mrs. Young said. "I just wanted to bring her some heavier clothes."

"You must realize by now that everything he told you was a lie," Miss Morey said.

"I'll be certain to point that out to him when I see him again," Mrs. Young said with some asperity.

"Looks like your friend is finally coming back," the guard said, peering out the front window.

Gideon and the two women hurried to meet O'Brien at the door.

Elizabeth couldn't remember why the idea of a walk had sounded so appealing. After a breakfast of wormy mush, skim milk and greasy coffee too bitter to drink, they'd been put to work sewing underwear for the male inmates again. Then came a lunch of split pea soup made from peas that had not actually been cooked, and before they went back to the sewing room, Matron Herndon had invited a few of the ladies for an afternoon stroll. Elizabeth should have known better.

The woods surrounding the workhouse were stark and leafless, but being outside was a welcome change. At first the cold air had invigorated her, or maybe it was just being away from the stench of the workhouse, but they hadn't gone far before Elizabeth had to stop. Leaning over, hands on her knees, she gasped for breath. The cold air seared her lungs, and her head swam. What on earth was wrong with her?

Two days without proper food had already taken a toll, and not just on her. The others had stopped, too, leaning against the damp tree trunks or each other. They all looked unnaturally pale and drawn, making Elizabeth glad she didn't have access to a mirror herself.

"Is this the best you can do?" Herndon said the third time the women stopped, gasping and panting. "I don't know how you suffs manage to walk around the White House if you can't walk a few steps in the woods."

Luckily, Elizabeth was too weak to do what she really wanted to do. She would have ended up at the workhouse for the rest of her life.

"I don't think I can walk another step," Anna said. "What will she do to me if I can't go on?"

Before Elizabeth could answer, an eerie howl drifted to them through the trees. The hairs on the back of her neck stood up.

"What's that?" someone asked.

Herndon grinned. "That's the hounds. Somebody must've escaped. We'd better hurry and get back."

"Will the dogs attack us?" Miss Findeisen asked. She was one of the younger women, and she obviously came from money, if Elizabeth could judge from her boldness in daring to address Herndon.

Herndon nodded, as if acknowledging an especially astute question. "That's exactly what they'll do."

The baying grew louder. Elizabeth saw her own terror reflected on Anna's face and took her arm.

"Come on."

Every muscle screamed in protest, but she forced her weary body to move. She needed to escape, but she couldn't leave the rest of them behind. Not bothering to ask herself why she should care, she poked and prodded the others.

"Let's go. We have to get back."

"I can't," Anna said.

"You have to." She gave her a shove to get her moving.

She'd heard what dogs could do, and even though she didn't think Whittaker would dare let the suffragists get mauled, she wasn't sure Mrs. Herndon cared one way or the other.

With Anna moving, Elizabeth herded the rest of them in behind her. One woman started to protest, but something in Elizabeth's expression stopped her, and she fell into step with the others.

Too weak, she couldn't run, even though every instinct demanded it. Stumbling and staggering and driven by the haunting wail of the dogs as they searched for their prey, Elizabeth moved forward, sometimes leading, sometimes following, as the others made their own uncertain way. Half falling, she felt a hand on her arm, reaching out to help. Her gaze locked for a second with a woman whose name she did not know.

"Careful," she said.

"Thank you," Elizabeth said. Words she rarely used and seldom meant.

The hounds were louder, closer now, their baying like echoes out of hell.

Miss Findeisen stumbled, trying to hurry, and Elizabeth caught her arm. "Careful," she said.

Miss Findeisen smiled weakly.

Anna staggered and nearly fell. "I can't go on," she sobbed, slumping against a tree.

Elizabeth grabbed her arm. "You have to. The dogs will tear you to pieces."

Her eyes widened, but she didn't move.

Desperate, Elizabeth pulled Anna's arm over her shoulders. "Lean on me."

"You can't carry me!"

"We can do it together," Miss Findeisen said, taking Anna's other arm.

They lurched off, half dragging, half carrying her. Elizabeth's lungs burned with each breath and all her muscles screamed in agony at every step, but still she put one foot in front of the other over and over until her legs at last refused and her knees buckled. But someone caught her and took Anna's weight from her shoulders, and someone else linked arms with her, urging her on.

Breathless and terrified and nearly hysterical, clinging to each other until no one knew who was really helping whom, they finally staggered back to the hideous safety of the workhouse. Only when they reached the familiar sewing room could Elizabeth be certain the baying of the hounds was now just an echo in her head.

Elizabeth and the other six women who had been out with her collapsed onto their chairs at the sewing machines, unable to do anything but gasp for breath. After what seemed an age, when she could breathe almost normally again and finally became aware of her surroundings, she sensed a current of unease that had nothing to do with their return.

The women who had stayed behind were stiff and silent, their eyes guarded, their lips pursed.

"What happened?" Elizabeth asked the one nearest her.

The woman glanced around to make sure no guard was near. "They took Miss Burns."

Elizabeth looked around, too. Sure enough, the woman with the fiery red hair was nowhere in sight. "Where?"

"No talking!" the guard called from across the room.

Elizabeth muttered a curse.

She had to wait until after supper to find out. In the last hour before they went to bed, the women were herded into the large "recreation" room and allowed some time to socialize. Weary beyond bearing, they all sought the chairs placed around the edges of the room and sat in numbed silence.

The regular prisoners were there, too, the ones wearing rags so the suffragists could have the "nicer" clothes. They sat in clusters apart from the suffragists, talking and picking nits out of each other's hair.

Elizabeth found Mrs. Bates and sank onto the floor beside her chair because the chairs beside her were already taken. "What happened to Miss Burns?"

"She asked to see Whittaker. She wanted to repeat her demands that we be treated like political prisoners. He came into the sewing room and . . ." Mrs. Bates shuddered at the memory. "He came in furious. I'm not sure why he was already so angry, but he just wanted to know what nonsense—that's the word he used—what nonsense Miss Burns had to say now. She told him she wanted to see an attorney and find out the status of our case, but he told her to shut up or he'd put her in a straitjacket and a buckle gag."

There it was again. "What's a buckle gag?"

Mrs. Bates shuddered again. "It's a device they use on insane people to keep them from screaming or biting."

Elizabeth winced at the thought. "I guess she didn't shut up."

"No, she didn't. She demanded her right to see an attorney, and Whittaker had her taken away."

"Where is she now?"

"No one knows."

Elizabeth doubted that very much. In a place like this, someone always knew something. "I'll find out."

She got wearily to her feet and strolled as non-chalantly as she could over to where some of the colored prisoners sat in a group. They eyed her warily, so she tried a smile. They didn't return her smile, but they didn't turn their backs, either.

"What you want, miss?" one of them asked. She was a little older than the others, and they probably considered her their leader.

"The warden took one of the suffragists today, Miss Burns."

"The one with red hair," she said with a nod.

"Yes, that's right. Do you know what happened to her?"

"I do."

She'd expect some kind of payment for the information. "I don't have anything to offer you in return. I was hoping that you'd help out of kindness from one woman to another."

The woman smiled, showing a missing tooth and little humor. "When did you folks ever do a kindness for us?"

"When women get the vote, it will help you, too. It will help all women."

They all grinned at that, and one even chuckled aloud.

"You ain't never gonna get the vote, miss. Might as well give up on that."

Elizabeth returned her grin. "Then help us because you feel sorry for us."

"Didn't think I'd ever feel sorry for no white ladies, but you folks is kinda sad, ain't they, girls?" The others nodded, enjoying themselves at Elizabeth's expense.

Elizabeth was perfectly willing to amuse them if she got the information she wanted. "Miss Burns?"

"They put her in the DT ward. You know what that is?"

Elizabeth shuddered. She knew only too well. "Thank you. I'm in your debt."

"I'll remember that."

Elizabeth was sure she would.

She hurried back to where Mrs. Bates waited. Anna had joined her, and they both watched anxiously as she crossed the room to them.

"What is it?" Mrs. Bates asked, seeing Elizabeth's expression.

Elizabeth sank down on the floor beside her chair. "They say he put her in the DT ward. Do you know what that is?"

"No."

"It's where they treat prisoners with delirium tremens."

"What's that?"

Elizabeth went cold at the memory, Jake's mother screaming in terror . . . "It's what happens when somebody who drinks a lot stops suddenly. They get the shakes and start seeing things that aren't there. I guess that happens to some prisoners when they're locked up here and can't drink anymore."

"So they'd probably put them in straitjackets."

"And buckle gags," Anna said in outrage. "But she's not crazy, and she doesn't have the delirium tremens. They can't do that to her!"

Mrs. Bates gave her a sad smile, as if to say they most certainly could, and of course they already had. They could do anything they wanted.

Elizabeth gritted her teeth against the rage boiling within her, the rage that had made her want to beat Mrs. Herndon and club Whittaker over his stupid head and shoot Thornton right between the eyes.

"Betty Perkins! Which one of you is Betty Perkins?"

Elizabeth's rage evaporated as she looked up at the female guard walking slowly around the room, staring each of the prisoners in the face.

"Come on, Betty. Somebody's paid your fine. Just speak up and you can leave," she coaxed, looking Elizabeth right in the eye.

Gooseflesh rose on her arms, but she stared the woman down until she turned to Mrs. Bates for a reaction. Then she tried to glare at Anna, but the girl had already gotten up to start spreading the word about Miss Burns, so the guard moved on.

"I don't understand," Mrs. Bates said. "Why don't they know who this Betty Perkins is? They certainly took every bit of information about all of us that they could. They must know who all their other prisoners are, too."

Elizabeth could have explained it, of course, but she said, "Maybe she didn't use her real name."

"Why would she do that?"

Elizabeth tried to imagine being so innocent that she couldn't think of a reason to lie about her identity. "Maybe she's ashamed to be in jail and doesn't want her family to find out."

"None of the suffragists are ashamed to be here, so it can't be one of us."

"Is that true, ma'am?" a girl sitting on the other side of Mrs. Bates asked. She was one of the regular prisoners, a white girl with a sharp, thin face and hair the color of poppies growing in black at the roots.

"Is what true?" Mrs. Bates asked.

"That this Betty Perkins isn't one of you ladies."

"I'm sure she's not."

Elizabeth got gooseflesh again as the idea

formed in her mind. She leaned around to see the girl better. She had a gleam in her eye that told Elizabeth she might be bold enough to take a chance. "Why do you ask?"

The girl shrugged and made a face she must have thought looked innocent. "Just curious."

"I guess this Betty Perkins isn't one of the regular prisoners, either."

"Oh no. Who'd miss out on a chance to get out of here? Except for you ladies, I mean."

Elizabeth returned her innocent look. "Why don't you tell them you're Betty Perkins, then?"

Mrs. Bates frowned. "That would be dishonest."

Elizabeth didn't bother to remind her that the girl was already in jail, for heaven's sake, and the girl herself didn't seem at all bothered by the prospect of some more dishonesty. "Now, that's a thought. But do you think they'd believe me?"

Elizabeth pretended to consider the question. "They might, and then you'd be out of here."

"But what if they don't?"

"Then you're no worse off, are you?"

"Are you sure that's wise, Elizabeth?" Mrs. Bates asked. "She might get in trouble."

"I can't get in much worse trouble than I'm already in," the girl said. "And this could get me out of it."

"Yes, it could," Elizabeth said. "If they want to know why you didn't speak up before, tell them you didn't want to give your real name because you didn't want your family to know you'd been locked up."

The girl gave Elizabeth a shrewd glance that saw more than Mrs. Bates ever would. "Thank you kindly, miss. You're a good one."

Elizabeth nodded and watched her scurry over to the guard, who gave her an earful for putting them to so much trouble finding her, and then the two of them left the room.

"That was very clever," Mrs. Bates said, although she didn't sound like she entirely approved. "However did you think of it?"

"I don't know," Elizabeth lied, giving Mrs. Bates her most innocent face. "It just seemed logical, and a kindness," she added quickly, "to help another female escape from this place."

Anna hurried back over, saving Elizabeth from any more inquiries. Plainly, she had some news.

"They said Mr. O'Brien was here today."

"Who did?" Mrs. Bates asked.

"One of the guards told Julia. She felt sorry for her. For all of us, I guess."

"Who's Mr. O'Brien?" Elizabeth asked.

"He's our attorney. What was he doing here?"

"The guard didn't know. She just said he came, and I guess they wouldn't let him see us, but there's more. Miss Burns has started a hunger strike, and Mrs. Lewis has joined her."

Chapter Five

O'Brien smiled at their eagerness as they met him at the door. "I found a friendly judge."

"Thank heaven," Mrs. Young said.

"You got the writ?" Gideon felt the first stirrings of hope that his mother would soon be free.

"Yes. All we have to do is find a deputy to serve it, and we can force the warden to present the prisoners in court."

"When can we see them?" Miss Morey asked.

O'Brien's smile vanished. "Not today, I'm afraid. Warden Whittaker made it clear to me that he is determined not to let us in unless a judge orders him to."

"But what about the writ or whatever it is?" Miss Morey asked.

"The writ will only get us before the judge," Gideon said. "Whittaker will know that, I'm afraid, and besides, it's Friday evening. Even if we find someone to serve Whittaker today, the soonest the judge can hear the case is Monday."

"Oh dear," Mrs. Young said.

"Which is why I'm going to ask Mr. Bates to take you ladies back to Washington," O'Brien said.

"I won't go back until I see Tilly," Mrs. Young said.

O'Brien frowned. "Please be reasonable. I can't leave you ladies here overnight, and I don't want to have to worry about your comfort while I'm trying to take care of everything else."

Gideon sighed out his frustration. "Surely, I can be of some assistance to you."

"Not here, but if you were back in Washington, you might be able to put some pressure on the right people."

"I suppose I could go see Mr. Tumulty again and tell him what's happening here," Mrs. Young said.

Miss Morey nodded her agreement. "We can also find some friendly reporters to do a story. If nothing else, we may be able to shame President Wilson into releasing them."

The guard cleared his throat. "I'll be glad to drive you folks back to the train station."

They all glared at him, but he only shrugged.

"We must let everyone at headquarters know our situation," O'Brien said to Gideon. "I need you to make sure these ladies get back safely, and I may need you to use your legal skills in Washington. You'd be doing me a great favor."

Gideon thought of his mother in that workhouse and wanted to put his fist through the wall, but he managed to swallow his fury. O'Brien was probably right. Staying here wouldn't help the prisoners, but he might do some good back in the district. "It will be my privilege to escort you ladies back to Washington."

Mrs. Young sighed in defeat. "If only I could leave these clothes for Tilly."

"You can give them to her yourself on Monday," Gideon said.

Hunger strike.

Elizabeth rolled the idea around in her mind. A few days ago, it would have been unthinkable, but that was before she'd eaten the food here.

"I think we should do it," Anna said, rejoining Elizabeth on the floor beside Mrs. Bates's chair.

"What would a hunger strike accomplish?" Elizabeth asked.

"It's an ancient tactic used by the powerless against the powerful," Mrs. Bates said.

Anna nodded. "In Ireland, if you had a grievance against someone, you'd sit on their doorstep and fast until you'd shamed them into giving you justice." Her eyes practically glowed with the enthusiasm of the fanatic.

Elizabeth knew better than to trust that enthusiasm. "How could starving to death shame somebody else?"

"The rules of hospitality were very strict in olden times," Mrs. Bates said. "Allowing someone to die on your doorstep was a great dishonor."

"Somehow I doubt Whittaker cares about his honor," Elizabeth said.

Mrs. Bates smiled. "You're probably right, but President Wilson can't allow forty respectable women to die in prison just because they marched in front of his house."

"He can't allow even one of us to die," Anna said. "Think of the scandal."

"We may not even have to go through with it," Mrs. Bates said. "If Mr. O'Brien was here today, we know he's working for our release. They might let us go tomorrow."

Elizabeth didn't want to get out tomorrow. She didn't want to get out at all, not with Thornton waiting for her. "Would we all have to do it?"

"None of us *have* to do it," Mrs. Bates said. "It would be completely voluntary."

Voluntary, my foot. Elizabeth saw the fanatic's gleam in Mrs. Bates's eye, too. She also saw the disapproval. A true suffragist would gladly starve for the cause. She glanced at Anna and saw only disappointment in her frown.

"Don't you want to do it, Elizabeth?" Anna looked as if somebody had just told her there was no Santa Claus.

For a few seconds, Elizabeth couldn't breathe. What was wrong with her? She didn't care what these women thought of her, so why did their disappointment sting so badly? "It's not that . . ."

Elizabeth looked back at Mrs. Bates, oddly desperate to get back in her good graces, but Mrs. Bates was already smiling at her. "Oh, I see. Anna, Elizabeth isn't thinking of herself. She's thinking of you."

"Me?" Anna smiled at Elizabeth, too, inordinately pleased about something.

"Yes, and so am I. You're already painfully thin, my dear. Even just a few days without food could make you quite ill."

Elizabeth was almost too surprised to take advantage of Mrs. Bates's mistake.

Almost.

"She's right," Elizabeth said. "You shouldn't do this. It's too dangerous."

Anna took Elizabeth's hand in both of hers. "You are a true friend to be so concerned, but I couldn't possibly sit by while the rest of you made such a sacrifice."

"Why not? If we shame them into letting us go, it doesn't matter if one of us starved or all of us."

"It matters to me."

And Elizabeth could see that it did. She turned back to Mrs. Bates. Surely, she could talk sense to Anna. The girl wouldn't last more than a few days without food.

"You must swear to me that if you become ill, you will start to eat again," she said instead. Elizabeth wanted to smack her.

Anna smiled sweetly. "Of course."

She was a much better liar than Warden Whittaker.

Oscar Thornton had dressed carefully this Sunday morning, but not because he was going to church.

Going to church was a waste of valuable time. Oh no. He had something much more important to do. He was going to see Miss Betty Perkins this morning. It would be the last time he saw Miss Perkins, and it would be the last time she saw anyone at all, so he'd dressed for the occasion.

Fletcher and Lester would have taken charge of her at the train station down in Virginia, and they would escort her here, to his hotel. Lester's telegram had estimated what time they would arrive, and when Thornton checked his gold pocket watch, he saw it wouldn't be long now. His hand trembled a bit with the thrill of anticipation. No one cheated Oscar Thornton and lived to tell the tale.

A woman's shrill voice raised in protest broke the silence. What the . . . ? He'd told them to keep her quiet. He hurried over and threw open the door. As he'd expected, Lester and Fletcher stood there with a woman between them, but the woman was not Betty Perkins.

"Is this him?" she asked, glaring up at him balefully.

The door across the hall opened and a curious face peered out.

"Get her inside," Thornton said, standing back so they could enter.

Fletcher gave the woman a shove and she staggered across the threshold. "Hey, watch what you're doing!" she said.

"Shut up," Fletcher said.

114

Thornton closed the door behind them. "Who the hell is this?"

Lester gave him a disgusted look. "Betty Perkins."

"That's not—"

"I know, but that's who they released from the workhouse after we paid the fine."

The girl was looking around the suite, obviously impressed. "This is all right. I wouldn't mind staying here myself."

Thornton turned on Lester, furious. "If you knew it wasn't her, why did you bring her here?"

"I thought you'd like to hear her story."

"It's a good one," Fletcher added.

Thornton ignored him. He studied the girl with distaste, taking in her garishly red hair, her cheap dress and worn shoes. "All right, young woman, what's your story?"

"My name is Betty Perkins, and I'm real grateful you got me out of that workhouse." She tipped her head and batted her eyes in a disgusting attempt at flirtation. "Want me to show you how grateful I am?"

"No."

This time she blinked her eyes in surprise. "These other two fellows wasn't so particular."

"I'm sure they weren't," Thornton said, glaring at them. They refused to meet his eye.

"Tell him what you told us, about how you got out," Lester said.

She sighed, obviously bored with the story. "They'd been coming around for a couple days, calling out for Betty Perkins. They said somebody'd paid her fine and she could go, only nobody ever owned up to being this Betty Perkins."

Thornton turned to Lester. "Don't they keep track of who they've got locked up there?"

"They told us they didn't have no Betty Perkins in there. She must've used another name when she got arrested."

"Why didn't you just go in and look for yourself?"

"They won't let anybody in to see those women. No visitors at all, not even if we paid." He said to the girl, "Tell him the rest."

"So last night, the guard comes around calling for Betty Perkins again, and this girl says to me why don't I tell them I'm Betty Perkins and they'll let me go."

Rage swelled inside him. "What did she look like?"

"I don't know. Auburn hair, I guess."

"Blue eyes?"

"I didn't notice."

Thornton gestured to Fletcher, who slapped the girl so hard, she fell to her knees.

"Jesus, Mary and Joseph! Why'd you go and do that?" she cried, clutching her face and cringing in terror.

"Blue eyes?" Thornton said.

"Yeah, I guess. I didn't pay much attention!" She yelped when Fletcher raised his hand again.

"It was her," Lester said. "She told Sally here to claim she was Betty. Who else could it be?"

Who else indeed? She'd tricked him again.

"Wasn't no need to hit me," she said. "I think you broke my jaw." She felt it gingerly.

For one blissful moment, Thornton considered breaking far more than her jaw, but then common sense prevailed. A hotel was too public a place for that. "Get her out of here," Thornton said.

"Not so fast," she said. "They said you'd pay me. I came here and told you what happened, didn't I?"

"Get rid of her," Thornton said.

Nearly three full days had passed since O'Brien had sent Gideon back to Washington with the ladies and still no word. Somehow Gideon had expected the case would be heard today, Monday, but if it had been, O'Brien hadn't seen fit to let them know. Gideon was pacing around the front room of the Woman's Party headquarters, earning black looks from the handful of women who hadn't yet left for the day, when Mrs. Young came in.

Gideon rushed to meet her, alarmed at how pale she was. "Are you all right?"

"What? Oh, yes, thank you, Mr. Bates. I . . . I'm just confused."

Gideon asked one of the women to fetch Mrs. Stevens. "Sit down," he said to Mrs. Young, pulling over one of the desk chairs for her. "Wouldn't Mr. Tumulty see you?"

"Oh, he saw me." She shook her head as if trying to dispel some unpleasant memory.

Mrs. Stevens came hurrying into the room. "Mrs. Young, were you able to—" She stopped when she got a good look at Mrs. Young's face. "What happened?"

"I was just telling Mr. Bates, Mr. Tumulty met with me. I don't know how he could have refused. I've known him almost my entire life, after all, but it was the strangest thing. He knew all about the writ that Mr. O'Brien had obtained. He even knew the judge's name. How could he have known that?"

"Someone at the courthouse probably told Warden Whittaker," Gideon said. "I'm sure Whittaker is keeping his superiors informed. What did he say about it?"

"He told me it was silly for us to go to all that trouble. He said if we would just wait a week, the prisoners would be released."

Mrs. Stevens huffed derisively. "If they're going to release them, why do they have to wait a week?"

"That's what I asked him, but he just started telling me how foolish the women were to start a hunger strike."

Gideon felt a chill of apprehension. "A hunger strike? Did he mean Miss Paul's hunger strike at the district jail?"

"No, he was talking about the women in Virginia."

"Of course," said Mrs. Stevens. "Lucy Burns is probably leading it. After the way the women were treated that first night, what else could she do?"

She could have thought about the safety of the other women, Gideon thought, imagining his mother wasting away in a prison cell. But that wasn't fair. His mother was just as likely to be the leader. "What in God's name is O'Brien doing? He should have gotten the women released by now."

The telephone rang, startling them all. Gideon ran a hand over his face as one of the women answered it. "Mrs. Stevens, it's Mr. O'Brien."

She hurried over and picked up the candlestick phone. "Mr. O'Brien? What's the situation?"

Gideon and Mrs. Young had followed and stood hovering, straining to make out O'Brien's words.

"Good heavens, are you sure?" she asked after a few moments.

"What is it?" Gideon asked, somehow resisting the urge to snatch the telephone from her hands.

"Yes, he's right here. Just a moment." She handed the telephone to him. "He wants to speak with you. He said he hasn't been able to find a deputy to serve the warrant."

"What?" Gideon lifted the earpiece. "You can't find a deputy?"

"No, they've all disappeared," the tinny voice said.

"What do you mean, *disappeared?*"

"I mean I've got a list of them, and none of them are at home or any other place where they can be found."

"That's impossible!"

"Yes, it is, which means that someone has instructed them to hide from me."

This was worse than they'd feared. "Mrs. Young just returned from seeing Wilson's secretary, Tumulty, and he told her if we just wait a week, the women will be released."

"A week? What will happen in a week?"

"I have no idea, but we can't wait a week. They've started a hunger strike."

"How do you know that?"

"Mr. Tumulty told Mrs. Young."

"How did *he* know that?"

"Probably the same way he knew you'd gotten the writ."

O'Brien swore eloquently. "It makes sense now. I've been followed all day. At first I thought I was imagining it, but now . . . They've obviously got some detectives watching me."

"I'm coming back down there. Maybe between the two of us, we can find a deputy to serve the warrant."

"Take the early train tomorrow. I'll meet you at the station."

The first day had been the hardest. Elizabeth's stomach growled and cramped in protest, but she looked at the pinched faces of the other women and thought better of complaining. Usually, the hunger pangs lasted three days, they'd told her, but she'd eaten so little since arriving at the workhouse last Wednesday that they'd stopped after only two. Strangely, she felt suddenly energetic, as if she'd like to go for a walk in the woods. Except for those cursed bloodhounds, of course.

The women were gathered in the gymnasium for their recreation hour before bedtime. Those who had experience with hunger strikes moved among them, sharing information.

"You won't feel hungry now for a while," one of them told her.

"How long?" Elizabeth asked.

"A few days, maybe even a few weeks. When you start to feel hungry again, that's when you have to worry."

"Why?" Anna asked.

"Because your body is starving then and starting to die."

"But they'll let us go before that happens," someone said. "That's why we're doing this, after all."

Anna slipped her hand into Elizabeth's. "I

couldn't do this if you weren't doing it, too. I'd be too frightened."

"They won't let us die," Mrs. Bates said. "Now that they know we're serious, they'll force-feed us. We need to be prepared for that."

Elizabeth remembered all too well the description of force-feeding she'd heard in the police van that day last week when they'd first been arrested.

The guards signaled to them that their hour of "recreation" was over and it was time for bed. The women rose and moved toward the door. When she stood up, Elizabeth had to stop for a minute and wait for her head to clear. The room swam before her, so she closed her eyes and drew a deep breath. A collective gasp startled her, and she opened her eyes to see Anna slumped on the floor. A dozen other women had already rushed to help her, but her face was chalk white and her eyes didn't even flutter when they tried to haul her to her feet.

"Leave her," a guard said. "We'll take her to the infirmary."

The other women backed away uncertainly, but Elizabeth squeezed in and dropped to her knees beside the unconscious girl. "Anna, wake up!" She grabbed her wrists and tried chafing them.

Mrs. Bates laid a hand on Elizabeth's shoulder. "It's for the best. They'll feed her there."

"*Force*-feed her," Elizabeth said, outraged at Mrs. Bates's complacency. "And she'll be terrified if she wakes up all alone."

Mrs. Bates squeezed her shoulder. "She won't be alone for long. Look around."

Elizabeth looked up at the circle of faces and for the first time really saw the changes: the hollow cheeks, the shadowed eyes, the pasty complexions. Even the spark of fanaticism Elizabeth had noticed before was gone from their eyes, replaced by a dull determination.

"Get moving!" the guard shouted, prodding the women into motion. "Don't worry about your little friend there. We'll take care of her." She grinned viciously.

Elizabeth jumped to her feet, ready to scratch her eyes out, but Mrs. Bates grabbed her arm. "You won't do Anna any good," she whispered fiercely, stopping Elizabeth in her tracks.

As weak as she was, she probably couldn't do the guard much damage in any case. With the frustrated fury still boiling in her, she stepped away from where Anna lay and followed the others as they filed out of the room. When she reached the door, she glanced back. A guard stood over Anna, nudging her with her foot.

Damn them. Damn them every one.

Gideon paced the platform as the New York train pulled into Union Station. He'd asked David not to come to Washington, but he really couldn't blame him for ignoring that request. David must have been terrified for Anna and feeling helpless after Gideon told him about their failure to find a deputy to serve the writ on Warden Whittaker. Gideon had returned to Washington just that morning himself. He only wished that being in Washington could actually help.

Finally, he saw David's familiar figure step down from a car farther down the track. He hurried toward him.

"Gideon!" David called, waving.

Gideon shook his hand, then noticed the men who had emerged behind him, two plug-uglies and one well-dressed fellow who was probably the last person Gideon wanted to see right now.

"Gideon, you remember Oscar Thornton."

"Of course," Gideon said. David must have encountered Thornton on the train and hadn't been able to shake him.

"Good to see you, Bates," Thornton said, shaking his hand. "Vanderslice has told me about your mother and the other suffragettes."

Gideon felt the heat rising in his face as he glared at David. What was he thinking to confide in Thornton? Mother would be furious. Since her cousin Marjorie's tragic death, she'd had absolutely no use for the man.

"Thornton came to see me at my office yesterday about . . . about some business," David said quickly, seeing Gideon's reaction, "and I had to tell him I couldn't even think about business until Anna was safe. Gideon, he believes he can

124

help. Or at least his men here can." He nodded at the plug-uglies, and they grinned at Gideon, making him even angrier.

"Exactly how can they help?" Gideon asked, not bothering to hide his skepticism.

"Vanderslice told me your man in Virginia hasn't been able to locate any deputies to serve the writ," Thornton said. "I'd like to let my boys here have a try."

Gideon studied the two men with their bowler hats pulled low over faces marked by fights past. Were they the kind of men to beat the administration at their own game? Now, that was an interesting idea. David had no business dragging Thornton into this, but Gideon couldn't let his offended pride stand in the way if Thornton really could help.

"Let's find a more comfortable place to discuss this, shall we?" Gideon said.

Thornton left his "boys" to collect the luggage. The three men climbed into a cab and headed for the Willard Hotel.

"Have you heard anything at all about how the women are doing?" David asked when they were on their way.

"We finally got a firsthand report. They released Mrs. Nolan today."

David remembered. "The elderly lady."

"Yes. She'd only been sentenced to six days, so her sentence was up."

"What did she say? Had she seen Anna?"

"She didn't know very much about the other women. They'd kept her in the infirmary the entire time. Probably afraid she'd die on them. Anyway, she only saw Miss Burns and Mrs. Lewis. They were in the infirmary, too, because they're on a hunger strike."

"I thought all the women were."

"Apparently, those two started the hunger strike. They're quite ill, according to Mrs. Nolan. She's not well herself. Even though she wasn't on the hunger strike, the food was so bad, she could barely eat."

Thornton had been following the conversation closely. Now he said, "What else have you been doing to get the women released?"

Gideon studied him for a moment. "Why are you so interested in this, Thornton? Are you a supporter of women's suffrage?"

Thornton cleared his throat. "As I explained to Vanderslice, any gentleman would be outraged at the way those women are being treated."

"Not really," Gideon said. "A lot of men think they're getting just what they deserve for daring to challenge the right of men to rule them. Even David here doesn't completely approve of their tactics."

"Why, I never—" David began, but Gideon silenced him with a gesture.

"Don't bother to deny it. It's no disgrace to

want your sister to stay at home where she's safe. But before we take Thornton up on his offer of help, I'd like to know why he made it."

Thornton studied Gideon in return. "I see you suspect my motives."

"Let's just say I wonder what they are."

Thornton gave him a crafty little grin. "You are wise to do so, because I must confess, they are entirely selfish."

Chapter Six

At first, refusing to work was a protest. Political prisoners were not required to work, or so Mrs. Bates had explained to Elizabeth. After a few days, however, Elizabeth simply could not have worked. Her limbs felt heavy and walking made her gasp for breath. Lying on her bed was about all she could manage. She and the others spent their time using what little strength they had to talk.

". . . and Miss Anthony was arrested for voting in the presidential election of 1872," Mrs. Bates told her as they lay curled up on their cots in the twilight of the winter evening. Mrs. Bates had moved to Anna's bed so they could talk more easily.

"Arrested? Is it actually illegal to vote?"

"It is if you're a woman."

"Why did she try it, then?"

Mrs. Bates smiled. "She had decided that the Fourteenth Amendment gave everyone in America the right to vote."

Elizabeth had never thought the garbage they'd taught her in school was all that important, and she couldn't remember what the Fourteenth Amendment was for. "Why did she think that?"

"Because it does, you see. It was passed to give Negro men the right to vote after the Civil

War, of course, but the wording doesn't say that exactly. Instead, it specifically gives all the rights of citizenship to 'All persons born or naturalized in the United States.' "

"*All* persons? I see; that should include women, too."

"But that wasn't what Congress had intended, of course, no matter what the law actually said. So when Susan Anthony voted, they arrested her."

Elizabeth smiled at her across the two feet of space separating their cots. "Did they charge her with obstructing traffic?"

"Oh, Elizabeth! Anna's right. You are very funny. No, I'm not sure what they charged her with, but her trial was much like ours. The judge refused to allow her to testify, and he instructed the jury to return a guilty verdict. When they did, he read an opinion that he'd written before the trial even started."

"Just like they got things ready for us here before we were even arrested."

"Exactly."

"Did she go to jail?"

"No, they just gave her a fine, but she never paid it."

"Good for her." Elizabeth sighed. "That was so long ago, and nothing's changed a bit since then."

"Oh, women have been working for suffrage even longer than that. They held the first Women's Rights Convention in 1848."

Elizabeth did the math in her head. "Sixty-nine years."

"Yes. Can you imagine a group of men fighting for something for so long?"

"Now *you're* being funny, Mrs. Bates."

The older woman grinned at her, making Elizabeth's chest go tight. When had Elizabeth begun to care so very much what Mrs. Bates thought of her? At first she'd been nervous, afraid she'd make some mistake and Mrs. Bates would know she wasn't really a lady like the rest of them. But if she had, Mrs. Bates either hadn't noticed or hadn't cared. She'd just accepted Elizabeth the same way she accepted Anna. The thought made her want to cry.

Before she could think why, the guard called, "Suppertime!"

The women groaned their protest at having to move, but the guards strode through the room, prodding them up to their feet. Even though they refused to eat, they still had to walk to the dining hall three times a day. Each time, Elizabeth got up more slowly and wondered how many more times she'd have the strength to do it. Each time they went, one or two of the women would collapse, and the guards would carry them away to the infirmary.

Mrs. Bates had been right. Anna hadn't been alone for long.

As she filed out of the ward with the others

and shuffled to the dining hall that evening for a dinner they would not eat, Elizabeth realized how much she hated the enforced silence they had to endure during mealtimes. She got to spend the rest of the time with Mrs. Bates and the other women, talking about the movement and the women who had come before them and the things they had done. Elizabeth found the stories fascinating.

How odd that she had reached the ripe old age of twenty-one without learning the joys of being with other women. Elizabeth could not remember ever having an actual conversation with her own mother. Of course, she'd been only thirteen when her mother died, so perhaps things would have been different if she'd lived until Elizabeth was older. Elizabeth would like to think so, but maybe not. She'd never know now, and in the years since, she'd spent her time with men. Men didn't have conversations with women. They just told women what to do and then waited until they did it.

Women, she was learning, were very different creatures.

Elizabeth followed the line of women up to the kitchen window, where the workers handed each of them a plate of slop. The plate, she noticed, was getting heavier each time, just as the walk from the ward to the dining hall had gotten longer each time. Slowly, deliberately, she put one foot in front of the other and took her turn, but unlike the other women, she didn't dump her dinner into the garbage can. Instead she carried it over to the table where the colored prisoners sat and set it down in front of the woman who had given her the information about Lucy Burns. The wormy mess was poor payment, indeed, but the regular prisoners were grateful for it.

Then Elizabeth picked up a cup of water, as she had been instructed, and carried it to a table.

"No talking," the guard said, even though no one had said a word.

Mrs. Bates sat down beside her. The older woman's cheeks were sunken, and dark circles rimmed her eyes. How much longer until she collapsed and had to be carried away? How Elizabeth would miss her wisdom. Impulsively, she reached out and laid a hand on her arm.

Mrs. Bates looked up and smiled. "Drink your water. That's very important."

"No talking!" the guard shouted.

Elizabeth drank her water.

After what seemed an age, the regular prisoners had finished their meals and started getting up to leave.

"You suffs, stay where you are." Elizabeth looked up in surprise to see the matron glaring at them.

How odd. Mrs. Herndon never came into the dining hall.

When the regular prisoners had gone, Herndon said, "Listen up. This is Mr. Ingalls." She nodded to a well-dressed man who lurked in the doorway as if afraid to venture any farther into the room. Maybe he thought this ragtag bunch of starving women would attack him. The thought made Elizabeth smile. "He's an attorney for the president of the United States. He wants to talk to each one of you, so you'll take your turn. Sit here until we call you."

"The president!" someone whispered.

"They're getting serious," Mrs. Bates said.

"Quiet!" Herndon said, hushing the buzz of conversation.

One by one the women were summoned. At last, Elizabeth made her way out and down the hallway to an office, where the attorney sat at a table. Elizabeth took the chair opposite him, glad for a chance to rest and catch her breath.

"I'm pleased to meet you, Miss Miles," he said, although he didn't look pleased at all.

Elizabeth waited.

"You look like an intelligent young lady."

"I'm in jail, Mr. . . . What was your name again?"

"Ingalls."

"I'm in jail, Mr. Ingalls. How smart is that?"

"You don't fool me, Miss Miles. I know you suffragettes are quite clever."

133

"Suffragists."

"What?"

"We like to be called suffragists. The word 'suffragette' is demeaning."

He stared at her for a long moment. "I see."

"Do you?"

"Well, perhaps I should just tell you why I wanted to meet with you."

Elizabeth waited again. She figured he didn't need any encouragement.

He gave a little cough. "You see, as Mrs. Herndon said, I'm an attorney. Not for the president, exactly, but for the administration. President Wilson asked me to come and assure you ladies that he has no intention of keeping you locked up here for three months. In fact, he plans to see that you're released in a week. Just one week."

He paused, probably to let this wonderful news sink in. Elizabeth wished she wasn't so weak. She should be able to figure out what he was up to, but her brain just didn't want to make the effort. "Herndon could have told us that."

"Yes, yes, she could, but you see, the president wanted you to hear it from an official source because, well, because some people are working to serve the warden with a writ of habeas corpus, and we wanted you to know you should refuse the writ. There's no need for you to go to court and involve a judge in this matter."

What was this writ he was talking about? Mrs.

Bates had mentioned it, she was sure, but she couldn't pull up the right memory just now. She didn't really need to know, though, did she? Oh no. She knew just what Mrs. Bates would tell her to say, Mrs. Bates who had a family full of lawyers. "I think I'd like to see my own attorney before I make a decision about that, Mr. Igloo."

"Ingalls," he said. "But there's no need for that. You have my word that you're going to be released in a week, so there's also no need for a hunger strike. Why should you ladies make yourselves ill for no purpose? I assure you, President Wilson is determined to give you your freedom."

"Then why not just release us right now? Why wait a week?"

"It's a legal matter," he lied. She could tell by the way he blinked, glad to discover she wasn't completely addled. "Some paperwork needs to be prepared. But it's just a week, and then you'll be allowed to go home to Wisconsin."

"South Dakota." She remembered that, at least. She was supposed to be from South Dakota.

"Yes, that's such a long trip, and you'll want to be well and strong when you're released, won't you?"

If she'd had the energy, Elizabeth would have slapped herself on the head for being stupid. Of course! They were going to wait a week in hopes the women would end their hunger strike and be recovered. How embarrassing to release a bunch of women who had to be carried out on stretchers. "I'd still like to speak to my attorney before I decide. I'm afraid I just don't understand all these legal things."

She smiled and batted her eyes in a parody of innocence.

Ingalls frowned. "I hope you will reconsider, Miss Miles. It's for your own good, you know."

How many times had men said that to women when it wasn't for their own good at all?

"May I go now, Mr. Ingledew?"

"Ingalls. Yes, yes, you may go."

Elizabeth took her time. No sense wasting energy rushing. It was just like Mrs. Bates had said. They couldn't force-feed forty women, and they couldn't allow them to starve to death, so they had to let them go. Still, they didn't want to release sick women and let the public get a look at them. Oh no. So they were trying to trick them into ending the hunger strike.

Good luck, Elizabeth thought as she made her way to the recreation room to tell Mrs. Bates what she'd figured out.

"Your motives are selfish?" Gideon echoed as their carriage swayed around a corner. "Just because you know Anna and my mother?"

"You could also add that they were such good friends to my dear wife," Thornton said with his oily smile. "But I wouldn't expect you to believe that. The reason I happened to call on Vanderslice in the first place is because I was going to ask him to assist me in an important business transaction, but he won't be of any use to anyone until his dear sister is home safe and sound."

Gideon didn't bother to hide his skepticism. He'd met too many men like Thornton in his career, men who came to him because they'd crossed one line too many in their business dealings and needed a bit of legal help to get them out of trouble. They always tried to pretend they'd only broken the law to help some poor soul in need. Thornton had always had that same self-righteous smugness, and it still set Gideon's teeth on edge. "Are you saying you're willing to help free the women so David will be available to help you with a business deal?"

"Would you believe me if I said I'm concerned only for the welfare of the women?"

Gideon stared at Thornton in grudging admiration. The man was an even bigger scoundrel than Gideon had thought, and he didn't even care if they knew it. He was also absolutely right. Gideon wouldn't have believed that for a second, but he had no trouble at all believing Thornton's claim of selfishness. "How do you think you can help?"

"As I said, I think my men would have better

luck finding these missing deputies than your people have."

"I was down there myself, and I assure you, we made every possible effort to locate them."

"I'm sure you did, but my men will look places you wouldn't go, and they'll spread around a little cash to encourage the flow of information, which I suspect you did not do. I've found that combination of efforts to be foolproof."

Gideon's experience confirmed his observation, but he didn't say so. "Where would they get the cash?"

"From me, of course. I expect to make a large profit on the business arrangement Vanderslice is going to assist me with. This would be an investment in my own future."

"You see, Gideon," David said, "when he explained all this to me, I knew we had to let him help."

Although Gideon found himself despising Thornton even more than he'd remembered, he said, "If your men can really find a deputy to serve the warrant, we would be forever in your debt."

"Forever is a long time, Bates. I would settle for a few weeks."

Elizabeth opened her eyes and instantly slammed them shut until the world stopped spinning. When she cautiously opened them again, a hoarse voice asked, "Are you awake?"

She turned her head slowly, mindful of how precariously she seemed to be balanced on the earth at the moment. A woman gazed at her from the next bed, her eyes enormous in her taut face. At first Elizabeth didn't know her . . .

"Anna?"

She smiled, showing bloodstained teeth.

"Your mouth . . ."

"It's from the forced feeding." Her voice sounded like sandpaper rasping softly against wood. "Don't fight them."

Elizabeth glanced around. She'd never seen this room before, but, obviously, it was the infirmary. Rows of beds filled with emaciated women lined the walls. Her nose burned from the smell of vomit and carbolic acid. "How did I get here?"

"You fainted, just like the others," a woman in a uniform said as she bustled by. One of the nurses. She didn't look like any angel of mercy Elizabeth had ever imagined, though. Her hard eyes and pinched mouth told of impatience and frustration with her charges.

"I don't remember fainting," Elizabeth said. Feeling a bit steadier, she pushed herself up a little so she could see the other beds. "Is Mrs. Bates here?"

"I haven't seen her," Anna said.

Elizabeth winced at the sound of her voice. "Don't talk. It must hurt."

Anna had been slender before, but now she was

skeletal. The skin of her face was paper-thin, the veins on her forehead were dark blue, and her hair lay limp and lifeless.

"Don't fight them," Anna said. "You can't stop them, and it only makes it worse."

"I said, don't talk! Anna, you promised that if you got sick you'd start eating again. Mrs. Bates made you promise. I remember. You've got to eat."

Anna smiled serenely for a second or two before a noise made her eyes widen in terror. Some of the others groaned, and one woman said, "No, God, please, no."

"What is it?" Elizabeth strained to hear, trying to identify the sound that had frightened them.

A familiar sound, a tapping and cracking, that spoke of warm kitchens on winter mornings. Eggs. Someone was cracking eggs. Lots and lots of eggs.

The nurse returned, her mouth pinched even more tightly now. She pushed a cart loaded with an odd assortment of things—medical equipment Elizabeth didn't recognize—and a big bowl. A bowl filled with raw eggs. A man wearing a suit came with her, followed by several of the regular inmates. They didn't look happy, and they didn't look at Elizabeth at all.

"Miss Miles, I'm Dr. Stanislov. You've been brought to the infirmary because you fainted from hunger. It is my duty to ask if you will agree to cease your hunger strike and voluntarily take some nourishment."

He spoke with an accent of some kind. Russian, probably, given his name. Elizabeth didn't have the strength to figure it out. She was too busy trying to figure out the expression in his dark eyes. She hadn't seen it in a man's eyes for so long that she hardly recognized it, but there it was, unmistakable: kindness.

How odd. But even in her current state, she was sure. He didn't like this any better than she did. But that didn't change anything.

"No, I won't eat," she said.

He sighed with what might have been resignation or maybe admiration. Elizabeth thought she must be delirious if she couldn't tell the difference. "I'll have to force-feed you, then. It's not a pleasant experience, Miss Miles." He picked up a piece of black rubber tubing from the cart. "I will insert this in your throat, and we will pour a liquid mixture of eggs and milk into your stomach. Are you sure you won't reconsider?"

Elizabeth glanced over at Anna, whose enormous eyes were squinched tightly shut, as if she could close out his words by not seeing him. Elizabeth thought of the blood in Anna's mouth and her raspy voice and the fear in her eyes. She thought of the groans of the other women, who had fallen completely silent now as they waited for her reply.

What would the Old Man tell her to do? He'd tell her she was a fool. He'd tell her to look after herself. He'd tell her she shouldn't be mixed up in somebody else's fight.

Except this wasn't somebody else's fight anymore.

"No, I won't reconsider."

The nurse grinned, her gimlet eyes sparkling with anticipation, but Elizabeth glared at her with her rich woman's glare and said, "We're doing this for you, too, you know. We're doing this for every woman who has ever been beaten down and abused."

The nurse blinked, and her grin faltered, and the doctor said, "Help me here," and she moved to help him. She wasn't grinning anymore.

"When I put the tube in your mouth, try to swallow it. That will make it easier."

Don't fight them, Anna had said, and she tried, she really did, but it was no use.

The tube tasted bitter and filled her mouth.

"Hold her," the doctor shouted because she was thrashing, swinging her head—or trying to—until something grabbed it in a vicelike grip. She tried to push him away, tried to grab the tube, but something caught her arms and held them fast, and a heavy weight bore down on her legs. The tube was down her throat, gagging her, choking her, ripping and tearing its way down inside of her, a searing pain like a hot poker against naked flesh. She gasped, desperate for air, but she couldn't breathe, couldn't speak, even though she was screaming inside. They were holding her, crushing her, suffocating her, killing her. Dark spots danced before her eyes, then everything went black.

Gideon and David found Thornton waiting for them in the hotel bar. They'd hurried back from the Woman's Party headquarters when he'd telephoned them saying he had news. He was sitting with his two plug-uglies, Lester and Fletcher, and another large man Gideon didn't know. Gideon thought he looked like he should be pushing a plow instead of drinking in the Willard Hotel.

Gideon and David pulled chairs up to the already crowded table and sat down.

"You said you had some important news," said Gideon, still eyeing the newcomer with suspicion.

"I do. Whittaker is in Washington."

"What?" David almost shouted.

"Lower your voice," Thornton said, glancing anxiously around the nearly empty room. "Everyone in this town is on the government payroll." Fortunately, everyone on the government payroll seemed to be still at their offices, working. "We found out Whittaker has been hiding here in the city the whole time we've been looking for him."

Gideon muttered a curse. "And who is this?" He nodded at the big farmer.

"Mr. Bates and Mr. Vanderslice, meet Deputy Klink," Thornton said.

Klink nodded politely.

"The deputy you found to serve the writ," Gideon remembered. Lester's telegram had said they found him hiding out on his brother's pig farm. Buying a transfer of his loyalty had been surprisingly cheap.

"Yeah, and he tried to serve it six times, but he never could find Whittaker, either at home or at the workhouse," Fletcher said.

"Because, as we found out this morning," Lester said, "he's been here in Washington since the writ was issued, hiding from us."

"Where is he?" David asked.

"At a cheap hotel, but it don't matter. Deputy Klink, here, he don't have no jurisdiction in Washington."

"We need to get Warden Whittaker back to Virginia," Deputy Klink said. He didn't seem to notice the black look Thornton gave him.

"And how do you propose to do that?" Gideon asked.

The three men looked at each other for a minute or two. Finally, Lester said, "We was hoping you'd have an idea."

"Good help is so hard to find," Thornton muttered, and for once Gideon had to agree with him.

"If we know where he is, why can't we just go talk to him?" David asked.

Thornton turned his black look on David. "What do you propose we talk to him about?"

"About releasing the women, of course."

"David," Gideon said patiently, "Whittaker couldn't release the women even if he wanted to, and we have no reason to think he does. He is bound by the law to keep them until ordered to do otherwise by a judge. That's why we need to get him to court." He turned to Thornton. "We do need to get him back to Virginia. What have your men found out about him?"

Thornton gave the men an impatient glance and said, "Just that he lives not far from the prison and he hasn't been home in days."

"Does he have family?"

"A wife."

"Good. She's going to send him a telegram telling him . . ." He gazed off into the distance, considering the possibilities.

"Why would she send him a telegram?" David asked.

"She wouldn't," Thornton snapped. "We'd send a telegram and sign her name."

"Oh, I see. Yes, of course. We could tell him she's sick or something."

Thornton seemed a little shocked by David's lack of insight. Apparently, he didn't really know him very well.

"And do we just hope Whittaker cares enough about his wife to go rushing home?" Gideon said. "Would that bring *you* rushing home, Thornton?"

Thornton smiled grimly. "Not if the president of the United States wanted me to stay in hiding."

"I think Whittaker would agree," Gideon said. "Maybe the president will send him a telegram instead."

This earned him a nod of approval from Thornton, but David said, "Does the president send people telegrams?"

"No, but I'll bet his secretary does," Gideon said. "And I just happen to know his name."

Don't throw up. Don't throw up. Deep breaths.

Air had never smelled so sweet, even the foul air of the dispensary. She wanted to tell Anna how happy she was to breathe, but she couldn't speak yet. Her throat burned and her jaws ached and every muscle in her body throbbed.

Don't throw up. They'll just do it again. The others had told her. Deep breaths.

The mess they'd poured down her throat lay like lead in her stomach. She tasted the sharpness of iron. Blood, she knew, seeping from the cuts in her mouth. She probed them gingerly with her tongue, testing each one, teasing the ragged skin and savoring the delicious twinge of pain because it proved she was alive.

"Elizabeth?"

She opened her eyes. Anna's wasted face came into focus. Elizabeth smiled to show she was all right.

"Miss Miles?"

Elizabeth flinched at the sound of his voice, but when she looked into his face, she saw the kindness again. She was lucky to get him, they'd told her. The other doctor enjoyed hurting the women.

"How are you feeling?" Dr. Stanislov asked.

"Terrible," she croaked, or tried to.

"I know that is not a pleasant experience, but we have no choice. We cannot allow you ladies to die."

Just what Mrs. Bates had told her.

"I must tell you how much I admire your dedication," he said, his dark eyes moist. "I would never have believed American women could care so much for freedom. I have seen women in Russia suffer for their ideals, but if I had not seen this with my own eyes, I would not have believed it."

"Do women in Russia go to prison?" Anna asked.

"Yes, my own sister did, when she would not betray her friends. Her friends were wanted by the government. She went on a hunger strike, too. They fed her after three days, but you women have been striking for almost a week."

"Doctor," one of the nurses called, and he hurried away.

"They took Lucy Burns and Mrs. Lewis away yesterday," Anna said.

"Where—" Her ravaged throat convulsed, silencing her.

"They don't tell us anything, but they were very sick, so maybe a hospital."

Anna needed to go to a hospital. Where was Mrs. Bates? She'd make Anna eat.

Her stomach roiled, and she swallowed hard, ignoring the searing agony.

Don't throw up. Deep breaths.

Gideon pretended to gaze out the train window at the passing scenery, but it was far too dark to see anything. Instead, he watched the reflection of the man he was learning to hate.

Warden Whittaker sat across the aisle of the railcar reading a newspaper but making little progress. He'd actually spent most of his energy tapping his foot and checking his pocket watch.

Gideon hated his ugly face and the spiderlike birthmark on his temple and his stubby hands and his fat feet. He wanted to slam Whittaker's ugly face into the train window and find out exactly how many times he'd have to do it before the glass shattered.

How fortuitous that his new friend, Mrs. Young, knew President Wilson's secretary so well. Mr. Tumulty's message urging Whittaker to return to Virginia at once had worked beautifully. The only problem had been convincing Thornton's henchmen that he didn't need their help following Whittaker from the hotel to the train station. They'd finally agreed that the dumb one, Fletcher, would wait at the station with Deputy Klink, and Lester would accompany Gideon. Two men having a conversation on a street corner wouldn't attract much attention, and so Whittaker had rushed right past them in front of his hotel in his search for a cab.

On the train, he'd split Lester and Fletcher up, one in the car ahead and the other in the car behind with Deputy Klink. Gideon didn't trust any of them not to betray themselves during what had begun to feel like the longest train ride in history. Finally, the conductor came bustling through to announce their stop. Gideon waited until Whittaker rose and started for the end of the car, then followed at a discreet distance.

When the train had rolled to a stop and the conductor released them, Fletcher came out of the car to his left, and Deputy Klink and Lester descended from the one on his right. A lone wagon stood outside the station, ready to transport any late travelers to their final destinations, its driver slumped inside his overcoat against the evening chill.

Whittaker hurried toward it, but Klink stepped in his path. "Say, ain't you Warden Whittaker, from Occoquan?" he asked pleasantly.

"What's it to you?" the hideous little man snapped.

" 'Cause if you are, I've got something for you."

Before Whittaker could blink, Klink slapped the writ into Whittaker's stubby little fingers.

"That's a warrant, Mr. Whittaker, and you've been served. You've got to show up at court tomorrow to see the judge. Oh, and you've got to produce your prisoners, too."

"Why, you son of a—"

"All forty of them," Gideon said.

Whittaker whirled to face him, and then he saw Fletcher and Lester and his beady little eyes widened in fear. "What's going on here?"

"We just want to make sure you understand," Gideon said. "That's a writ of habeas corpus, and we'd better see you at the courthouse tomorrow with all of your suffragist prisoners."

"And who do you think you are?"

"I'm an attorney for the Woman's Party, and if you aren't there, I'll make sure you're charged and arrested. I wonder how the guards would like to have you as a prisoner in your own workhouse, Whittaker."

Whittaker cursed them roundly, questioning the legitimacy of their birth and their ancestral heritage in terms Gideon had seldom heard outside of a saloon. He was so annoyed that he didn't offer to share the wagon with Gideon when they left the station.

• • •

The clanging of metal bedpans jarred Elizabeth awake. Disoriented, she needed a minute to remember where she was.

"Get up," a nurse said. "You're going to court today."

She tried to say, "Court?" but her throat rebelled, and the word came out a croak.

"Court!" Anna said. "I knew it! The hunger strike worked."

The hunger strike or the lawyers. Elizabeth's money was on the lawyers. She pushed herself up to see what was going on. The nurses scurried around, prodding the women awake and urging them to get up. Some inmates came in carrying bundles that proved to be sacks containing the prisoners' personal belongings. They were, it seemed, to dress in their own clothes for court.

Still weak, Elizabeth eased her legs off the bed and gingerly tried to stand. Oddly, she felt a little better than she had yesterday. Much as she hated to think it, the force-feeding had done her some good after all. A nurse plunked one of the sacks onto her bed, and she saw it bore a tag with *Elizabeth Miles* scrawled on it.

Apprehension shivered over her. Would it still be there? The money she'd sewn into her corset? The Old Man had taught her that. Always keep a stash for an emergency. If nobody had found it, she would be all right. She could get to New York and pick up her share of the Thornton score from the Old Man. She'd have to answer for what had happened to Jake, but she'd face that when she had to. First, she had to get out of here and make sure Thornton didn't find her.

She pulled open the bag and emptied it onto the bed. Everything was there. She wouldn't check for the money. No telling who might be watching. She glanced over to see how Anna was doing and found her struggling to sit up.

"Don't move!" The words snagged in her ragged throat, but she forced them out. "Let me get dressed and then I'll help you."

"I don't want to be a bother."

Elizabeth just glared at her until she slumped back down onto the bed obediently. Satisfied Anna would wait, she started stripping off her prison clothes. Without any obvious searching, she managed to find the hidden pocket inside her corset and felt the reassuring crinkle of banknotes. Relief flooded her. She'd be all right now. She just had to make a plan.

The other women were also trying to dress, with varying degrees of success, depending on how debilitated they were. Some, like Anna, couldn't even sit up. Those who were able dressed themselves and then helped the others. Ella Findeisen came over to assist her with Anna. The poor girl could hardly move her limbs. She was so thin, Elizabeth wondered why Anna's bones didn't break right through her skin. She already had open sores on her elbows and heels from shifting on the rough sheets.

Ella caught her eye at one point and whispered, "She won't be able to walk."

Elizabeth nodded, wondering how they could possibly even get her out of the bed.

But they needn't have worried. When the time came, those who couldn't walk were strapped onto stretchers and carried out to the waiting wagons. The rest of them straggled out, weak and weary but still avidly searching for the friends from whom they'd been separated. Elizabeth scanned the faces of the women climbing into the wagons. She saw Mrs. Bates, but her wagon pulled away before she could get to her. At least she was well. Elizabeth would find her when they got to the courthouse.

She would have to be clever, especially now because she wasn't strong. The judge might release them, and if he did, the news probably wouldn't hit the newspapers until tomorrow. That would give her a head start on Thornton and his thugs, at least. But she wasn't sure she was strong enough to get to New York without help. She'd have a much better chance if she could have a few days to rest up first. Was it too much to hope that the judge wouldn't release them at all? That something would happen so they could end the hunger strike but stay in jail for a while to recover? Probably. So she'd have to figure out something herself, some way to get herself to New York ahead of Thornton so he wouldn't kill her like he'd probably killed Jake.

That shouldn't be so hard, should it?

Chapter Seven

Gideon had been waiting on the courthouse steps with David for what seemed like hours. He hadn't known waiting could actually be painful. He'd paced and stood still and even tried to make conversation with David. None of that had been able to distract him from the awful anticipation or relieve the knot of tension burning in his chest. Would Anna and his mother really be released today? And even if they were, what condition would they be in? He had no doubt his mother would have joined the hunger strike, but what about Anna? She'd always been so frail. David was nearly frantic with worry. They both knew she wouldn't be able to survive for long without food.

Then, finally, something changed. He couldn't have said what it was. Perhaps just some sixth sense had warned him, but this time when he looked down the street, he knew they were coming. Indeed, only a few seconds later the first of the wagons came into view.

"They're here," he told David, then shouted it so they could hear him inside the courthouse.

O'Brien came rushing out. "Thank God," he muttered as they waited on the steps while the wagons drew up, then hurried down to meet the women.

Gideon searched each face as they climbed down, but his mother wasn't in the first group, and neither was Anna.

"Dear heaven," David breathed beside him. "Look at them."

He was looking at them, and what he saw horrified him—haggard faces, sunken eyes, bodies moving carefully, as if they'd aged decades in only weeks.

Fear roiled in him like a poisonous snake. Where were they?

The next wagon rumbled to a stop, and once again he searched each face, trying not to register how emaciated they were, looking only for the blessed one that had kissed him every night for his entire childhood. Where could she be?

"Gideon!"

He looked again and even then almost didn't recognize her. "Mother?" His heart lurched.

He lunged for her, but a billy club caught him in the chest. Pain exploded along with rage.

"You can't touch the prisoners," a burly guard informed him, shoving him out of the way.

He would have shoved him back, but O'Brien grabbed his arm. "Don't be a fool! He'll crack your skull open, and what good will you be to us then?"

"Mrs. Bates, where's Anna?" David called.

"I don't know," she managed before the guard shouted, "No talking!" and herded the women up the courthouse steps.

Gideon watched her go, not certain if he felt any relief at all from seeing her when she looked so awful.

"What does she mean, she doesn't know?" David asked of no one in particular.

"She was in the infirmary," one of the other women managed before the guard silenced her as well.

Two more wagons had arrived, and if Gideon thought the other women looked ill, these women looked to be at death's door. The guards had to assist them getting down, and even when they were on the ground, they had to cling to each other for strength. Their pale faces and haunted eyes told of suffering he could only imagine.

"This must be the group from the infirmary," he told David.

"Then where is she?"

Only a few women were on the final wagon, or at least that's what Gideon thought at first, seeing only a half dozen heads visible above the sides and none of them Anna's. Those women climbed down with difficulty, and then a couple of the guards climbed up and started handing down stretchers.

Stretchers?

"Are they dead?" David asked wildly when they realized there were women strapped to the stretchers.

"They can't be dead," Gideon insisted, although

the words were more a prayer than a certainty.

"Anna!" David cried, hurrying over to where the guards were carrying the first of the stretchers away from the wagon and up the courthouse steps. Gideon was close behind.

One of the women who'd climbed down on her own looked up at David's shout. "She's here."

Gideon had never seen this woman before, he was sure. He would have remembered. Her startling blue eyes took them both in as they reached the stretcher that had just been handed down.

"No talking to the prisoners," one of the guards told them, but neither of them paid him any mind.

Gideon looked at the shrunken figure strapped to the stretcher. She did look dead. Her eyes were closed and her face stark white.

"Anna?" David reached out but a guard blocked him.

"She's all right," the blue-eyed girl said. "Or she will be."

A guard shoved her. "No talking!"

Fury blossomed in her wonderful eyes, but she didn't spare the guard so much as a glance. "You're David," she said.

This time she ducked out of the way and the guard pushed thin air.

"Yes, her brother," he replied.

She simply nodded and went on, following Anna's stretcher up the steps.

The guards lowered another stretcher, and Gideon pulled David out of the way. "Who is that girl?"

David shook his head. "I never saw her before."

"Go after them. See if they'll let you talk to Anna," Gideon said. "I'll wait here until all the women are inside."

Luckily, there were only a few women on stretchers. They all seemed to be alive, too. Some even smiled weakly when he checked each of them. They wouldn't be alive much longer if they didn't end the hunger strike, though. He was certain of that.

By the time he got inside, the courtroom was in chaos. The women from the first wagons were trying to learn the welfare of those who had apparently been confined in the infirmary, and all of the women wanted to check on the women on the stretchers, in spite of the guards' attempts to silence them all and get them seated.

When Gideon located his mother in the crowd, she was embracing the girl with the amazing eyes, and the look on his mother's face told him how much the girl meant to her. She must be one of the leaders of the movement. How strange he'd never seen her before.

His mother released the girl and bent down to check on Anna, whose stretcher lay at their feet. David called out to them from where the spectators were being contained on the other side of the room, but she must not have heard him over the din.

Gideon could see that Anna's eyes were open now, and she was responding to his mother. Thank God for that.

Meanwhile, the women who still had some strength were assisting the weaker ones to lie down on the benches. Others sank down wearily, leaning on each other for support. Finally, his mother took a seat on the bench nearest Anna's stretcher, and the other girl—who on earth was she?—sat down on the floor beside Anna and took her hand.

Only then did Gideon find David and squeeze onto the bench beside him.

"Did you see Anna?" David asked.

"My mother and that other girl are looking after her. Her eyes were open just now, and she seemed to be talking."

David ran an unsteady hand over his face. "If the judge doesn't release them, I swear I'll carry her out of here myself."

The bailiff was trying to bring the room to order, and after a few more minutes he finally succeeded. The press were the last to find their seats in the very back of the room, and when even they were quiet, the bailiff told everyone to rise. Judge Waddill swept into the room.

He was, Gideon had learned, a true Southern gentleman who could be counted on to be fair. That was all they could ask.

• • •

Don't talk," Elizabeth whispered to Anna, who had been trying to tell her something for a while now, but the room was too noisy and Anna's voice too weak for her to hear.

Elizabeth was pretty weak herself. She heard the fellow up front call out, "All rise," but she didn't think she had the strength to do it. Mrs. Bates, bless her, put a hand on her shoulder and held her down in case she felt like trying, which she didn't. Many of the other women didn't rise, either. Some didn't even seem to be conscious.

The judge came out in his black robes, but she didn't get a good look at him until everybody sat down again. He didn't look cruel, but you could never really tell about some men. Sometimes the most charming ones were the meanest in the end. This one started talking, and Elizabeth found she liked his voice, all deep and slow and easy with his Southern accent.

She knew she should pay attention. This was important. She really needed to know what was going on, because she needed to know what was going to happen to her. If they let her go, she'd have to figure out how to keep Thornton from finding her. But somewhere between the workhouse and the courthouse, her head had started to ache. Now it was pounding, and she couldn't seem to concentrate for more than a few minutes at a time. At least she was sure Thornton and his goons weren't here. That was really all she needed to know.

Through the haze, she did see Whittaker. He'd brought some of his thugs along with him, too. They were all done up in their Sunday best, which reminded her of a poster she'd seen once with a picture of a gorilla in a dress suit. The comparison made her smile.

The judge wasn't happy about something. Miss Burns wasn't here. And Mrs. Lewis. That was it. They'd disappeared from the infirmary days ago, she knew. Whittaker was supposed to have produced all the prisoners, though, and the judge wanted to know where they were. Too sick to come, Whittaker said. He'd sent them back to the D.C. jail. Matron Herndon was there, too. She was trying to look concerned, but she just looked like she was constipated.

The attorneys argued for a while, and Elizabeth's attention wandered. She could see the back of David Vanderslice's blond head from here. Poor Anna. Her brother had certainly been blessed. Not only was he a male, he'd also gotten more than his fair share of good looks. How sad to have a brother who was more beautiful than you. At least Jake wasn't prettier than she was. If he was still alive. Poor Jake. She wanted to cry for him but didn't have the strength.

And that other fellow, the one with David. Who was he? Maybe Mrs. Bates's son. He was

162

a lawyer, Elizabeth knew, but he wasn't up at the front with the others. She supposed the women had enough lawyers and didn't need his help.

Some man got up on the witness stand and swore on a Bible to tell the truth, although Elizabeth could tell just by looking at him that he wasn't going to do it. Not only was he blinking, he was shifting in his chair and wringing his hands and looking everywhere but at the attorney asking him questions. After a bit she realized he was the warden at the D.C. jail. He was explaining to the judge why he'd sent all of them to the workhouse in Virginia instead of keeping them in his jail like he was supposed to. The judge didn't like his answers, and no wonder. He didn't have a single good one to his name.

Anna was asleep again, or at least her eyes were closed. Good for her. There was no sense wasting energy trying to listen to all this claptrap. The rest would do her good. Elizabeth wanted to sleep, too, but she thought Mrs. Bates might be disappointed in her, so she tried to listen some more.

They were talking about Mrs. Nolan now, the really old lady who'd disappeared that first morning. Nobody had seen her for days, and since her sentence was up, they all thought she'd been released. But the judge called her name, and to Elizabeth's surprise, she stood up. She was on the front row and looking a lot more spry than the last time Elizabeth had seen her. Then a lot of people seemed surprised about something. Elizabeth was amazed when the judge said the old lady was only seventy-three years old, although that was still plenty old for going to a workhouse, she supposed.

Mrs. Nolan sat down, and the judge lit into the warden again. Something about how they'd all been arrested and sentenced in Washington, D.C., and why were they imprisoned in Lorton, Virginia?

Elizabeth couldn't figure it out, either, probably because her head ached so badly. She rubbed her forehead, but it didn't help. She tried to pay attention, but the words didn't make sense anymore, no matter how closely she listened. She thought it must be the rushing sound that was filling her ears and her head, and why was the room getting so dark when it wasn't even noon yet . . . ?

Someone screamed, and Gideon saw that the blue-eyed girl had slumped to the floor in a faint. Before anyone else even moved, he was out of his seat and beside her.

"Get her out of here, Gideon," his mother whispered.

He lifted the girl into his arms and carried her to the back of the room. One of the guards opened the door, and he stepped out into the hallway. An ancient sofa sat against the wall, and Gideon carried her to it and laid her down.

He didn't have a lot of experience with ladies who fainted. At least he hoped she'd just fainted. But even if she had, he didn't have the slightest idea what to do for her. Luckily, he didn't have to do anything. After he'd stared at her for a few minutes, admiring the curve of her cheek and the smoothness of her skin, her eyes fluttered open.

Those beautiful eyes. This time, they filled with alarm.

"You fainted," he hastily explained. "I carried you out to the hall."

"I never faint," she said a bit petulantly.

"You probably never go on hunger strikes, either."

She blinked a few times as if trying to bring him into focus. "You're Gideon, aren't you?"

"How did you know that?"

"You're with David."

"You know my mother and Anna, then."

She started to nod, then winced and lifted a hand to her head.

"Would you like to sit up? That might help."

"Nothing will help, but yes, I would."

Ordinarily, he wouldn't have taken the liberty of putting his arm around a young lady whom he had just met, but since he'd already carried her bodily from the courtroom, he figured the regular rules didn't really apply in this situation. He slipped his arm under her shoulders and helped her sit up.

For a moment, she looked as if she would faint

again, but she fought it off and, after a few deep breaths, she looked up at him. "Why aren't you in there with the other lawyers?"

"Because I'm here with you. And how did you know I'm a lawyer?"

"Your mother brags about you."

That made him smile.

She smiled back, a glorious sight indeed.

"My mother didn't brag about you," he said. "Who are you?"

"Elizabeth," she said, and her smile vanished. "Miles," she added after a moment, as if she'd had to remember it. "Elizabeth Miles."

"I'm honored to meet you, Miss Miles. Are you ill?"

She frowned at that. "I've been on a hunger strike, remember?"

"No, I meant your voice. You sound like you've got a cold."

"Oh." She touched her throat. "No, not a cold. Force-feeding."

Rage boiled up in him again. His mother had told him the stories of other suffragists who had been jailed. "Did they hurt you?"

Amazingly, she smiled again. "Of course they did. What's going to happen to us now?"

Gideon needed a moment to control his anger. "We're hoping the judge will order all of you sent back to Washington, to the jail there."

"He's not going to set us free, then?"

"He doesn't have that authority, I'm afraid. In fact, our legal argument is that you shouldn't have been sent outside the District of Columbia in the first place. We're trying to get you out of that horrible workhouse and back to D.C. Then we can work on getting you released."

"So we'll still be in jail."

"I'm sorry, but yes, probably. We hope it won't be for long, though."

She closed her eyes and sighed, and he silently cursed himself for causing her distress. "Of course, when you get back to D.C., we're going to ask that judge to release you, and he might grant you bail while he decides."

She didn't seem too pleased about that. "But we can refuse to pay it, can't we?"

"Of course you can, and it might even be in your best interest to do so. Where are you from?"

"Uh . . . South Dakota." She'd had to think about that, too. She must have been even more ill from the hunger strike than he'd thought.

"You're a long way from home. Many of the other ladies are, too. If you're released on bail and go home, and then the judge decides you need to serve out your full sentences after all, you'd just have to come back here again."

She nodded her understanding and closed her eyes again. She must have been exhausted.

"May I get you something?"

She opened her eyes and glanced meaningfully

around the barren hallway. "What did you have in mind?"

"I'm sorry. I guess it's just the habit of a life-time to offer help to a damsel in distress."

"Do you meet many of those?"

"Not many, and certainly none as interesting as you, Miss Miles."

"If you're flirting with me, Mr. Bates, you're wasting your time. I'm sure I won't remember any of this."

"I'll remind you."

"You'll probably never see me again."

"I think I will. My mother likes you. She won't let you get too far away."

She smiled again, but this time her lovely eyes looked sad. "We should go back inside. I want to find out what the judge decides."

Gideon did, too. "Can you walk?"

"I hope so, but you'll help me, won't you? The habits of a lifetime and all that."

"Of course." He helped her to her feet, which luckily involved putting his arm around her again. It felt so good, he left it there and supported her with his other hand beneath her elbow. "Are you sure you want to go back in?"

She sighed again. "Your mother will worry if I don't."

"Yes, she will, but if you really don't feel well . . ."

"Let's go."

He matched his pace to hers, savoring the nearness of her. She smelled of disinfectant, and her auburn hair was limp and her clothes creased, but he didn't think he'd ever seen a more beautiful female. He really had no idea if his mother planned to keep her near, but he would suggest it to her at the first opportunity. At least he didn't have to worry about her disappearing of her own accord. There were a few advantages to a woman being in police custody.

A guard opened the door for them, and he escorted Miss Miles back into the courtroom. No one noticed their return because the judge was chastising Whittaker and his bunch again. Some of the women on the back row moved over to make room for Elizabeth, and he relinquished her to them with regret. The next time they met, all the rules of propriety would be back in force, and he wouldn't be able to hold her in his arms.

At least not at first.

He found a spot along the back wall to stand, just behind her. He wanted to stay close in case she fainted again, he told himself.

A murmur of surprise rumbled through the courtroom, distracting him from thoughts of the luscious Miss Elizabeth Miles. The judge banged his gavel for silence, and when he had it, he gave them his decision. Like all judges, he had to explain his reasoning and cite some laws, but in the end, he said all the women would be remanded to the custody of the superintendent of the Washington jail.

Judge Waddill had to bang his gavel again for order, and the government's attorneys jumped up and announced they would appeal the verdict.

"In that case," Judge Waddill said, taking obvious delight in thwarting their maneuver, "all the prisoners are at liberty to be paroled to the custody of their legal counsel until such time as the appeal has been heard."

"No!"

Gideon glanced at Elizabeth in surprise. Had she really said no to being released?

Mr. O'Brien was thanking the judge, but Elizabeth was signaling that she wanted to speak with him. The women around her started whispering, probably questioning her about why she'd protested being freed, and when she'd whispered back her reply, they all started waving for O'Brien.

Having little choice, O'Brien asked for a moment to confer with his clients. The judge allowed a brief recess, during which no one actually left the courtroom while the women conferred, first with each other as Elizabeth explained her concerns, and then with their attorneys. Gideon tried to join them, but a couple of the guards escorted him back to the spectators' side of the room, where he sat down beside David again.

"What's going on?" David asked.

"Apparently, the women aren't too happy about being released." Miss Miles hadn't been, at least.

"That's ridiculous! Why wouldn't they want to be released?"

Gideon figured he knew. He'd just explained it to Elizabeth out in the hallway.

After a few more minutes of hushed discussion among the women and their legal counsel, O'Brien and his cohorts returned to their seats, and the judge called everyone to order again.

"Your honor," O'Brien said. "I have conferred with my clients, and they have reminded me that many of them have come from great distances to join in the demonstrations at the White House. They would all like to return to their homes, but if the appeal is not decided in their favor, they will have to return to Washington to serve the remainder of their sentences. Their only other option is to remain in Washington until the appeal is heard, at great expense and personal inconvenience. Therefore, they would like to be allowed to remain in custody at the Washington jail to serve out the remainder of their sentences while the appeal is being decided."

The judge considered this very unusual request and allowed that he could see the logic in it. Hearing no objection from the government's attorneys, he again remanded the prisoners to Warden Zinkhan's custody.

Gideon managed to catch Elizabeth's eye across the crowded courtroom, and to his gratification, she smiled.

Elizabeth wondered what the Old Man would say if he knew how happy she was at the prospect of staying in jail. But after she'd gone to so much trouble to get there, she couldn't lose her safe haven just yet. She was still amazed at how easy it had been to convince the other women to stay in jail, and thank heaven Gideon Bates had given her the idea. At least they'd be going to a slightly more comfortable place and the hunger strike could end. Anna wouldn't last much longer if it didn't. Neither would she, come to that. Now she could get her strength back and be ready to make her escape when they finally were released.

The guards were rounding up the women now, herding them to the wagons. They'd be going straight to the depot to catch a train to Washington. Elizabeth pushed her way through the milling women to find Anna. She still lay strapped to the stretcher, but she was smiling up at Mrs. Bates when Elizabeth reached them.

"We're going back to Washington," Anna told her.

"I know. You're going to get better now. It's just a few more hours."

"How are you, Elizabeth?" Mrs. Bates asked. "I was so frightened when you fainted."

"I'm fine," she lied. Her head still felt as if someone were hitting it with a mallet, but she didn't see any point in complaining. All the women were miserable. "Are you feeling all right?"

"I can't believe I'm doing better than both you girls, but yes, I'm fine, too."

They had no more time to talk. Two guards picked up Anna's stretcher and they had to hurry to keep up. The trip to the station was one final agony of bouncing on wooden seats over rutted roads, but at last they were on the train. Elizabeth got Anna tucked into the seat beside her, and Mrs. Bates found them as the train pulled away from the station.

"How long do you think they'll let us stay at the jail?" Elizabeth asked her.

"What an odd way to put it," Mrs. Bates said, taking a seat across the aisle from her. "You sound as if you want to stay in jail."

She did, of course, but she said, "I'm just wondering how long until the appeal, because surely, they'll let us go then. I'm worried about Anna," Elizabeth said, surprised to realize it wasn't a lie.

"I'm worried about her, too, but it won't be much longer before they let us all go."

"It won't?"

"Oh no. Only a matter of days, I expect. They can't force-feed forty women any better at the Washington jail than they could at the workhouse, and they can't afford for any of us to die just a few blocks from the White House."

Elizabeth managed not to flinch. "Then we're continuing the hunger strike."

"Of course. It's our most valuable weapon in the struggle. I know it's hard, but it won't be much longer now, I promise you."

"What about Anna?"

Mrs. Bates glanced over to see if Anna was listening, but she appeared to be asleep. "I'm going to tell her she must end her strike. She's proven how brave she can be, and the rest of us can carry the burden from now on."

"She won't listen," Elizabeth said.

Mrs. Bates reached across the aisle and took Elizabeth's hand. "We won't let her die, I promise you."

The train ride from the courthouse in Alexandria to Washington wasn't long, but when they pulled into the station, the guards told the women to remain in their seats.

"What's going on?" Elizabeth asked when she saw the women on the other side of the car peering out the windows.

"Mr. O'Brien is having some sort of discussion with Warden Zinkhan," Mrs. Bates said.

Elizabeth got up and moved to where she could see for herself. Zinkhan gestured excitedly and O'Brien frowned back at him. Gideon Bates and David Vanderslice stood by with the other attorneys. Nobody looked happy, so Elizabeth figured whatever they were discussing would mean more trouble for her and the other women.

"Maybe they're having trouble getting transportation for us," Mrs. Bates said. "The judge didn't give them much notice we were coming."

This was much more than a transportation problem, though.

"What is it?" Anna asked groggily. "Why is the train stopped?"

Elizabeth slipped back into her seat and managed a smile. "We're in Washington. We're just waiting for them to come and get us off the train."

That seemed to satisfy her, and she closed her eyes again. Elizabeth wished she could believe her own lies.

After a few minutes, Mrs. Bates said, "Mr. O'Brien is getting back on the train."

Oh good! Maybe they were going back to Virginia or someplace else where Thornton couldn't find her.

O'Brien entered the car and asked for their attention, which he already had, since every woman in the car had been watching him for ten minutes.

"Warden Zinkhan has notified the judge here, the one who originally sentenced all of you, that he does not have the facilities to take all of you, particularly if you plan to continue the hunger strike, which I assured him you do. Consequently, the judge has reduced your sentences to time served, and you are all now free to return to your homes or go wherever you wish."

The women burst into applause and began to hug each other. Mrs. Bates threw her arms around Elizabeth, but she had to force herself to hug her back. Her mind was racing, trying to decide what she should do. She was already at the train station. It would be a simple matter of catching the next train to New York. News of their release wouldn't be in the newspapers until tomorrow, so even if Thornton knew where she'd been, he wouldn't know she was free until she was well on her way. The only question was whether she could make the trip by herself.

She turned to Anna. "We're free. You can go home now."

"Oh, Elizabeth, what will you do? Will you go back to South Dakota?"

For a minute, Elizabeth couldn't think why she would want to go to South Dakota. "I don't know," she said. "I'll have to let my aunt know I'm all right. Maybe I'll stay here for a few days to rest before I go on home."

"You could come to New York with us and rest there. My mother would love to have you, and she would take such good care of you. Mrs. Bates, tell Elizabeth she should come home with us."

"Oh, yes, do," Mrs. Bates said. "You aren't in any condition for a long trip like that alone."

She was going to New York herself, of course,

but she couldn't afford to let them slow her down. She had to get well away before Thornton and his thugs got wind of it. "You're very kind, but I couldn't possibly—"

"Of course you could," Mrs. Bates said. "Please at least consider it. You'll want to stay here in Washington tonight. You'll have to go back to your hotel to get your luggage if nothing else."

"My luggage?" Elizabeth thought of the things she'd left behind in the hotel room when she'd fled for her life. Coleman was going to take them to New York for her if he'd managed to escape Thornton and his men, so she had nothing to collect.

"Where were you staying?" Mrs. Bates asked. "We were at the Willard."

"I . . . no, not at the Willard," she lied, unable to think of another hotel at the moment.

"Mother!"

Mrs. Bates looked up and smiled lovingly at her son, who was hurrying down the aisle toward them. "Gideon, they're letting us go."

"I know. David has gone to get a cab. We thought we'd take you and Anna back to the hotel for the night. You can get something to eat and a good night's sleep. Then, if you're feeling well enough, we'll take you home tomorrow."

About halfway through that speech, his gaze had drifted away from his mother and found Elizabeth.

"Elizabeth, this is my son, Gideon," Mrs. Bates said with a knowing smile.

"Do you remember me, Miss Miles?" he asked with a knowing smile of his own.

"Not at all," she tried, knowing she couldn't encourage him.

"You remembered my advice, though."

For all the good it had done her. "I have no idea what you're talking about," she said.

"Gideon, she's my dearest friend," Anna said, oblivious to the undercurrents. "She's from South Dakota, but I've invited her to come home with us for a while. Tell her she must."

"You must," he said.

But Elizabeth knew she mustn't. "You're all very kind, but I couldn't possibly impose, and I really must get back home to my aunt. She'll be worried sick."

"You can send her a telegram," Mrs. Bates said. "Tell her kindly people are looking after you."

"Gideon!"

David Vanderslice hurried down the aisle, squeezing by the women who had begun to make their way out of the car.

"I have a cab waiting. Anna, don't worry, we'll take care of everything."

She smiled up at her brother. "David, this is Miss Miles. We must take care of her, too."

David nodded politely. "Of course we will. Anna, can you walk?"

Anna said she could, but Mrs. Bates told David to carry her, so that's how she was taken off the train. Mrs. Bates followed, leaving Gideon to escort Elizabeth.

"Can you walk, Miss Miles?" he asked with a wicked gleam in his eye. "Because I'm perfectly willing to carry you again."

"I can walk, Mr. Bates," she assured him, pretending not to notice how he was smiling at her. She followed the others, and Bates came along behind her.

"It's futile, you know," he said.

"What is?" she asked in alarm, wondering what he knew about her.

"Trying to resist my mother. She always gets her way."

"I really can't—"

"And what about poor Anna? How can you cause her any more distress?"

If he only knew the kind of distress Elizabeth could attract. "You're very persuasive, Mr. Bates," she said. She knew better than to continue an argument she couldn't afford to lose. She'd simply excuse herself to the ladies' lounge and then disappear. It would be kinder to everyone.

The porter helped her down the metal stairs to the platform, and she paused to get her bearings. She saw the doors into the station and the ticket windows beyond. And then she saw Thornton's thugs, standing at the end of the platform and watching every woman who got off the train.

"Are you all right?" Bates asked.

She wasn't all right at all. She ducked her head, praying they hadn't seen her. "I feel a bit faint," she said quite truthfully.

"You never faint," he reminded her. "Would you like me to carry you?"

"No!" She couldn't cause a scene. They'd see her for sure. "But if you'd let me take your arm . . ."

"Of course." He offered it, then laid his other hand over hers.

She turned her face, nearly burying it in his shoulder as they walked past the two men who would kill her, given the chance. Surely, they wouldn't dare accost her if she was with Gideon. She didn't even glance at them to see if they recognized her, but her heart hammered so loudly, she imagined they could hear it. Surely, Gideon Bates could hear it.

And then they were through the terminal and outside again, where a row of vehicles waited to carry passengers to their destinations.

David Vanderslice's shout drew them to a motorized cab, and Elizabeth let Gideon Bates hand her inside and onto the seat beside Anna.

"Oh, Elizabeth, I'm so glad you're coming with us."

"You're right. I do need to rest before I try to go home," she said as Gideon and David took their seats up front with the driver. She'd go to the hotel with them for the night. Maybe she'd even travel to New York with them. She'd be safe from Thornton's men if she wasn't alone.

"So tell us, Gideon," Mrs. Bates said. "How were you able to get Whittaker to release us?"

"I didn't have anything to do with it at all," he called back to them. "It was David and an old friend of ours."

"What friend is that?" Anna asked.

"You won't believe it," David said. "I hardly believe it myself, come to that. It's Marjorie's husband, Oscar Thornton."

Chapter Eight

Oscar Thornton?

Elizabeth's whole body went numb. She couldn't have heard that right.

"That's an unkind joke, David," Mrs. Bates said.

"It's not a joke, Mother," Gideon said. "Thornton found out you and Anna had been arrested, and he offered his help. Honestly, I don't think you'd be free if he hadn't."

"What on earth could Oscar do that you couldn't?" Mrs. Bates asked. Elizabeth had never seen her so angry, not in all the time they'd been mistreated and abused at the workhouse. "And how did he find out we were arrested in the first place?"

"I'm afraid I told him," David said. "He came to me with a business proposition and—"

"What kind of business proposition? I hope you aren't planning to get involved with him."

"Mother, please, don't upset yourself," Gideon said.

"I'm not upsetting myself. Oscar Thornton is upsetting me. How dare he approach any of us after the way he treated Marjorie?" Mrs. Bates said. "And then he expects David to help him in some business arrangement?"

"I have no intention of it," David assured her. "I'm afraid I used Anna's situation as an excuse to avoid having to turn him down directly, though, and then he offered his assistance. When it seemed as if he really could help, I had to listen."

"And he really did assist us," Gideon said.

"In what way?" Mrs. Bates asked skeptically.

"He sent his bodyguards out to find a deputy to serve Warden Whittaker with the writ to force him into court today," Gideon said.

"Gideon and Mr. O'Brien—he's the attorney for the Woman's Party—had been trying to find a deputy for days, but they were all hiding," David added.

"What do you mean they were hiding?" Mrs. Bates asked.

Elizabeth's head pounded as she tried to follow the conversation and make sense of it at the same time. David and Gideon explained how President Wilson or someone had hidden the deputies so they could keep the women in prison, which seemed very strange to Elizabeth. How would the president hide deputies? But somehow Thornton and his thugs had outsmarted someone or other and saved them all. Mrs. Bates couldn't believe it, but that was only because she didn't know Thornton wasn't trying to save her and Anna at all. Oh no. He was trying to get his fat hands on Betty Perkins. Elizabeth shuddered, remembering poor Jake out in the alley.

"I simply can't believe this of Oscar," Mrs. Bates said. "I actually saw him a few weeks ago. That first morning we were in Washington, I think. In the hotel dining room. I'm afraid I was terribly rude to him."

Elizabeth looked over at her in surprise. She remembered that morning only too well. Mrs. Bates had been the woman who'd cut Thornton dead the day they dropped the leather. How could she not have known? She hadn't seen the woman's face, but still . . .

"He has apparently forgiven you," David said.

"Or else he didn't even notice you were rude," Gideon added with a sly grin. "You've always believed he lacked genuine human feelings."

Another thing Mrs. Bates and Elizabeth agreed on.

"I shall have to send him a note to thank him," Anna said, her voice still a whispered croak from the forced feedings.

Mrs. Bates patted her hand. "I'm sure he'd appreciate that."

Elizabeth was so addled, she couldn't tell if Mrs. Bates was being sarcastic or not. "Who is this Oscar Thornton?" she managed to ask. What she really wanted to know was who Thornton was to them, so she'd know how he planned to use them to get to her.

"No one you need to worry about, dear," Mrs. Bates said.

"He was married to our cousin Marjorie," Gideon said.

"And he made her life miserable," Mrs. Bates said.

Thornton had mentioned being married, of course. He'd even bragged that his late wife had come from an "old money" family. But who could have imagined the wife would be related to Mrs. Bates? "Did she divorce him?"

For an awkward moment no one spoke, and Elizabeth wondered if perhaps they found the mention of divorce too shocking to discuss in polite company. Then Gideon said, "Marjorie died."

Mrs. Bates drew an unsteady breath. "They said it was an accident." But plainly, she didn't believe it.

Elizabeth didn't believe it, either.

"Here we are," David said with forced enthusiasm.

The cab had pulled up in front of the Willard Hotel. Elizabeth's stomach lurched at the memory of her last visit here, when she'd seen Jake beaten bloody and fled in fear for her life. Where was Jake now? And would she ever see him again?

But she couldn't think about that now. She was too exhausted to think about anything except getting out of the cab and somehow finding a place to lie down.

"We have a suite reserved," Gideon was telling

185

them. "David and I moved into it yesterday in hopes that we'd be bringing you ladies back here today. He and I will share one of the bedrooms, and you and Anna can take the other, Mother. We weren't expecting Miss Miles, but I'm sure we can find a room for her—"

"Oh, Elizabeth, don't leave me," Anna begged, her eyes enormous in her drawn face. "She can stay with us, can't she, Mrs. Bates?"

"If she doesn't mind being a little crowded. We'd be happy to have you with us. You can help me take care of Anna, and I can look after both you girls," she added with a smile.

Elizabeth couldn't stand the thought of being alone in a hotel room where Thornton could find her. "I don't mind being crowded. It can't be worse than the workhouse."

Anna slipped her arm through Elizabeth's and snuggled up to her. "You're so funny. I'm so glad you stayed with us."

The men helped them out of the cab and into the bustling lobby. Elizabeth ducked her head when she passed the doorman, hoping he wouldn't recognize her from her last visit. The elevator carried them up to the top floor, and Mrs. Bates ushered the two younger women into one of the bedrooms in the luxurious suite. Someone ordered food, and the women took turns bathing in the big, claw-footed tub. The luggage Mrs. Bates and Anna had left behind at the hotel when they were arrested miraculously appeared, and Mrs. Bates loaned Elizabeth a nightdress.

"We'll see about getting your things from your hotel later," Mrs. Bates told her. It was the last thing she heard before she fell asleep.

On the second morning, Elizabeth woke up feeling almost human again. Good food and real rest had quickly restored her strength, which made her anxious to make her escape. Anna wasn't responding as quickly, however, which was why they'd stayed an extra night, and for some reason, Elizabeth couldn't leave her.

"Eat just a little more," Elizabeth urged her as they sat at the tiny table in their crowded bedroom. Neither Anna nor Elizabeth had bothered to dress since they'd been at the hotel, so they'd been confined to their bedroom. They couldn't take a chance of being seen in their nightclothes by the two young men sharing the suite. Which was more than fine with Elizabeth. She wasn't too worried about spending time with David Vanderslice. He didn't seem particularly bright, so he presented no danger to her. She did worry about Gideon Bates, though. He'd already taken too much of an interest in her, and he wouldn't be as easy to fool. She'd have to be careful with him, so the less often he saw her, the better.

Anna obediently ate one more forkful of the scrambled eggs, but Elizabeth could see how much effort it took her to swallow it. "There," Anna said, laying her fork down. "Really, I'm stuffed. I feel fine, Elizabeth. So much better than when we first got here. Stop worrying about me."

Elizabeth wanted to; she really did. And she really should. She couldn't take care of Anna and get away from Thornton, too. Why should she even want to try?

Mrs. Bates came into the bedroom, being very careful not to open the connecting door too wide and give the gentlemen a glimpse of the girls. "How are you two feeling this morning?" she asked.

"Not as well as you," Elizabeth said. Mrs. Bates was dressed and had been taking her meals with David and her son.

"I never thought being a bit plump would be an advantage in life," Mrs. Bates said, "but if you're going to participate in a hunger strike, I highly recommend it." She stopped beside the table and looked at their plates with a critical eye. "Can't you eat just a little more, Anna?"

"No, she can't," Elizabeth said, earning a grateful glance from Anna. "I already nagged her."

"All right, then," Mrs. Bates said with false enthusiasm. "I've been thinking. I don't believe any of us will recover completely until we're home. If you feel up to it, I'd like to take the afternoon train, Anna. The sooner we get you back to your mother's loving arms, the better."

"What a wonderful idea," Anna said. "But what about Elizabeth? Surely, you aren't going to send her all the way to South Dakota by herself."

"I really don't think it would be a good idea," Mrs. Bates said. "I think it's too soon for her to make a trip like that, and I'm hoping she'll come home with us for a while, but that's Elizabeth's decision."

"No, it isn't," Anna said, surprising both of her companions. "She's coming home with me until she's completely recovered. Mother can take care of both of us."

"Are you sure your mother wouldn't mind?" Elizabeth didn't really care if the mother minded or not. Sticking with Anna was the safest course for her right now. Besides, she wanted to stay with Anna and she certainly needed to get to New York.

"If it makes her daughter happy, she won't mind a bit," Mrs. Bates said. "So that's settled. All we need to do now is get your luggage from your other hotel, Elizabeth, and we can be on our way."

She said something else, about how she'd had the maid freshen up the clothes Elizabeth had worn to the workhouse, but Elizabeth was no longer listening. How was she going to go to some hotel where she'd never stayed and retrieve luggage they didn't have?

"I'm glad to see you looking so much better, Miss Miles," Gideon Bates said while they waited on

189

the sidewalk for the Willard Hotel doorman to summon a cab.

"Are you saying I looked terrible before, Mr. Bates?" Elizabeth replied.

But instead of being chastened, he said, "Yes, I am. I've hardly ever seen a woman look worse. You were practically at death's door."

"Oh, please have mercy, Mr. Bates. Your charm is overwhelming me."

"Which, of course, was my intent all along," he assured her with his overwhelmingly charming smile.

Somehow Elizabeth managed to remain unmoved by it.

A cab had pulled up and the doorman opened the door for them. When they were settled inside, Elizabeth gave the driver the name of the hotel she'd gotten from one of the bellmen when she'd asked him to suggest a respectable hotel where a single woman alone might stay.

The cab chugged off, leaving her nothing to do now but talk to Gideon Bates. If only he wasn't quite so handsome and quite so appealing. She'd wanted David Vanderslice to accompany her. She could have told him any kind of tale, and he wouldn't have dreamed of questioning her. But Mrs. Bates had insisted that Gideon go with her.

"Do you really think they'll still have my luggage?" she asked, laying the groundwork for the misfortune that was going to befall her.

"Why wouldn't they?"

"I don't know. It just seems . . . Well, it might have been stolen or something. I've been gone a long time."

"I suppose that's possible, but not likely in a hotel like that."

Elizabeth frowned, hoping she looked like a helpless young woman with little experience of the world. "Does that happen often?"

"What?"

"That someone staying in a hotel disappears and leaves their luggage behind."

"I doubt it."

Which just proved how much he knew. It happened all the time. Grifters always carried a cheap suitcase stuffed with newspapers that they could leave behind when they ran out on the bill so the hotel staff wouldn't know they were gone until it was too late. "Then they might not realize they should keep the luggage until the person returns."

"Don't worry," he said with that wonderful smile that made her really want to believe everything was going to be all right. "I'll make sure they find your things."

Which was the last thing she wanted. She could have groaned. "Mr. Bates, would you mind . . . ? I mean . . ." She frowned her helpless frown again.

"I'll do whatever you wish, Miss Miles," he said, and she was sure he would at least try.

She rewarded him with a smile of her own. "I'd like to go in alone, if you don't mind. No, wait. Hear me out. You see, it's very . . . embarrassing to admit one has been in jail, even for the best of causes."

"Which is why I'm happy to do it for you," he argued.

"No, please. If there's any hope at all, a young woman alone is much more likely to win their pity than her overbearing escort."

"Overbearing?" He seemed genuinely offended.

"As I'm sure you would become on my behalf if you felt I wasn't receiving the right treatment."

He couldn't argue with that, and he didn't try, but she didn't like the way he was looking at her now, as if he'd seen something disturbing. What had she done to earn that look? She really needed to be more than careful with him.

Finally, he said, "So you want to go into the hotel alone to request your luggage, is that what you're telling me?"

"Yes, if you don't mind too terribly much. And rest assured, if I have any trouble at all, I'll summon you immediately."

He considered this for a long moment before he said, "All right, but don't let them fob you off."

"Oh, I won't," she lied, and rewarded him with another smile.

She left him waiting with the cab and walked into the quiet elegance of the hotel lobby. This

192

place was tiny compared to the Willard, and no political hacks sat in the lobby waiting for someone important to walk by. Instead, a few well-dressed gentlemen read newspapers in the comfortable chairs, and bellmen moved soundlessly over the carpeted floors, carrying things here and there.

She walked up to the desk, in case Bates was watching her, and asked the clerk for the time. Then she mentioned she was meeting some other ladies and went over to an empty chair and sat down. A lone female wouldn't sit long in a hotel lobby, but Elizabeth needed a moment to think. She could lie to Gideon and tell him her things had been stolen, but then he'd insist on seeing the manager and making a fuss. She thought of several other versions of the same lie, but they all ended with no luggage and Bates making a fuss. She could always tell him the truth, of course, that she was a grifter on the run who had never stayed at this hotel at all, but that didn't seem like a very good idea, either. The only other alternative was for her to find a back door, sneak out and disappear. She had money in her purse and more in her corset. She could go to the station and take a train for New York. She'd be safe from Thornton and she wouldn't have to lie to Gideon. It was the only sensible thing to do, after all. That's what the Old Man would say, she was sure.

So why was she still sitting here?

Because she could imagine how frantic Gideon Bates would be and how upset Mrs. Bates would be and how devastated Anna would be if she just disappeared. How they would have the hotel searched and summon the authorities. And how very, very frightened they would be for her. She tried to tell herself they were nothing to her, so what did she care? They'd forget all about her in a week.

Except that wasn't true. They would never forget her, just as she would never forget them.

Which was why she was still sitting there when the elevator opened and a heavily laden luggage cart rolled out. One of the Negro bellmen was taking great care that the enormous stack of matched luggage on it didn't tip.

A young woman and an older man came out behind him. "Be careful with that," she snapped at the bellman. "Do you have any idea how expensive those cases are?"

"Yes, ma'am," the bellman murmured.

"Honestly, where do they find these creatures?" she asked her companion. "He's so stupid and clumsy. An ape could do this job better."

"It's all right, my dear," the man soothed.

She heaved a dramatic sigh and sashayed around the luggage cart, stepping right in front of it so the bellman had to jerk it back to avoid running her over. The sudden stop upset the delicate balance of the luggage, and the smaller cases on top of the pile crashed to the floor before he could catch them. He only just managed to keep the entire load from falling over.

"You stupid idiot!" she screamed. "What's the matter with you? I should have your job for that."

"Now, darling, there's no harm done," the older man said.

"No harm?" she screeched. "Those cases are ruined. I want them replaced!"

The man continued to soothe her while she continued to heap abuse on the poor bellman, although Elizabeth had stopped listening. She watched them closely as the bellman picked up the cases and reloaded the cart. The woman was about her size. And the bellman—who was at least thirty—was moving the way someone moves when they're furious but don't dare let anyone know. And he wouldn't dare, either, not if he wanted to keep his job. A man like that, a colored man serving rich white people, had silently taken a lifetime of abuse with no hope of any retribution. This time the white woman had caused the accident herself and berated him in front of everyone in the lobby. She might well try to get him fired, too, and after all that, the man probably wouldn't even give him a tip.

But Elizabeth would.

She waited until the couple went to the front desk. They were still arguing, and it would take a few minutes for them to check out. More than a few, because the woman was making a complaint. The bellman had finished reloading the luggage, so Elizabeth strolled over to him. She slipped a five-dollar bill into his hand, which was probably more than he made in a week, and said, "These are my things. My cab is right outside."

His eyes widened, and he glanced over to where the couple was still arguing at the desk. She saw him silently weighing his options. Anger flared in his eyes, and then he smiled grimly. "Yes, ma'am." He pushed the cart a little faster.

Elizabeth followed, giving no indication she was with him. Outside, she saw Gideon pacing beside the cab, which had pulled down to the far end of the driveway. "Here we are," she called and strolled down to where he waited. The bellman followed with the cart.

Gideon's expression was priceless. "Is that all yours?"

Elizabeth had no idea. She turned to the bellman, who grinned. "Oh no, sir. Only the green cases is the lady's." The rest, Elizabeth supposed, belonged to the man who was with her.

The cab driver opened his trunk, and they managed to get most of the green cases into it. The rest went into the front seat.

"Will you get into trouble?" she asked the bellman when the driver and Gideon were busy trying to squeeze the last of the cases into the cab.

"Oh no, ma'am. They won't remember which

one of us took their luggage. We all look alike to folks like them. When my boss gets around to asking me, I'll say the cart was just sitting in the lobby and a young lady told me it was hers and would I take it out for her."

Which, of course, was almost exactly what had happened.

When all the luggage was loaded, Elizabeth made a show of reaching into her purse for a tip, but Gideon waved her away and produced a silver dollar for the helpful bellman.

"Thank you, sir," he said, beaming with pleasure at the exceptionally large tip. Combined with Elizabeth's fiver, he'd had a very good morning. "You have a nice day now, miss."

"I'm sure I will," she replied.

Gideon watched Elizabeth Miles from the corner of his eye as the cab carried them and her enormous pile of luggage back to the Willard. He would have been surprised to see any female carrying that amount of luggage, but somehow he hadn't thought Miss Miles to be the kind of woman to require that much. Or to be wealthy enough to own enough clothing to fill it all. He considered himself a good judge of people, and seldom had he been so very wrong about someone.

"Did they give you any trouble at the hotel?" he asked.

"Oh no. After I settled my bill, they were more

than happy to return my things. They didn't even charge me for the days I was in jail."

"They must've been surprised to hear where you'd been," he said, watching her face.

She didn't even blink. "They were actually very sympathetic. It seems the manager supports women's rights."

"That's fortunate," he said, thinking it was more than fortunate. So much for her concerns that her luggage might have somehow disappeared. He should be pleased, and he was, he supposed. He hadn't expected any real trouble, but he had expected his own services to be needed. And appreciated. Maybe that was why he felt something wasn't quite right with this situation. Maybe he was just suffering from wounded pride. Every other female of his acquaintance would have not only allowed but expected him to take charge.

But maybe Miss Miles was completely different from every other female of his acquaintance.

His mother had hinted at that very thing, hadn't she? "Mother told us what you went through at the workhouse."

She didn't seem pleased by the change of subject. "Did she?"

"Yes. She said you were very brave."

"All the women were brave."

"Mother said you saved Anna that first night."

She shook her head. "Hardly. I just picked her up off the floor when the guards threw her down."

"And you tried to talk Anna out of participating in the hunger strike."

"Anyone with sense would've done the same thing."

"And you endured force-feeding instead of giving up the hunger strike."

"I told you that myself."

"Then you do remember," he teased.

She almost smiled at that. "Only vaguely."

"I don't understand why you won't let me compliment your courage."

"And I don't understand why you want to."

Why did he want to? Because he wanted her to know that he admired her, and not just because she was so lovely. "You're a very unusual woman, Miss Miles."

"No, I'm not," she said, sounding oddly defensive. "I'm just like every other woman."

"Every other woman would've waited in the cab and sent me in to fetch her luggage."

She turned to him in surprise and studied his face for a long moment, giving him the opportunity to admire her amazing eyes. Were they the color of periwinkles or the sky on a cloudless day?

"Did I insult your manhood, Mr. Bates?"

"Thoroughly, Miss Miles. I may never recover."

She almost smiled again. "Then I apologize most humbly."

He pretended to consider her offer. "I'm afraid that's not enough."

"Then what more can I do to make amends?"

Gideon could think of many things he'd like her to do, but she wasn't likely to do any of them, and she was very likely to be outraged if he suggested any of them, so he said, "You can tell me how you became a suffragist and why you decided to make the trip to Washington."

He'd expected her to really smile at that and to happily tell him all about the amazing women who had influenced her awakening. Every suffragist he'd ever met was only too happy to speak of her conversion, and they all did so with great enthusiasm. To his surprise, however, Elizabeth Miles merely looked dismayed. Or at least he thought dismay was the emotion that flickered across her face before she said, "I can't believe that story is of interest to anyone but me, and I refuse to bore you with it. You'll have to think of something else."

"All right, then, tell me why you've decided to go back to the city with us."

"You should be able to guess that. Your mother willed it."

"Ah, of course. And Anna, too, I'm sure."

"And I was powerless to resist them."

"Oh, Miss Miles, I don't imagine you've ever been powerless."

Once again that strange emotion flickered across her beautiful face. Why had his compliment disturbed her?

"Women are by our very nature powerless in so many ways, Mr. Bates. As the son of a suffragist, you should know that only too well."

And he did, of course, but still . . . "Whatever your reasons, I'm glad you've decided to go with us."

He'd half expected her to coyly ask him why, the way the society girls he knew would have, but instead she said, "And I'm sure after all you've been through, you'll be glad to get back home."

"I'm glad this ordeal with my mother is over, at least."

"And we're very grateful for your help. I'm sure the rest of the ladies will be, too, when they learn what you did."

Gideon's pride finally started to feel a little better. "That's what attorneys do, Miss Miles. We keep our clients out of jail."

"Your profession must give you a great deal of satisfaction, then."

Gideon had never considered whether it did or not. He was an attorney because young men like him who needed a profession often became attorneys. And because his father had been one.

"Is something wrong?" she asked.

"What? No, of course not."

She didn't look convinced. "You looked like something was wrong. I didn't mean to . . . Did I cause offense?"

"I'm not offended," he said, sounding offended even to himself. "I just, uh . . ." He said the first thing that came to mind. "I just remembered my employer told me I could only be gone three days, and if I didn't come back then, I'd lose my position."

"And how long have you been gone?"

"Over a week. More like ten days."

"Oh dear."

But that wasn't really what was bothering him. Oh no, not at all. She'd just brought him to the realization that his career gave him no satisfaction. None whatsoever. In fact, the possibility that he might never have to return to Devoss and Van Aken was oddly cheering.

"They wouldn't really dismiss you, would they?" she asked with a worried frown that cheered him even more because it meant she might actually care.

"I doubt it," he said with regret.

"I should hope they wouldn't punish you for saving all of us. As you pointed out, that's what attorneys do."

"Well, that's not really what I usually do."

"It isn't?"

"No. What I usually do is prepare wills and manage trusts and make sure rich people's children stay rich." He thought of Ernest Pike and his musical daughter, Eugenia.

"That must be . . . interesting," she tried.

"Not very."

"Oh," she said uncertainly. Then, "I'm sorry."

"Don't be. They pay me well enough, so I shouldn't have any complaints."

"And yet you do." Her blue eyes sparkled. Was it with mischief?

"Not really," he lied. "I was only complaining so I could mention that I'm comfortably fixed, so you'll know I'm a good catch."

That brought the smile he'd been seeking. "Do you frequently manage to work that into your conversation?"

"Never before until today."

Those lovely eyes widened just a tiny bit, but instead of giving him the flirtatious grin he'd been hoping for, she turned away.

"Now I'm afraid I've given offense," he said, willing her to deny it.

When she turned back, she said, "Don't be silly." But her smile was forced and her eyes troubled. "I'll be sure to mention that you're comfortably fixed to every suffragist girl I meet." Meaning, of course, that she had no interest in the information for herself. He could have accepted that with good grace if she hadn't looked so sad about it.

How odd. She didn't seem like the kind of girl to get all vaporish from a little flirting, even if he had been half-serious. Or maybe more than half, if he were honest. Elizabeth Miles was the most interesting woman he'd ever met. But she'd folded her hands in her lap so tightly, he would have bet her knuckles were white beneath her gloves.

"Miss Miles, is something wrong?" he asked, echoing her words.

Her forced smile relaxed. "Of course something is wrong. Women are downtrodden and have no voice in their government and no rights as individuals."

Before he could think of an appropriate reply, their cab lurched to a halt, and the driver said, "Here we are, folks, and just in time, I'd say."

By the time they had all traveled from the Willard Hotel to Union Station, sat for half an hour in the massive waiting area and walked down to the tracks and finally boarded their train to New York, Anna was exhausted and Elizabeth wasn't feeling much better. Thank heaven they had the two young men to handle their luggage and make sure it was all loaded onto the train. Elizabeth cringed a little when Mrs. Bates raised her eyebrows at the amount of her luggage, but fortunately she said nothing, so Elizabeth didn't have to justify it. She only hoped there was something in those many cases that she'd be able to wear without looking as snobbish as the woman she'd stolen them from.

Elizabeth found a section of empty seats and guided Anna into one before collapsing beside her. Anna fell asleep before the train even began to move.

Mrs. Bates took a seat across the aisle from them, and the two men sat behind them. Elizabeth found the rumble of their deep voices comforting, as long as they weren't asking her any questions she didn't want to answer. Or hinting that they'd like to court her, as Gideon had done this morning. He already suspected something was different about her. She couldn't give him a chance to discover even more.

Once the train was on its way, Elizabeth finally relaxed and fell into a light doze until she heard Gideon Bates say Thornton's name.

Every nerve in her body jumped to attention, and she strained to hear over the clatter of the wheels.

"Don't worry," David said. "I'm not going to help him."

"What is it he wants?" Gideon asked.

"He has some rifles he wants to sell to the army."

"Rifles? Where would Thornton get rifles?"

"How should I know? I assume he bought them. That's what he does, I understand, and how he made his money in the first place. He buys things and sells them at a profit and probably for more than they're worth. I wouldn't have given him the time of day, but Senator Wadsworth sent him."

"How does Thornton know a senator?" Gideon asked, echoing Elizabeth's own question.

"He's got money, Gideon. Politicians know everybody who has money."

"And why did the senator send him to you?"

David cleared his throat, and Elizabeth imagined him squirming under Gideon's relentless gaze. "The senator appointed me to a committee. We're advising the army on purchasing materiel."

"Materiel? Do you even know what that is?"

"Of course I know what it is. Supplies. Armaments."

"And what do you know about armaments? Or supplies, either, for that matter?"

"I know how to bring people together to do business, and it's my patriotic duty to help with the war effort."

David sounded a little whiny, but Elizabeth thought he made a good argument. Gideon obviously did not.

"Just make sure Oscar Thornton isn't one of those people you bring together."

"I told you not to worry. I'm going to string him along for a while until he loses patience with me and goes someplace else. He's probably going to sell his rifles to the government, though, whether I help him or not."

"I understand that. Just don't make it easy for him," Gideon said. "And whatever you do, keep him away from my mother."

David muttered some kind of promise to do just that, and Elizabeth vowed to stay as close to Mrs. Bates as possible until she could collect her money from the Old Man and get out of New York City.

Chapter Nine

"And, Mother, this is my very dearest friend, Elizabeth Miles," Anna said after her mother had tearfully embraced her and welcomed her home.

Anna drew Elizabeth forward for her mother's inspection. Mrs. Vanderslice was an older version of Anna, fair and frail and more than overwhelmed by the thought of her only daughter spending time in jail. "I'm very pleased to meet you, Miss Miles."

"Elizabeth saved my life," Anna said, shocking her mother completely.

"Oh dear," Mrs. Vanderslice murmured, and for an awful second, Elizabeth feared she might actually faint.

"Anna is exaggerating," Elizabeth said quickly. "Our lives were never really in danger, and Anna was just as much a comfort to me as I was to her."

"Miss Miles is being modest," David said. "Mrs. Bates told Gideon and me some of the things she did, and you should have seen her in the courtroom."

Before Elizabeth could even register David's endorsement, Anna was at it again.

"Elizabeth lives in South Dakota, so we couldn't let her go all the way out there alone when she just got off a hunger strike. That's

207

why I convinced her to come home with us, and I've invited her to stay here for as long as she wants."

"Oh, yes, of course," Mrs. Vanderslice said, managing a rather stiff smile. "We're happy to have you, Miss Miles. David wired me that Anna was bringing a guest, so I've had the spare room made up for you. Let me confirm Anna's invitation to stay as long as you like."

Elizabeth didn't think that would be very long at all once she managed to sneak out to find the Old Man, but she thanked Mrs. Vanderslice and let Anna take her upstairs to her room.

"Oh, Elizabeth, I'm so glad you're here," Anna said, linking arms with her as they climbed the stairs. The Vanderslice home was an old one, with dark, heavy paneling and large, heavy furniture. They'd probably once had money, but now they carried on in genteel poverty, or at least not more than comfortable circumstances. David obviously worked, just as Gideon did, and Elizabeth was sure he didn't do it just to keep from being bored. Too bad he wasn't going to help Thornton. She could probably show David how to make a small fortune off that rat.

Anna pointed out her own bedroom, which was right next door to Elizabeth's. The servants had started carrying up their baggage, and once again Elizabeth felt a twinge of regret for having stolen so very much luggage. Nothing she could do about it now, though.

"Can I watch you unpack?" Anna asked. "You must have some lovely things."

"I . . . uh . . . I wasn't sure what I would need here, so I brought everything I own," Elizabeth lied. She opened one of the smaller bags to find an impressive array of toiletries and a set of silver-handled brushes and combs.

While Anna oohed and aahed over them, Elizabeth chose a larger case and opened it to find several stylish day dresses carefully wrapped in tissue paper. She silently thanked her benefactress for having packed something Elizabeth could actually wear.

"What's in that one?" Anna asked, coming over to see.

"I'm not sure what's in any of them," Elizabeth said quite truthfully, but she had to come up with another lie to explain why. "The hotel maids packed them after I was arrested."

Anna seemed invigorated by the chance to examine Elizabeth's wardrobe, and together they checked the contents of every one of the cases. Anna was shocked speechless by the elaborate evening gowns that Elizabeth couldn't imagine ever having occasion to wear. At least they found some sensible shirtwaists and skirts along with some needlessly fancy night-dresses.

"Are these real?" Anna asked, opening a jewel

case to find a tangle of sparkling necklaces and bracelets.

Good heavens! "Of course not," she said, pretty sure they were.

"This could be a trousseau," Anna marveled with an uneasy smile. "Is there something you haven't told me?"

"My aunt is very . . . Well, she insisted I have new clothes to wear in the East. I told her I was visiting an old friend from school, and she didn't want me to be embarrassed." Elizabeth was a little alarmed at how easily the lies were coming to her. She shouldn't have been, though. She'd always been an excellent liar. The Old Man said it was her best skill.

So why did lying suddenly bother her?

Anna didn't seem quite convinced. Elizabeth obviously needed to give more thought to her lies. She couldn't have Anna doubting her. "I was afraid you were going to tell me you're engaged to some fellow out West."

"Not likely. I'm not even sure I want to get married at all." Which wasn't a lie. The thought of putting herself into the power of some idiot man held no appeal for her. She'd seen too many women live to regret their choices.

"Really?" Anna said. "I don't want to get married, either. I thought I was the only girl alive who felt that way. They used to laugh at me at school when I said it, but the thought of having to live with some man day after day and sleep in his bed . . ." She shuddered delicately.

"Maybe you just haven't found the right man yet."

"That's what Mother always says, but I don't think any man would be the right one. Oh, Elizabeth, wouldn't it be wonderful if you and I could live together instead? We could get a little house of our own, and we'd never have to worry about a man telling us what to do."

"That does sound wonderful," Elizabeth agreed.

"I was telling the truth when I said you are my dearest friend. I never felt this way about anyone else, not even the girls I've been friends with all my life."

Elizabeth stopped rummaging through the latest suitcase and turned to look at Anna. She was sitting on the bed, her eyes wide and suspiciously moist.

"You're my dearest friend, too," Elizabeth said. And her only one.

Anna jumped up and threw her arms around Elizabeth. "I love you."

"I love you, too." It was, Elizabeth marveled, the truth.

"This is the last one, miss," the maid said, bringing in one last suitcase.

Anna and Elizabeth broke apart. Anna laid a

hand over her heart and gave a little titter of delighted laughter.

"I brought your case up, too, Miss Anna," the maid said, not even looking at them. "It's in your room."

Anna took both of Elizabeth's hands in hers. "Promise me you'll stay here forever."

"I can't do that, but I'll stay until you get tired of me."

"Then that will be forever!"

"Anna, dear," her mother said from the doorway, "you must give Miss Miles a chance to rest from the trip, and I'm sure you should also lie down for a while before supper. You've been through quite an ordeal."

"Your mother is right," Elizabeth said, noticing again the dark circles under Anna's eyes and the sunken hollows of her cheeks. "You should get some rest."

"All right, but only because you asked me," Anna said, and started for the door.

"Oh, I almost forgot why I came up," Mrs. Vanderslice said. "Some flowers just arrived for you girls."

"Flowers?" Anna said.

"Yes, an enormous arrangement. I had it put on the dining room table. It was addressed to both of you, and you'll never believe who sent it."

Anna gave Elizabeth a questioning glance. Elizabeth thought fleetingly of Gideon Bates, but he didn't seem like the type to send flowers for no reason. "I have no idea."

"Who was it?" Anna asked her mother.

"Oscar Thornton."

The card did indeed have both of their names on it, Elizabeth confirmed at supper that evening, and Thornton had used the name she was going by now to prove he knew it. She shouldn't have been surprised. Thornton's thugs had obviously seen her getting off the train with Gideon Bates in Washington and had probably been watching her ever since. They could have asked any of the other women what her name was, or even David or Gideon. Of course, it wasn't her real name, but it was her name for the moment. How well done on Thornton's part. He not only knew her name but where to find her.

She'd never intended to stay with Anna forever, but now staying here at all was no longer safe. She'd have to get out of the city as soon as possible.

"What a lovely gown," Mrs. Vanderslice said when they were seated.

"Thank you," Elizabeth said. It fit rather well, too, she was happy to discover. The maid who helped her dress had loosened her corset laces slightly when the gown proved a bit big. Elizabeth blamed it on her recent hunger strike. "It's so much nicer than our prison clothes."

Mrs. Vanderslice blanched at this, but Anna giggled. "Oh, Mother, you would have fainted dead away if you'd seen me in my prison dress. The fabric looked like mattress ticking."

"You girls have been through so much," Mrs. Vanderslice said as the maid came in to serve them their soup. "I hope it hasn't coarsened you."

"It's made me stronger," Anna said. "I don't think I'll ever be afraid of anything again."

David leaned sideways in his seat so he could see her around the mound of flowers. "I might just test you by releasing a mouse in your bedroom."

Anna glared playfully at him, and his mother said, "David, don't tease your sister."

He leaned the other way so he could see Elizabeth. "And what about you, Miss Miles? Do you fear nothing now, too?"

"Oh no. In fact, being in the workhouse only increased my fear of mice, I'm sorry to say."

David started to say something else, then sighed and rose from his chair.

"David, what are you—" his mother began, then stopped when he picked up the flower arrangement and moved it to the far end of the long table.

He resumed his seat. "There. Now I can see you. See you both," he added diplomatically to Anna.

Elizabeth rewarded him with a smile, glad he'd

given her an opening. "Which reminds me: I'm not used to receiving flowers from gentlemen I've never met. Who is this Mr. Thornton and why was he so helpful to us?" The more she knew about Thornton, the better.

"Oh my," Mrs. Vanderslice said, "he's no one you'd care to know, I'm sure."

"Mrs. Bates thinks he killed his wife," Anna whispered, probably so the maid wouldn't hear, although Elizabeth was sure the maid knew anyway.

"I did get that idea," Elizabeth said.

"To answer your question," David said in a normal voice to let her know he was taking charge, "Oscar Thornton is a newcomer to the city. He made his fortune in nails or something like that. He bought a lot of them at a bargain price and sold them for a profit. Then he kept on buying and selling until he could set himself up in style here in the city."

"He did this just with nails?" Elizabeth asked.

"Oh no. He'd buy anything he thought he could sell at a profit."

"And when he came to the city, he met Marjorie Behrend," Anna said.

"Mrs. Bates's cousin," Elizabeth remembered.

Mrs. Vanderslice sighed. "She was such a sweet girl."

"But almost thirty and unmarried," Anna added.

"And no dowry to speak of," David said.

Elizabeth frowned. "But how on earth did she meet Mr. Thornton?"

The women wouldn't meet her gaze, but David said, "He put it out that he was looking for a wife. He'd done pretty well for himself up North, but he wanted to do even better here. He figured he'd need society friends for that, so he wanted a wife who already had those connections."

"Is that true? Did he really need connections?"

"It never hurts." David laid down his spoon. "So Thornton courted Miss Behrend and married her because she came from an old family. But things didn't work out the way he expected."

Elizabeth already knew she wasn't going to like the way this story ended. "Why not?"

"Because instead of including him in their invitations, people dropped her," Anna said.

"He was too aggressive," Mrs. Vanderslice said. "People found him . . ."

"Coarse," Anna supplied.

"Abrasive," David added.

Elizabeth had no trouble at all imagining Thornton wearing out his welcome with the upper classes. "How sad for his wife."

"Sadder still when she died," Anna said.

"She fell down the stairs," Mrs. Vanderslice said sharply. "It was an accident."

But Mrs. Bates didn't believe that. "Was there any reason to believe otherwise?"

216

"Only if you knew Thornton," David said. "And the families who wouldn't receive him before shun him now. But it hasn't stopped him from making money."

"And now he wants to sell something to the army, I believe," Elizabeth said.

David grinned at her. "How did you know that?"

Mostly because Thornton had bragged about it so much, but she said, "I heard you and Mr. Bates discussing it on the train today."

"I hope we didn't disturb you."

"Not at all, but I couldn't help overhearing. What is it he wants to sell?"

"Rifles. He called them Ross rifles, whatever that means. I'm not that interested in firearms myself. But Thornton says the Canadian troops use them, and he's ready to sell some to our army."

If only she knew more about how these things worked. She'd really like to throttle Thornton for what he'd done to Jake, but that wasn't likely. She only knew how to swindle people, and she could do that pretty well. Taking him for another score could provide a little satisfaction. Too bad she didn't dare get close enough to Thornton again to get her revenge. "I suppose the army will buy a lot of rifles now that we're going to fight the Germans."

"Yes, but I've promised Gideon I won't help Thornton make the right contacts to sell his. Marjorie was a cousin to Mrs. Bates."

"First cousin once removed," Mrs. Vanderslice said.

The maid came out to remove their soup bowls. No one spoke until she returned to the kitchen.

Elizabeth turned back to David. "Didn't you say Mr. Thornton will still be able to sell his rifles, though?"

"Oh yes. Someone will help him, but it won't be me."

"Even after what he did for us?" Anna asked.

David winced a little at that. "Yes. Mrs. Bates holds him responsible for Marjorie's death, and she feels very strongly about it."

"I don't know much about business," Elizabeth said, "but wouldn't you stand to benefit if you helped Mr. Thornton?"

"Sometimes loyalty overrides profit, Miss Miles. I'm sure you can understand that."

Elizabeth didn't understand it at all, but she smiled sweetly as her mind raced. Maybe the Old Man would have some ideas. The maid returned to serve them the next course, and Elizabeth let Anna change the subject. She wanted to tell them how wonderful Elizabeth had been to her when they were in the workhouse, and Elizabeth could only protest modestly while David Vanderslice's gazes grew more and more admiring.

After supper, they sat in the parlor for a while. Anna soon started nodding off, so they sent her on to bed. David moved over to take Anna's place next to Elizabeth on the sofa. His gaze was still admiring.

"What do you think of our city, Miss Miles?"

"I haven't seen enough of it yet to form an opinion," she lied.

"I hope you'll allow me to show you some of the sights."

Oh dear. Now David Vanderslice was flirting with her. "I'd like that very much." Too bad she wouldn't be around long enough to actually do it.

"It's a shame you're here in the winter. I'd love to take you to Central Park or out on the ferry to the Statue of Liberty, but at least there are the museums."

"You must take Miss Miles to see some plays, too," his mother said, looking up from her sewing.

"You'll never see better theater than in New York," he said.

Elizabeth could have agreed, since she'd lived in New York her entire life, but she said, "That sounds lovely."

"I hope you're planning to stay for a while," he said.

"I promised Anna I would stay until you grew tired of me."

David gave her a devastatingly beautiful smile. "Then you'll be here forever."

Elizabeth had to force herself to smile back.

• • •

She'd been afraid she would have trouble finding a time she could slip away without anyone noticing and insisting that she needed a companion. Fortunately, the opportunity came the very next day. Mrs. Vanderslice had some sort of committee meeting after lunch, and Anna's doctor, who had come to examine them both that morning, had recommended an afternoon nap for both of them for at least two weeks.

With Anna tucked away, Mrs. Vanderslice out of the house and David at his office, Elizabeth made her escape. She was pretty sure even the servants hadn't noticed her departure. What day was it? She'd lost track, but the bite of the wind told her winter was closing in, and she hastened her step.

The street was busy, and she saw no sign of Thornton's goons. He was probably satisfied with knowing where she was now and didn't need to continually have her watched. She hoped that was true, at least. Just to be safe, however, she hopped on a trolley car at the very last minute and switched cars several times unnecessarily until she finally arrived at Dan the Dude's Saloon in Chelsea. The streets in this neighborhood were even busier, and she melted into the crowd of working-class people moving down the sidewalk until she reached the alley. She ducked into it and hurried to the side door. When she raised her hand to knock, she realized it was shaking.

But she had nothing to fear now. She was safe.

Her coded knock brought someone to open the sliding panel to see who might be outside. The eyes peering out widened in surprise and the mouth beneath muttered what was probably a curse before the door flew open. Spuds was the best lookout in the business, but he hadn't even bothered to close the spy panel.

"Lizzie!" He glanced around to make sure she was alone, then grabbed her arm and hauled her inside. "Are you all right? Nobody knew what became of you, girl!"

"I'm fine, Spuds, and what became of me is a long story. Is the Old Man here?"

"Of course he is." He hesitated. "Best you wait here, though, so I can prepare him. The shock . . ." He looked her over one last time, as if making sure she was really there, then hurried down the short hallway to the large room in the back of the saloon that served as the hangout for the Old Man's crew.

Spuds was a fireplug of a man of indeterminate age who had earned his moniker because his face resembled a dried-up potato. Elizabeth couldn't remember a time she hadn't known him. He threw open the door at the end of the hall and called, "Boss!"

Then, "It's the Contessa . . ."

Contessa? They'd never used that term of honor for her before.

"No, it's her," Spuds said. "She's here."

Her breath caught when she saw him, snagging on something sharp in her chest that was half joy and half dismay. He came toward her, tall and dignified as ever, his silver hair neatly brushed, his suit exquisitely tailored, his handsome face displaying an emotion she'd never seen him wear.

"Lizzie," he said when he reached her. He threw his arms around her and crushed her to his chest. Tears sprang to her eyes. She couldn't remember that he'd ever hugged her before, not in all the long years she'd known him. "Thank God," he whispered. "We thought you were dead."

He released her then but kept his hands on her shoulders as he studied her face. His eyes were suspiciously moist, and she marveled. She didn't think she'd ever seen him express a single genuine emotion. "Are you all right? Did the mark get you?"

"No, I got away, and I'm fine."

"Texas John came right away to tell me what happened. He brought your suitcase, and he thought you'd be here waiting for it." Texas John, the man they'd called Coleman for the con. "We thought for sure they got you."

"Let the Contessa come inside, where it's warm," Spuds said, using that term again. "She said it's a long story, and she can tell all of us at once."

"Of course." He released her shoulders and

took her by the hand, as if she were a child, to draw her down the hallway.

"Wait, first . . ." She had to swallow before she could ask. "Jake?"

"Jake will be glad to see you, too."

Relief flooded her, but he was coaxing her along, willing her to move, and before she could even make sense of it, she was in the big room with the rest of them. About a dozen men had been sitting at tables, playing cards and swapping lies. She knew every single one of them.

At the sight of her, they stood, all but one.

"Jake," she said, hurrying over to where he was struggling to rise. His arm was in a sling and his face was a patchwork of fading bruises. She laid a hand on his shoulder to hold him in his chair. "I thought they'd killed you."

He gave her a lopsided smile that seemed to hurt him. "I thought they'd killed you, too, Lizzie."

"What happened? How did you get away?"

"Those two goons of Thornton's, they left me when he called for them. He told them to go after you. I would've gone after them, but . . ."

"You wouldn't've caught me, either," she said, making him smile again. "Did Texas John find you? He said he would."

"Yes, he had to carry me out of the alley. He took me to a doctor he knows. They patched me up and let me hide out until I could travel."

"He's only been back three days himself," the Old Man said. "But at least we knew where he was all that time. Now we want to know where you were and why you didn't send us word."

Elizabeth grinned. She knew they liked nothing better than a good tale, and she had one to tell. "I couldn't send you word because I was in jail."

"Jail?" Spuds cried. "How on earth did you end up in jail?"

"Don't you boys read the newspapers? For obstructing traffic at the White House. I'm now a suffragist."

That made them laugh, all except the Old Man. He was looking at her in a completely new way, as if he'd never really seen her before.

"Somebody get the Contessa a chair and something hot to drink," Spuds said, "and we'll get the whole story from her."

They sat her next to Jake, who kept looking at her as if he was afraid she'd disappear, and they brought her coffee with a dollop of whiskey in it, and she told them everything up to and including Thornton's deal with the Ross rifles.

"Are you thinking he's good for another touch?" the Old Man asked when she was finished.

"We took him for fifty," she said. "He'll be anxious to make that back."

"Do you think he can raise enough to make it worthwhile?"

"He raised the fifty with no trouble at all," Jake said.

"And what about this Vanderslice fellow?"

"He's a lop-ear," Elizabeth said, "but he won't do business with Thornton, so Thornton will be looking for somebody else when Vanderslice cuts him loose."

"Too bad you and Jake can't get in on this," Spuds said.

Elizabeth sighed. She would have liked nothing better. "Not only can't I get in on it, I need to get out of town. Someplace Thornton won't find me."

"Texas John brought your share of the score," the Old Man said. "I've been holding it for you."

Jake nudged her with his good elbow. "I tried to convince him to give it to me, but he wouldn't do it."

"If you steal my cut, you'll have your other arm in a sling," she replied, nudging him back.

That made the others roar with laughter.

When everyone had had a chance to tell her how glad they were she wasn't dead, the Old Man took her into his office and closed the door.

"How much do you need? Texas John brought you eleven thousand."

"I don't want to take it all. How about two? That'll keep me for a year, if I need to stay away that long. You keep the rest of it for me."

He opened his safe and counted out the bills. She stuffed them into her purse.

"You should leave right now. Go straight from here to the station and take a train to Florida or somewhere. Just leave your things behind. You can buy what you need when you get where you're going."

He was right, she knew, but when she thought of Anna and Mrs. Bates . . . "I'll leave tomorrow. Can you send me a telegram? I'll tell them it's from my aunt in South Dakota and she's sick, so I have to go back right away."

"Lizzie, you don't owe these people anything."

He was wrong, but he'd never understand. "I know, but if I just disappear, they'll look for me, and Thornton will help them. I can't take that chance."

He sighed and shook his head. "Just be careful, and send me word if you need anything. In fact, send me word just to let me know you're all right."

"I'm sorry I couldn't let you know this time, but I didn't realize you'd be so worried."

For a second, he looked unutterably sad, and he laid a hand over hers where it rested on his desk. But only for a second. Then his mask was back in place, and he cleared his throat and rose to his feet. "You'd best be on your way before it gets dark. Those people you're so concerned about will be wondering what's become of you."

She had to say good-bye to all of them before they'd let her go. Jake was the hardest, but at least now she knew he was safe. He took her hand. "Be careful, Contessa."

"Why are you all calling me that?"

"Because you earned it, girl," Spuds said.

When she stepped out into the alley, she needed a moment to compose herself before making her way back to the street. She'd just missed a trolley, but there'd be another along in a few minutes, so she waited on the corner.

"Cab, miss?" a voice called. The driver stood on the curb, ready to open the door for her.

She thought about the long, cold ride back to the Vanderslice house and the two thousand dollars in her purse, and she said, "Yes, thank you."

He seemed oddly delighted with her answer, and he pulled the door open with a flourish. She had only a moment to register the odd bundle lying on the floor before someone shoved her from behind. She fell onto the bundle, which sprang to life, and the man who had pushed her climbed in on top. She scrambled up, or tried to, but two sets of hands grabbed her and dragged her up onto the seat. When she could see again, the cab was moving, and the two men were Thornton's thugs, one sitting on each side of her.

Fear coiled in her stomach, but she knew better

than to show it. "What do you think you're doing?"

"We're taking you for a little ride," one of them said. "Mr. Thornton wants to see you." He looked a little too happy about it, too.

"This is kidnapping. You'd better stop this cab and let me go at once."

"Or what? You'll call the cops?" he asked, still grinning.

"And when Mr. Thornton gets through with you, you won't be able to call nobody," the other one said.

"Shut up, Fletch," the first one said.

But she didn't need them to tell her what Thornton would do to her. If he'd killed his own wife, he wouldn't hesitate to kill her, too. She tried to assess her chances of escape. The cab was crawling through the late-afternoon traffic, so she'd have no trouble jumping out of it. The problem would be getting by Fletch and his pal. They sat on either side of her, prepared to hold her down or catch her if she tried to flee. And even if she did get away, she'd never outrun them. Could she count on help from the people on the street? Probably not.

She was helpless, with no one to save her but herself, and no strength to rely on except her wits. She allowed herself one moment of bitterness at the plight of females who were always at the mercy of unscrupulous men. Then she began to plan.

Where are you taking me?" she asked after what seemed like a long time of threading through the crowded city streets.

The two men exchanged a glance, as if trying to decide whether to answer her.

"We told you," the first one said. "Mr. Thornton wants to see you."

"But where is he?"

They were in a residential neighborhood now, and the streets were quieter here. A few well-dressed people strolled along the sidewalk, but the busiest time of the day was over now. People were heading to their homes. The cab suddenly stopped in front of a brownstone. She thought they were in Murray Hill.

Fletch jumped out and handed the driver a wad of bills. The other one grabbed her arm and jerked her out of the cab and onto the sidewalk. Fletch came around and took her other arm. Together they guided her up the front steps.

She could have screamed, but she doubted anyone in the surrounding houses would hear or come to investigate even if they did. People in neighborhoods like this minded their business. Besides, one of the thugs would probably have hit her, and she didn't want to be injured when she saw Thornton. She'd need all her faculties if she hoped to survive.

The front door opened before they reached

it, and Thornton stood there, watching with his piglike eyes. The advice she'd given Anna back at the workhouse echoed in her head. Don't let them see your fear. She couldn't quite manage a smile, but at least she was sure she didn't look as terrified as she felt.

"Good evening, Miss Perkins, or should I call you Miss Miles?" he said, stepping back so the thugs could push her into the house. One of them closed the door behind them.

"You may call me either one," she said.

Thornton wasn't amused. "Which one is your real name?"

"Perkins, of course. I gave a false name when I was arrested so you wouldn't be able to find me."

"That was very clever, Miss Perkins. In fact, it was too clever for the innocent young woman you were pretending to be when I met you and your brother on the train."

"And yet that's exactly what I am."

He slapped her then. He just wanted to frighten her. And it worked. She clapped a hand to her burning cheek as every thought in her head jangled in protest. For a full minute the pain literally blinded her.

"Take her in there," Thornton said, and the thugs grabbed her arms and dragged her into the parlor, where a straight wooden chair had been placed in the middle of the floor. They forced her down onto it.

By then her jangled thoughts were settling and her vision had cleared. The stinging pain in her face would at least keep her alert. "What do you want with me?"

"Haven't you figured it out yet? I want my money back."

"But I don't have your money. You lost it on those stocks."

"No, your brother lost it, or at least he said he did. He said he bought the shares when Coleman had told him to sell, but do you know what? After you and your brother disappeared, I went back to the brokerage. They told me he never bought any stock at all that day."

Elizabeth gritted her teeth to hold back the curses she wanted to heap on Jake's head. That's what happened when you played it against the wall. If they'd had a setup with a fake brokerage, Thornton would have found an empty office when he returned. Instead they'd only pretended to buy and sell stock at a real brokerage. "If he didn't buy stock, what happened to the money, then?"

"Oh, Miss Perkins, you lie so prettily," Thornton said. "Don't you think so, boys?" The boys nodded, their ugly faces grinning stupidly. "You know perfectly well what happened to the money. He kept it. He kept it all, my fifty thousand and Coleman's ten. Maybe he even kept yours, too, for all I know." At least he hadn't realized Coleman was in on it.

"If he kept it, then you should've found it on him when you beat him up."

"That's what we thought, too, but since we didn't, I figured you must have it."

"Me? How would I have it?"

"I'm sure he figured out some way to get it to you, and now I want it back."

"But I don't have any money at all. And even if I had it then, what would I have done with it? I went right from the hotel to the White House, where I got arrested. Your boys here saw it themselves. Then I went to the workhouse. If I had fifty thousand dollars—"

"Sixty."

"Sixty thousand dollars, what would I have done with it while I was in jail?"

"She's right, boss," the one named Fletch said. "They never would've let her keep that much cash."

"Shut up," Thornton said.

"So if I don't have it and Jake didn't have it, he must have lost it buying the stock, like he said. I don't know what else could've happened to it, and Jake is stupid like that."

"Where is Jake now?"

"I don't know. I've been in prison, remember? I hope he's at home, but I didn't have any money to get home to find out. That's why I've been staying with Anna Vanderslice. Maybe you'd lend me train fare, and if I find him, I'll let you know."

For a second Thornton looked like he wanted to tear her head right off, and she knew real fear. Then he smiled, and her blood practically froze in her veins. "I'm going to let Lester here hit you a few times, and when he's finished, I'm going to ask you again where my money is. If you don't tell me, Lester and Fletcher are going to tear your clothes off and each of us will take a turn with you. After that, I imagine you'll do anything I ask, but if not, we'll dump you naked in the gutter in front of some brothel and you'll have to beg them to let you in."

Elizabeth was quaking now, but even if she did tell him, he wouldn't like the answer, and as soon as she did, he'd still do all those things and probably kill her in the bargain.

Thornton stepped back and Lester stepped forward. He'd taken off his coat. Fletcher wrapped an arm around her neck to hold her in place and Lester drew back his fist.

"Wait!" she cried. "If you hurt me, David Vanderslice will never help you sell those rifles to the army!"

Chapter Ten

Thornton grabbed Lester's arm. "What did you say?"

"I said you'll never sell your Ross rifles to the army if you hurt me."

"What do you know about that?"

"I know everything. I know you need David Vanderslice to help you sell them, and I also know David promised Gideon Bates not to help you."

"How do you know all this?"

"I heard them talking on the train yesterday. David is going to string you along, but he's really going to make sure the army never buys anything at all from you ever. That's what he promised Bates, and that's what he'll do unless I help you." This was a bit of a stretch, but he had to think she was his only hope.

Thornton smiled again, but he didn't look a bit happy. "And how can you possibly help me?"

"I can convince David to change his mind."

"Why would David listen to you?"

"Because we're engaged. We're going to be married, and he'll do anything I ask him."

"Married!" Thornton scoffed. "You've only known him a few days."

"I only knew you a few days, and you would've married me."

"Not *married* you."

"You would've done it if you had to." She was right, and the truth of it was on his face. "David thinks he has to, so we're engaged."

"You're a clever little minx, aren't you?" His tone told her it wasn't a compliment, so she didn't respond. For a long moment, no one moved. Then Thornton said, "Let her go."

Fletch reluctantly removed his arm from her neck, and she drew an unsteady breath.

"How do I know I can trust you?" Thornton asked.

"Because I know what you'll do to me if I don't help you. The question is, what will you do if I'm successful and you sell your precious rifles?"

"Don't tell me you want a commission."

That almost made her smile. "I'm not stupid. All I want is for you to leave me alone. I don't have your money, and I don't know what happened to it, so the best I can do is help you make some more by selling the rifles."

"What about your brother? If he really is your brother."

"He can take care of himself, and if he really did steal your money and didn't share it with me, then I hope you do find him." Except he'd never find Jake now. The Old Man would keep him safe.

"Well, then."

Did she dare hope that she'd convinced him? "Well, then what?"

"How are you going to convince Vanderslice to help me?"

"By using my feminine wiles, of course, and reminding him that we owe you a tremendous debt for finding the deputy to serve the warrant on Warden Whittaker. He thinks I've never even met you, so I won't understand why he'd refuse to help someone who rescued me from prison."

"You really are clever." He obviously hated her for it, too.

"And in return, you forget we ever met."

"I don't think I will ever forget you, Miss Perkins, but I'll be happy never to see you again."

At least they agreed on something. "Then we have a deal?"

"Yes, but don't think for a minute you can trick me again. If you even try, you know what I'll do."

"Throw me down the stairs?" she said before she could think better of it.

But he only raised his eyebrows at her. "You've been listening to gossip."

"Isn't that the way you killed your wife?"

This time his smile made her skin crawl. "No, it isn't. I choked the life out of her after I'd beaten her nearly to death. I enjoyed it, too, Miss Perkins, and she hadn't even done a thing to deserve it."

And, of course, Elizabeth had. His message was plain. She swallowed the terror clogging her throat and wrapped her arms around herself to keep from shaking. "I need to get back to the Vanderslice house before they miss me."

"And how do I know you won't just hop on a train and disappear?"

"Because I give you my word."

He actually laughed at that, an odd bark that made the hair stand up on the back of her neck. "And because my boys will be watching you, so don't get any ideas."

"Yeah," Fletch said. "We followed you today, didn't we? Even though you tried to lose us."

She didn't bother to reply. "Fine. You'll know I'm keeping my end of the bargain when David contacts you. I'm ready to leave now. Where's my purse?" she asked, suddenly realizing she'd lost track of it during the ordeal of the taxicab ride. If they'd left it in the taxi . . .

Neither of the goons replied, and Thornton frowned. "Which one of you has it?"

Fletch reluctantly pulled the small drawstring bag she'd been carrying out of his pocket. She reached for it, but Thornton snatched it away. To her dismay, he pulled it open.

"What's this?" he demanded, snatching out the wad of bills. "I thought you didn't have any money."

"I didn't until today. I went to see an old family friend and borrowed it."

"What family friend is that?"

She sighed as if put upon. "Dan Kelly, also known as Dan the Dude."

"That's the fellow who owns the saloon where she went this afternoon," Lester said. "He claimed he'd never heard of her when we asked him, though, and then he threw us out."

Of course he did. Dan wouldn't give Thornton or his goons the time of day, so they'd never know if she was telling the truth or not.

"Your family has interesting friends," Thornton said, stuffing the money into his own pocket.

"What are you doing? That's mine!" she cried.

"And if I let you keep it, you could very easily leave the city. You're more reliable when you're penniless, Miss Perkins." He dropped the empty purse into her lap. "Take her back to the Vanderslice house and make sure she stays there," he told his goons.

"David wants to take me around to see the sights," she said.

He gave her a murderous glare, but he said, "Just make sure she doesn't leave the city."

"I couldn't fall asleep, so I thought I'd just go for a little walk," Elizabeth explained to David and Anna. "I wanted to send my aunt a telegram to tell her where I am, but then I couldn't find my way back. I was hopelessly lost, and everyone here is so unfriendly, I was afraid to ask for help."

"You poor thing," Anna said, taking both her

hands. They were sitting in the parlor where Anna had taken her after she arrived back on the front doorstep, disheveled and unnerved from her encounter with Thornton.

"You should never have gone out alone," David said.

"I know that now," Elizabeth said, not even having to force the tears that flooded her eyes. "Back home, I walked out alone all the time."

"You're not at home now," David said, "and New York can be a dangerous place for a female alone."

How well she knew. "I've learned my lesson, and I'm so sorry I worried you."

"I was terrified when I woke up from my nap and you weren't here," Anna said. "You should have at least told one of the servants where you were going. We didn't have the slightest idea even where to look for you."

"I think Miss Miles has been chastened enough, Anna," David said. "I blame myself. I should have stayed at home so I'd be available. If I had, I could have sent your telegram for you."

"I'd hate to take you away from your work, Mr. Vanderslice, but I certainly would have appreciated your help today." Elizabeth gave him her best smile and wondered if she could really get him to propose to her in the next day or two. He already seemed smitten, but that was still a long way from a marriage proposal.

"It's settled then. I promised to show you the city, and that's what I'll do."

"And I'll go with you," Anna said a little petulantly. "We have to make you fall in love with New York so you'll stay here forever."

David smiled. "Yes, forever."

Maybe a marriage proposal wasn't entirely impossible.

At supper, Mrs. Vanderslice said, "I've invited Hazel and Gideon Bates for dinner on Thanksgiving. I felt we all had much for which to be thankful this year, so we should celebrate together."

"Oh my, I'd forgotten all about Thanksgiving," Anna said. "I guess I lost track of the time when we were in prison."

Elizabeth hadn't given it a thought, either. In her world, holidays weren't very important. She refused to analyze too closely why her heart had lurched a bit at the thought of seeing the Bates mother and son, though. She'd missed Mrs. Bates, but Gideon could only cause trouble. He'd probably remind David of his promise not to do business with Thornton, and he'd also try to flirt with her. She'd have to make sure to be engaged by Thursday to put an end to Gideon's interest in her. She managed not to groan out loud.

"What do you think, Elizabeth?" Anna asked.

"I'm sorry. I was woolgathering."

"David suggested we go to the Museum of Natural History tomorrow."

"That sounds lovely." It really sounded awful, but Elizabeth needed to spend some time with David. Having Anna along would be a distraction, but she couldn't break the poor girl's heart by saying she didn't want her to come. In truth, she was better company than David.

"You'll have to be careful, girls," Mrs. Vanderslice said. "You don't want to exert yourselves. Remember what the doctor said."

"Don't worry, Mother. We'll be home in time for our naps," Anna said. "And this time, I'm sure Elizabeth will take hers."

Elizabeth wasn't so sure. She had a lot to do before Thursday.

Were there really hundreds of different types of birds in the world? Until today, Elizabeth had had no idea. And who in heaven's name would take the trouble to catch, kill, stuff, mount and label every single one of them? And put them in a museum? It was almost as big a mystery as why anyone in their right mind would make a trip to a museum to see them all.

And yet, here she was, strolling down the long aisle to marvel over each and every bird as David read the descriptions aloud to them. How long could she endure this before she started screaming?

Anna had linked arms with her the moment the taxicab had dropped them at the museum's front steps, so David hadn't been able to offer his arm to her. Instead he trailed behind them and managed to move to Elizabeth's side as often as possible. He really was a handsome man, so she had no trouble at all gazing at him adoringly. If she hadn't sensed Anna's disapproval, she would have actually enjoyed the flirtation. Instead, she had to keep a careful balance of holding David's attention while not encouraging Anna's ire. Why would Anna disapprove, though? If Anna wanted her to stay in New York, Elizabeth's marrying David would guarantee it. Maybe Anna was afraid Elizabeth was just leading David on, and since that was the truth, Elizabeth couldn't fault her. In fact, she admired Anna for wanting to protect her brother's tender feelings. But when it came down to Elizabeth's life or David's feelings, Elizabeth had her priorities.

Deciding she should pay more attention to Anna, Elizabeth turned to say something about the current bird, which had unusually beautiful plumage, but the words died in her throat when she saw Anna's face.

"Are you all right?"

Anna smiled, or tried to, but her face was gray. "I think I'd like to sit down for a minute."

"Mr. Vanderslice," Elizabeth said, but he'd already taken Anna's other arm.

"You should've said you were tired," he scolded his sister as the two of them supported her over to the nearest bench.

Elizabeth had wondered why they had benches here. Who would want to sit and stare at a bunch of dead birds? But maybe people were regularly overcome by boredom here and needed to rest.

"I'll be all right in a minute," Anna assured them, but plainly she would not be.

"You never should have come," David scolded. "You aren't strong enough yet."

"I think Anna has been chastened enough," Elizabeth said, echoing David's words from yesterday and making both brother and sister smile. "But I also think we need to get you home, Anna."

"I hate to spoil your outing," she said.

"The birds will be here another time," Elizabeth said. And she'd never agree to see them ever again. "But we mustn't endanger your health."

When Anna felt stronger, they left the museum and David hailed a cab for them. They tucked Anna between them for the ride home. Anna clung to Elizabeth's hand, and after a few minutes, she laid her head back against the seat and closed her eyes.

Elizabeth watched her face, glad to see a little color returning to Anna's pale cheeks. She'd been selfish, dragging Anna out today so she could spend time with David when she knew

Anna wasn't strong enough yet. One more day wouldn't have made any difference.

Something warm covered her hand where Anna still clutched it tightly. When she looked down, she saw David had covered it with his own. She looked up in surprise, and when she met his gaze, he squeezed her hand and smiled.

She wanted to snatch her hand away and say there'd been some mistake, she didn't mean to give the wrong impression, but she couldn't do that, not if she wanted to live. So she smiled back.

When they arrived home, a telegram awaited her. She'd asked the Old Man to send it, and when she opened it, the message read, "Gravely ill. Come home at once." It was to be her excuse for leaving immediately, but she couldn't go anywhere, not immediately or otherwise.

"Good news, I hope," David said when she'd read it.

"My aunt is glad to know I'm being well taken care of."

"You should invite her to join you here. We'd love to have her visit as well."

Oh yes, she'd happily invite her imaginary aunt for a visit. "She doesn't like to travel, but I'll pass along the invitation when I write to her." Which she would do immediately. The Old Man needed to know she hadn't left the city. He also needed to know there'd been a big change in plan.

· · ·

The doctor insisted that Anna remain in bed all day the next day, especially if she wanted to participate in Thanksgiving dinner the following afternoon. That left Elizabeth and David to their own devices.

"Dress warmly, Miss Miles," he said after lunch. "I have a surprise for you."

Elizabeth had a surprise for him as well, so she found the warmest dress in her stolen wardrobe and dug out the white fur collar and matching hat and muff she'd found in one of her many suitcases.

David hailed a cab for them on the next corner, and she looked at him in surprise when he told the driver, "Central Park."

"Isn't it late in the season for visiting a park?"

"They have carriage rides all year round, and it's going to be almost sixty degrees today, so I thought we should take advantage of what is probably the last pleasant afternoon until spring."

Elizabeth could not have agreed more. She'd seen the carriages many times but had never dreamed of riding in one.

A line of carriages waited, the horses' heads drooping. David approached the first one in the line and paid the fee. The driver helped them into the open vehicle and covered them with a lap robe. The air was crisp but mild, and the sky was actually bright.

"Are you two on your honeymoon?" the driver asked, slamming the carriage door.

Elizabeth had to cover her mouth to keep from laughing out loud, and David actually blushed. "Oh no, nothing like that. At least not yet."

"I understand," the driver said, tipping his top hat to them.

Elizabeth didn't have to feign her astonishment, but David's face was the picture of innocence when he turned to her. "Are you warm enough?"

"Oh, yes."

The carriage started with a jerk. David had given a lot of consideration to their outing today, choosing a very romantic activity. Under the lap robe, he could sit as close to her as he liked, although he was currently maintaining a respectable few inches' distance. Although Central Park was far more appealing in any other season of the year, it would always hold a certain charm, with its acres of woodland nestled in the center of the busiest city on earth.

"I think I'm beginning to fall in love with your city, Mr. Vanderslice."

"I hope you're also developing a fondness for its residents as well."

"For some of them, at least. You and your family have certainly made me feel welcome."

"After Mrs. Bates told me how you'd conducted yourself in Virginia, how could we do anything less? We will be forever in your debt for the way you looked after Anna."

"We all looked after each other, Mr. Vanderslice. I didn't do anything special." Which was perfectly true.

"Not according to Mrs. Bates. Honestly, Miss Miles, I don't think I've ever met another female quite like you."

Which was also perfectly true. David Vanderslice had certainly never met a grifter before. "I'm not sure that's a compliment."

"Oh, it is. The more I learn about you, the more I want to know."

He wouldn't like a lot of what he'd learn if he really got to know her, of course. "Knowing me would take a long time, I'm afraid."

"I'm prepared to make the effort. Didn't I tell you I'd like you to stay here forever?"

"And I'm sure you know I couldn't possibly do that."

"Why not?"

She shook her head at his teasing. "Because my home and my family is in South Dakota. An unmarried woman can't just go to a strange city and start a new life." Although that's exactly what she was planning to do if she could escape Thornton, she realized.

"You're right, an unmarried woman could not. Are you opposed to marriage, Miss Miles?"

"Why would I be?" she asked.

247

"Many of the suffragists are. They don't like the idea of being under a man's control."

Of course they didn't, but she couldn't tell him she disapproved of marriage. "When you put it like that, I'm not fond of the idea. But not all men look upon marriage like that."

"No, we don't," he said, clearly putting himself into that winning category.

"Does your mother approve of rights for women? I haven't heard her express an opinion."

"She isn't as outspoken as Mrs. Bates, of course, but I think she supports the cause in her own way."

"Even after Anna was arrested?"

David winced a little. "She wasn't too pleased about that, as I'm sure you can understand, and that may have tempered her enthusiasm a bit."

"Enough so she'll forbid Anna to participate in any more protests?"

"I'm hoping Anna herself will decide that. She isn't strong, as you know, and no one expects her to give her life for the cause."

Elizabeth thought about the hunger strike and how none of them had hesitated to join it, especially Anna. No one had died, but many had been close to it. She only hoped the men in Congress came to their senses before someone did. But as the Old Man would undoubtedly remind her, she had a more urgent problem. "I have a feeling Anna won't be sensible about her dedication to the cause."

"Which is why she needs friends like you to advise her."

"I'll continue to advise her as long as I'm here." She sighed. "But I don't know how much longer that will be."

"Miss Miles, if you don't mind my asking, is there any reason you need to return to your home?"

"You mean besides the fact that it is my home?"

"Yes. For example, do you have any, uh, attachments there?"

Elizabeth feigned innocence. "My aunt, of course."

"Uh, no, I mean any, uh, romantic attachments, for example. Is there someone special in your life?"

"Oh no, not at all. I've never . . . Well, if you'd ever been to South Dakota, you'd understand." Of course, Elizabeth had never been to South Dakota, either, but she had no trouble imagining. "And to answer your question, no, I have no romantic attachments."

"I'm sorry, that's really none of my business, is it?" David said, color blooming in his face.

"Isn't it?" she asked coyly. "I wouldn't have answered if I thought so."

"I'm glad to hear it. We hardly know each other, but even in the short time since I've met you, I've come to respect and admire you."

And he'd continue simply admiring her for

weeks if she didn't take matters into her own hands. "Why, Mr. Vanderslice, is this a proposal?"

"Oh, uh, I didn't mean—"

"Because I've come to admire and respect you, too," she hurried on before he could deny it. "But I never dreamed my feelings would be returned. I'm just a simple girl, and I'm not familiar with the way things are done in the city. I'm very glad you had the courage to make a declaration first, so I didn't embarrass myself."

"You are?" He looked shocked but, mercifully, he also looked pleased.

She looked down demurely. "Of course I am. No matter how she feels, a woman must wait for the man to speak first, and if he never does, well, she has to return to South Dakota broken-hearted."

"I wouldn't want that. Oh no, I'd never want that," he said, growing more confident by the second.

"So was it? A proposal, I mean? I know it's forward of me to ask, but I have to be sure . . ."

"Yes! I mean, Miss Miles, you would do me the greatest honor if you would agree to become my wife."

She managed not to sigh with relief. "And you do me the greatest honor by asking. How could I refuse? Yes, Mr. Vanderslice, I would be delighted."

He looked so pleased, she almost felt guilty,

but she knew he couldn't possibly be in love with her, at least not yet. And he wouldn't like the way she was going to conduct herself over the next few weeks, either. She'd give him more than enough reason to rue his hasty engagement and to be relieved when his fiancée disappeared. In the meantime, however . . .

"You have made me the happiest man alive, Miss Miles."

"I think you may call me Elizabeth now that we are engaged."

"And you must call me David. I can't wait to tell Mother and Anna. Anna will be so pleased! Now you really will stay here forever."

Anna wouldn't be pleased when Elizabeth deserted all of them. Elizabeth wouldn't be pleased, either. She'd never had a friend before and probably never would again. "Do you really think your mother will approve? I don't know anything about New York society, and I don't have much of a dowry."

"Everyone will want to know you. The old families get a little stuffy, so we need some new blood every now and then to freshen us up."

"I hope you're right, but you haven't said what your mother will think."

"She'll just be relieved that I'm finally getting married. She's been wanting grandchildren for ever so long."

Elizabeth ducked her head at that. Hopefully,

he'd think it was modesty, when in reality it was horror at the thought of bearing David's children. If she ever did have children, she'd want their father to be someone who hadn't needed to be tricked into a proposal.

"I didn't mean to embarrass you, Miss . . . I mean Elizabeth."

She managed a shy smile. "That's all right. It's just . . . The idea of marriage is a bit overwhelming."

"Yes, indeed, and we should make some plans. We'll live in my house, of course. What about your aunt? Do you think she'll want to come here to live as well?"

Since her aunt did not exist, Elizabeth doubted it. "I have no idea. I'll have to ask her. But first things first. How shall we announce it?"

"We'll send a notice to the newspapers, of course."

"And I'll write to my aunt, of course. Oh, and we can tell the Bateses tomorrow when they come for Thanksgiving dinner."

"Yes, that will make the day even more special. Oh, wait, why don't we keep it a secret from Mother and Anna until then, too? We can announce it to everyone at the same time."

Was that really a good idea? What if Anna and her mother really didn't approve? On the other hand, if they didn't, they probably wouldn't say so in front of company. Once they'd told outsiders, it would be harder for David to back out as well. "What a wonderful idea."

David started chattering about things in which Elizabeth had no interest, like how long they should remain engaged before they married and where they should go on their wedding trip. Since she wasn't ever going to actually marry him, none of it mattered, as long as he agreed they wouldn't marry until after Christmas. That should give her plenty of time to get Thornton's rifles sold and break free of him.

They'd reached a rather secluded section of the park, and the driver turned in his seat. "Congratulations, young man, and if you want to kiss her, this would be the perfect place."

Elizabeth smiled at David's chagrin, but when he turned to her, she had to admire his expression of determination. He leaned down and brushed her lips with his in the barest promise of a kiss. Its sweetness almost broke her resolve, until she remembered Thornton's face when he described how he'd murdered his wife. After that, she didn't even feel guilty anymore.

Elizabeth was sure Anna and her mother would guess their secret from the way David kept staring at her all evening. But Mrs. Vanderslice was distracted by her plans for the holiday dinner the next day, and Anna was determined that Elizabeth not notice David at all. She dragged out some photograph albums and insisted on showing

Elizabeth every photograph the Vanderslices had ever had made. Poor David never even caught her alone for so much as a good night, much less another of his tepid kisses, which was just fine with Elizabeth. Tomorrow would be soon enough to start pretending affection in front of other people.

Gideon had never looked forward to a visit with the Vanderslice family with more enthusiasm. Hardly an hour had gone by since his return to the city that he hadn't thought of the fascinating Elizabeth Miles. He probably should have dropped by to see her, but he hadn't wanted her to guess how enamored he was. That would never do. He didn't know her well, but he suspected she could be merciless to a man who loved her. Unless she loved him back, which he had no reason at all to suspect. No, he wasn't going to reveal his true feelings until he'd learned more about her, and that, he was sure, would take some time. Something about her was just not quite right. She was probably the most mysterious female he had ever met.

His mother seemed to be equally as eager for the visit, and when they entered the Vanderslices' parlor, she went straight to Elizabeth, even though by rights she should have greeted their hostess first.

"Elizabeth, my dear, I'm glad to see you looking so well, and what a lovely gown."

It was a deep blue that matched her eyes, and it looked as if it had come from Paris or at least some place more exotic than South Dakota or even New York. She glowed like a precious jewel in the Vanderslices' mundane parlor.

Elizabeth made no effort to hide her joy at seeing his mother. Elizabeth said something about how well his mother looked, too, and they kissed each other the way women did, except with genuine affection.

David distracted him by shaking his hand. He looked inordinately happy to see them. "Important day."

"Is it?" Gideon said. "I suppose so. We've got our women back safe and sound."

David smiled mysteriously. "Yes, that, too."

But he didn't have time to worry about David and his cryptic hints. He exchanged pleasantries with Mrs. Vanderslice, then turned to Anna, who didn't look nearly as well as Elizabeth. He teased her a bit, as he always did, and got her to smile a little. Then he turned to Elizabeth, hoping he'd managed to wipe all trace of eagerness from his expression.

"Miss Miles, you're looking well."

"I wonder how long it will be until my health is not the first thing people mention when they see me."

"Then I apologize for mentioning it. I had no idea how tedious it must be to have people constantly concerned with your well-being."

"Now you make me sound disagreeable. Who wouldn't want to have people concerned about her well-being?"

"You, apparently, but rest assured, I will never inquire after your health again."

"Thank you, Mr. Bates. It will be a great relief to me."

"What is Gideon saying to make you smile like that, Elizabeth?" David asked.

Since when did David call her by her given name? And why was he standing so close to her? He had a decidedly proprietary air about him, too.

"Nothing but nonsense," she said.

"Has she mentioned that I've been showing her around the city?" David asked.

"Not yet." How enterprising of David. Now Gideon was really annoyed. He had been a fool not to visit sooner, but he'd had no idea David had any interest in her.

"Oh yes. We saw the Museum of Natural History, and yesterday was so fair that we took a carriage ride in Central Park."

"How . . . nice." But it wasn't nice at all, especially considering the way David was looking at her now. He was thoroughly smitten. At least Gideon saw no indication she returned his affections. And how could she? David was far too ordinary for a woman like Elizabeth Miles.

Gideon might also be too ordinary for her, but he intended to explore the possibility anyway.

His mother returned to Elizabeth after satisfying her duty to greet her hostesses and filled the time before dinner by telling her and Anna what was happening in Washington City with the movement. At last, the maid came to announce that dinner was ready, and Mrs. Vanderslice delighted Gideon by placing him next to Elizabeth at the table. Of course, David was at the head, with Elizabeth on his right, but Gideon felt sure he could draw her attention from him.

When the oyster soup had been served, Gideon turned to Elizabeth. "What did you think of our Central Park?"

"It was quite a surprise. I certainly didn't expect to find a wilderness in the middle of the city."

David chuckled for no apparent reason. "I don't think I ever really appreciated it until yesterday, either."

Elizabeth gave him a polite little smile, because of course she knew what he meant, and Gideon was very much afraid he did as well.

She turned back to Gideon. "And how are you faring, Mr. Bates? Are you still comfortably fixed or did your employer make good on his threat?"

"What threat was that?" his mother asked in alarm.

"Devoss told me I could have three days to

rescue you, but if I was gone any longer, I'd lose my position."

"He wouldn't dare," David said, outraged, and the ladies murmured their agreement.

"And he didn't dare," Gideon said. "I think he might have made a fuss, but when I handed him the note you wrote him, Mother, he was instantly contrite and congratulated me on my success."

"But all I did was thank him for letting you come," his mother protested.

"Exactly."

"It sounds like we have a lot to be thankful for on this festive occasion," Mrs. Vanderslice said. "I know I'm very thankful to have my beloved daughter and my dearest friend safely at home again."

"And Anna and I are thankful that Elizabeth has consented to remain in New York for a while," his mother said.

"We certainly are," Anna said.

Gideon was, too, and he'd just opened his mouth to say so when David interrupted him.

"If we're sharing our blessings, I have one to announce."

Beside him, Elizabeth drew a sharp breath and stiffened in her chair, although her smile never wavered.

David actually rose to his feet, and when everyone had stopped eating to look at him, he said, "I have asked Elizabeth to marry me, and she has accepted."

Gideon watched in horror as David took her hand and raised it to his lips. He wanted to grab her wrist and wrench it away, but before he could move, before anyone else could even absorb this information, Anna made a strangled sound of protest.

She jumped up, knocking over her chair, and gave Elizabeth the most anguished look Gideon had ever seen on a human face. "No!" she cried and ran from the room.

Chapter Eleven

For a long moment no one moved. Elizabeth's heart convulsed in her chest. She'd expected Anna to be surprised and perhaps even dismayed, but not horrified. She glanced up at David, but he appeared too shocked to even react.

"Oh dear," Mrs. Vanderslice said, and made as if to rise, but Elizabeth knew she wouldn't be any help at all.

"I'll go," she said, dropping her napkin on the floor in her haste to be gone.

Anna's bedroom door was closed but not locked, and Elizabeth didn't bother to knock. Anna lay sprawled across her bed, sobbing. She looked up at the sound of the door opening.

"How could you?" she demanded, her face twisted in agony.

Elizabeth shut the door and hurried to the bed. "I thought you'd be pleased. We'll be sisters," she said, hating herself for the cold comfort of the lie, since she had no intention of ever marrying David. "You wanted me to stay forever, and now I can."

"I wanted you to stay with me! You said you didn't want to get married, either. You said we'd get a house together. You said you loved me!"

"I do love you. You're my very dearest friend."

Elizabeth sat down beside her on the bed, and Anna pushed herself up, her eyes blazing.

"Then you don't need him. We don't need him. Don't you see, Elizabeth? This is our chance to be independent women. We can be so happy together, just the two of us! Oh, Elizabeth, I love you so much!"

Anna took Elizabeth's face in both hands and kissed her, right on the mouth. The kiss was far more passionate than David's had been, and a much bigger surprise. When Anna pulled away, they stared at each other in shock for a long moment.

"I don't know why I did that," Anna said faintly.

Elizabeth did, though, and now she understood just how deeply her betrayal would cut. "Oh, Anna, I had no idea."

"No idea about what?"

"That you loved me."

Anna scowled impatiently. "But I told you."

"Yes, you did, but I thought you meant like a friend."

"But I do!"

"Friends don't kiss each other like that."

Anna clapped a hand over her mouth, then lowered it slowly. "I'm sorry. I didn't mean to."

Why did life have to be so complicated? The Old Man was right: you should never get involved with other people. At least breaking

David's heart wouldn't cause him much pain, but breaking Anna's would devastate her.

"Anna, I really do love you, like a friend, but I think you're in love with me, in a very different way."

"What do you mean? What other way could there be?"

"The way men and women love each other."

"That's ridiculous! Women don't love each other like that."

"Some of them do."

"What are you talking about?"

Elizabeth winced and rubbed her forehead. How had she gotten into this? "I don't have time to explain it to you right now, and I wouldn't really know how, even if I did. Everyone is waiting for us, and we have to go back downstairs, but will you trust me?" She took Anna's hands in hers. "If you trust me, tomorrow we'll . . . I'll take you to meet someone I know, and she can explain it to you."

"Someone you know? Here in the city?"

"Yes, it's a long story, and . . . Well, I'll explain that tomorrow, too. Please, will you trust me?" It was a stupid question. No one should ever trust her.

"I don't have any choice, do I?"

"Oh, Anna, you have lots of choices. I just hope hating me isn't one of them."

"I could never hate you, Elizabeth."

She knew that wasn't true, of course. By the time this was all over, Anna would despise her. "Good, then we'll sort all this out tomorrow. In the meantime, we need to go back downstairs."

"Oh no!" Anna covered her face with both hands. "I couldn't possibly face them after the way I acted."

"But it's Thanksgiving," Elizabeth argued.

"I don't care. Tell them I'm sick. Tell them whatever you want, but I just can't."

It was probably for the best. She'd have enough trouble pretending to be the happy bride-to-be without having to look at Anna's tragic expression across the table. "I'll tell them to send you up a tray."

Anna's sad smile almost broke her heart. "And tomorrow everything will be better?"

"Everything will be clearer at least."

Gideon watched Elizabeth go, then looked at David. How could his friend have won Elizabeth's heart in just a few days? How could he have won her heart *at all?* It didn't make any sense. Hadn't he just decided she had no tender feelings for David? He would have seen it when she looked at him, the way he'd seen it when David looked at her. But he hadn't. So, what was going on? Why would David propose marriage to a woman he hardly knew, and why would she accept when she was plainly not in love with him? And why was Anna so very horrified by the very thought?

"Maybe I should go, too," David said.

Gideon was surprised to hear his own mother say, "Oh no, dear. Let Elizabeth handle it."

"Are you sure?" Mrs. Vanderslice asked.

"I'm sure. I think Elizabeth can handle just about anything."

Gideon had to agree.

"But why is Anna so upset over such happy news?" Mrs. Vanderslice asked.

"It's just the shock, I'm sure," his mother said. "You've surprised us all, David." She met Gideon's gaze with an unspoken question that he didn't want to answer, so he looked away.

He'd risen automatically when Elizabeth had, so now he and David both took their seats again.

"Should we wait for them?" David asked.

"I think we should continue with the meal," Mrs. Vanderslice said quite sensibly. "The soup is getting cold."

The four of them began to eat, but the soup was like acid in Gideon's stomach. He had to do something. He couldn't let Elizabeth ruin her life by marrying David Vanderslice. He couldn't let Elizabeth ruin his own life by marrying someone else.

"I'm afraid that in all the excitement, we haven't congratulated you, David," his mother said. "I'm sure we all wish you and Elizabeth much happiness."

"Thank you, Mrs. Bates. I can't imagine it would be otherwise."

"And I have to agree with you," Gideon said, although the words wanted to stick in his throat. "You're a lucky man."

"I am indeed." David grinned and Gideon wanted to punch him.

Instead he said, "Have you set a date for the wedding?"

"Not until after Christmas at least, and of course we need to discuss it with our families."

"Will you be married here or at Elizabeth's home?" his mother asked.

"Oh, here surely," Mrs. Vanderslice said.

"We're thinking it will be here, yes," David said.

So, Gideon had at least a month to figure out a plan. His mind was racing, but he was too angry to really think straight at the moment. And how was he supposed to disrupt this engagement with Elizabeth living right here under David's roof and . . .

That's when it came to him.

The maid cleared the soup course and then brought out the turkey and all the side dishes. Mrs. Vanderslice had ordered a traditional meal with chestnut stuffing, cranberry jelly, mashed potatoes and gravy, creamed onions, squash and chicken pie. They were still passing around the dishes when Elizabeth returned.

Gideon and David stood up, and Gideon pulled out her chair before David could think of it. She hurried in and sat. "I'm so glad you didn't wait for me. She's fine, really. We had a little talk, and she's very happy for us, David." She gave him a fleeting smile. "She's sorry for becoming emotional, though, and is too embarrassed to come back down. She wants us to enjoy our dinner without her."

"Are you sure she's all right, Elizabeth?" Mrs. Vanderslice said. "Do you think I should send for the doctor again?"

"I think she would be mortified if you did. Thank you," she added as Gideon passed her the meat platter. "I promised her that she and I would have an outing tomorrow, just the two of us." She smiled at David again, which Gideon found extremely annoying. "She may be a tad jealous, so I want to reassure her that our friendship won't suffer."

"I should think you would become closer," Mrs. Vanderslice said. "You'll be sisters, after all."

"Which is what I plan to impress upon her. Now let's change the subject, shall we? I'm sure Anna would hate to know we talked about her all during our dinner."

"We were wishing David happy while you were gone, my dear," his mother said. "So we must wish you the same."

"You're very kind."

"I hardly know what to think," Mrs. Vanderslice said. "I never even suspected . . . Well, how could I have? But Hazel speaks so highly of your character, Miss Miles, that I must feel honored to have you as my daughter-in-law. You have obviously made David very happy, and we look forward to welcoming you to our little family."

Elizabeth murmured some clichéd reply that Gideon didn't believe for a minute. Then she looked at him expectantly. Did she think he'd congratulate her for marrying another man?

He picked up his wineglass. "Let me propose a toast to David and Elizabeth. May you have all the happiness you deserve."

Elizabeth picked up her glass and allowed him to clink his against it, but her eyes told him she understood his toast better than the others. What she didn't tell him was what she thought of it.

David clinked his glass with so much enthusiasm, Gideon was surprised it didn't break. He didn't dare meet his mother's eye when he touched her glass with his, and Mrs. Vanderslice was gazing fondly at her son, so she didn't even look at Gideon.

Mrs. Vanderslice had a lot of questions for Elizabeth about the wedding plans. Elizabeth answered them very patiently while they proceeded to pass the serving dishes and eat their meal. By the time they had devoured the mince and apple pies, they all knew that Elizabeth felt a long engagement was in order, so she and David could get to know each other better, and she agreed with Mrs. Vanderslice that a New York wedding made perfect sense.

Gideon waited for a lull in the conversation while they passed around the fruit, nuts and raisins and sipped their after-dinner coffee to make his comment.

"It just occurred to me, David, that since you and Miss Miles are now engaged, it's no longer proper for her to be living under your roof."

"Why, you're right, old man. I never thought of it, but it's decidedly improper."

"It certainly is," Mrs. Vanderslice said in dismay, "but what can we do? We don't want to send Elizabeth home to South Dakota, do we?"

Gideon glanced at Elizabeth, expecting to see surprise or perhaps even a spark of understanding because she'd guessed at his intention. Instead he saw an absolute terror in the instant before she dropped her gaze. He'd hardly registered it before his mother said what he had fully expected her to say.

"Sending Elizabeth home would hardly accomplish her goal of getting to know her intended better, but I'm sure we'd be happy to have her come and stay with us, wouldn't we, Gideon?"

He tried to look surprised. "Of course we would."

Elizabeth looked up at that, and this time he did see understanding. And a hint of anger before she said, "How very kind of you, Mrs. Bates. I'm not familiar with New York customs, I'm afraid, so I had no idea this would be a problem. I wouldn't want to cause a scandal."

"We're happy to help," his mother said, "and believe me, I'm being selfish. I'd like nothing better than to have your company for the next few months."

"I would enjoy that, too," Elizabeth said with all the warmth Gideon could have wanted.

She didn't show any of that warmth to him, though. The ladies retired so David and Gideon could enjoy some brandy, but David was in a hurry to rejoin his beloved, so they didn't linger. In the parlor, Mrs. Vanderslice had set up a card table with four places. Since there were five of them without Anna, Gideon wondered who would sit out until Elizabeth excused herself to pack her things. The ladies had apparently decided she should leave that very night. She'd take just one bag this evening and they'd send the rest of her things over in the morning.

She must have spent some time with Anna, too, because she didn't return until it was time to leave. Even then, she refused to meet his eye, and he sensed her anger, even though she took pains to hide it from everyone else.

269

"I'm so sorry to see you go," Mrs. Vanderslice said as Elizabeth kissed her cheek. "But I suppose we'll see you tomorrow in any case."

"Oh, yes. Anna and I have our outing all planned."

"Then you must dine with us tomorrow evening, too," David said.

She gave him her hand and a dazzling smile that made Gideon grit his teeth. "Of course I will. Until tomorrow."

"Take good care of her, old friend," David said to Gideon, slapping him on the back.

Gideon intended to.

Then they were ready. The Bateses' home was only two blocks away, so they were going to walk. Gideon picked up Elizabeth's suitcase and almost staggered under its weight. Could she have put rocks in it?

"Are you sure you can manage that, Mr. Bates?" she asked sweetly.

"Oh yes." He was gritting his teeth again. Sometimes getting what you wanted wasn't such a good thing.

Gideon hadn't expected to see Elizabeth at breakfast the next morning, but she was already at the table when he came down. She looked fresh and beautiful until she saw him. Then she looked fresh and beautiful and angry.

"Good morning," he said, determined not to

notice her hostility. "This is a delightful change. Usually, all I have to look at in the morning is the newspaper."

She completely ignored his implied compliment. "I need to send a telegram this morning."

"All right," he said, nonplussed. "Just write out the message, and I'll be glad to send it on my way to my office."

"I would prefer to send it myself, but after what happened the other day, your mother suggested I ask you to escort me to the telegraph office." The Vanderslices had told them at dinner yesterday how Elizabeth had become lost when she'd tried to send a telegram. He couldn't blame her for not wanting to repeat that unpleasant experience, and he was grateful for an opportunity to spend a little time with her, even if he was a bit disgruntled to learn she didn't trust him with her messages.

"I'd be happy to escort you. It's right on my way. I suppose you want to give your aunt the happy news of your engagement," he said in an attempt at conversation.

"Thank you." She rose from her seat. "I'll be waiting in the parlor."

Gideon's face burned with humiliation as he watched her leave. Only then did he notice the remains of her breakfast. She'd made sure to be finished before he came down. If he thought he could win her away from David by having her here, he was obviously going to have to work a lot harder than he'd expected.

By the time he'd finished his own breakfast, he'd given the matter a bit more thought, and now he had a completely new question: why was Elizabeth so angry with him for taking her away from the Vanderslices?

Could he have misjudged? Was she really madly in love with David and furious at being parted from him? Was he just an infatuated fool for thinking otherwise?

Or did she have another reason to be angry?

And why did these new questions make her even more fascinating to him?

By the time he reached the parlor door, she was waiting for him with her coat and hat on. He put on his own coat and hat, then opened the front door and gave her a little bow.

Did she really roll her eyes? Fortunately, he liked a challenge.

She hesitated on the front stoop while she put on her gloves, although he thought she was also surveying the neighborhood. What was she looking for? Signs of wealth? She wouldn't find many in this part of the city. Those with true wealth had moved uptown ages ago.

When she was satisfied with her gloves, she started down the steps. He followed and fell into step beside her. He'd been debating how to start with her, and he decided to be reckless.

"He's not rich."

She looked up in surprise. "What?"

"I said, he's not rich."

"Who isn't rich?" she asked, but he could see she knew full well.

"David."

"Do you think I'm a gold digger?"

He hoped not, because he wouldn't be in the running, either. "I just thought you should know."

"I only expect him to be comfortably fixed," she said with a sly grin that reminded him he'd used those very words to describe himself.

He absorbed the sting of that barb and soldiered on. "I sense that you're angry with me, Miss Miles."

"Why would I be angry?"

"I was hoping you would tell me."

She pretended to consider that. "Perhaps I'm put out with you because you separated me from my fiancé."

"I hope not, because Mrs. Vanderslice would have realized the problem soon enough, and if she didn't, her friends would have, and they would have descended like a flock of hens to make you notorious."

"And you saved me from that."

"I did indeed."

"Do you think I should be grateful?"

"That is my sincere hope, although I suspect I will be disappointed. I also know my mother is very fond of you, so I thought she would invite you to stay with us, which would make her very happy."

"Then you were only being a thoughtful son."

"And a good friend to David for keeping you so close. His mother might have sent you back to South Dakota."

"I'm afraid I'm going to have to change my opinion of you, Mr. Bates."

"You are?"

"Oh, yes. You are far more devious and conniving than I originally thought."

"You wound me to the quick."

"I doubt it."

They'd reached the corner and she stopped, waiting for him to indicate in which direction they should head. He pointed to the right, so she went in that direction.

"How can you question my motives, Miss Miles?"

"Easily."

"Then what do you think they are?"

"I hesitate to guess."

Gideon couldn't resist. "Do you think I hope to steal you away from David?"

She looked up at him in surprise, then turned her face away again. "How could you hope to steal me away from the man I've fallen in love with and plan to marry?"

"Because that's impossible."

This time she frowned, apparently confused. "It's not impossible. We're engaged."

"It's impossible that you've fallen in love with him."

She stopped dead in her tracks, nearly causing the people behind them to knock them over. "How dare you!"

He took her arm and pulled her into the safety of the nearest shop doorway. "I've known David all my life. There's nothing about him that would make any woman fall in love in a few days, much less a woman like you."

"And exactly what kind of woman am I?"

"You're smart and spirited and strong, and you deserve a man who's your equal."

Every ounce of that spirit flared in her remarkable eyes for an instant, and then someone clapped a hand on his shoulder.

"Is this gentleman bothering you, miss?"

Gideon turned to shove the interloper out of the way, but he stopped when he realized it was Thornton's man, Lester. "What are you doing here?"

Lester stepped back and held both hands up in a sign of surrender. "Nothing much. Didn't realize that was you, Mr. Bates. I just saw what looked like some man forcing his attentions on this lady here."

"I'm not forcing my attentions on her." Well, maybe he was.

"That right, miss?" Lester asked.

"Of course it is. We were just having a serious discussion, but this is not the time or the place, is it, Mr. Bates?"

"No, it's not."

"Thank you for your concern, sir," she said to Lester. "Now if you'll excuse us, we'll be on our way."

Lester moved back some more and Gideon gave him a hard stare as he allowed Elizabeth to step out into the flow of pedestrians in a hurry to get wherever they were going. Lester didn't look the least bit contrite, though. What was he doing here at this time of day if he was working for Thornton? But Gideon didn't have time to worry about Lester—or Thornton, either—just now.

He hurried to catch up to Elizabeth. "We need to cross the street here," he said when they reached the corner. "The telegraph office is on the next block."

She didn't reply. She didn't even glance at him. All the color had drained from her face, and regret stabbed at him. What had he been thinking? If he'd had any chance at all of winning her from David, that chance was gone now. The most he could hope for was preventing her from marrying David, and that would probably mean he'd never see her again.

They'd reached the telegraph office, and he

hurried to grab the door handle before she could. He held it, preventing her from entering and forcing her to look at him.

"I'm sorry—"

"Thank you for your assistance, Mr. Bates. You may now be on your way." Her gaze chilled him.

"Can you find your way back?"

"Yes. I paid particular attention this time. May I go inside now?"

He turned the knob and opened it. She went in without a backward glance, and he closed the door behind her. Left with no other choice, he headed down the street to the offices of Devoss and Van Aken.

Elizabeth needed a moment to compose herself before approaching the counter. What was she going to do about Gideon Bates? She'd thought he would mind his manners if she treated him with disdain, but she'd underestimated him. Her disdain only made him more interested in her. And how dare he try to ruin her engagement to David when that was what would save her very life? Gideon Bates was infuriating.

"Can I help you, miss?" the clerk asked, gazing at her from under his green eyeshade.

"I want to send a telegram." She stepped up to the counter and took a blank form and pulled a pencil from the can. She scratched out the address of Dan the Dude's Saloon and the message:

"Cannot leave town. New plan. Meet at Cybils today eleven."

"That's exactly ten words," the clerk said when he'd looked at her message.

She paid him and waited while he sent it.

By then she figured Gideon would be well away, and when she turned, she was not surprised to see Lester peering at her through the plate glass window.

She stepped outside.

"What do you think you're trying to pull?" he demanded.

She gave him her haughtiest look. "Would you please explain to Thornton that an engaged woman cannot live in the same house as her fiancé, so I have gone to live with Mrs. Hazel Bates. This will in no way affect our arrangement." She started to walk away, then stopped and turned back before he could recover his wits. "Also, do not be alarmed to see that I am going to visit Anna Vanderslice this morning. We are then going to visit friends in Greenwich Village, and I will return with her to have supper with her family."

"How is that going to convince Vanderslice to help sell those rifles?"

"Is that your business?"

"No, but Thornton will ask," he said with a grin.

"Vanderslice will be at his office all day, so

I'll be ingratiating myself with his family. Is that good enough?"

"I guess it'll have to be."

"Fine. Now if you give me a head start, I'll try to make it easy for you to follow me back."

She didn't like the hard glitter in his little pig's eyes, but she didn't let it show. She took her time walking back to the Bateses' house, pausing to look in shop windows on the way, just to annoy Lester. She wasn't going to forget he was the one who would beat her if she failed. That was one reason she'd asked Gideon to go with her this morning. She certainly could have found the telegraph office herself, but after she'd moved into a completely different house, she didn't want to explain it to whichever one of Thornton's goons was on duty this morning until she was in a very public place.

Now she had to figure out how to deal with Anna and her inconvenient infatuation.

"I don't think I've ever known anyone who lived in this neighborhood," Anna said when the taxicab had dropped them off in front of Cybil's house in Greenwich Village.

It was a ramshackle place close to a hundred years old, and Elizabeth felt the sting of tears when she saw it. She couldn't give in to emotion now, though. She took Anna's arm. "Come on."

Anna needed a tug to get her started up the walk. "Are you sure this is the right place?"

"I told you, these people are good friends of mine." More than friends, if the truth were known, but Anna was going to get enough truth of her own today. She didn't need Elizabeth's.

Ordinarily, Elizabeth would have just walked right in, but she didn't want Anna to know exactly how familiar she was with this house. Cybil saved her the trouble of knocking, though. She threw open the door just as they reached the front stoop. The Old Man must have told her Elizabeth was coming.

Cybil stood half a head taller than Elizabeth, but she had the same auburn hair and bright blue eyes. Today she wore a red silk kimono over a pair of baggy black trousers gathered at the ankles. On her feet were peacock blue satin slippers. Elizabeth thought Anna's eyes might pop right out of her head.

"Lizzie!" She threw her arms around Elizabeth, shocking Anna even more. Cybil started to say something else, but Elizabeth jerked her head toward Anna, silencing her. She took Anna in with one shrewd glance. "And who's this now?"

"Cybil, this is my dearest friend, Anna Vanderslice."

"Pleased to meet you, Miss Anna, but where would you be meeting somebody named Vanderslice, Lizzie?"

Elizabeth smiled with delight. "We met in jail."

Cybil smiled back with delight. "Then you'd best come inside and tell me all about it."

They took off their coats, and Cybil led them into the cluttered parlor, which was furnished with a collection of mismatched furniture chosen primarily for its ability to provide comfort or function, preferably both.

"Zelda, Lizzie's here!" Cybil called, and in another moment, a tiny, blonde woman came bustling in. If Cybil was outrageously dressed, Zelda was as prim and proper as any lady Anna's mother might have known. "And she's brought a friend," Cybil added in warning.

Zelda greeted Elizabeth with a kiss on both her cheeks. "I've just made some tea. I'll bring it in and we'll have a chat."

When they'd been served, Anna seemed to have recovered from her initial shock. Zelda was the perfect hostess, asking the right questions so that Anna was able to tell the story of their arrest and the growth of their friendship in a perfectly natural way. When Zelda got up to refill the pot, Elizabeth went with her.

"Who is this girl and why have you brought her here, sweetheart?" Zelda asked when they were in the kitchen.

"Zelda, I need your help."

Zelda smiled and shook her head at Elizabeth's foolishness. "The Old Man told us what happened to you and Jake with that mark and how you ended up with the suffragettes."

"Suffragists."

"What?"

"Never mind. I told him to meet me here."

"And he's been here for an hour, but we didn't think you'd want your friend to see him."

"No, I don't. Thank you. But there's a reason I brought Anna with me." Quickly, she explained about Anna's reaction to Elizabeth's engagement to her brother.

Zelda's well-bred jaw dropped. "You're engaged to a mark?"

"David isn't a mark. I'm just using him to . . . Oh, it doesn't matter. However I explain it sounds horrible. Anyway, I'm not worried about that part of it. I'm worried about Anna and what's going to become of her after I'm gone. I thought maybe you and Cybil could talk to her and . . . and explain things. She thinks she's in love with me, and I can't stand the thought of hurting her."

"Maybe you're in love with her, too," Zelda suggested gently.

"I wish it was that easy. I do love her, but only as a friend."

"We've told you before, it's so much easier if you love another woman."

"I know, men are so . . . complicated."

"And unreasonable and smelly and—"

"Believe me, I understand! I wish I were like

you and Cybil. Anna and I get along so well, too. But . . ." She thought of Gideon Bates and how deliciously complicated and unreasonable he was, although he did smell very good indeed. Her life would be much simpler if she really did hate him. "Anna needs to understand her feelings and what they mean, or at least what they could mean."

"Cybil and I will figure out if this is just a schoolgirl crush or if she really is one of us. Now why don't you go see the Old Man? He's probably pretty worried by now."

Nothing ever worried the Old Man, but she nodded and thanked Zelda and went upstairs to the room she used when she stayed here. Unlike the rest of the house, this room was in perfect order. He sat reading a newspaper in the overstuffed chair Elizabeth had bought with her first score. At the sound of the door opening, he'd crushed it and tossed it aside.

"What happened? Are you all right?" he asked, jumping to his feet.

"Didn't you say that the last time I saw you?"

"I thought you were leaving the city."

"Thornton's thugs picked me up right outside of Dan's."

He swore. "If they laid a hand on you . . ."

"They were going to, but luckily, I knew enough about Thornton to figure out how to get away from him." She sat down on the neatly made bed and explained what she had done.

"You're really engaged to this Vanderslice fellow? How did you manage that?" he asked with some amusement.

"I told you he's a lop-ear."

"But that was dangerous. What if he hadn't proposed?"

"He *didn't* propose, and I'm still engaged to him. Sometimes I don't think you appreciate my talents."

"You may be right. So now we need to figure out how to work the deal with the rifles. I have been thinking about it. We were going to approach Thornton directly when this Vanderslice wouldn't help him. All we need to change is that we'll approach Vanderslice instead and ask him to help us deal with Thornton. Can you convince Vanderslice to cooperate?"

"Just tell me what you need, and I'll make sure he does."

He smiled at her fondly. "You're right. I have never truly appreciated your talents."

Chapter Twelve

Elizabeth could hear Anna sobbing before she was halfway down the stairs. She flew down the rest of the steps and raced into the parlor.

"What have you done to her?" she demanded, hurrying to Anna's side.

"We didn't make her cry. You did," Cybil said.

"How could I make her cry? I wasn't even here," Elizabeth said, sitting down beside Anna and taking her hand. "I'm so sorry I left you. I don't know what they said, but they were supposed to make you feel better!"

Anna dabbed at her tears and managed a reassuring smile. "They did make me feel better. Oh, Elizabeth, you have no idea. All these years, I knew I was different from other girls, and I thought I was the only girl alive who didn't care if boys noticed me. Once I even told my mother that when I grew up, I was going to marry a girl because girls are prettier."

"Girls *are* prettier," Zelda said.

Anna smiled at that. "I think that was one reason I was attracted to the suffrage movement, too. So many of the ladies are unmarried and not interested in men. Cybil says some of them are probably like us, too."

"I'm sure they are, dear," Zelda said.

Anna turned back to Elizabeth. "You can't imagine what a relief it is to know there are other women like me."

"Then why were you crying?" Elizabeth asked.

"She was crying," Cybil said, "because we told her *you're* not like us."

"And you'll never love me the way I love you," Anna said, tearing up again. "And I'll have to watch you marry David."

"But I'm not going to marry David," Elizabeth said. Only when she saw Anna's shock did she realize the mistake she had made. She clamped a hand over her mouth, but it was too late.

"What do you mean, you aren't going to marry him?"

"Oh dear," Cybil said, rising. "I think we need to leave these two alone, Zelda. They have some things to talk about."

Zelda stood, too, but she stopped to take Anna's hand before she left. "You are always welcome here, my dear girl, at any time of the day or night. And we have a salon every Monday evening. I hope you will come by sometime and meet our friends."

"Thank you for everything. You've both been very kind."

Cybil discreetly closed the pocket doors behind them, leaving Elizabeth to explain herself to a very confused Anna.

What could she say? The Old Man always said stick to the truth as much as possible. It's easier to remember than a lie. "Anna, a lot of what I told you about myself wasn't true."

"I may be naïve, Elizabeth, but I'm not stupid. I'd already figured that much out at least."

"You did?" Elizabeth asked, horrified.

"Of course. How many times did I tell you that you aren't like anyone I've ever known? And you didn't seem to know much about the suffrage movement for someone willing to go to jail for it. And when we were unpacking your luggage . . . Well, I knew something wasn't right almost from the first."

"I didn't want to lie to you, but I had very good reasons. I just hope when you hear them, you'll be able to forgive me."

"I'm very anxious to hear them, and I probably shouldn't tell you, but I'm very anxious to forgive you, too."

That probably wouldn't last long, but Elizabeth swallowed down her natural reluctance to tell the truth and began. "As you probably have guessed, I'm not from South Dakota. I live here in the city. Here in this house, in fact, when I'm in town."

"I gathered as much from Zelda and Cybil."

"A few weeks ago, my brother and I were traveling to Washington City."

"Your *brother?*"

"I told you I'd lied about some things. Yes, my brother, Jake. We met Oscar Thornton on the train."

"Thornton? The man who helped get us out of the workhouse?"

"The very same. He and Jake became fast friends, and we were staying at the same hotel. The Willard."

"But you said . . . Oh, more lies."

"Exactly. While we were there, Thornton and Jake met a man who was making a lot of money in the stock market. He offered to help Jake and Thornton make some money, too, and for a few days they did very well. Then something went wrong. I don't really understand what, because I don't know much about that sort of thing," Elizabeth lied, "but Jake and Thornton lost a lot of money because Jake made some sort of mistake."

"How dreadful."

If Anna only knew! "Even more dreadful because Thornton blamed Jake. He thought Jake had taken the money or something. Thornton's men beat him very badly, and then they came after me."

"You! Whatever for?"

"Thornton thought I could make Jake give him his money, I guess, or else he was just going to get some revenge. At any rate, I escaped just in time, but they were chasing me. I didn't have any place to go, and then I remembered the women were demonstrating in front of the White House, which was just down the street."

"And that's when you joined the demonstration. I remember, you looked a little anxious, but I thought it was just because you'd never demonstrated before."

"You know the rest of the story, up until we came back to the city."

"So Thornton knew you were in the workhouse with us," Anna mused. "That's probably why he helped all of us get released."

"It was. I knew he still wanted his revenge, so I was going to sneak out of New York at the first opportunity, but I had to go see my brother first, to make sure he was all right. That's where I went the day I told you I got lost."

"You were in a state that day. Did seeing your brother upset you so much?"

"No, he's recovering nicely, but Thornton's men had followed me, and after I visited Jake, they forced me into a cab and took me to Thornton's house."

"How awful. But you escaped!"

"No, he let me go, but only after he threatened me with unspeakable things. He was going to kill me, Anna. He wanted his money back, but Jake and I don't have it, so I did the only thing I could think of. I promised to convince David to help Thornton sell his rifles to the army."

Anna gaped at her. "How on earth did you think of that?"

Oh dear, Anna really was innocent. "I don't

know. It just came to me. At first Thornton didn't believe that I could convince David of anything, so I told him we were engaged."

Anna considered this for a moment. "But you weren't engaged then."

"I know, which is why I had to . . . uh . . . encourage David to propose so quickly."

"And you said you have no intention of marrying him. That's very cruel to poor David."

"Oh, Anna, he doesn't really want to marry me. I tricked him into proposing, and I'm not going to break his heart. I'm going to be a terrible fiancée, not the girl he thought I was at all, and he'll be very relieved when I break it off with him after the rifles are sold."

Anna stared at Elizabeth for a long moment, and Elizabeth held her breath, waiting for the final judgment. After what seemed an eternity, Anna smiled. "Elizabeth, you are amazing."

"No, I'm not. I'm desperate. And of course now you can tell David I'm a liar and a cheat who tricked him, and he won't help Thornton and—"

"Don't be silly! Of course I won't tell him. In fact, I'll help you convince David. I don't want anything to happen to you, either, Elizabeth."

Surprisingly, Elizabeth felt the sting of tears. No one had ever loved her so unconditionally.

"And don't you dare cry," Anna scolded, "because then I'll start, and we'll never get anything done. First of all, are you sure this will work? Will it satisfy Thornton, I mean? Enough so he'll give up his plans to harm you?"

Elizabeth obediently blinked away the moisture in her eyes. "Honestly, I don't know, but I was planning on taking a long trip as soon as Thornton gets his money, someplace where he's not likely to find me."

"That's a wonderful idea. I could go with you."

Elizabeth smiled at Anna's eagerness. "I'd like that, but I'm not sure it would be safe."

Anna waved her concerns away. "We'll worry about that later. Now we need to make some plans for persuading David. You don't know him as well as I do. I've been talking him into things my whole life."

Poor David. He'd gotten the good looks, but his sister had gotten the brains. Over the next hour, she proved it, too.

"Have you and Elizabeth decided where you're going on your honeymoon?" Anna asked her brother that night at dinner. She looked so innocent, Elizabeth could hardly believe they'd planned this whole conversation. Anna would have made a good grifter.

David grinned broadly at the mention of a honeymoon. "We haven't discussed it yet."

"It should be special, don't you think? You only have one honeymoon. Elizabeth, where would you like to go?"

"Oh, I really don't care. Wherever David decides is fine with me." She gave him her sweetest smile, which clearly charmed him. "As long as we're together, it will be wonderful."

"But you must have an opinion," Anna insisted. "Isn't there some place you've always dreamed of going? Now is your chance, while David is still besotted with you!"

"You're being silly, now," Mrs. Vanderslice scolded good-naturedly.

"But it's true!" Anna said. "Confess, Elizabeth. What is your heart's desire?"

Elizabeth hemmed and hawed and let Anna coax her a little more before she finally admitted, "I've always dreamed of taking a European tour. Oh, I know it would cost a fortune and David couldn't possibly be away that long, but . . . Well, that's what I've always dreamed about."

"It wouldn't cost that much," Anna said. "And David could probably do some business in Europe while you're there, couldn't you?"

David was a little disconcerted, but to his credit, he rallied quickly. "I might be able to."

"As for the expense," Anna continued, "didn't you say that Oscar Thornton wanted your help with something? There would certainly be a big commission in that."

"I also said I wasn't going to help him."

"But why not? Papa always said not to let sentiment interfere with business."

"I'm not sure your papa ever said that," Mrs. Vanderslice said.

"I know Mrs. Bates doesn't approve of Mr. Thornton," Elizabeth said, although the words wanted to stick in her throat, "but he did help get us released from the workhouse. I can't help feeling very grateful for that."

"I don't think that's enough to earn Hazel's forgiveness," Mrs. Vanderslice said.

"I don't, either," Anna said, "but I can't think why Mrs. Bates even has to know about it if it would upset her. And Mr. Thornton will think us very rude indeed if you refuse to do business with him after what he did for your sister and your fiancée, David."

"You don't know what you're asking, Anna," David said.

"And I'm not going to be the kind of wife who makes demands," Elizabeth said, glad she was so good at lying. "I know you'll make the right decision, David."

"Of course he will," his mother said, ending the discussion.

After dinner, the family retired to the parlor. Mrs. Vanderslice wanted to play cards for a while since Elizabeth made a fourth, or so she said. But when they were settled, with David beside Elizabeth on the sofa, he turned to her with a beaming smile and presented her with a small box from Tiffany.

Elizabeth didn't have to pretend to be surprised. She hadn't even considered the possibility that she would receive an engagement ring. At least when this was over, she'd have some jewelry to show for it. She bestowed a grateful smile on her intended and opened the box to reveal the ugliest ring she had ever seen.

Fortunately, Elizabeth had been carefully schooled in how to hide her true emotions. "Oh, David, it's . . ."

"It was my grandmother's," he said, which meant it was really old, in addition to being old-fashioned. For some reason he seemed proud of this fact. "Anna helped me pick out which one to give you."

Elizabeth risked a glance at Anna, who looked so smug, Elizabeth had to bite her cheek to keep from laughing out loud. Elizabeth would get even with her later. "I don't know what to say." Which was the absolute truth for once.

"I hope it fits," he said, taking the box from her unresisting fingers. He removed the ring—how could he present it in a Tiffany box and deceive her like that?—and slipped it on her finger.

"It's perfect," she declared, holding out her hand to admire it. It looked even worse out of the box.

"David thought you might want a new ring," Anna said, "but I told him you'd appreciate something that had been in the family for generations."

"You know me so well," Elizabeth said.

Anna ignored Elizabeth's sarcasm. "What parts of Europe did you especially want to see, Elizabeth?" Anna asked to remind Elizabeth of their purpose.

Over cards, Elizabeth admitted being torn between London and Paris but being especially interested in seeing Rome and Venice. David, she noticed, didn't say much. She suspected he was trying to figure out how to please his intended bride without bankrupting himself. She might have felt sorry for him if she hadn't known he'd never have to face that choice.

Gideon was beginning to understand what hell must be like. Hell was having the one you wanted near enough to touch and not being able to touch her. Not even being able to get her to speak to you, in fact. The weekend had been torture, with Elizabeth flitting in and out, visiting the Vanderslices and having them visit here, and seeing David possessively tuck her hand into the curve of his arm and sweep her away. And she continued to ignore Gideon, giving him just the barest notice when forced to acknowledge his presence and speaking only the most banal platitudes when forced to address him.

And the very worst part was all of that only made him want her more.

For once, he'd been glad to leave for his office this Monday morning. While he couldn't hope to forget about her completely, at least he didn't have to see her or hear her voice all day. But now his day was over, and he had to go back to his place of torment. With any luck, she would have already left to spend her evening with the Vanderslices, and he wouldn't have to see her at all today.

Of course, the thought of not seeing her at all depressed him beyond bearing, and he entered the house with a resigned sigh.

He was shrugging out of his coat when David stepped out of the parlor. "Gideon, old man, glad you're home. I've been waiting for you."

Gideon managed a smile for his old friend. "Have you?"

"I need your advice on something."

Hopefully, he wasn't looking for marriage advice. "Of course." Gideon hung up his coat and followed David into the parlor. As he'd expected, Elizabeth was there, sitting on the sofa and looking so beautiful, it almost stopped his heart. "Miss Miles."

She didn't smile. "Mr. Bates."

David sat down beside Elizabeth, as was his right, and Gideon took a chair opposite them. The gas fire burned in the grate, but Gideon still felt chilled. "You said you wanted some advice. You could've come by my office, you know."

"This isn't legal advice, at least not technically. It's more . . . personal." David exchanged a look with Elizabeth, and Gideon managed not to groan.

"I'm the last one to give personal advice," Gideon said.

"It's about Thornton."

Not at all what Gideon had expected to hear. "What about him?"

"That deal with the rifles he wants to sell to the army. Well, someone came to see me today, a General Sterling. Retired General Sterling, I should say. The president appointed him to some committee that's authorized to buy supplies for the troops, and Senator Wadsworth sent him to me. He'd sent Thornton to me, too, which is why he knew I could help the general."

Gideon glanced at Elizabeth, but her face revealed nothing. "You said you weren't going to work with Thornton."

"I'm . . . uh . . . having second thoughts."

How interesting. "Why?"

David glanced at Elizabeth, giving her the lovesick smile that made Gideon want to vomit. "I've been thinking about what he did for us. He's the one who found the warden and got the warrant served. He got Anna and Elizabeth and your mother out of that workhouse. Without him, they might still be there."

Gideon sincerely hoped they would have been released by now, but he couldn't know for sure, so he couldn't argue with David's logic. "And you want to show your gratitude."

"It's the decent thing to do. It's not like I'm buying the rifles myself. I'm just going to help him make the right contacts, and I'll be helping the army get the supplies they need, too."

"And someone is going to earn a fee, so it might as well be you."

David stiffened but he didn't back down. "A man has to think about these things when he's planning to marry."

Of course he did. "I have it on good authority that Miss Miles isn't interested in your money."

At last she met his gaze. Her look was sharp enough to draw blood, but he held it until David said, "I know, but she does want a European tour for a honeymoon."

"I told you, that doesn't matter," she insisted.

David took her hand and patted it, making Gideon grind his teeth. "Which is why you're going to get it. So you see, Gideon, this benefits everyone."

Not everyone deserved to benefit, but David probably didn't want to hear that. "You said you wanted my advice. It sounds like you just want my approval, but you don't really need that, either. You can do whatever you think is right, David."

"Of course I value your counsel," David said. "I just . . . Well, your mother might be upset. I wouldn't want to lose her good opinion."

Gideon was sure of that, and now he thought he

298

understood David's concern. "There's no reason she even needs to know about this, then. I certainly won't mention it to her."

"I would appreciate that."

David was still holding Elizabeth's hand, and Gideon didn't think he could stand seeing that very much longer. "If that's all," he said, starting to rise.

"One more thing," David said, stopping him.

Gideon sat back down and somehow didn't sigh. "Yes?"

"Could you join us when I get the general and Thornton together?"

Elizabeth's chin snapped up, and she turned her razor gaze on David. "Why would you impose on Gideon when you know how he feels about Mr. Thornton?"

A very good question.

"Now, Elizabeth, you don't need to concern yourself with this. It's business, and Gideon understands we put our personal feelings aside." David turned to him. "I'd like to have your help on this, to make sure everything is legal and aboveboard. You'll be paid for your time, of course."

Of course he would. Devoss and Van Aken would insist upon it. "Do you have any reason to believe something wouldn't be legal?"

"Not at all, but this is so new, everything to do with the war, and I don't want to leave anything to chance. I'd like to have someone I trust involved in drawing up the papers."

Gideon couldn't argue with his logic. He only wished David was more considerate of his feelings. But of course David didn't know the extent of Gideon's feelings as they pertained to Elizabeth. And maybe Gideon could at least influence this general not to overpay for the rifles. No sense in making Thornton any richer than necessary. And if his mother found out, well, he'd have that to tell her, at least. "All right. Just let me know when you're meeting."

"Thank you, Gideon," David said with obvious relief. He rose and offered his hand. Gideon rose, too, and shook it. Only then did he notice Elizabeth's frowning disapproval. Should he be touched that she'd wanted to keep him out of it? Somehow he didn't think so. "I'm sorry, but I have to go," David said. "I have a previous engagement this evening that I made before I actually became engaged, and Elizabeth has graciously agreed to forgo my company this evening. I will leave her to your tender care."

David took his leave, and when the front door had closed behind him, Gideon hazarded a glance in Elizabeth's direction.

"Why did you agree to that?" she asked.

"Because David is my friend and he asked me."

"You don't have to do it. Just tell him you're busy when he has the meeting set up."

"I don't lie, especially to my friends."

"Don't be silly. Everyone lies."

"I don't." Why was she so angry? And so adamant that he not help David? "Do you want this deal to fail?"

"Of course not. Didn't you hear what David said? He's taking me on a European tour."

"I also heard what you said, that you don't care about the tour."

"Of course I do, but I don't want him to think I'm a gold digger."

"I think we've already established that if you were a gold digger, you'd be digging in a richer vein."

She reached up and pinched the bridge of her nose, as if he were giving her a headache. She was certainly giving him one. Then he noticed something else. "What on earth is that on your hand?"

Did she actually wince? "My engagement ring." She certainly sounded defensive.

He leaned in for a closer look, and she quickly covered it with her other hand.

"It was his grandmother's."

"I'm sure it was." Could David really have given her such a hideous ring?

Before he could decide, Elizabeth looked up at him and tried to smile, although the effort was strained. "Let's not quarrel, Gideon. I'm trying to save you from compromising your principles by helping this man Thornton, whom you obviously despise. Anna and I are grateful for his role in getting us released from the workhouse, and David feels a need to repay him somehow, but you are under no obligation. If you don't want to lie, simply tell David the truth and beg off. No one will think less of you."

"Why do you care?"

"What?"

"Why do you care about my moral dilemmas?"

"I don't, but I know you wouldn't hurt your mother for the world, and if she found out you'd participated in this, she'd be devastated."

She was right, of course, but she was also lying. Or at least not telling him the whole truth. Her reasons sounded logical, but he didn't know why she should even need reasons. Why should she be concerned about him at all? She seemed to want the deal to succeed, but she didn't want Gideon involved, even though he could probably ensure it. Did she not know that?

"Maybe you don't understand that David needs me there to make sure he doesn't foul things up."

"Are you serious?"

"Perfectly serious."

"You can't mean . . ."

"I can't mean what? That David isn't very bright? Surely you've noticed that by now."

The color bloomed prettily in her cheeks and anger made her eyes flash. She'd never looked more beautiful. "Are you still trying to convince me not to marry him?"

"Of course I am."

He thought the emotion that flickered across her face was dismay, but he couldn't be certain. "But why? You said yourself that David is your friend. Don't you want him to be happy?"

"Of course I do, but he won't be happy with you, and you won't be happy with him, either."

"You sound very sure of that."

"I am. There's a fire in you, Elizabeth. You need a man who won't be consumed by it."

"A man like you?" she scoffed.

He would have reached for her then, but the doorbell jangled, startling them both.

"That's Anna," she said with what sounded like relief, and before he could react, she had darted around him and out into the hall to greet her friend.

Gideon rubbed a hand over his face and took an unsteady breath. He had almost taken Elizabeth into his arms. He didn't want to admit what he would have done then, but all of it would have been a betrayal of his oldest friend. What was he thinking?

He hadn't been thinking at all, of course. Elizabeth had that effect on him.

"Hello, Gideon."

He looked up to see Anna smiling at him from the parlor doorway. "Hello. Are you dining with us tonight?"

"Oh no. Elizabeth and I are going out to a . . . a meeting." She came into the room. "I passed David outside just now. He said you're going to help him deal with Mr. Thornton."

He glanced past her, but Elizabeth was nowhere in sight. "Yes, I am."

"That's very generous of you. I know how you feel about Mr. Thornton."

"Yes, well, David is a friend."

"But that's asking a lot, even of a friend, so be sure you charge him a large fee. It's the least he can do for taking advantage of you."

"He's not taking advantage."

"Of course he is. We both know he wouldn't be able to do this on his own, but we both love him too much to mention it."

Gideon blinked a few times to make sure his vision was clear. Was this really Anna Vanderslice? He'd never known her to express an opinion about anything before, much less an insightful one. And now that he noticed, she seemed different somehow. Was she taller? No, that wasn't possible. Maybe it was the way she held herself. But something had definitely changed. "You're looking very . . . well this evening," he said, searching for the right words. "I guess you've recovered from your ordeal."

"Oh, yes. I wouldn't want to do it again, but I'm almost glad we got arrested. So many wonderful things came out of it."

He could only think of one. "You met Miss Miles."

Her smile widened at that. "Yes, I've never known anyone quite like her."

"Neither have I."

Her smile turned puzzled, but before she could question him, Elizabeth swooped into the room. She'd put on her coat and hat and was pulling on her gloves. "I'm ready. Shall we go?"

"Is Mother going with you?" he asked.

Both women turned to him, instantly sobered. "No, why would she?" Elizabeth asked.

"Anna said you were going to a meeting. I naturally assumed it was one of her endless committee meetings."

"Oh no," Anna said with what appeared to be forced cheerfulness. "We're going to a literary salon."

That sounded odd. "I didn't know you were interested in literature, Miss Miles."

"There are many things you don't know about me, Mr. Bates."

That was only too true.

"It's mostly to introduce Elizabeth to the right people," Anna said. "She needs to know all our friends."

Of course she does, if she is going to marry David.

"We should go," Elizabeth said brightly. "We don't want to be late."

305

She wouldn't even meet his eye. Of course not. She was still angry at him for some reason he hadn't figured out yet, and not because he had insulted her fiancé. In fact, she hadn't cared about that at all.

He should probably be heartbroken over the way she treated him, but if she didn't really care about him, why was she so angry? And so worried about him compromising his principles? And so anxious to keep him away from David's general?

He would just have to figure that out.

When they were safely away from the house, Elizabeth turned to Anna. "A literary salon?"

"It was the first thing that popped into my head," Anna said with a giggle. "I didn't think I should tell him where we're really going."

"No, you shouldn't. Have you ever been to a literary salon?"

"A few times. It's terribly boring. They just talk about books and argue about what they mean."

"Are books supposed to mean something?"

"Apparently. What was going on with you and Gideon when I came in?"

"Nothing."

Anna made a rude noise. "Don't tell me that. I could've cut the air with a knife. Poor Gideon was practically boiling."

"*Poor Gideon* is trying to ruin our plans."

"What do you mean?"

"David asked him to help with the Thornton deal."

"I know. David told me when I passed him on the way over."

"But why would he do that?"

Anna sighed. "Because David is hopeless at business. He's simply too gentlemanly to drive a hard bargain, and he never seems to know what's in his own best interest. Gideon has been saving him for years."

"Oh." Elizabeth's assessment of David had been too correct. He really was a lop-ear. "Well, I don't think he can ruin this. It sounds like this general is determined to buy Thornton's rifles. What could go wrong?" Nothing, of course, because the general would make sure of it.

"I don't know, but believe me, we want Gideon by David's side, just to be sure. If something goes wrong, I'm sure Thornton will blame you."

Elizabeth was sure he would, too. "I guess there's no hope for it, then. Gideon is going to be involved." She would have to get a message to the Old Man and warn him. He would know how to handle Gideon, or at least she hoped he would. She didn't think grifters did much business with people like him, though. In fact, she hadn't even known there were people like him. The Old Man always said you can't cheat an honest man, but it was a joke. Nobody was truly honest, or at least that's what she'd always thought.

"Don't sound so discouraged," Anna said. "Everything will work out just like we planned. You'll see."

Elizabeth hoped she'd see. At least it wouldn't be too much longer. A few days or a week maybe, and the game would be over and she'd be on a boat for Cuba. Or maybe Bermuda. If only she could feel excited at the prospect. For some reason, the thought of leaving New York made her want to cry, even though staying in New York put her life in danger.

"Now tell me what I should expect this evening," Anna was saying. "I'm so excited to meet Cybil and Zelda's friends, but I'm terrified, too. They'll think I'm a hopeless innocent, I'm afraid."

"They'll love it that you're a hopeless innocent," Elizabeth said, and proceeded to reassure her until they'd found a cab and traveled to Cybil's house in Greenwich Village. She didn't even bother to check to see if Thornton's goons were following them. She just assumed one of them was lurking in the shadows. He'd see them doing nothing unusual this evening, although he might be a bit shocked by the colorful crowd that gathered at Cybil's.

Zelda greeted them both with a hug and a kiss and then promptly took Anna off into the living room to meet some people. Elizabeth saw both male and female professors from Hunter College, where Cybil and Zelda taught, as well as some students and former students. Another woman she recognized as a rather successful novelist. She wore a lacy dress and was smoking a cigar. Maybe Anna would get her literary evening after all.

She was just about to follow Anna and Zelda when Cybil caught her arm. "He's upstairs if you want to see him."

"Good," she said with relief. "I was going to have to send him a message."

"I told him you'd probably be here tonight, and he decided to take a chance, since nobody would notice one more person coming into the house."

"Look after Anna while I'm upstairs, will you?" Elizabeth said.

"I don't think that will be necessary." Cybil nodded to where Anna was shaking hands with the cigar-smoking lady novelist. "I think she'll be just fine."

Chapter Thirteen

Gideon wasn't sure why he needed to see David. He just knew he did. Luckily, he didn't have any scheduled appointments that morning, so he told the good folks at Devoss and Van Aken that he had to go visit a client. It wasn't a lie.

He walked the short distance to David's office, which was a cluster of rooms in a tastefully insignificant building just off Fifth Avenue. No one sat at the front desk. In fact, it was so tidy, Gideon imagined no one had sat at it for a while. None of David's partners appeared to be in, either. Their office doors stood open to reveal equally tidy and empty desks. Of course, the partners only appeared when there was money to be made, and even then not before noon.

David's office door was closed, but Gideon had telephoned, so David was expecting him. Gideon knocked perfunctorily and went in without waiting for permission. To his surprise, he saw David had a visitor. "Excuse me. I didn't mean to interrupt."

"Gideon," David said with obvious delight. "We've been waiting for you."

David and his guest had both risen, and Gideon saw he was a tall man who held himself perfectly erect. His expensive suit was severely tailored so it resembled nothing so much as a uniform, and his silver hair was trimmed short and neatly combed. Gideon had an overwhelming urge to salute.

"General Sterling, may I present Gideon Bates?" David said.

Gideon shook the general's hand. In spite of his age, his firm grip was just short of painful.

"Pleased to meet you, young man. Vanderslice here was just singing your praises."

"I'm glad to hear it."

The general didn't smile at that. Instead he studied Gideon with his icy blue eyes as if taking his measure. Or judging his fitness for combat.

"Please, sit down," David said after an awkward moment. "I was just telling the general that you're going to provide legal advice for the transaction, Gideon."

Too late to back out now, Gideon supposed. "That's right."

"But Vanderslice is concerned because you've got some sort of grudge against this man Thornton," the general said.

More than a grudge, but how to explain it? "He was married to a cousin of mine. He treated her badly." A shocking understatement, but he couldn't very well accuse a man of murder with no proof beyond his mother's intuition.

"But the wife, your cousin, she's left him now?"

"No, she's . . . dead."

The general had no reaction to that. None at all. "I see. And you blame him. That's natural. But I'll tell you, Bates, this is war. We have to put our personal feelings aside. I'd be willing to do business with the Devil himself if it meant I could get the equipment our boys need to fight the Kaiser."

Gideon didn't doubt it. "I'm sure the army appreciates your dedication."

"I don't give a damn whether the army appreciates it or not. I'm doing this for my country, young man, and because the president asked me to step forward. And because good men will die if I don't. In any case, you do know that you'll collect a handsome fee for your time? That's usually enough to convince most people to ignore their principles."

Gideon stiffened. "My principles are not for sale."

The general raised his eyebrows. "And nobody wants to buy them, young man. We only need for you to come to terms with them. Now, I need to make contact with this Thornton fellow, and if you object to doing business with him, you can step aside. Nobody will think less of you for it."

"I don't have any objection," Gideon heard himself say. Surprisingly, it was the truth.

"I'm glad to hear it, Gideon," David said. "So very glad. Now all we need to do is arrange a time when we can all meet—"

"You know, you've got me thinking, Bates," the general said, ignoring David. "Maybe I should think twice about doing business with Thornton myself."

"Oh no," David said, sounding almost desperate. "I mean, you said yourself, the Devil and all that. And Thornton isn't so bad. No worse than a lot of men, at least."

"Even still, maybe I should meet him first. Judge for myself."

Not a bad idea. Maybe the general would call off the deal himself. "Like David said, we could arrange a meeting," Gideon said.

"Not a meeting. Men like Thornton, they know how to act in a meeting. You don't get the true measure of a man. No, I'd like to see him socially. Could you arrange that, Vanderslice?"

"Certainly," David said without bothering to consider.

"Maybe a dinner at your home. Or do you live in one of those bachelor apartments?"

"No, no, I live in my family home. With my mother and sister."

"Oh, yes. Ladies. That's even better. A man is always uncomfortable when ladies are present. A little on edge, am I right, Bates?"

He'd never thought about it, but, "I suppose so, sir."

"Yes, yes. On edge and afraid of making a fool of himself, which means he's almost certain to do it. And, Vanderslice, didn't you say you'd just got yourself engaged?"

"Yes, sir, I did. To a lovely young lady who—"

"Invite her, too. How about you, Bates? Do you have a lady you can invite?"

"No, sir." He wasn't going to bring his mother to this debacle.

"Too bad. Well, we'll make do. Four men and three women. That's not even, and Mrs. Vanderslice will probably complain, but it will have to do. Let's set it for tomorrow night if you can arrange it, Vanderslice. The next night if not. That all right with you, Bates?"

"Yes, sir." A dinner with Elizabeth. This should be interesting.

"Good." The general rose again to his impressive height. "I'll expect to hear from you at my hotel, Vanderslice." They shook hands across David's desk. The general turned to Gideon, who had also risen, and offered his hand. "Good to meet you, Bates. I'm expecting you to perform well."

With that, he left, leaving the door standing open behind him.

"What do you suppose he meant by that?" Gideon asked.

"I have no idea. The man is a force of nature. My mother will be furious at having to put together a dinner party on such short notice."

Mrs. Vanderslice's fury was hardly something

314

to be feared, but she certainly had a right to be dismayed at the inconvenience. "Tell her it's business and you can't help it. That's what your father always did."

"I'm just worried about *your* mother," David said. "Won't she be upset that we're entertaining Thornton?"

"I have no intention of telling her."

"How will you explain that you and Elizabeth are dining at my house but that she's not invited?"

"I'll tell her the truth. That it's a business dinner with a client. You need me there for advice, and you want Elizabeth to practice being your hostess. Elizabeth certainly isn't going to tell her any different, and Mother will be happy to miss it."

"Of course. Well . . ." David rubbed his hands together. "I think this is going to work out splendidly, don't you?"

He did not, but he said, "The general seems determined that it will, and he also seems to be a man used to getting his way."

"He does, doesn't he? Well, what do we need to do to prepare for this dinner?"

"Find out if Thornton is available, although I suspect he'll make himself available to meet the general."

"I'll do that right away. And then tell Mother. I hate to upset her, but it can't be helped."

"Can't Anna be of some assistance?"

David frowned. "She never has been. And she's been acting so peculiar lately."

So David had noticed it, too. "In what way?"

"I don't know. Suddenly she has opinions. I wouldn't be surprised if she refused to attend this dinner, for example."

"Why wouldn't she?"

"Just to be contrary, although if Elizabeth is there, she'll probably come. Will you tell Elizabeth? You'll see her before I do."

Oh, yes. Gideon would like nothing better than telling her David was requiring her presence at a dinner. "I'd be happy to."

"Good. Then I'll contact Thornton and the general. And warn Thornton to be on his best behavior. As soon as we calm the general's fears, we can get the rifles sold."

"And you can be off to Europe with your bride," Gideon said, pleased that he didn't sound the least bit sarcastic.

Why, then, did David frown?

Elizabeth checked her reflection one last time before heading downstairs to begin what promised to be a very trying evening. She did look fabulous. The purple silk gown from the trunk of stolen goodies fit perfectly and showed off her slender figure. She'd found some amethyst jewelry that matched, and she'd pinned a small tiara with a peacock feather in her hair.

The matching shoes were a little big, but she'd stuffed tissue paper into the toes, so they'd do. The long, white kid gloves were the final touch.

Satisfied that she had managed to create every advantage available to an attractive young woman, she wrapped her confidence around her like a cloak to conceal the quiver of terror hiding deep inside of her. So many things could go wrong tonight, and she had no one to whom she could turn. Even Anna didn't know the whole truth, and if she ever found out . . .

Elizabeth shrugged off that horrible thought and practiced her smile in the mirror. There, that should do it. Of course, she wouldn't need it until she reached the Vanderslice house. She had no intention of smiling at Gideon Bates on the way over.

As she made her way down the stairs, however, she almost forgot her resolve when she saw the expression on his face when he caught sight of her. He already had his coat on, so plainly he'd been waiting, but any signs of irritation or impatience dropped away instantly.

She was gratified to note that he had to swallow before he could speak. "You're looking exceptionally lovely tonight, Miss Miles."

"Indeed you are, Elizabeth," Mrs. Bates exclaimed. She'd just come out of the parlor and beamed her approval.

"Thank you. I wanted to make a good impression. For David's sake," she added. "I wish you were joining us."

"And I'm glad to be spared an evening of trying not to say anything controversial," Mrs. Bates said. "Those stuffy men David does business with are so narrow-minded."

"Is that what my life will be from now on?" Elizabeth said with feigned dismay.

"Only occasionally, I'm sure," she said. "And when we get the vote, it won't matter anymore."

"May I help you with your wrap?" Gideon asked.

Elizabeth had carried down the black velvet cape she'd chosen to wear over her gown, and she held it out to him. He shook it out and wrapped it around her with an ease that surprised her. If his hand lingered on her shoulder just a second too long, she pretended not to notice.

"Will that be warm enough?" he asked.

She looked at him in surprise, and Mrs. Bates actually laughed.

"Of course it won't be warm enough," Mrs. Bates said, "but a woman can't think of that when she's trying to look fashionable, can she, Elizabeth?"

"Certainly not. Besides, it's not far. I'm hardly likely to freeze." She took a moment to tie the ribbons at her throat. Then Gideon opened the door, and Mrs. Bates told them to have a lovely evening, and in another moment they were alone out on the quiet street.

Gideon offered his arm, but she ignored it and set as brisk a pace as her ill-fitting shoes allowed. Why couldn't David have come for her so she didn't have to be alone with Gideon?

"You don't have to be nervous," he said, easily matching her pace.

"What makes you think I'm nervous?" she asked in alarm.

"I just supposed you might be. It's the first time you're acting as David's hostess."

"All I'm doing is having dinner. Mrs. Vanderslice is our hostess."

"We both know you're expected to make an impression, and in that outfit, you certainly will."

"And I suppose all that's expected of me is that I look lovely and make charming conversation."

"And don't mention women's rights, I suppose. I don't know where the general stands on the issue, but I'd guess he's not very open to the idea."

"What about Mr. Thornton? Surely he supports the movement."

"Don't let his recent behavior fool you. He only helped us get you ladies out of the workhouse because he wanted David's assistance with this deal."

"So neither of them would be sympathetic if I asked for their support?"

"I doubt it."

"So you and David are our only male friends at this event?"

She'd expected him to confirm that statement. It was one area where he might win her good opinion, but he said nothing.

She gave him a few more paces to reply, and when he didn't, she said, "Aren't you a supporter, Mr. Bates?"

He turned his gaze on her, and the heat of it made her forget the thinness of her cape. "You know I am."

"Then what . . . ? Do you mean that David isn't?"

He smiled mirthlessly. "Far be it from me to speak ill of your fiancé, Miss Miles."

Was he serious? "But he allowed Anna to go to Washington to demonstrate."

"Against his better judgment, and he had no idea she'd be arrested, much less end up in that workhouse."

She hadn't really discussed the matter with David, so she had no idea if Gideon was right. Except that Gideon didn't lie, or so he claimed. "How do I know you aren't just trying to change my opinion of David?"

He smiled at that. "Could I?"

Honestly, he was so infuriating. "Absolutely not." Her opinion of David could hardly get any lower.

"I was afraid of that. I guess I'll just have to rely on David to do it."

At least he'd given her a subject with which she could disagree with David to begin their estrangement. "What if I told David the things you say about him?"

"Go right ahead. In fact, I think he'd be happy for an excuse to tell you that he doesn't want you involved in any more demonstrations."

He really was infuriating. And hopefully right. She couldn't wait to bring up the subject with David.

"Aren't you going to argue with me?" he asked when she didn't reply. Did he sound disappointed?

"What would be the point? Like most men, you assume you're right, and no amount of argument will convince you otherwise."

"You have a low opinion of most men."

"Based on experience, I'm afraid."

"I think you'll find it confirmed this evening when you meet Thornton and the general."

Elizabeth was sure of it. "I'll try to keep an open mind."

They'd reached the Vanderslices' front steps, and she climbed them without waiting for assistance from Gideon. The fewer times he touched her, the better.

The maid had been waiting and opened the door instantly at their knock. After taking their coats, she showed them into the parlor, where the Vanderslice family waited.

They greeted Elizabeth warmly, and all three of them kissed her cheek. Anna told her she looked beautiful, and David murmured something complimentary as well. They greeted Gideon only slightly less warmly, and David pumped his hand and slapped him on the back and thanked him profusely for coming.

Elizabeth sat down next to Anna on a sofa. Mrs. Vanderslice had sunk into a nearby chair looking forlorn.

"Mother is worried the dinner won't be a success," Anna told her.

"It was rather short notice," Elizabeth said diplomatically.

"I don't know why these men can't do business in an office," Mrs. Vanderslice said. "There's no reason we have to be present. We'll only be bored while they natter on about contracts and such."

Elizabeth knew why, but she couldn't say so. She just let Mrs. Vanderslice natter on about how unhappy her staff was about being rushed and how was she supposed to seat people when she had an odd number of guests? Mrs. Vanderslice stopped abruptly when they heard the doorbell, and everyone turned. The wait for the guest to be admitted, relinquish his coat and be escorted the short distance to the parlor seemed interminable, but no one spoke or moved the entire time. Finally, Oscar Thornton entered the room.

The sight of him sent a frisson of alarm skittering down her spine, but she stiffened that spine. He couldn't hurt her tonight. She was perfectly safe here, at least.

Thornton looked terribly uncomfortable in his evening clothes, which gratified Elizabeth to no end. She wanted to see him far more than uncomfortable, but this would do for the moment. David greeted him, and Gideon shook his hand, although without much enthusiasm, Elizabeth noted. Mrs. Vanderslice also went to welcome him. Then David brought him to the sofa where Elizabeth and Anna sat.

"You remember my sister, Anna," David said. "And may I present my fiancée, Elizabeth Miles?"

Not wanting to touch him, Elizabeth kept her hands primly folded in her lap, but she nodded politely. "A pleasure to meet you, Mr. Thornton. I believe we owe you our gratitude for your help in Virginia."

"I was happy to be of assistance, Miss Miles," he said with his smarmy smile. It still made her skin crawl, but she held his gaze without flinching. "And your young man is going to return the favor many times over."

Elizabeth was spared having to reply by the sound of the doorbell.

"That will be the general," Mrs. Vanderslice

said. She sounded more resigned than happy that the guest of honor had arrived.

Everyone turned to the doorway except Thornton. He leaned in a bit closer and whispered, "This deal better go through, or you *and* your brother will both be sorry."

Elizabeth instinctively recoiled, but she somehow managed a smile, as if he'd said something pleasant.

Only Anna had seen the exchange, although she couldn't have heard what he said. She knew the danger Thornton posed, however, and she immediately came to Elizabeth's rescue. "Mr. Thornton, allow me to add my thanks to Elizabeth's. You can't know how grateful we are to be free from that horrible place."

"It was my pleasure, Miss Vanderslice."

"General," David said a bit too loudly, which mercifully drew Thornton's attention away from the two women. He instantly left them to meet the newly arrived guest.

"Oh my," Anna whispered to her. "David said the general was imposing, but I had no idea."

Indeed, the general seemed to fill the room with his presence. He was a magnificent figure in his evening clothes, holding himself perfectly erect and with his silver hair gleaming in the electric lamplight. He bowed over Mrs. Vanderslice's hand and told her he'd taken her for David's sister.

Then he pumped Thornton's hand and told him how pleased he was to meet him. When David brought him over to them, Elizabeth and Anna instinctively rose. Anna gave him her hand and blushed at his lavish compliments. Then he turned to Elizabeth, who offered her hand as well while David made the introductions. The general's grip was surprisingly gentle.

"My opinion of Vanderslice just improved immensely," the general said, his blue eyes sparkling. "He must be quite a man to have won your heart, young lady."

"Surely you already suspected as much, General."

"A man likes to be sure, Miss Miles." He turned back to David. "I can see I was right to insist on having ladies present. The evening is always more pleasant with them in attendance."

"Are you a married man yourself, General?" Mrs. Vanderslice asked.

"I'm afraid not. I lost my beloved wife many years ago."

This news perked Mrs. Vanderslice up immediately. "I'm so sorry to hear it. I know how lonely that can be, since I lost my dear husband, too."

The two of them commiserated for a while, and then the maid came to tell them dinner was ready to be served. The general escorted his hostess, while David instructed Thornton to take Anna into the dining room. Then he paired Gideon with Elizabeth and followed them alone.

Elizabeth almost would have preferred being paired with Thornton.

"How do you find the general?" Gideon asked.

"He's charming."

"With the ladies, certainly."

"But not with the gentlemen?"

"Not that I've noticed, but then he doesn't have to be, does he?"

"I suppose he has to drive a hard bargain for the rifles."

"Not really. He's not spending his own money, and people tend to be less careful with other people's money."

"But it's not other people's money. It's the government's money."

He gave her a pitying look. "Where do you think the government gets its money?"

Elizabeth had never thought of it at all. "From . . . uh . . . I really have no idea."

"From taxes. Which the government collects from people like you and me."

Elizabeth had never paid taxes in her life, but she decided not to mention it. "Is that true?"

"I told you, I don't lie. And yes, it's very true. The only money the government has is what it takes from its citizens. So you and I are paying for Thornton's rifles and everything else the government buys."

Which sounded like the biggest con of all. She couldn't mention that to Gideon, though.

"Then the general should be more careful with our money."

"Be sure to mention that to him, will you?"

"What are you saying to make Elizabeth frown like that?" David asked when they reached the dining room.

"I was just explaining how taxation works."

"Do you think that's appropriate conversation for a young lady?" David scolded him. "No wonder she's frowning."

"My apologies, Miss Miles," Gideon said, relinquishing her to David with a small bow.

She would have been gratified if she'd thought for one second that he meant the apology. "Dear me, I don't think anyone has ever apologized for boring me before."

Gideon laid a hand over his heart, as if she had struck him there, but his eyes danced with amusement in the moment before he turned away to find his seat.

Mrs. Vanderslice directed them to their places. As the most important guest, the general was on David's right, and Thornton was on hers. Elizabeth was between Thornton and David on one side of the table, and Gideon and Anna sat on the general's side, with Anna in the middle. Because they didn't have enough ladies, Elizabeth would be tasked with skipping over

David to entertain the general when conversation turned that way. Given the general's personality, she didn't anticipate that would be difficult. What would be hard was conversing with Thornton, who sat to her left.

"Where are you from originally, General?" Elizabeth asked as the soup was being served.

He regaled them with the story of his upbringing on various military bases, since his father before him had been a lieutenant colonel. The military, it seemed, was in his blood. When they'd exhausted that topic, David asked if he'd served in Cuba during the war with Spain nearly twenty years earlier. As it happened, he had been sent to the Philippines, where the climate had been horrible and the people had shown little appreciation for being liberated from Spain.

Then, halfway through the main course, Mrs. Vanderslice turned the table, and Elizabeth had to turn her attention in the other direction, to Oscar Thornton. At least there were only the two of them on this side of the table, so he wasn't close enough to actually touch her. She could still feel the way his man had wrapped his arm around her throat and the terror that had gripped her when Thornton told her what he was going to do to her. Her expression betrayed none of that, however. The casual observer would have thought Thornton a stranger to her, as he was supposed to be.

"Do you do business with the government often, Mr. Thornton?"

"I've dealt with the State of New York a time or two, but this will be my first experience dealing with the federal government, Miss Miles." His eyes glittered like broken glass. He was probably remembering his threats, too.

"I suppose it's pretty much the same."

"Yes, except for the size of the sale."

"Indeed, that's true, Thornton," the general said, breaking protocol to address Thornton across the width and length of the table. "I can purchase as many cases of rifles as you can lay your hands on."

"I've got a hundred ready and waiting for you, General."

The general's smile faded to nothing. "Only a hundred?" He turned to David. "You told me this sale would be worth my time."

"But, General, that's two thousand rifles," David protested.

"Which wouldn't outfit even one brigade. I've got a whole army to equip, son. It'll take me years to do it if I have to deal with every mother's son who has just two thousand rifles to sell me."

Elizabeth hazarded a glance at Thornton, and he looked thunderstruck.

"Please, General," Mrs. Vanderslice said gently. "We're trying to enjoy a pleasant dinner, and we ladies have no interest in armies or rifles and certainly not in wars."

"I beg your pardon, dear Mrs. Vanderslice. I'm afraid I've been too long out of genteel company, and I've forgotten my manners. Can you forgive me if I promise not to discuss this matter again in your company?"

"Certainly," she said with her sweetest smile. "You're very understanding, General."

"But we will discuss this when the ladies have left us, won't we?" Thornton said.

"Of course, of course," the general said, waving away Thornton's concerns with a flick of his hand. "I shouldn't have been eavesdropping in the first place. I will now return my attentions to the lovely Miss Vanderslice."

Anna seemed a little disconcerted, but she recovered quickly. Society girls were taught to make conversation under even the most adverse circumstances. She quickly asked the general to tell her which, of all the places he had lived, was his favorite place on earth.

Elizabeth turned back to Thornton, who was now an unbecoming shade of scarlet. His eyes were like hot coals in his ruddy face. "He better not change his mind," he said softly, so as not to be overheard.

"He'll buy your rifles. David will make sure of it," she promised rashly, keeping her voice low, too.

"And if he doesn't?"

"He will! You heard him; he actually wants

more rifles than you have to sell him. A lot more! Why don't you just buy more so you'll have more to sell him?"

"It's not that easy," he said through gritted teeth.

"But you have contacts," she reminded him. "You got that first batch of rifles, didn't you? Maybe you can get more."

"Since when are you an expert in firearms, Miss Miles?"

She didn't miss the quiet menace in the question, but she smiled the way she'd taught herself to smile no matter what the situation. "I'm not, of course. I'm just a silly woman who knows nothing about rifles or armies or war, but I'm sure David will help you with whatever needs to be done."

Thornton's gaze slid past her to where David was watching the exchange. "Yes. He'd better."

Elizabeth glanced over to see Gideon watching them with a slight frown. Did he have any idea what they'd been discussing? She gave him what she hoped was a reassuring smile.

After that, Thornton practically ignored her. She was left to chatter on about the weather and the museums David had taken her to visit, so the others would assume they were conversing. She almost wept with relief when Mrs. Vanderslice rose, which was the signal for the ladies to retire so the gentlemen could smoke their cigars and drink their brandy and discuss whatever men discussed when women left the room. She gave the general a big, hopeful smile and followed Anna and her mother out of the room.

Gideon watched the women go, or so he told himself. Really, he just watched Elizabeth go. She'd done yeoman's service in trying to engage Thornton. The man was an impossible bore and rude into the bargain. He'd known other men suspected of murder who could still manage to conduct themselves properly in society, but Thornton apparently didn't consider proper behavior necessary. Which he proved the next time he opened his mouth.

"Did you mean you won't buy my rifles at all, General?" he asked as David filled the brandy snifters.

The general waited until David had handed him his before responding. "Of course I'll buy them, Thornton. I've got to buy every weapon I can get my hands on. It's just less trouble for me to buy them all from one man, or at least as many as I can."

Gideon accepted a glass of brandy. "So you'd suggest Thornton increase the number of rifles he has to sell?"

The general selected a cigar from the humidor David had set on the table, slid it beneath his nose and inhaled rapturously. "You lawyers have such a nice way of saying things, but yes, that's exactly what I'm suggesting."

"How many rifles will you need, General?" David asked.

The general pulled out his pocketknife and cut the end off his cigar. "We'll probably put a million men in the field before this war is over, gentlemen. The French and the English have made a hash of things so far, and it's going to take some time to sort it out. So you see, I'll probably be buying supplies for years to come, but I want to get as much as I can up front so we make a good showing when we get over there." He leaned in with his cigar and puffed as David held a match for him.

"And how am I supposed to pay for a million rifles?" Thornton asked. Even though the room wasn't particularly warm, he'd begun to sweat.

"No one expects you to get them all," David said. "Just as many as you can find."

"I think Thornton understands that," Gideon said quickly, before Thornton had a chance to explode. "But he's already got a small fortune tied up in the rifles he just bought. He's justifiably concerned, I think."

The general puffed on his cigar for a long moment. "I can't tell you how to run your business, Thornton, but the government is paying more than anyone else for all sorts of weapons now, double or triple their real value, and that was last week's prices. Next week it'll be even more. If it was me, I'd beg, borrow or steal every penny I could get my hands on and use it to buy anything that shoots. I'll buy it all from you in a few days at a tidy profit, and you'll pay off your debts and walk away a much richer man."

"And, of course, you'll buy the rifles he originally offered you and be glad to get them," David said quickly, his gaze on Thornton's sweaty face, "if that's all he has to offer."

"Of course." The general puffed his cigar and blew a rather excellent smoke ring that floated lazily up to the ceiling. "If that's all he has to offer. But, Thornton, you strike me as a shrewd businessman. Whenever there's a war, there's money to be made if you're willing to do whatever it takes."

Thornton pulled out his handkerchief and mopped his brow. Only then did he take a taste of his brandy. "Whatever it takes," he murmured, setting down his snifter.

But the general wasn't listening. The excellent cigars and even better brandy had reminded him of a time he'd dined with an old Spanish family in the Philippines and how they'd tried to arrange for him to compromise their daughter so he'd be forced to marry her.

Gideon enjoyed the story, although he didn't believe a word of it, and he also enjoyed watching Thornton, who wasn't even pretending to listen.

Plainly, the general had inspired all sorts of ambitions in Thornton. Gideon had no idea how much cash the man might have access to, but he was willing to bet Thornton would be investing it all in guns of whatever type he could find for sale. How much would he have to pay for those guns, now that everyone knew the army wanted them? And how much would General Sterling pay for them to make it worth Thornton's while? Gideon saw his plans to prevent Thornton from profiting too much evaporating.

He'd have to stand by and see him become a millionaire instead.

Chapter Fourteen

The general didn't wait long after the men joined the ladies in the parlor to claim a prior commitment and make his excuses to leave. He'd accomplished his goal for this evening, whatever it may have been, and Gideon suspected it was far more than getting to know Thornton better. Before he left, the general made his rounds, addressing each of the ladies in turn and spouting more lavish compliments.

"You must come and see us again, General," Mrs. Vanderslice said.

"I expect to be spending a lot of time in the city for the next few months, so I will happily accept your invitation, my dear lady."

He left Anna blushing from hints that her great beauty must be a grave concern to her brother. Finally, he approached Elizabeth, who had wandered away from the rest of them as if trying to avoid him. Gideon couldn't imagine why she would want to, especially when he saw her expression when she looked up at the great man and allowed him to take her hand in both of his.

He'd never seen her eyes shine quite so brightly, which seemed odd, considering the nonsense he was spouting about how he'd give David some competition if he were only twenty years younger. Could she really be flattered? Or even attracted to such an old man? For some reason, Gideon found himself drawing closer to them. He wasn't jealous. How could he be? No, he just felt some natural urge to protect her, although he could not have said from what.

Elizabeth gave a little trill of laughter at the general's parting remark, and as it died, he whispered something that transformed her whole expression for just one second. That one second told Gideon something alarmingly important, however.

Something he hadn't allowed himself to realize until this moment, and something that changed everything.

Fortunately, Elizabeth saw Gideon approaching out of the corner of her eye before she replied to the general's whispered words. Had he heard? She couldn't tell from Gideon's face, but he was good at concealing his feelings. And had she given anything away with her own face? Surely not, but she schooled her expression to one of polite interest just in case. "I hope we'll see a lot of you while you're in the city, General."

He'd obviously seen her gaze shift ever so slightly to Gideon, and he followed her lead, releasing her hand and bowing slightly. "You can be sure of it, my dear girl." He turned then and, seeing Gideon, stuck out his hand. "Bates,

I'm looking forward to our next encounter."

"So am I, General." Did he sound different? Was his enthusiasm forced?

Then the general moved on to speak to Thornton, and Gideon turned to her. What was he thinking? Why did he look so somber? Why didn't he say something?

But she was being ridiculous. He couldn't have heard anything or seen anything or sensed anything. He was just being his normal, aggravating self. She said, "I'm afraid I didn't have an opportunity to speak to the general about being profligate with our taxes."

He blinked, and for a second she thought . . . But then he said, "Sadly, neither did I. But I'll have other opportunities. Perhaps you will, too."

What did that mean? "I will if the general is as good as his word about visiting us again."

"Yes, that, too."

She wasn't imagining it. Gideon was behaving strangely. But even if he'd heard something, she could convince him he was wrong. She knew how to play a mark. He wasn't exactly a mark, but she could play him just the same. She had to.

David was escorting the general out, leaving Thornton as their only guest. Mrs. Vanderslice moved to attend to him, inviting him to join the rest of them for cards. The thought of socializing with Thornton over a card table made Elizabeth want to scream, but to her relief, she heard him say he also had another engagement and wouldn't be able to stay.

Her relief lasted only a moment, however, since Thornton decided he needed to speak to her one more time before he left. For once, she was thankful for Gideon's presence.

"What a pleasure to finally meet you, Miss Miles," Thornton said with his phony smile. How could a smile make someone look more evil?

"You are too kind, and thank you again for your assistance, Mr. Thornton."

"This deal with the general will more than repay me, if it goes through."

She heard the warning. She only hoped Gideon did not.

"It will go through," Gideon said. "I think the general is as eager as you are."

"Then why was he so disappointed?" Thornton made no attempt to hide his anger now that the general was gone.

"Because he wants you to sell him even more rifles so he can pay you even more money." And Gideon made no attempt to hide his impatience. "Most men would be thrilled."

"I'll be thrilled when the deal is closed."

David was back, and he came straight over to them. "The general seemed very pleased. He said he looks forward to doing business with us."

"Don't spend your fee just yet, Vanderslice," Thornton said.

David refused to be discouraged. "I understand your concern, Thornton, but I'm sure we'll find more rifles for the general."

"You mean I will," Thornton said. "And don't bother to offer your help. I wouldn't trust you not to bypass me and sell directly to the general."

"I can see why you've been so successful in your business dealings, Thornton," Gideon said.

Thornton obviously missed the sarcasm in Gideon's tone. "You'd do well to follow my example, Bates. Your family fortune could use some fattening up, couldn't it?"

His smirk told Elizabeth he thought he'd insulted Gideon, but he'd underestimated his victim.

"I prefer to get by on less and maintain my belief in my fellow man."

"More fool you, then."

"Thornton, really," David said in exasperation. As host, he couldn't stand by while his guests insulted one another, but he couldn't afford to alienate Thornton, either. "We can work this out. I have contacts, and—"

"And if you hear of anyone selling rifles, I'm sure you'll let me know. Meanwhile, I'll be taking care of my own business."

"And you'll let me know when you're ready to close the deal?" David said a little anxiously.

This time Thornton's smile was pure evil. "Only because the general would probably insist on involving you, but don't worry, you'll get everything you have coming to you."

With that, Thornton turned and walked out.

"I warned you about him," Gideon told David.

"I'm sorry you had to see that, my dear," David said to Elizabeth.

"So am I," she said quite honestly.

"Elizabeth, are you all right?" Anna exclaimed, hurrying to her side. "You're white as a sheet."

"Am I?" Elizabeth asked, hoping it wasn't true. Thornton's little tantrum shouldn't have disturbed her so much. With any luck, she wouldn't have to see him again, but luck wasn't something she counted on. "I'm just a little tired. Did your mother say we were going to play cards?"

"Yes, but I don't know what we can play with five players. Happy Families perhaps?"

They all laughed at the prospect of playing the silliest of card games, breaking the tension Thornton had left behind.

"If Elizabeth isn't feeling well, perhaps she would like to go home," Gideon said.

Why was he suddenly so concerned about her? Elizabeth stared at him, trying to judge his mood, and by that his intention, but he only stared back, his face innocent of expression. No, she wasn't going home with him just now, and not alone with him at all if she could help it. She would have to avoid being alone with him until the deal with Thornton was done, too. That shouldn't be too hard, should it?

"Now that you mention it, maybe I will go along," she said, turning to David. "Darling, would you see me home? I don't want to ruin Gideon's evening."

"Of course, my dear," David said, glowing because she'd called him darling in front of everyone.

Was Gideon frowning? Of course he was. He didn't like being outmaneuvered, but that was too bad.

And so she escaped for one night. How many more did she have ahead of her?

The next morning, Elizabeth stayed in bed until she was sure Gideon had left for his office. She would have to plan her days carefully to avoid him. Mrs. Bates was just finishing her breakfast when Elizabeth went down.

"How was your evening?" she asked as Elizabeth served herself from the buffet.

"Very nice. David's client is a retired general. He was quite impressive. I think Mrs. Vanderslice is smitten."

"Poor Clarissa would love to remarry." Obviously, Mrs. Bates thought such a notion foolish. "Oh, did I tell you that you've been invited to the National Woman's Party conference?"

"They're having a conference?"

"Well, it's not exactly a conference, but the

officers and the National Advisory Council are having a meeting, and they are apparently inviting everyone who was jailed to attend as well. I suspect they have some sort of honor for us. The meeting is this weekend, though, so it's very short notice, but I'm thinking they just decided to invite us."

Elizabeth didn't dare leave the city in the middle of everything. "I certainly don't feel I deserve any honors, but you should go. Where is it?"

"In Washington City. I can't leave you alone here with Gideon, though. It wouldn't be proper."

Elizabeth didn't dare be alone with him, proper or not. "Couldn't I stay with the Vanderslices for a few days?"

"Not really, but in any case, I'm not going. I have far too much to do here. Which reminds me, today is the day I volunteer at the hospital, so I will see you at dinner."

Elizabeth bid her good-bye and finished her breakfast while she thought about being honored for spending time in the workhouse while trying to escape Thornton. The others might deserve it, but she certainly didn't.

After she finished her breakfast, she wandered into the parlor to see if Gideon had left the newspapers. Anna was coming over later so they could go shopping, and with Mrs. Bates gone, Elizabeth would have a peaceful morning, at least.

She was already in the middle of the room when she realized her mistake. Gideon rose from where he'd been sitting in the corner near the door, out of the way so she wouldn't see him until it was too late.

"You startled me," she said in dismay, watching him close the parlor doors behind her.

"I apologize. I didn't mean to frighten you."

She doubted that very much. "Why did you close the doors?"

"Because I need to talk to you, and I don't want to be overheard."

She managed a smile. "How very mysterious."

"I'm not the one being mysterious."

"Now you're being confusing."

"I don't think so. I think you know exactly what I'm talking about, Lizzie."

She managed not to flinch at the sound of her nickname on his lips. So he had heard the general last night. "Lizzie? Where did that come from?"

"I think you know. I think it's what people who know you well call you."

"And what if they do? What business is it of yours?"

"It's my business if you're acquainted with General Sterling and plotting something behind my back."

"Where would you get an idea like that?"

"From the general himself. Last night I heard him say to you, 'Good job, Lizzie.' He thought no one but you could hear him when he said it."

She tried for outrage. "So you were eaves-dropping on our private conversation?"

"Don't try to play the wounded party. You know I just happened to overhear. So you do know the general."

What should she say? How much would satisfy him and how much could she reveal without damning herself? "He's . . . an old family friend. That day you took me to the telegraph office, I sent him a message to tell him I was in town. When I saw him later, he told me what he's doing here, so naturally, I sent him to David." There, enough of the truth to sound reasonable.

"He told David the senator had sent him."

Dear Gideon, such a stickler for details. "Would you and David have been so helpful if he'd told you I sent him?"

"Of course we would!" He sounded insulted.

"Well, I couldn't be certain and neither could the general. I knew David didn't want to do business with Thornton, so he might have used any excuse to turn the general away. I suspect you would have, too."

His troubled frown told her she was right. "But why were you so interested in helping the general?"

"I told you, he's a family friend."

"A man like that doesn't need your help to make contacts."

He was right, of course. "I . . . I wanted David to benefit. So we could go to Europe on our honeymoon."

"You said you didn't care about going to Europe."

"I lied!" she snapped in exasperation. "When you told me David wasn't rich, I knew it was up to me to change our fortunes."

"But you already knew he wasn't rich when you agreed to marry him."

Elizabeth rubbed her temples, which were starting to ache. Gideon always brought out the worst in her. She needed to stop arguing and start playing him. She took a deep breath and smiled. "I'm afraid I'm not as unworldly as you believe. Yes, I did know David wasn't rich, but I wasn't satisfied to have him remain so. I was planning all along to encourage him in that direction."

"And how many business deals do you think you'll be able to conjure up for him in the next forty years?"

"What are you talking about?"

"I'm talking about how idiotic your plan sounds. If you want David to be rich, you'll have to find dozens of Thorntons and General Sterlings over the entire course of your married life, because David isn't capable of it, as I think you know perfectly well."

"How do you know what I do and do not know? And how dare you accuse me of . . . of . . . ?"

"Of what? Of not having a good enough story to cover up what you're really doing?"

Elizabeth's breakfast curdled into a ball of acid in her stomach. How could he know that?

"And while you're thinking," he added, as if being helpful, "you can think up a reason why you're so afraid of Oscar Thornton."

"Why would I be afraid of Thornton?" she asked, outraged that he had seen it.

"I have no idea. I only know that when you met him last night, presumably for the very first time, you actually recoiled when he got too close to you, and he treated you with complete contempt at dinner and afterward. And don't bother denying it. The two of you obviously have a history. So how do you know Oscar Thornton?"

"That's none of your business," she tried, knowing she couldn't tell him the story she'd told Anna. Even if it could explain everything, which it couldn't, he'd never accept such a patched-together mess of truth and lies.

"I suppose you're right, but what *is* my business is why you're so determined to make him rich."

"I'm not!"

He peered at her in that way he had that made her think he could see into her very soul. "And yet everything you're doing will accomplish that."

Suddenly, she knew just how to play this. Gideon didn't want Thornton to succeed any more than she did, and she could actually tell him some of the truth to convince him to help her. "It only looks that way."

Now she had his interest. "What do you mean?"

"I mean that this deal will end up ruining him."

"And how do you—and the general, I assume—plan to accomplish that?"

"I . . . I'm not sure, exactly," she lied. She figured Gideon would believe a mere female wouldn't know the intricacies of business. "The general is handling that part of it. My part was just to get the two of them together and give things a nudge now and then if necessary."

"And why do you want to ruin Thornton?"

"I . . . It's a long story," she hedged, her mind racing. "Maybe we should sit down."

He gestured to the nearest sofa. She sat at one end, assuming he'd sit beside her, but he took a chair at right angles to her, the better to see her face. She silently cursed him even as she smiled as sweetly as she could manage.

"A long story, you said," he prodded when she hesitated.

"Yes, well, you see, Thornton ruined my family's business."

"What kind of business was that?"

"A mill. A textile mill." Details always made a story more believable.

"In South Dakota?"

"Yes. My father was . . . not a very good businessman. The mill was failing, and he needed an investor. Thornton stepped in and . . . and eventually, he forced my father out. We were bankrupt." There. Take that, Gideon Bates.

He stared at her for a long moment, his face expressionless. "And I suppose your poor father shot himself in despair."

"What?"

"Isn't that how these stories usually end? And then Thornton tied you to the railroad tracks to force you to sign the business over to him."

"What on earth are you talking about?"

"I'm talking about your sad story, Miss Miles, which sounds too much like a penny dreadful to be true. You really need to embellish it if you expect to get sympathy. You need to work on some of the details, as well. For example, there are no textile mills in South Dakota, and I doubt Oscar Thornton even knows where South Dakota is, much less that he has ever invested in anything there. I'm even starting to wonder if you've ever been to South Dakota yourself."

"Are you calling me a liar?" she demanded with frustration that wasn't even feigned.

"I am, although I'm aware it's terribly ungentlemanly of me and my mother would be ashamed."

Which was exactly what she had intended to say, so she was momentarily speechless.

He took the opportunity to add, "I'm fairly certain that some of what you've told me is the truth. You do know the general and Thornton, and you obviously wish Thornton ill for some reason. Knowing Thornton, I'm sure it's a good reason, so I can't fault you for that. What I don't understand is why you won't just tell me what it is, when you know perfectly well that I'd also be happy to see Thornton ruined."

But what could she tell him? In the story she'd told Anna, she was an innocent victim simply trying to escape Thornton's revenge. That wouldn't explain why she wanted to cheat Thornton out of what remained of his fortune, though. Or would it? Perhaps it could, with just a few minor changes . . .

"All right, then, I'll tell you. You were right—I'm not from South Dakota. I'm from right here in New York. About a month ago, my brother and I were traveling to Washington, and we met Thornton on the train, and—"

"Stop."

"What's wrong?"

"What's wrong is I'm tired of your lies, so don't bother telling me a story about your mythical brother. I'll jump ahead and blow his brains out in despair so you don't have to. Now we can sit here all day while you dream up more stories, but we're not leaving this room until you tell me the truth."

The truth. She didn't think she even knew what that was anymore, and even if she did, telling it would hardly help. Telling it would also mean Gideon Bates would never look at her the same way again. Not that she cared how he looked at her. At least not very much. And what did it matter? As soon as the deal was done, she'd be leaving the city. She'd probably never see Gideon Bates again. Better for all concerned if he despised her. Oh, and if she told him, he also might ruin the whole plan. Which should have been her first consideration. And it was, really. Her life and Jake's were in danger after all. That was the most important thing. Really.

"Or maybe," Gideon said, his dark eyes glittering, "I should just ask Thornton why you would want to see him ruined. I'm sure he'd be happy to tell me."

"No, you can't!"

"But I can, and I will, unless you tell me first."

"All right! But you have to promise . . ."

"Promise what?"

What had she been going to demand? That he not tell his mother she was a liar and a thief? That he not hate her? Now she was being idiotic. "Nothing. I was going to ask that you not ruin the plan, but I don't think you will when you've heard everything."

He looked as if he might like to shake her, but he said, "All right, then, why are you out to ruin Thornton?"

"Because he's going to kill me."

"Don't be melodramatic, Miss Miles. Why would Thornton want to kill you?"

"Because Jake and I cheated him out of fifty thousand dollars."

His shock was almost comic. She expected many questions, but not the one he finally asked. "Who's Jake?"

"My . . . partner, and I'm not being melodramatic. Thornton almost did kill Jake, or at least his goons did, and they would've done the same to me if they'd caught me. I only got away from them by getting myself arrested with the suffragists."

"But what would make him do such a thing?"

"I told you," she snapped. "We cheated him out of fifty thousand dollars. That tends to make a man testy."

Gideon shook his head, as if he couldn't believe it. "How could a woman like you have done a thing like that?"

There it was. Now he would hate her. But it was the only way. "You don't know a thing about me, Mr. Bates. I'm a grifter, and I come from a long line of grifters. Cheating people is how we make our living."

He didn't believe her, or at least he didn't want to. She could see it on his face. And how could he? Sitting there in his mother's parlor in her fashionable gown, she must be the picture of female innocence. "How did you cheat him?"

She sighed. Here it was, the end of everything. "We ran a rag on him. He thought he was going to make a fortune, but Jake and I didn't have any money for a setup, so we had to do it against the wall, and—"

"You did *what?*" he asked, horrified.

She winced. "We ran a rag," she explained with deliberate patience.

For some reason, his face had turned scarlet. "No, the . . . the other thing you said."

"Oh." She gave herself a little shake. She should have realized he wouldn't understand any of that. He was just a winchell after all. "The rag is a stock market swindle. When you run the rag, you need to set up a store, a place where you can take the mark to make him think you're dealing with a real broker. It looks like a real broker's office and people are working there and it has telephones and tickers and everything. But we didn't have the money to set one up, so we had to play him against the wall. That means Jake just pretended he was going to see the broker, but he never actually took Thornton there."

This time Gideon said, "Oh," with obvious relief.

She frowned. "What did you think I was talking about?"

"Nothing."

But the truthful Mr. Bates was lying! "No, tell me. I need to know what I said that made you turn so red."

"I didn't turn red!"

"You were blushing like a schoolgirl," she informed him. "You must tell me. If I said something shocking, I need to know what it was so I don't do it again!"

Clearly, he didn't want to tell her, which meant it was pretty awful. Dear heaven, she'd actually shocked him. Finally, he cleared his throat. "Are you . . . are you and Jake lovers?"

Not at all what she expected him to say. "Of course not! He's my brother. And not my mythical brother, either."

He actually looked relieved. "You said he was your *partner.*"

"He was, in the con. And I was afraid to say he was my brother again because you already said you didn't believe that and blew his brains out. He's really only my half brother. We never even met until I was thirteen. And it was all his fault the deal curdled. I kept telling him Thornton wasn't really hooked, but he wouldn't listen to a woman. I was lucky to get away when I did, and . . . You still haven't told me what I said. Does it have something to do with Jake and me being lovers?"

Gideon ran a hand over his face, as if he wanted to make himself disappear. "This is extremely improper."

"I don't care. You have to tell me."

He sighed with resignation. "Do you know what a prostitute is?"

Oh dear. "Of course." She'd grown up surrounded by men, after all.

He looked a little shocked at that, too, but he soldiered on. "If a man wants to purchase the . . . favors of a prostitute, but he doesn't have enough . . . that is, he can't afford the cost of a room . . ." To Elizabeth's delight, he was blushing again. "They will find an alley, and she will . . . they will . . ." He gestured helplessly. "Against the wall."

She gaped at him. "Is that even possible?"

He made a valiant attempt to glare at her. "I wouldn't know."

She clapped a hand over her mouth to smother her laugh. She'd never imagined seeing Gideon Bates so discomfited.

He tried to cover his embarrassment with anger, but she wasn't fooled. "Now it's your turn, Miss Miles. Start at the beginning, and tell me everything."

Suddenly, she no longer felt an urge to laugh. This was worse than she could have imagined, but she'd already told him that she was a grifter, so she probably couldn't sink any lower in his opinion. She started with meeting Thornton on the train and running the con, then how it went bad and how Thornton's men beat up Jake and started after her, and how she joined the suffragists to escape, and finally how Thornton's men had captured her here in the city and taken her to him.

"He wanted to know where his money was,

and he was going to beat it out of me, and if that didn't work he and his men were going to . . . to violate me."

Gideon flinched at that, so at least he didn't hate her completely. "Dear God. Why didn't you just give him his money back?"

Was he serious? Of course he was. "Because I couldn't betray my friends and family to a man who'd kill them without a qualm," she said, certain he would understand that, at least. "Besides, the money . . . Well, I couldn't get it back even if I tried."

"Why not?"

"Because it's gone!"

"Gone where?"

"I don't know! You see, we only got half of it to start with. Less than half, forty-five percent. That's what the ropers get, and Jake and I were the ropers, the ones who roped Thornton in. Then Jake and I split that between us."

Gideon blinked. He'd probably consider even half of forty-five percent to be a fortune. "What happened to the rest?"

"Mr. Coleman got that. He paid the expenses out of it and kept what was left. Knowing him, he's probably gambled it away by now. In any case, I don't even know where he is."

"Assuming Jake would also be reluctant to part with his portion, you could at least have given Thornton your own share."

Elizabeth sighed. "I don't even have my share, and besides, I was still trying to convince Thornton that the money was really lost, because I knew I'd never be able to get it back. That's when I got the idea to help him sell his precious rifles. He'd been talking about them when we were in Washington, and I knew you didn't want David to help him find a buyer. So I told him that. I stretched the truth a bit and said that you were going to make sure no one else bought them, either, but that I could convince David to help him because we were engaged."

Gideon stiffened at the reminder. "How convenient."

"Yes, well . . . At least it worked. Thornton didn't beat me or . . . or anything else."

Gideon winced again. "Thank God for that. And Thornton believed you, and now David and I have played our roles. But how is your general going to ruin Thornton?"

"I don't know exactly. He's going to cheat him out of the rifles somehow." Was that enough information to satisfy Gideon? "So you see, Thornton will be ruined, and it will finally pay him back for everything, for what he did to Jake and what he did to Marjorie."

"We don't know for sure that he did anything to Marjorie," he said, always the stickler.

"But we do! I didn't tell you, but when he had me at his house, he admitted that he'd killed her."

"If you think that will convince me to help you—"

"I'm not trying to convince you of anything. It's true. He was trying to frighten me, even though I was already scared witless. I guess he wanted me to know he wouldn't hesitate to hurt a female or something. He told me he'd beaten her nearly senseless, and then he strangled her. If you'd seen his face when he said it . . ." She shuddered at the memory. "Anyway, you can be sure he killed her, and he got away with it. Nobody is ever going to punish him for it unless we do."

She waited for him to agree, certain that he would, but he only sat there, thinking.

"Gideon?"

"I can't do it. I can't take the law into my own hands. It goes against everything I stand for."

"Do you stand for letting murderers go scot-free?"

He frowned, but he didn't back down. "When we bypass the rule of law, civilization crumbles."

"It's not going to crumble just because one rotten apple gets what's coming to him. It's more likely to crumble because the law didn't notice what he did in the first place."

"I can't help you cheat someone, Elizabeth."

She managed not to groan. "You don't have to help. You just have to stay out of it."

"But I'm already in it."

"You can still beg off. Just tell David . . . Oh, I

know! Tell him your mother found out and asked you not to be involved with Thornton. You know she would, if she knew. I can even tell her, if you want."

"And who would draw up the contracts?"

"Ask someone else in your firm to do it."

"Ask one of my colleagues to help cheat someone?"

"Yes! Lawyers do it all the time!" In fact, she could name some she knew personally.

"I don't."

God save her from an honest man! "At least promise that you won't warn Thornton off."

She waited, hardly daring to breathe and watching the emotions play across his handsome face, as if he were in actual pain. Finally, he said, "I can't."

"Oh, Gideon, how can you say that? He's a killer! He killed at least one defenseless woman, and he had my brother beaten nearly to death."

"I'll go to the district attorney and have him charged."

"With what? Jake isn't going to court to say Thornton had him beaten after he cheated him out of fifty thousand dollars, and nobody is going to believe Thornton confessed anything to me, either. So he's not going to jail or even to trial, and if you warn him about the general, he'll just sell his precious Ross rifles to someone else and—"

"What did you say?" he demanded, straightening in his chair, all trace of pain gone from his face.

"I said he's not going to jail . . ."

"No, the rifles. What did you call them?"

"Ross rifles."

He leaned forward, his eyes blazing. "Why did you call them that?"

"I don't know. That's just what Thornton called them. All he could talk about when we were in Washington was his Ross rifles this and his Ross rifles that."

"Dear heaven," he murmured.

"Why? What is it?"

"Ross rifles. The Canadians used them early in the war, but they malfunctioned in combat. They would jam and the soldiers would be left defenseless in the middle of a battle. And there was some problem with the bolts, too. They'd sometimes fly off and injure a soldier, taking out an eye or even killing him."

"That's horrible!"

"Indeed it was, so Canada replaced all their rifles, but how did Thornton get his hands on some of them?"

"He bragged that he'd gotten them very cheaply. I wonder if he knew why."

"It doesn't matter if he did or not. I have to tell him so he won't sell them to our army."

"Do you think that will stop him?"

"Probably not, but I have to try."

"Gideon, he has money invested in these rifles. If he doesn't sell them, he'll lose that money. Don't forget, he just lost fifty thousand dollars, too. He really needs this deal to go through, so if you ruin our plan, he'll just go out and find someone else to buy them, someone else who also won't care that they might kill some poor American soldiers. Do you want that on your conscience?"

"Of course not!"

"Then let him sell his rifles to my general. If you do, I swear to you, no American soldier will ever even see one. It's the only way to make sure of it."

He got up and ran his fingers through his hair, then strode to the fireplace, where he braced his hands on the mantel and glared into the fire. Elizabeth followed him.

"You know it's the right thing to do, Gideon. You can prevent him from hurting any soldiers and you can punish him for killing Marjorie. That's the only justice he will ever get."

When he raised his head, his eyes were bleak. "That's ironic, you lecturing me on doing the right thing."

Stung, she lifted her chin in defiance. "You can't cheat an honest man, Gideon. Everyone I've ever conned knew he was doing something illegal and did it willingly."

"And how many men have you conned, Miss Miles?"

She couldn't claim just one. "A . . . a few."

He turned to face her. "Am I one of them?"

"What are you talking about?"

"Did you fool me about who you really are? Because I knew you were different the first time I set eyes on you. You're not like any other woman I've ever known, and I guess that's why I wanted you beyond all reason."

Her breath caught on something jagged in her chest, and her eyes stung with tears she dared not shed. She couldn't grieve for something that was never really hers, and though it broke her heart to do it, she said, "I'm not like any other woman, Gideon. I'm everything you hate."

"No," he said, reaching for her. "No, you're not."

"I know I'm early, but . . . Oh dear!" Anna said as Gideon jerked away and Elizabeth turned guiltily to face her.

Chapter Fifteen

For a very long moment, the three of them stared at each other, frozen in place. Then Gideon muttered, "Excuse me," and hurried out before either woman could manage a word.

Elizabeth laid a hand over her heart and realized she was trembling.

"What was going on in here?" Anna asked. "And don't tell me nothing again."

No, not nothing. Not at all. "Would you close the door?" she asked, making her unsteady way to the nearest chair. The servants didn't have to overhear whatever explanation she could manage to give Anna.

Anna closed the door and hurried over to where Elizabeth sat. "I knew it. How silly of me to think David was my rival. You're in love with Gideon, aren't you?"

"Don't be ridiculous!"

"Of course you deny it." Anna grinned with delight. "And he's in love with you, too. Of course he is. You're irresistible."

"Stop it, Anna. I'm engaged to your brother, remember?"

"But you have no intention of marrying him, and now I know why. But poor Gideon, he must be in agony. He's far too honorable to betray his oldest friend, although I think he was awfully close to it when I came in just now. Does he know about Thornton? And why you're engaged to David in the first place?"

"No, and I'm not going to tell him." That last part was true, at least.

"Good. I won't be the only one pining for you."

"Don't be silly, Anna. Gideon isn't pining for me."

"You're the one being silly if you expect me to believe that. He was just about to take you in his arms, wasn't he? If I'd been five minutes later, who knows what I would've interrupted."

Elizabeth didn't bother to stifle her groan as she rubbed her aching temples. How had everything gotten so out of hand? For a second or two, she considered telling Anna that Gideon knew what was going on, but then she realized Gideon knew far more than Anna did. She couldn't take a chance on the two of them comparing stories and discovering those stories hardly matched at all. "It doesn't matter."

"What doesn't matter?" Anna asked eagerly, taking a seat across from Elizabeth.

"None of it. Whether Gideon is . . ." She gestured helplessly, unwilling to say the words.

"Besotted?" Anna supplied.

"Or not. Nothing is going to come of it."

"You don't know Gideon as well as I do."

"You forget, I'm leaving the city as soon as this is over."

"Do you think Gideon will just let you disappear?"

"He won't have a choice."

Anna gave her a pitying look. "Elizabeth, if I thought there was a chance you'd love me back, I'd follow you to the ends of the earth."

Elizabeth wanted to weep, but tears weren't going to help anything. "Oh, Anna, I'm so sorry."

"Don't be sorry. I've done my grieving, and I'm happy to be your friend. But you do need to know Gideon isn't going to give you up without a fight."

Was Anna right? And did that mean he wouldn't betray her to Thornton? Did his desire for her outweigh his blasted principles? "Even if it means he's betraying his best friend?"

"Oh, I expect you'll be breaking your engagement to David soon enough, and the moment you do . . ." Anna patted her heart and assumed an expression of rapture. "And in the meantime, just tell me what I can do to help."

Help? No one could help now. If, by some miracle, Gideon decided not to warn Thornton, she'd still have to disappear when this was over, because Thornton would want revenge even more. She'd have enough money to travel around the world if she wanted to. The thought should have been exciting. Instead, she wanted to weep again. If only she could stay right here and still disappear . . .

"Anna, I just thought of something you can do. You'd have to be very, very brave."

Anna leaned forward eagerly. "Tell me what it is. You know I'd do anything at all for you."

"You may change your mind when you hear what it is."

But Anna shook her head. "I won't change my mind. I'd die for you, my friend."

Elizabeth didn't think she really meant it, but she said, "It's harder than that."

After his encounter with Elizabeth, Gideon threw on his coat and left the house, knowing only that he had to get away from her so he could think clearly. Eventually, he found himself at his office and decided that was as good a place to think as any. He shut himself in and paced until he collapsed into his chair in exhaustion, still no closer to a decision than he'd been before.

If he really wanted Elizabeth, he only had to tell David what he'd learned about her this morning. Surely, finding out that his fiancée was a liar and a thief would be enough for David to instantly break the engagement. But if it was, wasn't it also enough to prevent Gideon from wanting anything further to do with the duplicitous Miss Elizabeth Miles?

If only that were true.

He'd known something was different about her from the very first. She was too confident, too clever, too beautiful. Every time he thought he had her figured out, she surprised him with something new. He thought about the trip to the hotel where she'd retrieved her luggage, except he now knew she'd never stayed at that hotel. How had her luggage gotten there then? Even more intriguing was the way she had totally deceived his mother, the most discerning of females. Why hadn't Mother seen through her? Or had she seen something else entirely?

He might never know the answers to those questions, and the only way he'd get them was by telling his mother everything he knew about Elizabeth. He wasn't ready to do that just yet, though, at least not until he came to terms with all of it himself. He also had to decide what to do about Thornton.

Although the thought of Thornton's sins made Gideon furious, taking the law into his own hands was wrong. He'd be no better than a vigilante. The law was the only thing that separated man from the beasts, and it must be preserved at all costs. He truly believed all of that. On the other hand, as an attorney, he also knew the shortcomings of the law. He knew justice was a nebulous thing, seldom found by those seeking it. Men like Oscar Thornton, with money and influence, could act with impunity and never feel the hot breath of the law on their necks. Elizabeth was only too right when she said he would never be prosecuted for his crimes. No one would take her word over his, even if she were the woman she pretended to be and certainly not when they found out who she really was. If Thornton had truly killed Marjorie—and Gideon had no reason to doubt it now—he would never be punished by the law. Added to that was the issue of the rifles. Gideon could warn Thornton of the dangers and ask him to destroy the weapons, but once again Elizabeth was right: Thornton would always put his need to make money above the lives of any faceless soldiers.

Gideon had to make sure the U.S. Army never received those rifles. He also had it within his power to punish Thornton for Marjorie's death. It wasn't the imprisonment the law provided and he deserved, but in some ways, it would hurt Thornton just as badly. Thornton without his money would be a broken man, stripped of his pride and his power. Gideon could see how it was going to happen. The general's demand for more rifles and his suggestion that Thornton invest every penny he had into buying them was the first step. What would the general do next, though? Buy them with a worthless check, leaving Thornton penniless? No, surely he had a more sophisticated plan in mind. Would the general tell him what it was? And if Gideon knew the plan, what would he do about it? For all his blustering about his principles, he wanted to see Thornton broken, too.

But would he be so bloodthirsty if he weren't in love with Elizabeth Miles? If he didn't want to see the man who had threatened to rape and kill her punished? He didn't even want to know the answer to that. He didn't want to know any of this.

But he did know it. And now he had to decide what was more important to him: the law, to which he had dedicated his life, or a woman whose whole life was a lie?

"Oh, Lizzie, what am I going to do with you?" the Old Man asked.

She'd managed to get away from Anna and get to Cybil's house, with Thornton's man close behind her as usual. They were used to her going there now, she supposed. Cybil had summoned the Old Man, who had arrived at the back door in a wig and false mustache, dressed as a butcher and carrying a package of meat. But it wasn't meat, and Elizabeth was very glad he was able to get what she needed.

After she had told him about her conversation with Gideon, he sat shaking his head at her while he stroked his fake mustache.

"It's your fault!" she said when he made no further comment. "He heard you call me Lizzie last night."

He nodded. "So I guess we should be grateful that he's in love with you, because he might've said something right then and curdled the whole deal."

Elizabeth groaned. She wanted to deny that Gideon was in love with her, but he'd made it pretty clear that he was, as much as he hated himself for it. Even still . . . "What makes you think he's in love with me?"

"It's obvious, my dear girl, at least to me. The way he looks at you . . ." He shook his head in mock despair.

Was it obvious to everyone else? She didn't want to know. "So what are you going to do? If he tells Thornton—"

"I could have some of the boys collect him."

"Thornton?"

"No, Bates. We could hold him for a few days, until—"

"No!"

"They wouldn't hurt him. Just keep him unavailable until—"

"I said no!"

The Old Man sighed. "This would be a lot easier if *you* weren't in love with *him*."

"I'm not in love with him!" she cried, outraged.

The Old Man didn't blink. "Oh, Lizzie, you used to be a much better liar than that. No wonder you're having so much trouble."

"I'm not!" she tried again, resisting the urge to

stamp her foot, which would only make him laugh.

He rubbed his fake mustache again. "Maybe if he knew you returned his feelings, he wouldn't warn Thornton."

"I don't know if anything will keep him from doing that. He's so disgustingly honest!"

"You see, this is why women don't do well in the game. You let your heart rule your head and end up falling for a mark."

"He's not the mark."

"And it's a good thing he's not, because this really would curdle, but I think we still have a good chance. Tell Bates you're in love with him."

"I will not!"

He raised his eyebrows. "Why not?"

Why not indeed? "Because . . ." Because she couldn't bear for Gideon to know how much it would hurt when he turned his back on her, and besides, "It won't make any difference."

"What makes you think so?"

"Because he's so honest! He'll do what's right, no matter what I ask him to do."

"And if he thinks he can have you, he'll decide that what you ask him to do is the right thing."

"Don't you understand it yet? Now that he knows what I am, he won't want me anymore."

His eyebrows rose again, but he said, "All right, let's put it to the test, shall we? Let him know that you return his tender feelings . . . somehow," he added when she was about to protest. "Then find out what he plans to do. If he's set on warning Thornton off, I'll send the boys to get him."

"Isn't there another way?"

"We could forget the whole thing. I can smuggle you out of here and put you on a ship, and we can hope Thornton doesn't ever find you."

And she would be looking over her shoulder for the rest of her life.

Elizabeth knew when she was beaten. "I'll find out what he's going to do."

"And let me know?"

"And let you know."

Elizabeth entered the Bateses' home quietly, half-afraid of attracting Gideon's attention and half-afraid of not attracting his attention. But apparently he wasn't home yet. Mrs. Bates was in the parlor, reading her mail.

"Did you have a nice day, dear?" Mrs. Bates asked.

"Yes," she lied. "Did they wear you out at the hospital?"

"They always do." She held up the letter she'd been reading. "I received a note from Mrs. Belmont herself about the Woman's Party conference this weekend. She is urging me to attend. It's going to be a very big celebration."

"Then you should go."

"You and Anna should go, too. You both suffered far more than I did at the workhouse."

Elizabeth sat down beside her on the sofa. "I don't think Anna and I would enjoy a conference nearly as much as you would, and quite frankly, I don't think Anna is strong enough yet for another trip. I wouldn't dream of going without her, either."

Mrs. Bates smiled and patted her hand. "I can understand that. I do hate to disappoint Mrs. Belmont, though. She's done so much for the cause."

"Then don't worry about us. Surely, I can stay with the Vanderslices while you're away."

"I'm afraid not, but perhaps Anna can stay here with you and Gideon can stay at his club."

That sounded perfect. Anna would be delighted to spend time with her, and she wouldn't have to worry about seeing Gideon. Only one thing sounded strange. "Does Gideon have a club?"

"Everyone has a club, dear," Mrs. Bates told her with a grin. "Some men have more than one. Gideon doesn't spend much time at his, but he does belong to one."

Well, then. "I'll ask Anna tonight! That is, if you don't think Gideon would mind."

"It doesn't matter if he does or not. He'll do the proper thing."

Yes, that's exactly what Elizabeth was afraid of.

Elizabeth took the coward's way out and hastily changed her clothes so she could go right over to dine with the Vanderslices before Gideon got home. She'd have to face him sooner or later, but later seemed like a much better idea. As she had predicted, Anna was delighted at the prospect of spending more time with her. They passed a quiet evening playing cards and ignoring Mrs. Vanderslice's hints that they should invite the general over again very soon.

When David walked Elizabeth home, the hour wasn't late, but she felt oddly weary. The pressure of her plans weighed too heavily, she was sure. At the Bateses' doorstep, she lifted her face for David's chaste kiss, but he said, "You were awfully quiet tonight. Is something wrong?"

She hadn't expected David to be observant. How inconvenient. Now she had to make up a lie for him, too. "Not a thing. Perhaps I used up all my energy last night on the general."

"He is certainly an interesting man."

"Do you suppose your mother is really interested in him?"

"I'm sure she could be, if he were interested in her," he replied with a smile.

"I can't imagine they'd suit."

"Certainly not as well as you and I," David said with more confidence than he had any right to. "I wish you'd set a wedding date. People keep asking me, and it's embarrassing that I don't have anything to tell them."

What a stupid reason to set a wedding date! But

she said, "I'm sorry. I had no idea it was such a trial for you. I promise to set one soon. Anna and I will put our heads together while she's staying with me, and we'll figure it out."

He smiled, pleased to have gotten his way. He kissed her cheek and waited until the maid let her in before setting out for home.

When the maid had taken her coat, she looked up to find Gideon standing in the parlor doorway. "May I have a word with you before you go up?" It didn't sound like a request.

She laid a hand over the sudden quivering in her stomach and stepped into the parlor. Once again, he closed the door behind her. "Mother has already gone up," he said, so she knew they could speak freely.

He looked as uncomfortable as she felt, but she didn't give him any help. She just waited while dread coiled ominously through her limbs. After what seemed an age, he said, "I feel I should apologize for my behavior this morning."

Not what she wanted to hear. "What behavior is that?"

Was he blushing or was that just a trick of the light? "For laying my hands on you."

"Are you sorry for that?" she asked with some disappointment.

"Not really, but I should be, so I'm apologizing."

The coiling dread slipped silently away. "Is that all you wanted to say?"

"Of course not. I'm aware that you are most likely waiting to hear my decision about informing Oscar Thornton of your little scheme."

"Is that what you think it is, a little scheme?"

"Of course not. I'm just trying to annoy you."

"You hardly need try!"

"But you don't look very annoyed."

"Well, I am. In fact, I'm furious with you. I can understand that you think your principles are important, but I can't understand why you'd protect a man who'd sell faulty rifles to the U.S. Army and who murdered a woman—a woman who was your relative, no less—and who threatened to murder another."

"When you put it like that, it doesn't sound very logical, does it?"

"No, it does not. It also doesn't sound kind or generous or . . . or . . ."

"Loving?"

"Or loving." Why had she said that? Now *she* was blushing.

"You're right. It doesn't. Do you think a man should put aside his principles for love?"

Why was he looking at her like that? Like he could see into her soul? She didn't want anyone to see into her soul, least of all saintly Gideon Bates. "Why do you care what I think? You already know I don't have any principles."

"I think you have principles. They're just different from mine. And I'm curious. I want to know what goes on in that beautiful head of yours."

No, he didn't, or at least he wouldn't once he found out. "I think . . ." What did she think, really? She looked at him standing there, so upright and respectable. If she was unlike any woman he had ever known, he was unlike any man she had ever known, too. He cared little for money or power, and he always spoke the truth. He was, as she had said, disgustingly honest and honorable in a way she could hardly even understand. Could she change that? And even if she could, did she want to? "I think you should do what you think is right."

Surprise flickered across his face but it quickly turned to suspicion. He was right not to trust her, of course. "I suppose you're going to tell me what you think is right."

"No, I'm not. I already told you what I want you to do, but I'm not going to try to persuade you. The general . . . Well, I saw him today, and I told him that you know everything. He said I should . . ." Her voice broke but she cleared it and went on. "He said I should tell you I'm in love with you so you'd do what we want, but I'm not going to."

"And are you? In love with me, I mean?" Was it hope that made his eyes glitter like that?

"You don't really want me to answer that question, because whatever I say, you'd always suspect it was a lie."

This time she knew it was anger flashing in his dark eyes. "And what if I decide to tell Thornton everything?"

"Then we'll abandon our plans." She wouldn't let them kidnap Gideon no matter how much the Old Man argued. "The general will disappear and so will I."

"You? Where will you go?"

"Someplace where Thornton can't find me, hopefully."

"But a woman alone . . . How will you do that?"

"I have money put away."

He frowned at that. "I thought you didn't have your share of Thornton's losses."

"I don't." She could get it easily enough, but, "I don't need it."

"I see." He didn't, of course. He would never understand her world. "And if I don't warn Thornton, you'll go ahead with your plans?"

"Yes. I'm supposed to let the general know what you decide."

"Who is the general to you?"

"Does it matter?" It did to him, but she wasn't going to ease his suspicions. She needed him to doubt her.

Anger flashed in his eyes again. "All right, then, I'll tell you what I've decided. I don't know what your general is planning, and I don't want to know. That way, I don't have to warn Thornton. I'll do what David asked me to do and attend the

378

meetings and draw up the documents, but I won't lie to Thornton or anyone else."

"You won't have to," she promised rashly. "You aren't part of this at all, and you'll be just as shocked as everyone else when it goes wrong."

"Perhaps not quite as shocked as Thornton," he said with the ghost of a smile. "And when it's over, what will you do?"

"That will depend on Thornton. If he still blames me, I'll have to disappear." And he would, she was sure.

"I can help you with that."

Anna had warned her he'd follow her to the ends of the earth, but she would never let him do that. "We'll see."

"Yes, we will." He thought it was settled. She could see it in his face.

"I'll write the general a note and tell him what you decided." She turned to go.

"Elizabeth."

She stopped, and when she turned back, she nearly gasped at the naked longing on his face. "What are you going to do about David?"

She gave him what she hoped was a reassuring smile. "I never intended to marry him. I'll break the engagement as soon as everything is over." If she had time before she left, of course.

He nodded, and she thought she saw some of the tension drop away from him. She hadn't told him she loved him, but he believed there was

379

hope. She had no idea why he still wanted that hope. He knew what she was. How could he even imagine they could have a future together?

The Old Man would tell her not to worry about it. The important thing was that Gideon wasn't going to ruin everything. And if he got his heart broken, well, he asked for it, didn't he?

Elizabeth had asked for it, too.

The next morning, Elizabeth gave her letter to the maid to post. The Old Man would receive it that afternoon or the next day. Meanwhile, she had nothing more to do. The Old Man and his mob would take care of the rest of it. The general had told him the tale, and now Thornton was on the send, figuring out how to turn everything he owned into cash so he could buy up as many rifles as he could find. He was going to find them pretty easily, too, once he had the cash.

Mrs. Bates was packed, and they put her on a train to Washington City for the Woman's Party conference and the awards ceremony she wanted to attend. Gideon left for his club, and Anna arrived at the Bateses' house with her bag.

"We'll have such fun," she said, and although Elizabeth didn't feel like having fun, they still managed. They went ice-skating with David and shopping with each other and visited Cybil and Zelda, who were trying to convince Anna to enroll at Hunter College. Since she knew she would never marry, Anna needed a profession so she could support herself, they argued.

On Sunday, Elizabeth attended church with the Vanderslice family, and she spent most of the service wondering if she could ever be like the rest of the people sitting in the pews. The Old Man would say they weren't all as pious as they pretended, and he would be right. The question was if Elizabeth could pretend to be pious along with them. The hardest part was knowing Gideon was there, too. She caught him watching her a time or two from his seat on the other side of the church, and after the service, Mrs. Vanderslice invited him to join them for Sunday dinner.

As they sat around the table, David took the opportunity to inform Gideon that Thornton wanted to meet with the general on Monday to discuss terms. He was apparently buying up whatever guns he could find, and he needed to know how much the government would pay so he didn't overspend.

"I'm sure the general will pay whatever Thornton asks," Gideon said with a meaningful glance at Elizabeth.

"The general is the only one who can affirm that," David said. "Do you want to attend this meeting?"

"I probably should," Gideon said with another glance at Elizabeth. Was he seeking her opinion? Or perhaps her approval? She had no idea, but she saw no reason he shouldn't meet with the others. It would give the general an opportunity to see for himself how Gideon would act with Thornton. When she made no protest, he said, "Once they agree on terms, I can prepare the bill of sale and the other documents and have them ready."

"That's a good idea. I'm sure Thornton won't want any delay once he's ready," David said. "I heard he's even mortgaging the house."

"Marjorie's house?" Mrs. Vanderslice said in dismay. "Can he do that?"

"He owns it now," Gideon said. "He can do whatever he likes with it."

"But it's been in the family for years," Mrs. Vanderslice said. "What if he loses it?"

"He's only mortgaging it, Mother," David said. "As soon as he sells the rifles, he'll pay it off, I'm sure."

Marjorie's house. Elizabeth couldn't believe it. Even Marjorie would get some revenge.

"I'll be glad when this is over," Mrs. Vanderslice said. "You know I hate it when you discuss business at the table."

"I apologize, Mother," David said, his good humor undaunted by her disapproval.

"I think it's all very interesting," Elizabeth said. "And how nice that we can do something for Mr. Thornton to repay him for his help."

Elizabeth didn't dare meet Gideon's eye after making such a ridiculously hypocritical remark, and even Anna pulled a bit of a face. Poor David was oblivious, of course, and Mrs. Vanderslice shook her head.

"You'll change your mind after hearing years of it, I'm sure, my dear," she said. "Now tell me, Gideon, when do you expect your mother to return?"

"Tomorrow. Mrs. Belmont offered to bring her back along with some of the other former prisoners in her private railroad car."

"I can't imagine anything more boring than sitting in meetings and listening to lectures on women's rights," Mrs. Vanderslice said with a delicate shudder. "Oh, I know it's important," she added when Anna was about to protest, "but why do they have to have so many meetings?"

For some reason, Elizabeth felt compelled to defend Mrs. Bates. "I'm sure the meetings are very interesting."

"I hope you never have to find out, darling," David said. "You and Anna have already done more than enough to promote women's suffrage."

"But we've hardly done anything at all," Anna said. "We've only gone to one protest."

"Are you calling the time you spent in that horrible place 'hardly anything'?" David asked.

"Many of the ladies have been jailed several times," Elizabeth pointed out, glad for the time she'd spent with Mrs. Bates learning about the history of the movement.

"Ladies with no family to look after them, I'm sure," David said.

So David was showing his true colors. Elizabeth didn't dare glance at Gideon. "By 'families,' do you mean husbands?"

"It's a husband's duty to keep his wife safe, and you can be sure I take that responsibility very seriously, my dear."

"What about a brother's duty to keep his sister safe?" Anna asked with feigned innocence.

David, still oblivious, didn't notice she was feigning. "I take all my responsibilities seriously, which is why I won't allow either of you to put yourself in harm's way again."

"You won't *allow* us?" Elizabeth asked sweetly.

"A wife must be ruled by her husband," Mrs. Vanderslice said. "David only has your best interests at heart."

"Indeed I do, and while I know the suffrage movement is important, I can't let you subject yourselves to that kind of danger again."

So Gideon was right, as Elizabeth was sure he'd remind her when next they spoke privately. Except they'd probably never speak privately again. The thought made her want to weep.

"What if every husband felt as you do, David?" Anna argued. "What would become of the movement?"

"I'm sure the unmarried ladies would continue," David said.

"But I'm an unmarried lady."

"Yes, but—"

"And I have the time and energy to devote to the effort," Anna continued relentlessly. "I should be on the front lines of the struggle."

"But—"

"She has you there, David," Gideon said. "We should send her straight to President Wilson. I'm sure he'd be no match for her."

"But Anna is just a girl," her mother said.

"I don't think so," Gideon said, turning to Anna. "She's changed since she came back from Washington. Haven't you noticed?"

Anna beamed at him. "I'm glad someone has."

"But we can't allow her to go gallivanting off to protests and getting herself arrested," Mrs. Vanderslice said. "What young man would be interested in a girl who does things like that?"

"None of them, I hope," Anna said. "I've been thinking I might not marry at all."

Elizabeth only cringed a little bit. Anna's timing could have been better.

"Anna!" her mother cried. "What a terrible thing to say."

"It's not terrible at all. I could become a teacher or a social worker or—"

"Why would you want to do something like that?" David asked.

"To feel useful."

"Being a wife and mother is a very useful vocation for a woman," her mother said.

"Maybe we should go back to discussing business," Gideon said with a grin.

Elizabeth snatched up her napkin to cover her answering grin. Why did he have to be so appealing?

Mrs. Vanderslice knew how to control her brood, however. "David, what did you think of the sermon this morning?"

And David knew his role as well. He replied at length, successfully boring everyone until the meal was over.

Gideon took his leave shortly after they retired to the parlor. Elizabeth would have liked to acknowledge that he'd been right about David, but he probably would have been disgustingly smug about it, so it was just as well she never had the opportunity. Anna accompanied Elizabeth back to the Bates home for what was supposed to be their last night without Mrs. Bates, but at breakfast the next morning, the maid brought them a telegram. Mrs. Bates was going to remain in Washington for a few more days. As a result of the outstanding show of public support at yesterday's meeting, the Judiciary Committee of the House was going to consider the suffrage amendment immediately, and they needed everyone to call upon their representatives to encourage the House to bring it to a vote.

"What does she mean about public support of the meeting?" Anna asked when they'd both read it several times.

"I don't know. Let's see if the newspapers are here."

They were in the parlor, and Elizabeth and Anna read the account of the mass meeting held Sunday afternoon at the Belasco Theater, which had been packed to the rafters with four thousand people. The crowds were so thick on Madison Place that the president couldn't get out of his front gate to go for a Sunday drive.

"It says they presented every woman who had been jailed with a special pin," Anna said. "Do you suppose we are to receive one?"

Now Elizabeth felt terrible that she and Anna hadn't gone. "If we are, I'm sure Mrs. Bates will bring them to us."

But if Mrs. Bates stayed in Washington for a few more days, Elizabeth would most likely not be here any longer to receive hers. In fact, she might never see Mrs. Bates again.

Chapter Sixteen

Oscar Thornton looked positively jubilant. Gideon didn't think he had ever seen the man really smile until today. The meeting with General Sterling at David's office this afternoon had gone smoothly, with Thornton reporting he now owned over ten thousand rifles and expected to purchase several thousand more the next morning.

The general wanted to know the locations of all of these rifles so he could verify their existence. When Thornton worried about how long that would take, the general reminded him he would delegate that task to military officers stationed near the locations, rather than go himself. He wasn't interested in wasting time, either.

The two dickered a bit over the selling price for the rifles, but Gideon's assessment had been correct: the general was more than willing to pay whatever Thornton asked.

"It's the government's money, not mine," he pointed out, "and the government needs your rifles, Mr. Thornton." He glanced over to where Gideon sat at the end of the meeting table, taking notes. "Are you the one who does the figures, Mr. Bates? How much will the United States owe Mr. Thornton?"

Gideon was still marveling that the general

gave no indication he knew anything about Gideon's reluctance to participate in the scheme. As far as Gideon could tell, he might never have spoken to Elizabeth at all. Perhaps he hadn't.

But David was the one who was doing the calculations, and he answered the question. "It looks like a little over three-quarters of a million dollars," he said, turning the paper around so the other two men could see his exact total.

Gideon suspected more than half that amount would be profit for Thornton, even after David's commission.

Sterling didn't even blink. Nodding, he said, "Not bad, and you can come back to me later, Thornton, if you obtain more rifles."

Thornton frowned. "It's getting harder to find them, General, and the war is driving up the price."

"Which just means I'll have to pay you more, doesn't it?" the general said. "There's no help for it, though. The need will go on as long as the fighting does."

"Let's hope it doesn't go on much longer," Gideon said. "Isn't that why the United States got involved? Because we want to put an end to it?"

"Let's hope you're right, Bates," the general said. "Too many good men have been lost already trying to put the Kaiser in his place. But it's an ill wind that doesn't blow someone some good, eh, Thornton?"

The general slapped Thornton on the back and, amazingly, Thornton smiled again. "That's right, General. It's our patriotic duty to support our soldiers."

Thornton's brand of patriotism made Gideon want to gag, but he reminded himself that the general had no intention of buying Thornton's rifles. Or at least that's what Gideon had decided would happen. The general had tricked Thornton into sinking his entire fortune into buying rifles, and if he didn't sell them, he'd be ruined. Gideon hadn't figured out how the general would profit from this or how he could stop Thornton from selling his rifles to someone else instead, but Gideon kept reminding himself that wasn't his concern. The less he knew about it, the happier he would be.

"Calculate your commission," the general was telling David, "and I'll bring two bank drafts with me. Or three, if I need one for Bates, too."

"I'll pay Gideon out of my share," David said. "He is only charging for drawing up the documents."

"You'll never get rich that way, Bates," Thornton said with a malicious grin. Plainly, he thought Gideon a fool for not cashing in on this deal.

"I'm not interested in being rich."

"I'll never understand you people," Thornton sneered.

"What people is that?" the general asked, his startlingly blue gaze darting between Gideon and Thornton.

"The old New York families," Thornton explained, not bothering to hide his contempt. "The ones who call themselves Knickerbockers. They think they run the city, even though most of them don't have two nickels to rub together anymore."

"I'm sure the Astors and the Vanderbilts will be surprised to learn that," the general said with a laugh. "And how would you know about them? Are you a Knickerbocker yourself, Thornton?"

"Only by marriage. My late wife was a cousin to Bates, here, and one of society's four hundred, as she often reminded me."

The words set Gideon's teeth on edge. How dare he bring Marjorie into this? "I doubt she ever even spoke of it."

Thornton's sneer turned ugly. "Are you calling me a liar?"

"Of course he isn't," David said quickly, shooting Gideon a warning look. "And the general isn't interested in family squabbles, I'm sure. General, I can't thank you enough for coming today so we can get this all settled. I think the transaction will go very smoothly now. When can you be ready to close the deal?"

"The day after tomorrow, if that's not too soon for Thornton," the general said.

Thornton grinned with satisfaction. "Just tell me what time."

They settled on one o'clock, and Thornton left after shaking hands all around. Gideon ignored his triumphant smirk. Then it was the general's turn to shake their hands. As he clasped Gideon's palm in a bone-crushing grip, he said, "There's no shame in making money in business, son."

What did he mean by that? "I like to make my money from honest labor."

If the general was insulted, he gave no indication. In fact he seemed amused. "A very refreshing attitude in this day and age, Mr. Bates. You are a rarity, I'm afraid."

He turned to David before Gideon could think of a suitable reply, and then he was gone. The man was such a presence, his sudden absence seemed to rob the room of oxygen for a moment.

"I can't believe it's really going to happen," David said, almost giddy with his success. "Do you know how much I'll earn from this? I might take Elizabeth around the whole world instead of just to Europe! Do you think she'd like to see the Orient, too?"

"I'm sure she would," Gideon couldn't resist saying.

Oscar Thornton could hardly believe his luck. That little chippie Betty Perkins or Elizabeth Miles or whatever her real name was had turned out to be his lucky charm in spite of everything. He wasn't going to forgive her for the fifty thousand she and that son of a bitch brother or whoever he was had taken from him, of course, but he might not let Lester and Fletcher have her when he was finished with her. She'd be grateful, he was sure.

"We'll go straight to the bank when we leave Vanderslice's office," he told Fletcher. The two of them were in a cab on their way to the final meeting with the general. "I want to deposit the bank draft right away."

"Whatever you say, boss. I'll get a cab and have it waiting. You don't want to be standing around on the street with so much money in your pocket."

Finally, Fletcher was showing some intelligence. He'd sent Lester, the smarter one, to watch the girl today. He only needed muscle to guard himself, but she might try to slip away now that the deal was going through. He couldn't allow that. Victory wouldn't be nearly so sweet without a little revenge.

As the cab chugged through the crowded city streets, Thornton mentally went through all his calculations. He knew to the penny how much he'd receive after Vanderslice took his cut. Out of that he'd only have to pay off the mortgage on Marjorie's house and a ten-thousand-dollar loan he'd taken out to cover the cost of the last lot of rifles he'd bought just yesterday. The general had given him good advice, and he'd spent nearly every penny he had. At first he'd wondered why he'd been able to buy up so many rifles. Couldn't the owners just sell directly to the army like he was doing? But no. Some of the rifles, as it happened, hadn't been obtained legally. The current owners hadn't had proper documentation, but they were happy to provide some for the sale to Thornton. If it wasn't exactly legal, who cared? The papers he handed over to the general would all be in order as far as he was concerned.

And now that he thought about it, he'd sell Marjorie's house. What did he need with that crumbling pile? He could build himself a mansion on Fifth Avenue. He'd rub shoulders with the people who mattered in the city. They'd put him on to more deals like this one. Before he knew it, he'd be a millionaire. Too bad Marjorie wasn't here to see it. But since she wasn't, he was free to marry another society girl, the daughter of one of those old families who sold their girls to the highest bidder because they were down to their last penny. This time he knew how to make the most of his opportunities. They'd invite him to their parties and he'd join their clubs. They might turn up their noses in private, but in public, they'd acknowledge him and nod to him in his box at the opera and shake his hand at church.

The cab swerved to the curb and stopped with

a lurch in front of Vanderslice's office. Fletcher paid the driver, then jumped out and held the door for him. Thornton frowned at the building with its ancient bricks and wavy glass windows. The place had probably been there since the Revolution. From now on, he would only do business in offices located in tall, new buildings with elevators.

Inside, he looked askance at the fading wallpaper and age-darkened wainscoting. Even the clerk sitting at the lobby desk looked old.

"Welcome, Mr. Thornton. The others are already inside. Allow me to escort you."

Thornton left Fletcher to wait in the lobby. He didn't need protection from the general, and certainly not from Bates and Vanderslice.

Vanderslice greeted him. The poor fellow was practically giddy with excitement. The general, as he had expected, seemed merely pleased that this day had finally come. Bates, however, was grim. He'd probably realized how stupid he'd been not to demand a higher fee for his work.

When they were settled, Bates led them through the process of transferring ownership of the many, many rifles from him to the United States Army, making sure they had the addresses of the various warehouses where they were being stored so the army could collect them. Bates had contracts and bills of sale and other papers. Thornton signed and the general signed and occasionally Vanderslice signed as a witness. The final paper was a list of all the lots of rifles and the price the general was paying him for each, with a lovely total at the bottom. Vanderslice would get ten percent, but what was left would be more than triple what his fortune had been even before he'd met Betty and Jake Perkins.

He had to clench his hands on the tabletop to keep from rubbing them with glee.

"And here," the general said, pulling an envelope from the pocket inside his jacket, "are the bank drafts." He handed it to Bates. "If you'll make sure everything is in order, we can celebrate with a cigar." From another pocket, he produced a gold case engraved with a heavily stylized monogram. He flipped it open and offered one to Thornton.

He took it happily, running it beneath his nose to savor the rich aroma as he'd seen the general do. A fine cigar. He would have expected nothing less from the general.

"Maybe we should open a window before we indulge," the general said, getting up after handing the case to Vanderslice. While he opened one of the windows a bit, Bates and Vanderslice each selected a cigar. Vanderslice produced a knife and matches, and soon they were all puffing away.

Bates, he noticed, had peered into the envelope and seemed satisfied with what he found there. Then he turned to Thornton. "What are your plans now, Thornton?"

"What do you mean?" he asked, instantly wary. Bates would never ask him a question unless he had an ulterior motive.

"Just what I said. Are you going to stay in the city or go back to Albany or maybe travel or . . . ?" He shrugged as if the answer meant nothing to him.

"Perhaps Thornton is going to keep finding more ordnance to sell to the army," the general said with a smug smile.

"Perhaps I will," he said.

Everyone looked up in surprise at the sound of a disturbance in the front office. Nothing untoward ever happened to challenge the dignity of this building, so the echo of raised voices was doubly disconcerting.

"What on earth . . . ?" Vanderslice muttered, starting to rise, but he was hardly on his feet before the door to their meeting room flew open and slammed into the wall.

"Ah, there you are, General Sterling," the intruder said. He was some kind of army officer, his uniform fairly glittering with gold braid and brass buttons. Behind him came half a dozen enlisted men in their bright blue uniforms with equally shiny buttons, carrying rifles and wearing sidearms.

A tremor of alarm flickered over him, but Thornton reminded himself that the army didn't rob people. They couldn't possibly be in any danger.

"What is the meaning of this, Colonel?" the general demanded. He'd also risen from his chair, and Thornton and Bates had, too.

"I think you know why we're here, Sterling." The colonel's gaze skimmed the other three men, sizing them up. Thornton instinctively straightened and lifted his chin. "Which one of you is Vanderslice?"

"I am," Vanderslice said. "Who are you and why are you here?"

"Colonel Inchwood, at your service. Am I correct in assuming that you gentlemen are here because you believe you are selling something to the United States Government?"

"That's right," Thornton said. "I am."

The colonel looked him over again, this time with what might have been pity. "I'm sorry to inform you that General Sterling has no authority to purchase anything on behalf of the United States or anyone else." He nodded to one of the soldiers, who moved to the table and began gathering all the papers lying there.

"What are you doing?" Vanderslice cried. "You can't take those."

"Yes, I can," the colonel said. "That's evidence. I'm here to arrest General Sterling for war profiteering, among other crimes."

"You can't do this," the general said, outraged. "I'm a personal friend of President Wilson. He'll never allow it."

"When he heard what you were doing, he signed the warrant himself, General." The colonel nodded to two other soldiers. "Take him." They moved around the table and grabbed hold of the general, who seemed too flummoxed to even react.

Thornton suddenly realized with alarm that the first soldier had also picked up the envelope containing the bank drafts. "Wait, that's mine."

He would have lunged for the soldier, but the colonel held up his hand to stop him and snatched the envelope for himself. "What's this? Ah, yes, bank drafts." He looked up and shook his head. "Forged, I'm afraid, and worthless. The general was going to steal your property . . . What was he buying from you?"

"Rifles," Thornton said through the thickness in his throat.

The colonel nodded. "We've been watching him for some time now. The last time it was buttons for uniforms. The time before it was saddles for horses the army doesn't even use anymore. By the time you discovered that the drafts were worthless, the general would have sold your rifles to the army himself. Let's go, men."

The two soldiers shoved the general into motion.

"Vanderslice, do something," the general cried. "You can't let them take me."

Vanderslice turned his stupid face to Bates. "Can't you do something?"

"I'm afraid not. It's an army matter," he said.

"Will he be tried in a military court?" he asked the colonel.

"Yes," the colonel said. "I'm sorry to have shocked you gentlemen like this, but there was no other way. We had to catch him in the act. You'll all be called to testify, of course."

"But what about my rifles?" Thornton suddenly realized.

"What about them?" the colonel asked.

"Those papers you're taking, that's my bills of sale proving I own them."

"And you'll still own them. They'll be safe and sound wherever you're keeping them while we get this all settled."

"But I need to sell them immediately, and I can't without those papers."

"As I said, it's evidence. I'm afraid you'll have to wait until after the trial."

"But I can't wait!" Thornton nearly shouted as panic welled in him. He had a mortgage and a loan to pay and only a few hundred dollars left to his name.

"I'm sorry, sir, but there's nothing I can do. It won't be long, only a month or two, I'm sure. It's wartime and the army will want this settled quickly."

Quickly? A month or two wasn't quickly! And what was he supposed to do in the meantime? The general and his guards were gone and so was the soldier with the papers and Thornton's money. Without that, he wouldn't even be able to pay Fletcher and Lester. Which reminded him. "Fletcher!"

"Was that your man outside?" the colonel asked. "I had to take him into custody. He was threatening my men." He turned to Vanderslice. "You may call at the armory tomorrow. Ask for me. By then I'll be able to tell you more. Good day, gentlemen."

"Good God," Vanderslice said, sinking back into his chair when the colonel and his men were gone. "I can't believe it. I had the man as a guest in my home."

What did that matter when Thornton had lost everything? "You've got to get those papers back, Vanderslice."

"You heard what he said," Vanderslice said. "They're evidence."

"But I need them. I need to sell those rifles or I'm ruined."

"You heard the colonel," Bates said. "You can sell them after the trial."

Thornton closed his hands into fists, wishing he dared use them on the attorney. "I borrowed money against the house and I took out a loan. Both are due in thirty days."

"Can't you sell the house to satisfy the mortgage at least?" Vanderslice asked.

"If it sells that quickly, but there's still the loan."

"And you don't have the funds to pay that back?" Bates asked. Was he smirking?

He had to swallow his pride before he could speak. "I put everything I own into those rifles."

"I'm sure we can work this out," Vanderslice said with his phony enthusiasm. "The colonel said I should go down to the armory and ask for him tomorrow, so that's what I'll do. He can't possibly object to your selling the rifles yourself. Surely, the army still wants them."

"And what if you can't work it out? No, we're going to the armory right now, before this Inchwood has a chance to do anything. And I want those bank drafts returned. We only have Inchwood's word that they're no good."

Bates and Vanderslice just stared back at him, gaping like the stupid oxen they were. "Fletcher!" he shouted again. Where had that idiot gotten to? Surely, the soldiers hadn't arrested him, too.

Fletcher came staggering in, straightening his coat and looking dazed.

"Where have you been?" Thornton demanded.

"They grabbed me and dragged me outside." He rubbed his jaw gingerly. "Roughed me up pretty good. Then they threw that general into one of them ambulance trucks and drove off."

"Get me a taxicab. We have to go to the armory."

"Where's that?"

Thornton realized he had no idea. He turned back to Bates and Vanderslice.

"There's an armory on Lexington and Twenty-fifth," Bates offered.

"But isn't there one on Fort Washington Avenue?" Vanderslice asked.

"What about the one in Sunset Park?" Bates asked.

"Inchwood didn't say which one we should go to, did he?" Vanderslice asked.

Thornton swore. "Which one is closest?"

In the end, the cab driver took the four men to the 69th Regiment Armory on Lexington, but the idiot private at the front desk knew nothing about a Colonel Inchwood. They finally found a sergeant who sent them to the 7th Regiment Armory on Park Avenue, where a young lieutenant also knew nothing but sent them to the 8th Regiment Armory, where they finally found a colonel who listened to Thornton's story with a puzzled frown.

"Are you sure these were really soldiers?" the colonel asked when Thornton had finished his story.

What a stupid question! "Of course they were. They had on uniforms, and this Inchwood fellow told us to come to the armory to claim our property," Thornton said, stretching the truth a bit.

"And he didn't tell you which armory you should go to?"

"No," Thornton said, swallowing down his fury because shouting at this martinet wasn't going to get him what he wanted.

"That's very suspicious. You see, I'm not aware of any investigation into profiteering at all, and I've never heard of a Colonel Inchwood here in the city."

"What do you mean?" Bates asked. "Do you think this Inchwood was lying?"

"That's exactly what I think," the colonel said.

"But he arrested a general," Thornton nearly shouted. "A retired general, at any rate. And Senator Wadsworth had sent the general to Vanderslice in the first place."

The colonel frowned beneath his lush mustache. "Did you speak to the senator yourself?"

"Uh, no," Vanderslice said. "I mean, he'd already sent Thornton to me, so when the general told me the senator had sent him, too . . ."

"So you only had the general's word," the colonel said.

Thornton saw it all then. The general wasn't really a general at all, and he'd tricked Thornton into signing over all of his rifles to him. It was just like Inchwood had said, except Inchwood was in on it, too. They'd stolen his rifles, or at least they would now that they had the signed bills of sale, unless he could get them back . . .

The colonel was telling them there were a few more armories in the city they could visit, but he was sure they wouldn't find Inchwood at any of them. Thornton didn't even listen. As the four of them walked out of the armory, Thornton told Fletcher to get a cab.

"We can check the other armories," Vanderslice was saying. "This fellow might be wrong. If it's an investigation, maybe it's a secret."

A cab pulled up and Fletcher opened the door. "You can go to the other armories if you want," Thornton told the other two men. "But I know who's behind this and that's where I'm going." He climbed into the cab and Fletcher followed. He told the driver where to go, and the cab lurched away from the curb, leaving Bates and Vanderslice behind

"What did he mean that he knows who's behind this?" David asked as the cab pulled away.

Gideon knew only too well, but he said, "Why don't you visit the other armories, just to be sure? I've got to . . . I've got to go." He looked around frantically, but saw no cabs, so he started walking without even waiting for David's reply. Dodging the other pedestrians, he worked his way through the crowded sidewalks. The winter sun had already disappeared behind the tall buildings, and everyone was heading home for dinner. Traffic was jammed at each intersection, and he darted between the vehicles with no regard for his own safety.

All he could think about was Elizabeth alone at his house with no idea that she was in danger. Because surely that's who Thornton blamed for all of this. Rightly so, if Gideon had put all the pieces together correctly, but that didn't mean Thornton had the right to revenge. Or maybe it did, but Gideon wasn't going to allow it, not if he could beat him there.

He had a good chance, too, since the cab would be slowed by the traffic, but Gideon could dart right through, ignoring blaring horns and screeching tires and shouted curses. After what seemed an eternity of racing through the darkening streets and pushing past countless strangers, he reached his own street, panting and holding the stitch in his side, but refusing to slow his pace. As he'd hoped, the cab was just pulling away from the curb in front of his house. No sign of Fletcher, so he must have gone inside with Thornton. Where was the other one? What was his name? Lester, yes. Elizabeth said Thornton had one of his men watching her all the time, but he saw no sign of Lester, either. Had he gone in with them, too? How on earth would he protect her from all three of them?

He was running when he reached the stoop and had to grab hold of the railing to swing around and up the steps. The front door stood open, and inside Thornton was shouting. Gideon took the steps two at a time and launched himself down the hall and into the parlor, where Elizabeth faced Thornton.

"I don't know what you're talking about," she was saying.

"Leave her alone," Gideon said.

"Stay out of this, Bates," Thornton said, nodding to his men, who were both there, as Gideon had feared.

Before he could think, they'd grabbed him, each holding an arm in a vicelike grip. He struggled, but they held him fast. He was no match for them physically, but if he couldn't beat them with brawn, he'd have to use his wits. "She didn't have anything to do with this."

Thornton turned to him with interest. "And why would you say that unless you already knew why I suspected her?"

"Because she told me everything about how she knows you and how you threatened her."

"Gideon, don't!" Elizabeth cried. "Just leave. He won't dare hurt me."

"Won't I?" Thornton asked with a smile that turned Gideon's blood to ice. "And now that you mention it, I think it will be even better if Bates is here to watch. Make sure he doesn't get loose, boys."

Frantic, Gideon tore one arm free from his captor and would have lunged at Thornton but his other captor punched him in the stomach, driving the breath from his lungs and sending him to his knees, nauseated and gasping. As he fought for breath, he heard a new voice and thought he must surely be hallucinating.

"What's going on here?" Anna Vanderslice said

in a commanding tone he'd never heard her use before. She'd waltzed into the room like some kind of snow queen wearing a fur-trimmed coat and a white fur hat with her hands tucked into a matching muff. "Have you gotten yourself into even more trouble, Elizabeth?"

"Anna, this doesn't concern you. Get out of here!" Elizabeth cried. "And please, go find a policeman!"

"Yes, Miss Vanderslice," Thornton said. "Get out of here now, but don't bother with a policeman."

Anna glared at Thornton as if he were a bug she'd found floating in her soup. "Are you here to get your revenge on Elizabeth? Oh yes, she told me all about it, back when she thought we were friends, but now . . . Well, I'm sorry, Mr. Thornton, but I have a prior claim on her. She's a lying, scheming harlot, and she's betrayed me for the last time." Anna slipped her left hand out of her muff and pointed the muff on her right hand at Elizabeth.

The muff exploded.

The noise was impossibly loud, and for a few seconds they were all too stunned to move. But Elizabeth had clapped her hands to her chest, and blood began to ooze from between her fingers. She made a small cry of distress and sank to her knees as Anna began to scream.

"What have I done!" she cried, demanding it

408

over and over of every person in the room. "What have I done!"

Gideon staggered to his feet, forgotten by his captors, who were still too stunned to take any action at all. Thornton gaped at Elizabeth, who cried out again as blood dribbled from her mouth.

Anna was still screaming, begging Thornton to help her now, but he could only stare at Elizabeth as she toppled over onto her side.

"Boss," Fletcher said, "we need to get out of here."

Gideon sucked in as much air as he could and lurched to Anna. When she turned to him, he grabbed the muff and jerked it off her hand. A pistol fell to the floor.

"Yeah, the coppers will be here, and you don't want them pinning this on you," Lester said. They grabbed Thornton and started dragging him from the room. He didn't resist. He still couldn't seem to tear his gaze from Elizabeth, who lay deathly still as blood flowed from her mouth and slowly stained her shirtwaist.

"I didn't mean to kill her, Gideon!" Anna cried.

Was she insane? He didn't know and he didn't care and he couldn't deal with her now anyway.

He snatched up the pistol and stuffed it into his pocket as he sucked in another ragged breath and threw himself to his knees beside Elizabeth.

Anna was screaming again, begging Thornton

to help her, which sent him and his men scrambling out even faster.

Gideon's heart had stopped. He knew he was going to die, because no one could feel pain like this and survive. He reached out to her, longing with everything in him to save her and knowing of nothing that would help. A doctor? A hospital? Nothing could save her from a wound like that.

Was she still breathing? "Elizabeth?" he whispered.

Her eyes fluttered and opened just a bit. Could she see him? Could she hear him? Miraculously, she lifted one bloodied hand from the terrible wound in her chest and held it out to him. He took it in both of his.

"Elizabeth, I'm sorry, so very sorry. I never meant to judge you. I don't judge you. You did what you had to do. I'm sorry I was angry. It was just because I love you so much and I . . ." His voice broke and he had to blink away the tears. He could cry later, after she was gone.

"You . . . really . . . love me?" she asked in a broken whisper.

"Of course I do! I love you more than life itself. I want to marry you and spend the rest of my life making sure no one ever hurts you again."

She smiled at that, a sad, bloody smile that broke his heart into a million pieces, because they both knew the rest of her life was only minutes now. How would he ever live without her?

"Oh dear," Anna said. She sounded annoyed.

Annoyed? At some point she'd stopped screaming, and he'd forgotten all about her in his concern for Elizabeth. He glanced up to see her furtively peering out the front window. She *must* be insane. What else could explain all this?

"Mrs. Bates just got home," Anna reported. "Thornton is taking her taxicab."

"Gideon?" Elizabeth whispered, drawing him back, reminding him they had only minutes left. "Did you . . . say . . . marry me?"

"Yes!" he assured her. "I was going to propose as soon as you broke your engagement to David."

"Even though . . . I'm a liar . . . ?"

"I love you, Elizabeth. I love you for everything you are, and if you lie, well, everyone lies."

"You don't."

"It doesn't matter. None of it matters now. I just want you to know how very much I love you. Always remember that."

"They're gone," Anna reported from her post at the window.

To Gideon's amazement, Elizabeth smiled, and while it was still bloody, it was no longer sad. In fact, it was positively wicked. And then she sat up.

What the . . . ?

"It worked," Anna cried, clapping her hands in delight. "It was even better than the way we practiced!"

"You were marvelous, Anna," Elizabeth said in her normal voice, the one she used when she hadn't suffered a fatal gunshot wound.

Gideon looked from her face to the bloody spot in the middle of her chest and back to her face again. "You're shot," he said stupidly.

"Not really. Anna used blanks." She touched the bloody mess on her chest. "This is chicken blood." She pulled a handkerchief from the sleeve of her shirtwaist and wiped her bloody face. Then she removed something black from her mouth and wrapped it in the handkerchief.

"You aren't dead."

She smiled again, and this time she looked a little embarrassed. "Not yet at least."

"What on earth is going on here?" his mother demanded from the parlor doorway. "Oscar Thornton practically dragged me out of my cab and threw my bags on the sidewalk, and, Gideon, what are you doing on the floor and—"

Gideon scrambled to his feet and helped Elizabeth up as well, and then his mother saw the blood and nearly fainted.

"I'm all right," Elizabeth assured her over and over as they got her seated. "I'm not even hurt. It's all fake."

"But why? And what was Oscar Thornton doing here?"

"It is," Gideon said, "a very long story."

Chapter Seventeen

Telling the story this time was almost a relief, because this time she didn't have to lie, at least not very much. Anna and Gideon already knew most of it, even if Anna didn't know the worst of it. She couldn't bring herself to meet Mrs. Bates's eye, though, not when she knew what the good woman would think of her now. How could she bear seeing the disappointment and downright disgust Mrs. Bates would surely feel when she knew the truth?

"But what made you think of having Anna pretend to shoot you?" Gideon asked when she had come to the end of her tale.

They were all sitting in the parlor. Gideon had taken a seat beside Elizabeth on the sofa, and Mrs. Bates and Anna sat across from them.

"It's something grifters do when a touch comes hot . . ." She drew a breath, remembering they didn't know what any of that meant. "If a mark figures out that he's been swindled, he usually wants to go to the police or at least get his money back, so one of the grifters pretends to shoot the other one, and the mark does just what Thornton did, runs away so he won't be involved in a murder. The mark never comes back looking for the grifters, either."

"But where did all the blood come from?" Mrs. Bates asked. She hadn't spoken a single word until now.

"That's the clever part," Anna said, still so excited that their plan had worked that she could hardly sit still. "We put the blood in a rubber bladder and stuffed it inside Elizabeth's bodice. When I shot her, she clutched at her shirtwaist and popped it open. She had a smaller one in her mouth, too."

"I'll never forgive you for that," Gideon said, although the gleam in his eyes said differently. "You took ten years off my life."

"You weren't supposed to be here," Elizabeth said in exasperation. "It was just supposed to be Thornton and maybe his two goons, but no one else. I even gave the servants the afternoon off so they wouldn't interfere." She turned to Mrs. Bates. "And you certainly weren't supposed to come home just then."

"And if I hadn't, would I ever have known any of this?" she asked.

Suddenly, Elizabeth wanted to weep, which was getting to be a very familiar feeling. And why shouldn't she? She'd forever lost the respect of the woman she admired most in the world, and she'd never be able to win it back. Now that Mrs. Bates knew the truth, Elizabeth would be lucky if she let her spend even one more night in her house. But she didn't have the right to weep, at least not in front of Mrs. Bates. She'd do her mourning in private. "I hoped you'd never have to know what I am, Mrs. Bates. I was planning to just pretend I was going home to South Dakota and then you'd never hear from me again."

"Oh, Elizabeth, I've always known exactly what you are. Oh, not the details," Mrs. Bates added quickly when Elizabeth's mouth dropped open. "Not what made you, but I did know what you're made of. You're one of the strongest, bravest young women I know, and I know a few. The way you took charge when we were in the workhouse—"

"I didn't take charge!"

"Yes, you did," Anna said. "You knew just what we should do and how we should act and you weren't afraid to talk to the other inmates or stand up to the warden and the matron—"

"And the way you looked after Anna during the hunger strike was so practical," Mrs. Bates said. "It was obvious to me that your background was very different from . . . well, from anyone I'd ever known."

Elizabeth shook her head in silent denial. She'd been so careful not to show how much she knew about being in jail. They couldn't possibly have suspected anything.

"I thought it odd that you knew so little about the movement," Mrs. Bates continued, "but it was clear you truly believed in our cause, so it was a pleasure to teach you. Oh, I almost forgot in all the excitement. Gideon, hand me my bag, will you?"

Gideon jumped up and brought over the carpetbag she'd carried to Washington. She dug around inside for a moment and pulled out a small packet wrapped in brown paper and tied with string. "Remember I told you that Mrs. Belmont asked me to attend the conference because the women who had been jailed were being honored? Well, the theater was packed that afternoon. Everyone said there's never been a suffrage meeting like it. Mrs. Belmont got up and made a stirring speech, praising the courage of all the women who had endured the hardship and humiliation of imprisonment because they love liberty."

Seeing the glow on her face, Elizabeth could almost imagine being there. Mrs. Bates must have been so honored.

"We read about it in the newspapers," Anna said. "Did you really block the White House driveway?"

"Not intentionally, but so many people came, they couldn't help it. Then Mrs. Kent gave a speech. You remember, she was the leader of our picket line. She called all of us up to the stage and gave each of us one of these. I brought yours back for you." She unwrapped the packet and drew out two small silver objects. She handed one to Anna and one to Elizabeth. "Now everyone will know that you were jailed for freedom."

It was a silver brooch made with exquisite detail into the shape of a cell door, complete with a heart-shaped padlock and chain.

"How lovely," Anna exclaimed, instantly pinning it to her bodice.

Elizabeth couldn't take her eyes off the brooch. She had no right to wear it, of course. Her reasons for going to jail had nothing to do with the suffrage movement, so she couldn't claim the honor of having been jailed for freedom. She might never wear it, but she would always treasure it.

"Thank you," Elizabeth said. "For everything. I'll never forget . . . I'll never forget any of it. I suppose you'll want me to leave now, and that's all right. I'll just pack a few things and—"

"Leave?" Mrs. Bates and Gideon said in unison.

"Why would you leave?" she asked.

"And where would you go?" he asked.

"Because . . ." Elizabeth tried to think of a reason that didn't remind them of too many reasons why. "I'm a liar and a thief and I involved Gideon in a crime and—"

"I don't think Gideon minds too much, do you, Gideon?" Anna said with a wicked grin.

"Not too much," he admitted solemnly.

"I don't think he minds at all," Mrs. Bates said

archly. "And it's obvious you were simply trying to save your life."

"Which wouldn't have been in danger if I hadn't helped cheat Thornton in the first place," she reminded them.

"I'm afraid I can't feel sorry for Oscar Thornton," Mrs. Bates said, "not even in the interest of Christian charity. I always suspected he'd killed Marjorie, and now that you've confirmed it, I have no pity for him at all. And yes, what you did was wrong, but none of us are perfect. I can only wonder what I might be capable of in your situation. The important thing is what you do from now on."

What *would* she do from now on? She had no idea. Why had everything suddenly become so complicated?

"Which is why," Anna said, rising from her chair, "you and I should leave Elizabeth and Gideon alone, Mrs. Bates."

"We should?" Mrs. Bates asked.

"No," Elizabeth said, but Gideon said, "You should," at the same time, and Mrs. Bates rose also.

"Elizabeth," Mrs. Bates said, "you are welcome to stay with us as long as you wish, and I truly hope it is a very long time."

With that, she and Anna left, closing the parlor doors behind them.

Elizabeth couldn't bear to hear what Gideon

had to say, so she spoke first. "I'm sorry I frightened you. As I said, you weren't supposed to be here."

"I might not have been, but when we found out the army never heard of Colonel Inchwood—"

"Who?" she asked in surprise.

"The officer who came to David's office to arrest the general. Didn't you know what was going to happen?"

"I did, but I didn't know what his name would be."

"Yes, very creative. At any rate, he walked off with all the papers and the bank drafts, but he told David we could go to the armory tomorrow to get more information."

"A nice touch."

"It would have been, but Thornton decided we had to go right away and get the papers and the bank drafts back. We went to three different armories before a real colonel told us he never heard of Inchwood or any investigation. That's when it came hot. Is that the expression?"

"Yes, it is," she admitted with some amusement.

"So Thornton and his man jumped in a cab, but before he left, he said he knew who was behind it, so I was afraid he was coming here for you."

"And you were going to rescue me." Suddenly, she wanted to weep again. She was awfully emotional today, probably because she'd nearly died.

"And I would have failed miserably." Plainly, it pained him to admit it, too.

"But you were going to try. That was very brave."

He made a rude noise. "Luckily, Thornton was no match for you and Anna. When I thought you were dying—"

"Gideon," she said quickly, before he could say too much, "I won't hold you to anything you said then. I know you didn't mean it, but you were kind to . . . to . . ."

"To what? Make it easier for you to die? Is that what you think?"

She didn't think that at all, but, "I was wicked to tease you like that, to make you say things you didn't mean."

"I did mean them."

"All of them?" she wanted to ask, but she was afraid of the answer.

Gideon frowned. "Why do you look so frightened?"

"I'm not frightened," she lied.

"You already knew I was in love with you."

"Which is why I shouldn't have teased you."

"Were you teasing? Because you didn't say you loved me, too. Was that because you knew you weren't dying or because you don't love me?"

"I . . ." Even now, she couldn't say it. "I knew I wasn't dying."

"Then tell me."

"I can't! How could you ever believe me? How could you believe anything I say ever again?"

"I don't know, but I think it might be very interesting to spend the rest of my life figuring it out."

What was wrong with him? Why wasn't he angry or disgusted or appalled? He couldn't possibly want to marry someone like her, unless . . .

The very thought was too horrible. "You can't save me."

"What?"

"That's what you're thinking, isn't it? That you can reform me and turn me into someone like . . . like . . ."

"Like my mother?" he offered helpfully.

"I could never be that good, but maybe like Mrs. Vanderslice. Someone who will keep your house and raise your children and never cause you a moment's worry."

"Why would I want a wife like that? I'd die of boredom."

"I'm serious, Gideon. I'm not like you and I never could be."

"Thank God. Now, I'd made up my mind that I wasn't going to kiss you until you'd broken your engagement to David, but I can see this is an emergency situation."

Before she could think, he took her in his arms, and when his lips touched hers, all thoughts of protest vanished from her mind. All thoughts of everything else vanished, too, and her traitorous arms slipped around his neck and she lost herself completely. She even heard bells.

When they were both breathless, he broke the kiss, but he only pulled away far enough to say, "Tell me."

"I love you, Gideon. I truly do."

She thought she might really cry this time, but he started kissing her again, and she forgot everything else until someone rudely said, "What's this?"

They broke apart guiltily to find the Old Man glaring down at them. Apparently, the bells she'd heard were doorbells. "What do you think you're doing with my girl, Bates?"

"Your girl?" Gideon echoed in dismay, jumping to his feet.

Elizabeth rose, too, a little flustered, but very glad to see him. "I'm sorry. I completely forgot to telephone you."

He clasped her shoulders in his big hands, and his gaze found the blood on her shirtwaist. "The cackle bladder worked?"

"Perfectly."

"Oh, Lizzie, when you didn't call . . ." His hands slipped around her back, and he pulled her into a bone-crushing embrace. Two hugs now. The Old Man was getting sentimental in his old age.

"And who's this?" Mrs. Bates demanded.

The Old Man released Elizabeth, and they

turned to see Mrs. Bates and Anna in the parlor doorway.

"This is General Sterling," Anna informed Mrs. Bates slyly. "Although I suppose he really isn't a general. And, General, this is Gideon's mother, Mrs. Bates. She's really his mother, at least as far as I know."

The Old Man strode over to them and sketched a little bow. "I'm so pleased to meet you, Mrs. Bates. I have thoroughly enjoyed getting to know your son. You did a remarkable job raising him."

"Why, thank you," Mrs. Bates said, obviously charmed and not sure she should show it.

"And how delightful to see you again, Miss Vanderslice," he added, taking the hand she offered. "I hope you'll give my regards to your beautiful mother."

"That probably isn't a good idea," Anna said, grinning ear to ear.

"Anna is the one who shot me," Elizabeth said.

"Ah, so she is brave as well as beautiful, a dangerous combination."

"I hope so," Anna said, making him grin in return.

"Mr. Sterling, or whatever your real name is," Gideon said, not charmed at all, "you should know that Elizabeth is no longer *your girl,* and that she has agreed to become my wife."

"Really?" Mrs. Bates said, and Elizabeth thought she actually looked pleased, although it was probably just wishful thinking on her part.

"Is that right?" the Old Man said. "Well, Mr. Bates, you should know that Lizzie will always be my girl, and if you hope to marry her, you will have to begin by asking my permission."

Gideon could only gape at him, as if he hadn't quite understood. He turned to Elizabeth for clarification.

"That's right. He's my father."

For some reason, this made Gideon very happy. "Well, sir, in that case—"

"You're a bit premature, Bates," the Old Man said with a smirk, "since I believe she's currently engaged to someone else."

"And when she does become engaged to you, Gideon," his mother said, "I'll have to rescind my invitation for her to stay here, at least until after the wedding. For propriety, you understand."

Gideon muttered something that might have been a curse.

"And from what I saw a moment ago," the Old Man said, "I think I should take Lizzie home tonight to ensure that her virtue stays intact until the wedding."

"Really, sir," Gideon tried, but both Anna and his mother were laughing. He made a visible effort to regain his dignity. "Does Elizabeth live with you?"

"With my sister, Cybil, so it's all quite proper. When you come to ask my permission, Bates, we can also discuss the matter of Lizzie's dowry."

"She doesn't need a dowry," Gideon said, his dignity firmly back in place.

"Well, she has one just the same. She's rather a wealthy woman, in fact. I've . . . uh . . . been putting money aside for her since she was born."

He had, of course, because he'd never wanted her in the game. The nest egg was meant to provide for her so she never had to work, but she'd desperately wanted the Old Man's attention, the kind of attention he gave Jake when teaching him the game. So she had refused to resist the lure of the grift, which had brought her to this place. Elizabeth had added to her fortune considerably from the first Thornton touch, and she'd get a lot more from the second one. How much she could only guess at this point, but the Old Man would make sure she got her fair share. Gideon didn't need to know where the money came from, though. He might want her to give it back, and since it would most certainly be the last of her ill-gotten gains, she saw no reason not to keep it.

"Which reminds me," Elizabeth said. "What are you going to do with the Ross rifles?"

The Old Man smiled at that. "I sold them to the Canadian army."

"What?" Gideon almost shouted. "Didn't Elizabeth tell you how dangerous they are?"

"She did, but when I looked into it, I found

out that the Canadian army still uses them for training, and they were happy to get them. They are, in fact, on their way to the border at this very moment."

"Even though they explode?" Elizabeth asked.

"Apparently, they only 'explode,' as you call it, under combat conditions, when they get dirty or overused. They're fine for training."

"But how could you sell them? You didn't even have the bill of sale until today," Gideon said.

The Old Man merely shrugged sheepishly. "Not all attorneys are as honest as you are, Gideon."

To his credit, Gideon hardly blinked at this. "And what about the rest of the rifles? The extra ones you convinced Thornton to buy?" he asked. "Did you sell them all to Canada, too?"

The Old Man frowned. "Didn't you explain it to him?" he asked her.

"He didn't want to know," Elizabeth said.

The Old Man nodded. "The rest of the rifles don't exist," he told Gideon.

This time Gideon frowned. "But Thornton bought thousands of rifles in the past week."

"Yes, I know. Rifles that don't exist. He bought them from, uh, some friends of mine. Oh, we rounded up a few hundred to show him, but the rest of them were just boxes in warehouses." He turned to Mrs. Bates. "I'm sure this is distressing to you, but we had to make sure Thornton was completely penniless so he wouldn't have the resources to come after Lizzie again if he ever figured out what really happened."

"I'm not a bit distressed to hear that Oscar Thornton has been justly punished," Mrs. Bates said.

"I'm very glad to hear it," the Old Man said, and he really looked like he was. How nice that he was concerned with the good opinion of her future mother-in-law.

"So that's how it worked," Gideon said. "Not at all what I'd imagined. Very clever."

"Thank you, son," the Old Man said. He looked extremely pleased with himself.

"But what happens now?" Mrs. Bates asked. "With Thornton, I mean. What if he finds out Elizabeth isn't really dead? Or, heaven forbid, happens to see her in the street someday?"

"Thornton will soon be completely bankrupt," the Old Man assured her. "Then he will be dunned by bill collectors—some of them real and some of them in my employ—who will drive him from the city. He'll never dare return here again."

Mrs. Bates rewarded him with a beatific smile. "How very clever."

"Why, thank you, dear lady." The Old Man looked genuinely touched.

"Oh my, I'm afraid we've completely forgotten about supper in all the excitement," Mrs. Bates said quickly, as if to fill an awkward silence. "Elizabeth has dismissed our servants for the evening, but I'm sure I can find something in the kitchen, even if it's just sandwiches. Would you stay and eat with us, Gen . . . uh, I mean Mr. Sterling?"

"It's Miles, actually, and I'd be delighted."

"I'll help you, Mrs. Bates," Anna said, giving Elizabeth a wink.

"And so will I," the Old Man said. "I've learned a thing or two about the kitchen in my years as a bachelor." He gave Gideon a wink as he followed the two women out.

Gideon turned to her. "You're not really leaving, are you?"

"I think I'd better," she said with a grin. "I don't think I can be trusted to resist temptation if you're close."

He sighed. "Then you'd better break your engagement with David tomorrow so we can set a wedding date."

"Of course. And we can get married right away. I won't even need to have a trousseau made, with all those clothes I got in Washington."

"What? Do you mean those clothes weren't yours?"

"Of course not. I told you I'd never even stayed in that hotel."

"You mean you . . . *stole* them?"

"Stole" was such an ugly word. "I got them from a very unpleasant woman who was being rude to the bellboy, which is why he carried them

428

out for me. I'm sure her husband replaced them immediately, though. He looked quite rich."

"Are you going to keep them?"

This time she sighed. "This is what I was afraid of. You're already trying to save me."

He raised his hands in surrender. "No, I'm not. I won't say another word about it."

But he'd always know she'd stolen the clothes, and so would she. For some reason, and for the very first time in her life, the thought made her uncomfortable. "I'll send them back. There was an address in the trunks. It'll be a good excuse to get all new clothes anyway."

"You don't have to," he said. "I really won't—"

"I know, but I will. I want to start a new life with you, Gideon, and show you I can be a little bit good at least." Although she definitely wouldn't tell him where the money came from.

For some reason, he didn't look pleased, though. "I hope this doesn't mean you're going to be boring."

She laughed at that. "I promise I will never be boring. I will be the most interesting woman you've ever met."

Author's Note

I hope you enjoyed reading this book as much as I enjoyed writing it. Like many women, I was only vaguely aware of the story of the "suffragettes," and I had no idea what they had suffered to win women the vote. When I started reading more about it, I realized that, when my own mother was born, women weren't allowed to vote! Somehow understanding how recently this had occurred brought the issue home to me in a new way, and I wanted to tell their story.

Elizabeth's experiences with the suffragists are based on the true story of the women who demonstrated in front of the White House every day during 1917. They were indeed arrested on November 13 and sentenced to the Occoquan Workhouse. Everything I describe actually happened, including the awful events of their arrival at the workhouse, which became known as the Night of Terror. I condensed some of the events for dramatic purposes, but many of the individuals Elizabeth meets there were real people. The women did stage a hunger strike and were force-fed as I describe. Mr. O'Brien and others did spend days trying to locate a deputy to serve the writ on Warden Whittaker, but without the help of Oscar Thornton, I'm afraid. The deputies had really been instructed to hide, so no one was available to serve the writ. The courtroom scenes I describe really happened, and the women did refuse bail for the same reason I have Gideon explain to Elizabeth. In reality, they were transferred to the D.C. jail for a few more days until they were released because the jail could not accommodate so many women on hunger strike. Although the House of Representatives passed a suffrage amendment a month after this book ends, in January 1918, it would be almost two years before it passed both houses of Congress and yet another year until the amendment was ratified by enough states, in August 1919, and became law.

The con that Elizabeth and Jake run on Oscar Thornton is a classic "big con" and is known as the rag. Elaborate cons like this fell out of fashion by the middle of the twentieth century, although con men continue to create new ways to swindle the public.

Please let me know how you liked this book. You may follow me on Facebook at Victoria. Thompson.Author and on Twitter @gaslightvt and visit my website at victoriathompson.com to sign up for my newsletter.

Center Point Large Print
600 Brooks Road / PO Box 1
Thorndike, ME 04986-0001 USA

(207) 568-3717

US & Canada:
1 800 929-9108
www.centerpointlargeprint.com